Evelyn Hood is an ex-journalist and has been a full-time writer for many years, turning her talents to plays, short stories, children's musicals and the novels that have earned her widespread acclaim and an ever-increasing readership. She also writes under the name Eve Houston.

For more information about the author and her books, visit www.evehouston.co.uk and www.evelynhood.co.uk.

STAYING ON

Evelyn Hood

SPHERE

First published in Great Britain in 2001 by Little, Brown and Company
This paperback edition published in 2002 by Time Warner Paperbacks
Reprinted by Sphere in 2007
Reissued by Sphere in 2013

Copyright © 2001 by Evelyn Hood

The moral right of the author has been asserted.

A CIP catalogue record for this book
is available from the British Library.

ISBN 978-0-7515-5247-8

Printed and bound in Great Britain by
Clays Ltd, St Ives plc

Papers used by Sphere are from well-managed forests
and other responsible sources.

To my husband Jim

who never knows where he will have to go next,
or what he will be expected to research next,
but copes so well with the constant uncertainty.

Acknowledgements

—◆—

I am indebted to the following people, who assisted with background information for this book:

Robbie Sloss, James and Anne McAlister, Marion Ritchie and Elizabeth Currie for their time and patience in teaching me about farming on the beautiful Island of Bute. Any technical errors in this book are mine, not theirs.

Former Women's Land Army member Sheila Inglis, for her invaluable assistance.

Robin Taylor, who answered all my questions about the boat-hiring business.

Margaret Currie, who was evacuated to Bute during the Second World War and still lives there. As well as describing her war experiences in detail, Margaret kindly allowed me to use some of them.

Betty Greig and Ian 'Scotia' Scott, for their general assistance in connection with background information.

How could any writer possibly survive without libraries and the people who run them? My everlasting gratitude goes to the staff at Rothesay

Library; to librarian Eddie Monaghan and library
assistants Patricia Pollock and Patricia McArthur;
and to the librarians and staff of Ardrossan, Paisley
and Johnstone Libraries for their assistance with
research on Bute, farming, the Second World War
and the Land Army. You are all wonderful – and rest
assured that I will return to pester you again.

1

Albert McCabe leaned on the rail as the paddle steamer *Duchess of Fife* sailed across Rothesay Bay and began to pass a stretch of graceful waterside houses built in the nineteenth century by wealthy industrialists. He glowered down at the water, seeing no beauty in the way the bow-wave foamed creamy lace along the steamer's flanks, or in the approaching town, neat and clean beneath the June sun.

As far as the Glasgow docker was concerned, water was meant for cargo ships to sail on and towns were places for folk to live, and there was no beauty in either. His idea of a grand sight was a foaming beer mug at the end of a hard day.

He stood immobile at the rails, a great solid slab of a man, and his fellow-passengers, crowding excitedly to look at the splendid houses and their colourful gardens, the ruins of Rothesay Castle rising from a whirlpool of neat tenements, the long curving shore-line and the cool green slopes of the hills beyond the

town took care not to jostle him. There was something about Albert McCabe that sent out a warning
to anyone in his vicinity.

In any case, none of them wanted trouble, for they
were all on board the steamer with a single shared
intention: to enjoy a day, a week, even mebbe, for the
fortunate, an entire fortnight on this beautiful island
in the Firth of Clyde. They had struggled through to
the end of the second worldwide war suffered by the
century and they had survived.

War had touched the Island of Bute too. Its mark
could be seen in Rothesay Bay itself, where sleek
submarines nestled against a depot ship and another
vast salvage ship lay at anchor. It could be seen in the
Army vehicles parked along the embankment opposite
the shops, and in the rolls of barbed wire that had only
recently been drawn back from the beach. Even so
there was something about the town and the island
that held out the promise to war-weary travellers of
peace and a welcome, and the chance to move on from
the hardships and sufferings of the past six years.

Now it was time to celebrate before returning to
their normal lives. They were all in the mood for celebration and the small accordion band on board – now
playing, inevitably, 'Sweet Rothesay Bay' – had done
well when the collection box went round. Even those
who looked as though they scarcely had two pennies
to rub together had contributed.

Fools, Albert had thought, waving the box away
with a scowl. Why celebrate the ending of a war when

peace made little difference to working folk like them? Ahead of them lay the same hard graft as before, day in and day out, and probably the same old worry about whether they'd be working come next week.

For him the war's end had only one benefit – getting his wife and weans back home in Glasgow where they belonged. He should never have allowed Nesta to go with the weans when they were bombed out of their own home, but she had begged to be allowed to stay with Sam, the youngest, who suffered badly from asthma. And once she got to Bute she had turned a deaf ear to his demands that she leave the children there and return to take up her duties as his wife.

She'd had a grand war, Albert thought viciously, enjoying herself on a Clyde island while he managed as best he could in Glasgow, working in the docks and sleeping on a rickety sofa bed in his parents' tiny flat. Well, she was about to get her comeuppance, that was for sure.

A city man to his fingertips, he hated being out of the city. He had hated every minute of his journey, first by train and then by steamer. The minute he got his hands on Nesta and the weans, he'd have the lot of them off this lump of earth and back home.

As the steamer slid gracefully alongside Rothesay Pier, where men waited onshore to catch the mooring ropes, McCabe strode to where the queue was forming; parents and children and elderly relatives all coping as best they could with bags, cases and boxes carrying all they might need for their stay away from home. Impatient to find his family and get off the island as soon as possible, he jostled his way to the head of the queue, ignoring those who protested at being pushed aside or, if they were particularly vocal, turned to stare coldly until their eyes slid away from his. He was in no mood for niceties.

As soon as the gangplank was in place he was down it, striding along the length of the pier until he reached the road.

'Westervoe Farm,' he barked at a lad idling on the pier. 'Name of Scott. Where is it?'

'Westervoe? It's round near Stravanan Bay. You'll want that bus over there.'

'I'll walk.'

'Suit yourself,' the boy shrugged. 'It's miles.'

Albert hesitated and then stamped over to the bus stop. More money wasted . . . Nesta was going to regret giving him all this bother once he got her back home, he promised himself.

The bus, like the streets, was busy. After ordering the driver to let him know when he had reached his destination, Albert squeezed his bulk into a back seat and scowled at the floor as the vehicle jolted its way out of the main island town and into the country-side.

When he finally reached his destination he alighted, staring distrustfully about as the bus rattled on its way. Then, following the direction indicated by the bus driver with a jerk of the thumb, McCabe started down a rutted lane leading to a huddle of buildings, walking with long strides, impatient to collect his wife and children and be on his way home.

The lane opened into a central courtyard with buildings on all four sides. The place was shabby and run-down; even city-bred Albert could see that; some of the outhouses had an empty, neglected look and weeds grew in their guttering. At the far end of the yard two long trestle tables had been set out near an open door, with wooden seats and benches beside them. A plume of smoke rose into the blue sky from the chimney, indicating that that was the farmhouse. Hens clucking and scratching about the uneven paving stones scattered away from McCabe's large hobnailed boots. It looked, he thought as he bore down on the place, as though the folk who lived there were preparing for a party. Well, he'd party them, he promised himself, pleasure stirring in the depths of his mind at the prospect of meting out some hefty, well-deserved punishment. They'd learn, Nesta and the youngsters, what he thought of being made to come all this way! And it would be their own fault; if they had only heeded the letter he'd sent, ordering them back home, there would not have been any need for unpleasantness.

His huge calloused hands began to curl into fists in pleasant anticipation and then he halted as a familiar figure appeared in the doorway, bearing a tray so large that she had to turn slightly sideways to get through the door. The woman saw him, and was just narrowing her eyes against the sun to look more closely when McCabe roared, 'Nesta! Come here!'

She gave a high-pitched squeal, like a rabbit being nipped by a ferret, and dropped the tray with a crash. Then, instead of doing as she was told, she disappeared into the house, leaving broken plates and cups rolling about on the ground.

Almost at once a girl popped out of the door, shading her eyes with both hands as she stared over at him. 'Dad? Daddy!' She came rushing towards him, her face split by a huge grin. 'Dad, it's me, Senga. Have ye come tae take us home?'

'Where's your mother?'

'In the kitchen.' His daughter nodded with her chin towards the open door. 'That's the farmhouse. We bide over there, see, in that wee cottage.'

'Get yer things,' Albert grunted, shouldering her out of the way and making for the door.

It led straight into a low-beamed kitchen where most of the space was taken up by a huge table covered with dishes bearing bread and butter, scones, pancakes and oatcakes. A party right enough, he thought, and it was well seen that the folk who lived here knew nothing about the miseries of food rationing. A big man who worked hard and enjoyed his food as well as his drink, Albert McCabe had had a hungry war, even though his parents had gone without in a vain attempt to satisfy his appetite.

He snatched up a scone and crammed it into his mouth, blinking to adjust his eyes to the darkness of the kitchen after being out in the June sun. It took a moment for him to discover his wife, backed against a big range by the far wall.

'There ye are, Nesta!'

'Albert?' she quavered in reply.

'Oh, so ye know me now, do ye? And don't pretend ye didnae see me out there. What the hell d'ye mean by runnin' away when I called ye?' He grabbed the lapels of his jacket and jerked on them, a favourite gesture when he was working himself into a rage. 'I've come tae take the lot of yez back where yez belong. Why did ye no' come when I wrote for ye?'

Nesta McCabe's locked hands writhed nervously against each other. 'Did you not get my letter, Albert? I wrote back to say that our Sam was doin' awful well in the school and I didnae want to take him out till he was finished, with this bein' his last year. His chest's much better since he came here, Alb . . .'

'Oh aye, I got your letter.' He dragged it from his pocket and started tearing it into small pieces. 'Here's yer bloody letter,' he said through his teeth as he ripped at the paper. 'And here's what I think of yer damned cheek!'

The letter was nothing but confetti now; he threw the pieces across the table at her and she flinched as they fluttered down onto the food. 'Never mind our Sam's schoolin', he's near old enough to go out and work anyway. I'll not be defied, Nesta; I'm yer husband and ye have got no right tae go against my wishes. Have ye learned nothin' in all the years we've been married, woman?' His voice began to rise. 'Workin' all those years in the docks,' he raved at her, 'and havin' tae bide alone because my wife was away enjoyin' hersel' . . .'

'Your m-mother was there to look after you . . .'

'A mother's no' the same as a wife, ye daft bitch! I got married tae get away from my mother, and if I'd wanted tae go back tae her I'd have done it long since. Now fetch the weans, for I've found us somewhere else tae live. You're all going back where you belong, and the sooner the . . .'

He broke off as a child wailed. Peering across the room, McCabe suddenly saw that there was a little boy clinging to Nesta's skirt.

'What's this?' he asked. Then, his voice suddenly heavy with suspicion, 'Have you been . . . ?'

'Of course not! How could you think such a thing!' Shock gave strength to Nesta's voice as she bent and picked the little boy up. 'He's Jennet's wee lad . . . Jennet that lives here on the farm. Hush now, Jamie, it's all right. And I cannae just come back with you like that, Albert,' she added, facing up to him, 'for there's folk comin' in hungry from the potato howkin' at any minute, wantin' their dinners.'

'Well, they can just see tae their own bloody dinners. Get your things together . . . now!'

Nesta's mouth and chin quivered in the way that had irritated him right from the first days of their marriage. It always made the palms of his big hands itch and the only way to soothe them was to give her a good hard slap. 'Wh-why don't you sit down and have your dinner with us, Albert?' she suggested. 'I'm sure Mrs Scott wouldnae mind. Then you can meet her, and Jennet and her brother Angus. And afterwards we can talk about going home.'

'There's nothin' tae talk about, ye stupid bitch!' McCabe's temper suddenly snapped. 'You're comin' with me now, and the weans an' all! An' if you don't shut that brat up, I'll do it for ye!' he added as the little boy began to scream with fear, clutching Nesta's neck and burying his face in her hair.

'Albert . . . !'

'Right, that's it. You're needin' tae learn yer manners!' He began to make his way round the table towards his disobedient wife and then stopped as a man's voice asked from the yard door, 'What's going on here?'

Not so much a man, McCabe saw, as he swung round. More of a lad, and a cripple at that, with a crutch jammed beneath one armpit. He looped his thumbs into his belt and gave the newcomer a cold smile.

'What's goin' on is that I'm here tae take my wife and my family back tae Glasgow with me, and the sooner we can get out of this place, the better pleased I'll be. So ye can just step aside and let me tend tae my own business.'

'Is that right, Nesta? Is this your husband?'

'Of course I'm her man. D'ye think I'd want a poor-lookin' creature like that if I had my choice?'

'Nesta?'

Her head, already shaking with fear, managed a deeper bob. 'It's my Albert, come from Glasgow,' she said, her voice a mere thread floating through the room.

'D'you want to go with him?'

The effrontery of the question stunned Albert. 'It's got nothin' tae do with want! She belongs back in her own house with her own man, and that's all there is tae it!'

The younger man limped further into the room. 'Your wife's not a parcel, Mr McCabe, she's a person with a mind of her own. D'you want to go, Nesta?' he asked again.

By now she was too frightened to give a coherent answer. 'I . . . Albert . . .' she stuttered, and McCabe gave a jeering laugh.

'Are ye quite sure that she's no' a parcel? She's always seemed like one tae me,' he sneered. Then, his voice hardening, 'Of course she wants tae go home, it's where she belongs!'

'It's where we all belong!' Senga said from the door. She burst into the kitchen, lugging a cheap little cardboard suitcase. 'C'mon, Daddy, we'll get the next boat and the rest of them can come when . . .'

'Shut up, you,' her father said without taking his eyes from his wife. 'Nesta, get yer things together or leave them behind – it's your choice. Either way, ye're comin' home . . . today!'

'You don't need to bully her.' The younger man had

managed to ease himself round the table to take up his position in front of Nesta, without Albert realising what he was about.

'Bully her?' McCabe stared. 'How can a man bully his own wife! It's her duty tae do as she's told. Now get out of my way.'

'Angus, best do as he says,' Nesta said anxiously, but the newcomer dug the end of his crutch into the floor and stayed where he was.

'Not until I know what Nesta wants.'

Albert's docker's fists curled into two tight knots. 'Tae hell with what she wants, it's what I want that matters. Now . . .' He took a step forward, his head thrust forward, 'get out of my way, sonny boy, afore I make ye sorry ye were ever born!'

2

'Would you look at this place? They've not even set the tables yet.' Celia Scott's voice was sharp with irritation as the three women plodded into the yard.

'They'll be doing their best. Mollie and me can help get things right before the rest of them come in for their dinner,' Jennet said swiftly. After a morning spent lifting potatoes by hand beneath the sun's heat she was stiff and sore and certainly did not need one of her grandmother's outbursts.

'Of course we can, it'll not take a minute,' Mollie McCabe chimed in, massaging her back.

Celia strode forward, as erect as ever although she was in her seventies and she, too, had been working in the potato field all morning. 'Where's Nesta, and that lassie Senga? The folk'll be right behind us looking for their dinner and not a thing ready,' she raged. Then, as she rounded the nearest table and saw hens and cats busily scavenging the contents of a fallen tray outside the open farm door, her voice rose. 'Would you look at that mess? All that waste!'

'Out of my way,' a man's deep voice shouted from inside the house just then, 'afore I make ye sorry ye were ever born!'

Mollie's freckled face turned ashen beneath its grime as Gumrie, the farm dog, shot past Celia and made for the door, barking. 'That's my dad's voice. Oh, Mrs Scott, my dad's here! Where's Mam? Mam . . . !' She broke into a run, almost falling over Gumrie, and disappeared into the house.

'Quiet!' Celia ordered the dog. 'For pity's sake, Jennet, shut him into the byre while I go and see what's going on.' And she plunged after Mollie, the long mackintosh coat that she always wore for farm work billowing out behind her scrawny figure.

Jennet grabbed Gumrie, named by her brother Angus after Field Marshal Montgomery, and almost threw him into the empty byre in her haste to reach the kitchen. There she found her grandmother confronting a large and burly man who looked, with his head lowered and thrust forward belligerently between broad shoulders, and his small eyes gleaming with malice, for all the world like one of the island's bulls.

Nesta McCabe was backed as far as she could get into a corner by the range, Jamie in her arms, while Angus, supported by his single crutch, stood between her and the newcomer. Mollie's younger sister Senga watched from another corner, her eyes flickering between the adults while one hand, as usual, twisted at a lock of the auburn hair she had carefully been cultivating into a Veronica Lake dip over one eye. Steam curled from the big pots on the range and the room was fragrant with the smell of the stew Nesta had prepared for the folk coming in from the fields.

'I asked, what's going on here?' Celia was saying as Jennet arrived.

'And who are you when ye're at home?'

'I,' Celia said frostily, 'am Mrs Scott, and I *am* at home. Who are you?'

'I'm her man, that's who I am.' McCabe flung an arm out to indicate the cowering Nesta.

'Are you indeed? You'll forgive me for not recognising you,' Celia reverted to the ladylike voice she normally reserved for the Women's Rural Institute meetings, 'since in all the years your family have been billeted on this farm, you've not once visited them.'

'I've been too busy workin' tae come pussy-footin' down here! There's been a war on, missus.'

'There has indeed, and it is still going on in the Far East. And we have all been playing our part in the war effort, Mr McCabe, but even so most of us were able to find the time to do the right thing by our blood kin.' The words fell from Celia Scott's thin lips like icicles from the eaves of a house.

'Are you sayin' that I should have spent my hard-earned money comin' all the way tae this godforsaken place just tae see them enjoyin' themselves?' McCabe indicated the laden table with a sweep of one massive paw. 'I'd enough tae do, but now I've got us a new place tae bide and I've come tae take my family back where they belong!'

'Not at this moment, for we're picking the early potatoes and I need all the workers I can get,' Celia told him, her voice brisk and matter-of-fact. 'You are very welcome to come and collect your family in a week's time, provided you do so in a more civilised manner. Until then they're busy helping to feed the country.'

The man's eyes bulged in a face scarlet with temper. 'A week, is it? A week? Listen you to me, missus, they're comin' with me right now, whether you like it or not. Oh, I know about your kind usin' evacuees like my wife and bairns for cheap labour. My lassie here wrote tae me about the way ye've forced them tae work tae suit yer own ends.' He jerked his chin towards Senga, who thrust her artificially reddened lower lip out and stared at a point just behind Celia Scott's right shoulder.

'Albert, Mrs Scott never . . .' Nesta began timidly.

'Shut yer mouth, you!' her husband ordered without bothering to turn in her direction. She did as she was told, trying at the same time to cringe her way through the wall at her back.

'Cheap labour?' Celia's voice shot up half an octave. 'I've been housing and feeding your wife and your children for years, man. Of course they've worked to earn their keep – everyone works on a farm. Where d'you think I was when you arrived? Out in the fields, that's where, and me an old woman too! As for that precious daughter of yours . . .' she delivered a withering scowl at Senga, 'I'm surprised to hear that she could find enough words for a whole letter, let alone spell them. Her teachers at the school were always complaining about her lack of attention, and now that she's working in one of the Rothesay shops I've had nothing but complaints from them too, about her laziness and her time-keeping.'

'Daddy, are you going to let her talk about me like that?' Senga bleated, taking a step forward and then retreating when her father snapped, 'Hold yer tongue, you. Ye'll work all right when I get ye back tae Glasgow, for there's plenty needin' done there. The new house is like a midden. Ye're all goin' tae work hard when I get yez back home.' He rounded on the woman cowering behind Angus, pointing a huge fore-finger at her. 'For the last time of tellin', get yer things together!'

'Albert . . .' Nesta was white to the lips and shaking like a leaf. 'Did ye not see in my last letter that our Bert's got a good job with Mr Blaikie on the next farm? He likes it here, Albert, and he wants to stay . . .'

'Well, he can't. I've got him a place on the docks alongside me.'

'Just a wee while longer, just till Sam finishes the school? Please, Albert?'

'He doesnae need schoolin', he needs tae get work. That'll knock this asthma nonsense out of him once and for all. Now keep yer tongue still and get yer things. That's the last time of tellin', Nesta,' he added threateningly.

Nesta flinched again – like an ill-treated dog, Jennet thought, appalled by the sight. Mollie's mother was a good, kind, hard-working woman and it was terrible to see her so cowed and terrified.

'Just a minute,' Celia squawked, but the big man hunched his shoulders against her voice.

'Where's our Bert? And Sam?'

'They're both out working.' Mollie spoke up for the first time, edging carefully round her father in an attempt to reach Nesta. Her face gleamed white in the dim room and Jennet realised that her bullying father cowed even Mollie, who was never afraid of anything. For the first time she glimpsed something of the life Mollie and the rest of her family had known before coming to the farm as evacuees.

'I thought you said the lad was still at the school?' McCabe snarled at his wife. 'And now I'm told he's out workin'? What are ye tellin' lies for, eh?' He took a slight step forward and Mollie moved swiftly into his line of vision, using the chance to step between her parents.

'They've closed the schools, Dad, because the farmers need all the help they can get with liftin' the potatoes. They do the same at harvest time.'

'Oh, they do, do they? So much for all this precious schoolin', then. And would ye just look at yersel'?' her father said contemptuously. 'Ye're as filthy as a tink. Away and wash yer face and get some decent clothes on. I'd be ashamed tae be seen with ye in that state.'

'It's good clean earth,' Celia informed him. 'The lassie's been lifting potatoes along with the rest of us.'

'Well, she's goin' back tae a proper decent place where potatoes are bought in the shops, no' howked out o' the dirt. Senga, away and fetch yer brothers. Tell them we're all on the next steamer out of this place.'

'But Sam's out in the far field and I don't know where Bert is,' Senga whined.

'Then they'll just have tae follow along on the next boat. And if they don't,' McCabe added menacingly, 'they'll be in trouble. Now then, sonny.' He doubled his fists again and eyed Angus up and down. 'I'm takin' my wife and my lassies back where they belong, so ye can just get out my way afore ye get hurt.'

'You've heard Nesta . . . She wants to stay here on Bute for another week.'

'An' you've heard me, unless ye're deaf as well as lame.' McCabe leaned forward, bawling the next words into Angus's set face. 'My fam'ly belongs in Glasgow, no' on a wee scrap of an island in the Clyde. And they're comin' back home tae Glasgow, with me, right now!' A blunt, thick finger prodding at the air between them punctuated the final six words.

'Come on, Mam, Glasgow's a lot better than this dump,' Senga said eagerly, emboldened by her father's presence.

'I want to stay here an' all, Daddy.' Mollie reached

behind her for her mother's free hand, and clutched it tightly. 'You can't make us go back.'

'Oh, I can't, can I no'? I'm the head of this family,' he roared at her, setting Jamie off on another bout of tears. 'I'm Albert McCabe and I can make all of yez do anythin' I want yez tae do, as you well know, my lassie. And I'll no' stand for my own flesh and blood defyin' me! Now . . .' Again, the big finger swung towards Nesta, 'get movin', ye daft bitch!'

'Here, here . . .' Celia, outraged, poked the man's back with her own forefinger, shorter and thinner than his, but hard and sharp, as Jennet knew to her cost. 'I'll not tolerate such language in my house!'

'Will ye no', missus? In that case the sooner me and mine get out of yer house, the better pleased we'll both be. Come on!' McCabe swung back to his wife, 'Move!'

'Albert . . . !'

'Right, that's it!' He took a step forward, seizing Mollie by the shoulder and spinning her out of his way. With the other hand he reached for Nesta.

'That's enough!' Angus clamped his free hand on the man's arm and, to Jennet's horror, McCabe swung round on her brother, pushing him back so that he lost his fragile balance and reeled against the table.

'Don't you dare touch my grandson,' Celia screamed at the man. 'Can you not see that he's a cripple?'

'I'm no' goin' tae hurt him, ye daft old woman. I just . . .' McCabe began, turning his head to look at her and then he yelped as Angus, steadying himself against the table, lashed out with his crutch. The sturdy wooden support cracked down on McCabe's wrist and, instinctively, he drew back his other fist as he spun round on the younger man. With a screech that would have done credit to a witch, Celia snatched up the long-handled floor brush from where it stood against the wall by the door and swung it back over her shoulder. Jennet saw it coming just in time and ducked as it cut through the air above her head, then whistled round in a wide swing that ended with the bristles scraping across Albert McCabe's ear. He yelped and clapped a hand to his head.

'Old, am I?' This time Celia drew her elbow back and lunged forward with the brush instead of swinging it in the kitchen's confined space. It landed on the back of the man's neck. 'Daft, am I?'

As McCabe turned to face her, bellowing and more bull-like than ever, the wooden part of the brush head landed with a crack on the bridge of his nose.

'Don't you dare speak to me like that in my own house!' Celia shouted, dancing round the man until she was behind him and driving him out through the open door with more swift blows on his ears, his shoulders, the back of his head, his thighs. A lifetime of doing a man's work on the farm had given Celia Scott brawn, as well as the brains she had been born with. 'Get out of here . . . out, I'm telling you! Get back to Glasgow and don't ever set foot on my property again!'

'You'll be sorry!' McCabe yelped, his arms thrown

up to protect his head and the studs in his boots
sparking off the flags.

'Not as sorry as you'll be, if you don't get off my
land. The men'll be coming in from the fields any
minute now for their dinner. If they find you still here
they'll teach you to bully women and cripples. I'll set
the dogs on you!' Celia threatened while Gumrie, the
sole representative of his kind on the Scott farm,
yapped frantically from behind the byre door.

'I'm comin' with you, Daddy.' Senga pushed past
Celia and ran into the yard, clutching her case in her
arms. 'Wait for me!'

'Senga, no! Stay here with the rest of us!'

The girl scowled at her mother from the safety of
McCabe's side. 'Stay in this dump? Youse lot can do
what you want, but I'm for home with my daddy!'

'And ye'd better not stop her, or I'll have the polis
on ye for keepin' her against her will,' her father added
threateningly to Celia, who lowered the brush and
gave a contemptuous laugh.

'You think I'd want to keep that shiftless lassie a
minute longer than I have to? You're welcome to her.
Go on, the pair of you!'

She lifted the brush again and Albert McCabe spat
on the flagstones, then turned and stalked towards the
road with his daughter, weighed down by her bag,
wobbling after him on her high heels. Celia followed,
the brush held at the ready like a lance.

'Jennet,' she said over her shoulder. 'Make yourself useful. See to your brother.'

In the kitchen Mollie had lifted the fallen crutch and returned it to Angus.

'Are you all right?' Jennet asked.

'Of course I'm all right!'

He scowled at her, then at Mollie when the girl said, 'He was great, wasn't he?'

'I wasn't as great as my old grandmother.'

'You were wonderful,' Mollie insisted. 'You refused to let him get near me and Ma, and I've seen him beat a man so hard you couldnae tell who it was for the blood all down his face . . .'

'Stop fussing!' Angus snapped at her, while Jennet gathered two-year-old Jamie into her arms, holding him tightly.

'He's all right,' Nesta assured her nervously. 'Just frightened by the noise.'

'Right, that's them away. Come on, now, the folk'll be here any minute looking for their dinners!' Celia bustled back into the kitchen, the fallen tray in one hand and the brush in the other. 'Nesta, more bread to make up for what you dropped. Angus, you can mash the tea. Jennet, fetch the lemonade from the larder. These folks have been working hard in the field since early morning and they've got a long afternoon in front of them, too. They've every right to expect to see their dinner on the table when they get here.'

'They will, Mrs Scott,' Mollie panted, staggering out under the weight of a huge pot of steaming potatoes.

'It wasn't Nesta's fault, Gran,' Jennet protested, and earned herself a cold glare.

'Was it not? Who else is married to that . . . that animal?'

'Mrs Scott . . .' Nesta began, and was waved to silence.

'We'll discuss the matter later. They're here,' Celia said as the first of the potato howkers, worn out from their back-breaking toil, came slowly round the corner of the old stable and into the yard.

'These,' Mollie murmured to Jennet, 'will be the men your grandmother threatened my dad with?'

Jennet looked at the people filling the small yard and hoped that her sudden broad grin looked to them like a welcoming smile. 'It's as well he didn't stay long enough to see them,' she agreed as the motley band, mainly women of all ages and schoolchildren eager to earn some extra pocket money, sank gratefully onto the benches.

Westervoe was a small farm and during the war years, while her brother Martin was in the Army, Jennet and her grandmother and Angus had run it on their own with help from Jem, a man in his late seventies, and from the McCabes.

They had only planted one field of potatoes, and as those with larger farms on the Island of Bute had commandeered most of the able-bodied islanders, as well as all the Irish potato pickers, or howkers as they were known in that part of Scotland, who had come specially to harvest the early potatoes, the Scotts had had to make do with what they could get. Now some

of the people sitting at the trestle tables looked
exhausted.

Celia, who never seemed to tire, bustled about
organising everyone. 'You go and fetch the teapot,
Jennet. Mollie, you can hand the plates out when I've
filled them. Mrs McCabe, have you not started
pouring the lemonade yet? These folk are parched.'

It was strange, Jennet thought as she went back into
the house for the teapot, that in all the five years the
McCabes had been billeted on Westervoe as homeless evacuees, the two older women had never reached
first-name terms. But then, her grandmother was not
the sort of woman to invite such liberties. She had
been furious when Jennet fell into the way of calling
Mollie's mother Aunt Nesta, warning her that famil-
iarity could only lead to trouble.

In the kitchen thirteen-year-old Sam McCabe, too
thirsty to wait for the lemonade jugs, was downing a
cup of water from the tap. 'I'll carry that for you,' he
offered.

'You should be sitting out there getting your dinner.
You've earned it.'

'I'm just goin' and I might as well take the teapot
with me.' His face was glistening with sweat and filthy
from all the times he had wiped a hand over it.

'It's hard work, isn't it?' Jennet asked sympathetically, and he grinned.

'Aye, but it's grand!' he said. Then, the grin fading,
'Is everything all right?'

'Why shouldn't it be?' Best to let his mother and

sister tell him in their own words what had happened.

'My mam looks a bit . . . different. And where's our Senga? Have they had another row?'

'No, I don't think so. Go on now and get your dinner,' Jennet told him.

Outside, the potato howkers were all eating as though they had not seen food for weeks. Everyone was there . . . except Angus, Jennet noticed. Deciding that she would not be missed for a few minutes, she slipped into the kitchen and then through the inner door at the back. This led to a short corridor with stairs going to the upper floor, a door to the rear of the house and two other doors, one to the parlour and the other to a room that had been the best parlour, but was now her brother's bedroom.

There was no reply when she tapped on the door, but when she opened it cautiously she saw him sitting on the edge of his bed, staring out at the small garden where Celia and Jennet grew fruit and vegetables for the family's use.

'You'd best come for your dinner before it's all eaten.'

'I'm not hungry.'

'Don't let that man bother you, Angus, he won't come back.'

'You think I'd let the likes of him trouble me?' he asked. Then, his voice suddenly flat, 'Did you hear what she said, Jen? "Women and cripples." That's all she sees when she looks at me now . . . a cripple.' He banged a fist on his right leg, which had been badly crushed in a railway accident in 1939.

'She didn't mean it the way it came out. She spoke in the heat of the moment, without thinking.'

'When folk speak without thinking they say what's really on their minds. You know the thing that sticks most in my craw, Jen? I brought this on myself. If I'd got hurt or killed because of a tractor accident, like the one that killed poor Drew Blaikie at Gleniffer, there might have been some sense to it. But this happened because of my own stupidity!'

'How could you have known that the train was going to run off the rails?'

'I should never have been on that train, Jen. I should have been here when the accident happened, working on the farm. But, oh no . . . I was so desperate for a bit of adventure, so keen to get away from here for a wee while.' He groaned, burying his face in his hands. 'And look at me now, a cripple like Gran says, of no use to anyone.'

'You're not useless! Look at the way you defended Aunt Nesta and then gave the man a right good crack on the arm with your . . .' She stopped suddenly, shying away from the word, and settled on, '. . . when he tried to pull her out of the house.'

'And he would have beaten me to death for my cheek, if Grandmother hadnae gone after him with that floor brush. God, Jen, I wish I'd had a proper ending to it. I wish I'd died in that crash.'

'No!' Sick with horror at the very thought of a world without Angus, she dropped to crouch in front of him, grabbing his shoulders and shaking him.

'Don't you ever say that to me again, d'you hear?
Never! If anything had happened to you, I'd not be
able to bear it!'

'You'd have got over it in time, the way folk always
get over these things.'

'I wouldn't,' Jennet said fiercely. She did not
remember their mother, who had died when she was
a baby, and she only dimly recalled their father as a
kindly adult who had carried her about the farm,
talking to her about the animals. As she grew older,
Angus had become the most important person in her
life.

She straightened and looked down at him, trying
to find the words that might bring him out of his
depression. Once, he had been full of laughter and
mischief, always looking for new challenges. When
war broke out and Angus decided to enlist, though as
a farmer he would have been exempt from call-up, he
had persuaded his brother Martin and Struan Blaikie,
the son of a neighbouring farmer, to do the same.

Knowing that Celia Scott and Struan's parents
would have put a stop to their plan if they knew of
it, the three of them invented a story about being
invited to play in a football match on the mainland.
After they had enlisted Struan and Martin came
straight back to the island from Glasgow, while Angus,
keen to make the most of his day away from
Westervoe, travelled on to Saltcoats to visit a girl he
was courting. Just outside Saltcoats station the train
was derailed. Two people were killed and several

injured, including Angus, who was trapped in the wreckage.

Jennet, a schoolgirl at the time, still had nightmares about that first sight of him in a hospital bed, his face cut and bruised, both eyes blackened, one arm broken and a great mound under the blankets where they had placed a protective cradle over the crushed tangle of bone and flesh, nerve and sinew, which had been a strong, healthy limb only hours before. She had thought that he was dying.

'Jennet!' her grandmother shouted from the kitchen just then. 'Where are you? We're near ready to get back out to the field!'

'Just coming!' Jennet called back and then, to her brother, 'Come outside with me and get some dinner.'

He shook his head. 'You go. You earned your food, and you've still got a hard afternoon's work ahead of you. I can eat any time.' His voice was heavy with self-loathing.

3

Potato picking by hand was one of the worst jobs Jennet knew of. The howkers spent most of their time bent double, shuffling along each row, their boots sinking into mud in wet weather, at the mercy of rain, sleet, sun and wind. Today the weather was fine, but even so it was one of those jobs that never seemed to have an end.

Nervous in case Albert McCabe returned, Jennet had opted – against her grandmother's wishes – to bring Jamie out to the field with her. Now he toddled along the furrows, squatting to pick out a potato here and there and offer it to the nearest howker with a sweet smile.

'I wish I was his size,' Mollie said longingly from beside her. 'Then I'd not need to bend my back like a hairpin to get down to the ground.' Then, after a pause, 'I could kill my father, humiliatin' my ma like that.'

'It was brave of her to refuse to go back with him.

I couldn't have done that.' The memory of Albert McCabe with his big tough body and his bullying voice, storming and threatening in the farm kitchen, made Jennet shiver.

'If you knew him, you'd understand her tryin' tae say no tae him. One of the first things I can remember is him hittin' her. I mind when I went tae the school at first, I was surprised because the teacher didnae have a bruise on her face or her arms. It was the same for the rest of us; he just lashes out when he's got a drink in him.'

'If she did go back, would you go with her?'

'And leave you? Of course not. We're blood sisters, aren't we? Well, skin sisters,' Mollie said. 'It still makes us special, even if we didnae have the courage tae keep goin' with the blunt knife.'

They had known that they were special when they discovered, the day after Mollie and her family had come to Westervoe, that they had been born on the same day. Gashing their wrists and mingling their blood had been Mollie's suggestion; Jennet could still see her, trying in vain to tuck wisps of fiery red hair behind her ears, explaining that as blood sisters they would be pledged to befriend each other till death and beyond, a pledge that could never be broken. To Jennet, who had never had a real friend in her life, it sounded wonderful.

Unfortunately, the penknife Mollie produced – specially stolen for the occasion from her brother Bert and carefully sterilised beforehand in a fire

made from bits of dry stick – was blunt, and Jennet
had been unable to make the cut on her wrist deep
enough. Mollie had jeered, but when her turn came
she fared no better. Instead, they bound their wrists
together with grasses and pronounced themselves
skin sisters. 'One for both and both for one,' Jennet
had proclaimed while Mollie, not to be outdone,
added grimly, 'Let no man put us under.'

Now, popping another potato into the sack tied
about her waist, Mollie declared just as grimly, 'You
needn't think you're going to be rid of me that easy,
Jennet Scott. I'm stayin' on here, and so's my ma and
the rest of them. Senga's a right fool – we're better
shot of her. Right, that's another load in.'

'Me too.' They straightened, holding onto each
other for support.

'I feel as if my leg muscles have been cut in two
with a rusty saw,' Mollie moaned as they hobbled,
weighed down by the sacks of potatoes, to the end of
the row, where they emptied them into a large box.
When the box was full it would be heaved onto the
horse-drawn cart and taken to the farmyard. Westervoe
had its own tractor, but it was old and temperamental,
and the Scotts much preferred to stick to the tradi-
tional methods and use Nero, the horse, whenever
possible.

'The terrible thing is,' Mollie moaned on as they
returned to the row and coaxed their aching backs to
bend again, 'I know that I'll feel twice as bad
tomorrow mornin' when I try tae get out of my bed.'

'But you know it'll get better eventually,' Jennet consoled her.

'Thank you, Pollyanna,' Mollie growled.

Although they had their own living accommodation in the cottage adjacent to the farmhouse, the McCabe family ate in the farm kitchen, which was only fair since Nesta did most of the cooking.

Jennet had thought that her grandmother might mention Albert McCabe's visit during the evening meal, but Celia remained silent, her eyes fixed on her plate.

'If she's got something to say I wish she'd come out with it,' Mollie said that evening as the two girls shut the hens into the small portable hen coops known as arks.

'They'll need to be moved to the other end of the field soon.' Jennet closed an ark door and straightened her painful back, glancing about the field where the hens spent their days pecking and scratching for delicacies not provided in their daily food ration. The arks were on long carrying poles, so that they could be moved around to give the hens fresh ground. 'What can Grandmother say? What happened today's over and done with and we'll just have to hope that your father doesn't come back.'

Mollie shook her head. 'There's something about this silence of hers that minds me of a teacher I had back in Glasgow. She could say more with her mouth shut than most tongue-waggers could say in a month.'

'No, in there, you daft creature!' Jennet managed

to stop a hen that, halfway up the ramp leading into its ark, had suddenly decided to make a dash for freedom. Most arks had netting runs attached, but some runs, like the arks themselves, had fallen into disrepair and so the hens roamed free, which made things difficult at night. 'D'you want the foxes to get you?' she scolded, scooping the bird up and easing it in through the door. 'I don't know which is worse in the summer, getting Jamie to go to his bed or getting the hens to go to theirs.'

'I wish we could turn things round.' Mollie shut the door of the ark and straightened slowly and carefully before moving on. 'Wouldn't it be grand if the hens had to put us to bed? I'd go like a shot.'

'Me too, though I'd not want to be milked by the cows in the morning,' Jennet said, and they both shrieked with laughter.

Darkness was falling by the time all the hens had been shut in safely and the girls were free to make their way back to the farmhouse arm in arm . . . holding each other up, as Mollie put it.

'Imagine living in a city tenement when you could be here instead.' She lifted her freckled face to the sky, where the first stars were beginning to come through. 'Even if Ma did give in, I'd want to stay on this island. Our da can't make me and Bert go back – we're too old for that – and Sam will be fourteen come the summer.' Then, scratching with her free hand at her scalp, 'The midges are out. Come on quick, before they eat us alive.'

They separated in the yard, Mollie going to join her family in the cottage while Jennet went to the farmhouse. Sometimes she spent the evening in the cottage, but she knew that tonight, when Aunt Nesta would have to tell Bert and Sam about their father's arrival, the McCabe family were best left on their own.

Celia Scott was reading the weekly newspaper with the aid of a large old magnifying glass that had belonged to her mother. She had been using the glass for months now, but she refused to admit that there was anything wrong with her eyes, claiming that the newsprint was to blame. 'It's this war . . . nothing's right any more,' she kept saying. Now she looked up at her granddaughter. 'You're sure all the hens are in?'

'Every last one of them.' Jennet sank into a chair, wearied to the bone. 'Some of the arks are in a terrible state.'

'We'll mend them in the autumn after the harvest, when we've got more time.'

'There's a good half-dozen past mending. I don't know how they'll be moved again without falling apart.'

'We'll just have to mend them,' Celia retorted sharply. 'I'm not made of money; I can't afford to buy new all the time. Make a cup of tea.'

Jennet, who had been thinking of going to her bed, struggled to her feet to obey. When the tea was poured

she put a cup in front of her grandmother, who said,
'I've told Mrs McCabe that she and her family will
have to go.'

'Gran!'

'I'll not put up with another scene like this
morning's. We've more than done our Christian duty
by them, and nobody can fault us on that score. We
took them in when they had nowhere else to go and
now we can do no more.'

'What's the sense in taking them as evacuees, then
putting them out?'

'Don't be cheeky, Jennet Scott,' Celia said, as she
had said all Jennet's life, every time she tried to argue.
'When they came here their home had been bombed,
but now the war's over and you heard that dreadful
man say he'd found somewhere else for them to stay
. . . and so it's time for them to go back to Glasgow.'

'You can't send Aunt Nesta back to that man. He
hits her, Mollie told me. He hits them all! You saw
what he was like, Gran. What happened wasn't their
fault!'

'Mind your own business, young woman . . . and
your tongue as well. I took them in because I'd no
other choice. Just the same way I took you back when
you came running home with a fatherless bairn in
your belly,' Celia reminded her coldly. 'I've got a duty
towards you, since you're my own blood kin, but not
to them. Your brother Martin'll be coming home any
day now to take over the place and he'll not want
strangers here. When he marries and has a family of

his own, you, me and Angus'll have to find some-where else to live too.'

'Angus's the oldest,' Jennet said sharply. 'He shouldn't have to leave the farm if he doesn't want to.'

'And how could he run the place, the way he is?'

'He could manage, with help. Mebbe Martin will be willing to work for him.'

'Play second fiddle when he's the one who'll be doing most of the work? No, no, we're relying on Martin to take over the place now. If he chooses to let Angus stay, then that's his concern.'

'Aunt Nesta and Mollie aren't strangers – you can't treat them as if they are.' Jennet dragged the conver-sation back on course. Her grandmother frowned.

'Did I not say when you started addressing that woman as Aunt that it would cause trouble? It was just the same when you put names to the pigs and made pets of them. Then when they were slaughtered you broke your heart, year after year, over and over again. And now you're encouraging that bairn of yours to do the same.' She reached up to her straggly grey hair and pushed a hairpin back where it belonged. 'You're far too kind-hearted, I keep telling you so. Thanks to you, the McCabes probably think they've got a claim on us, but the sooner they're gone, the better pleased I'll be.'

'And how are we to keep the farm running without their help?'

'We'll manage till Martin comes back. I've told

Mrs McCabe that they can stay for a few more weeks; that should give them ample time to make other arrangements if they're so determined not to go back to Glasgow,' Celia swept on, folding her newspaper neatly. 'Time for us to get to our beds, so drink that tea and rinse the cups out.'

'I knew that we couldnae stay here for ever,' Nesta McCabe was saying in the adjoining cottage, 'but even so, I kept thinkin' . . . hopin' . . .'

'I wish I'd been here when Da came and spoiled everything.' Bert, just turned seventeen, doubled his fists on the table. 'I'd have had a thing or two to say to him.'

'He'd just have taken his belt to you, son.'

'It's been a while since he last belted me and I've been putting in some hard work since then. I'd be a match for him now.' It was not an idle boast. Bert was not tall, but he was broad-shouldered and muscular and not afraid of manual labour. Andra Blaikie, the farmer who had taken him on as a full-time labourer when he left school, had been heard to say that even though Bert was city-born, he put in as good a day's work as any of his other employees.

'I'm glad you were out of the way, for it would just have caused more trouble if the two of you had started fighting. But I'm worried about our Senga,' Nesta said, 'back in Glasgow with her daddy, and me not there to stand between them if he takes too much to drink.' Her roughened hands fretted with the

handkerchief she held and she sniffed constantly to
hold back the tears.

'Senga can look after herself. Listen, Mam, if you
don't want to go back to Glasgow and the life he
made you lead there, you don't have to.'

'What else is there for us to do? Where would we
live? How would we eat?' Nesta cast an irritated look
at the budgie, bouncing about his small cage by the
window and chirping happily. 'Sam, will you cover
that bird up? I'm not in the mood for his noise
tonight.'

'I'll do it.' Mollie talked softly to the little bird
before covering him, and he sidled along his perch
to listen, his head cocked to one side. When he first
arrived on Bute, huddled morosely in a battered cage,
Cheepy had looked sad and moth-eaten, having lost
most of his feathers in the explosion that destroyed
the McCabes' Glasgow tenement home. Now, in a
smart cage that Sam had found in a pawnshop in
Rothesay, his feathers all restored, he was a handsome and happy bird.

As Mollie draped a bit of old curtain over the cage,
a light tap was heard at the door. 'Come on in, Jennet,'
she called.

'Are you sure?' Jennet ventured in, eyeing them
nervously. 'My grandmother's just told me. I thought
you might not want to see me tonight.'

'Don't be daft.' Mollie bundled her friend into the
kitchen.

'I'm truly sorry,' Jennet said miserably as Sam

offered her his stool. 'I've tried to get Grandmother to change her mind, but she won't.'

'Ach, we'll be all right. It's not your fault,' Mollie told her robustly. Raised on the Glasgow streets, where she had learned at an early age that shy and retiring kids went to the wall, she had worked hard to instil some of her own confidence and bounce into Jennet when they first met. It angered her to see how easily Mrs Scott could crush and humble the girl. There were some folk, she reckoned, who could use their tongues instead of their fists and deliver bruises unseen by human eyes, but just as sore as any physical evidence.

Mam was right; lessons learned early in life stuck like glue. Her own home life had been far from perfect, thanks to her father's temper and his drinking binges, but she reckoned that even that was better than being raised by Jennet's old witch of a granny.

'It's all right, lassie.' Nesta's tears were banished and she spoke with quiet dignity. 'Your granny's right, we should have found somewhere else to stay before now and I'm grateful for all she's done for us since we first came here.'

'I'm staying on, no matter what,' Bert said defiantly. 'Mr Blaikie'll likely let me sleep in one of the bothies the Irish potato howkers use when they're on the island, and I'll be well fed as long as I work for him. But what about you and Mollie and young Sam here?'

'I can work alongside you when I leave the school,'

Sam piped up hopefully, and his brother reached out to tug gently on his snub nose.

'You're the cleverest of us all and you might be able to make something of yourself. There'll be no farmwork for you, if we can find something else that uses your brain instead of your muscles.'

'There's mebbe work to be found in one of the boarding houses in Rothesay,' Jennet suggested; then, brightening, 'My aunt and uncle might be needing more help this summer with their boarding house. Now that the war's over there'll be hundreds of trippers coming here in the summer.'

'That's right!' Mollie sat upright. 'Me and Mam could clean and cook and help with the holiday folk.'

'And I can clean boots and run messages,' Sam piped up, determined to do his bit.

'And help Uncle George with the boat-hiring,' Jennet suggested.

'I could do that no bother,' he said eagerly. Then, glaring at Bert, 'That surely takes brains, stopping folk from getting drowned.'

'D'ye think they'd want a whole family landed on them?' Nesta was doubtful.

'There would only be the three of you. The best way to find out is to ask. I'll go and see them tomorrow. You'd not mind sharing a room if you had to?'

Mollie beamed at her friend. 'We'd not mind sharing a bed, if it meant us being able to stay on the island. I knew you'd come up with the answer, Jennet

Scott. Have I not always said that you'd more brains than me?'

'And more beauty too,' Bert said, and got a clip on the ear from his sister for his cheek.

'Don't get too excited,' Jennet warned with the wisdom of one who had never been able to take anything for granted. 'My aunt and uncle might not be able to help you.'

'Ach, they will,' Mollie said confidently. 'You'll talk them into it, I know.' Then she yawned and stretched, wincing. 'I don't know about the rest of you, but I'm ready for my bed. I'm goin' to sleep like a log tonight.'

Jennet was so worried about the McCabes' future that she went to bed convinced that she would be unable to sleep a wink that night, but no sooner had she turned out the lamp and put her head on the pillow than she was roused by Jamie bouncing about in his cot and talking to his toys.

'Mummy!' he said gleefully when she lifted her head and blinked at him in the dawn light.

'Wha . . . ?' She reached for the old clock by the bed, then as she heard her grandmother's booted feet on the stairs she pushed it away and leaped onto the cold linoleum, gritting her teeth against the waves of pain radiating from her back muscles.

By the time she had splashed water from the jug she had filled the night before into a bowl, stripped off her night-gown and washed the remains of sleep

away with cold water and harsh soap, her back had
loosened up slightly. She ran the flannel over the
little boy, who squealed and squirmed as the chill
water came in contact with his sleep-warmed skin,
then towelled him briskly to warm him up, before
dressing him and combing his silky hair.

When she had been forced to return pregnant and
disgraced from Glasgow, where she had gone to take
up a nursing career, her grandmother had done everything possible to force her to reveal the name of
Jamie's father, but Jennet had held her tongue, even
when the words spilling from her grandmother's
vicious tongue sent her running from the house to
weep her heart out in one of the barns, huddled
against a bale of hay. Gumrie, she remembered, had
followed her in and lain beside her, his cold nose
pressed comfortingly against her neck.

Angus had found her there and said, 'Listen, Jennet,
you're the only one who knows who the lad is and
nobody else needs to know, not even Grandmother.
But I'm certain sure that this bairn you're carrying'll
bring its own joy to you. And whatever happens, I'm
here to look out for the two of you.'

Angus had been right . . . Jamie was a cheerful,
lovable and loving little boy who had brought a new
and much-needed pleasure into their grey lives. Celia
was over-harsh with him, but at the same time Jennet
feared that her grandmother was trying to take control
of him, as she had done of his mother and uncles.
Hers was a tyranny that had overshadowed their

childhood and sent Angus on the desperate break for freedom that had ended in a smashed railway carriage. Sometimes it seemed to Jennet that every day was a continuation of the silent struggle between herself and her grandmother over Jamie.

Now she took a moment to cuddle him as she carried him from the room, revelling in the fresh clean baby smell of him, the softness of his hair and skin against her face. Jamie, who had had his second birthday three months earlier, was now old enough to rebel against being fussed over.

'Not kiss face,' he reproved her, then, 'Down!'

He had been going up and down the steep narrow staircase for months now, at first on hands and knees and then on his feet, step by step. Even so, Jennet was nervous about it, so she slowly backed down ahead of him, ready to catch him if he should lose his footing. But he clung to the banister above his brown curly head, his round face a mask of concentration as he clambered down, until he reached the bottom and toddled into the outer kitchen, where he submitted impatiently to having his outdoor clothes pulled on.

Celia and Mollie, with Gumrie's help, were already bringing the small herd of cows along from their field when Jennet and Jamie arrived. The toddler skipped fearlessly among the huge animals, slapping a leg here, pulling at a tail there, roaring 'Ho!' and 'Get up will ye!' in imitation of the adults. The cows, as used to him as he was to them, paid him no heed as

they ambled along the lane and into the yard, a
familiar route that they took twice a day.

In the yard they milled about for a moment, forming
their usual line before going on into the byre. Each
cow knew her regular stall and objected if another
animal tried to take it. They always entered in the
right order, eager for the handfuls of hay that Angus
and Sam were putting into their individual racks.

By the time the milking was done, the herd returned
to the field and the milk cooled, Jem, the old farmhand who had come out of retirement to help after
Angus's accident, had arrived, just in time to help the
women and Sam manhandle the milk churns out to
the head of the lane, where they would be collected
by lorry and taken to the ferry. Then the byre had to
be cleaned and made ready for the afternoon's milking
before they were free to get their breakfast.

4

---·---

Andra Blaikie, tenant at Gleniffer, the neighbouring
farm, arrived while they were still breaking their fast.
A tall, burly man, he filled the doorway, blocking out
the light and darkening the kitchen.

'Young Bert tells me you'd some trouble last night,
Celia.'

'Just some vermin,' Celia said calmly from the
stove. Nesta, who was working beside her, flinched
slightly. 'I sent him packing with a flea in his ear.'

'You should have fetched me. I'd have given him
somethin' tae think about.'

'You're a good neighbour, Andra, but I can fight
my own battles. You'll have a cup of tea now you're
here?'

'I might as well.' He stepped over the threshold,
nodding to the room's other occupants, and settled
himself at the table.

'And you'd best put some good food in your belly
while you're about it.' Celia heaped a plate with

rashers of bacon, link-sausages and two fried eggs
and put it down before him. Although rationing was
in force the farming community, who raised livestock
and grew potatoes and turnips, leeks, cabbages and
grain in their fields and used a form of barter among
themselves, ate better than most. And as Celia kept
pointing out, they deserved to, since they had to work
hard to keep the country fed.

'Has there been any word from your Martin?' Andra
wanted to know as he picked up his fork.

'The occasional letter, but no word yet of him being
let home. Why they had to send him to Germany when
I've got sore need of him here, I don't know. What
about your Struan?'

'We'd word the other day, he'll not be long in
getting back.' Blaikie pushed a forkful of food into
his mouth, then swilled it down with half a mug of
hot tea. 'Martin might well be with him, since they
were both sent tae Germany.'

'Please God.' Now that everyone had been served,
Celia and Nesta brought their own plates to the table.
Jennet tied Jamie into the wooden high chair that she
and her brothers had used as babies, then sat down
beside him and started to feed him from her own plate.

'Jennet, Mr Blaikie's mug's empty,' her grandmother said almost at once.

'You're lookin' fit the morn, Jennet,' the farmer said
as she went to the range to fetch the teapot. 'I swear
that the lassie that first owned those trousers never
filled them as well as you do.'

'They're just right for farm work,' she agreed, embarrassed by the way the man was studying her, as though she was one of the Clydesdales that he, like many other Bute farmers, bred. It was Andra himself who had given her the sturdy corduroy jodhpurs left behind by one of the Land Army girls who had worked on his farm, which was much larger than Westervoe. Buttoned up the calves, and with a fullness at the thighs to make movement easy, the jodhpurs were ideally designed for heavy farm work and Jennet wore them most of the time.

'By God,' Blaikie went on with an unexpected burst of enthusiasm, 'it's been a while since I've had my arm about a nice wee waist like yours.'

'I'd not advise it.' Angus spoke for the first time. 'Not while my sister's got that big heavy teapot in her two fists.'

The farmer barked out a laugh. 'Ye're mebbe right there,' he said, while Jennet poured his tea.

'He'll be away home to eat another breakfast,' Angus said when Andra left.

'He's entitled to his meat,' Celia told him sharply. 'He works for it.'

'And if that's not a hint I don't know what is.' He levered himself to his feet, reaching for the crutch and tucking it into his armpit. 'Come on, Jamie son, you and me'll go and feed the hens, eh?'

'It's time we were going too,' Mollie told her brother. She had a job in a shop in Rothesay, the island's only town, where Sam went to school.

Because of the sudden rise in the population caused
by evacuees coming to the island, his classroom was
a converted shop in the town.

When the two of them had gone, Mollie riding on
Jennet's old bicycle and Sam on Angus's, Jennet said
casually, 'I thought I'd go to see Aunt Ann and Uncle
George tomorrow afternoon.' Then she added, as
Celia's lips pursed as they always did when her late
daughter-in-law's family was mentioned, 'It's been
six weeks or more since I was last there. I've scarcely
been off the farm in all that time.'

'Very well, if you must. I suppose you'd better take
some eggs and a few rashers of bacon from the pantry,'
her grandmother said somewhat ungraciously.

'I will. And some butter too,' Jennet said, and
winked at Nesta.

It was a struggle to get herself and Jamie, and the
bags she had packed for her uncle and aunt, onto the
small bus and into a seat, but Jennet managed it. As
the vehicle trundled placidly along the few miles
between the farm and Rothesay town, her sense of
freedom grew with every turn of the wheels.

'Look . . . look . . .' Jamie perched on her knee,
his hands sawing the air as he tried to point out everything that caught his fancy He stared wide-eyed when
they reached the town's outskirts, with its houses and
shops instead of the fields he was used to seeing, not
to mention the busy pavements. When they alighted
he clutched at her hand, nervous among so many

strangers, then he let out a squeal of excitement as he caught sight of the superstructure and funnels of a steamer lying at the pier.

'Let's go and have a look.' Jennet took a moment to organise her bags before leading him across the gardens, once a handsome stretch of smooth lawns and bright flowerbeds separating the street from the waterside, but sadly neglected now, since during the war the area had been used to park Army tanks and lorries. As she led her son onto the pier she relished the cool breeze about her legs, and the sensation of her skirt drifting about her knees. It made her feel feminine again, and it was so different from the heavy dungarees and the jodhpurs she wore on the farm. She didn't possess a pair of silk stockings, but she had put on leg make-up, and early that morning Mollie had found time before going to work to draw a 'seam' down the backs of her legs with an eyebrow pencil.

The steamer had almost finished loading by the time they reached her. Passengers hung over the rails, taking a last look at the town with its impressive glass-domed Winter Gardens and the curved splendour of the Pavilion Theatre further along the coast road.

'Horsie!' Jamie jiggled with excitement as a great Clydesdale was led along the pier towards the steamer. The horse jibbed at the gangplank and the farm lad leading it took off his jacket and tied it about the animal's head so that it could not see the boat. Then he managed to urge it step by step up the gangplank and onto the deck, where it was led aft.

The ropes were cast off and a bell clanged deep within the boat. Slowly she moved away from the pier, her bows swinging out and her paddles beginning to churn. Jennet led Jamie as close to the edge as she dared, so that he could watch the paddles turning within their box, slowly at first and then faster and faster until they could only be seen as a blur. Then the steamer turned away and headed out into the huge bay.

''Bye, horsie, 'bye!' Jamie waved so energetically that if she had not been clutching his hand he might have worked his way off the pier and into the green and white water foaming below. As the steamer beat her way across the great bay towards the mainland, leaving behind a train of sparkling white foam, Jennet was struck, as always, by the way the paddle boxes on each side gave the otherwise graceful boat the look, from directly astern, of a pregnant cow.

'Is that not a picture?' Ann Logan asked as she and Jennet stood at her parlour window watching the elderly man and the tiny boy walk along the pavement. 'George is that tall and your Jamie's that wee – the one has to bend sideways and the other has to reach away up, just so's they can link hands.'

'It's good of Uncle George to take the time to keep Jamie amused.'

'I think it's you that's doing him the favour, lending the wee one. He loved taking our Geordie down to the river when he was that size, and explaining everything to him.' Ann lifted a photograph from the small table in the curve of the window and looked down at the likeness of a young man in the uniform of an Able Seaman, his arms formally folded but his round face split by a huge grin.

'Enjoy every minute of your wee one, Jennet, for they don't take long to grow up,' Ann said. Then, putting the portrait back, she went on briskly, 'We'll just have a fresh pot of tea, will we? In the kitchen, for it's cheerier there. It's daft to feel like a visitor in my own parlour, but in the summer months this room belongs to the boarders, not to us.'

She whisked out of the room while Jennet returned to the window to catch a last glimpse of her son and her uncle, two men together, turn the corner and disappear from sight. Then she paused on her way to the kitchen to study her cousin's picture.

Geordie, who had spent most of his short life in and around the water, helping in the family boat-hiring business almost as soon as he could walk, had enlisted in the Navy when war broke out and had gone down with his ship in 1942. It was strange, and terrible, to realise that she would never again see him skipping deftly from dinghy to dinghy, or charming the lassies with his laughing eyes as he handed them into the motor boat, ready for a sail round the bay.

Jennet blinked several times, then picked up another framed photograph, this time of two attractive young girls not much older than she herself was.

Although Ann Logan was now grey-haired and

middle-aged, she still had the clear, sparkling eyes and wide smile of the girl on the left. Her sister Rose, the mother who had died when Jennet was less than a year old, was slimmer but she, too, brimmed with life and happiness. While Ann's hair had been plaited into long braids and wound about her head, Rose's hair, a mass of curls, was held back by a ribbon. Jennet had inherited her mother's hair, and although at times it got in the way of her work, she had steadfastly refused to give in to Celia, who referred to it on occasions as a burst mattress, and have it cut.

Celia had never spoken to her grandchildren about their mother's death, or her son's disappearance shortly afterwards. Jennet would never forget the day, in her first year at school, when an older girl had shouted to her in the playground, 'Your daddy ran away because he didnae want tae live with you!' Everyone had looked at her, and she had cried, but when she asked her grandmother about it, Celia had merely tightened her lips and then said, posting the words through the remaining slit, that gossips should never be listened to.

As ever, it had fallen to Angus to explain to his bewildered little sister that their father had just walked away one day, not long after their mother's death. He had looked at her, a long level look, and said, 'I don't know why he went, but it wasn't because of us, it was because our mother died. But that's all right, because you and me and Martin have each other, and we don't need anyone else . . . not even Grandmother, and not *him*, wherever he may be. We can manage fine without him! And if anyone else says that to you, don't let it hurt you, right? Just tell me and I'll bash them for you.'

Later, when Jennet came to know Aunt Ann and Uncle George and her cousins Geordie and Alice, Ann had explained as carefully as she could that James Scott had felt so alone when his wife died that he had not been able to stay at Westervoe.

'But he had us, and Grandmother,' Jennet had argued, puzzled. 'She's his own mother. Why didn't he want to stay with her?'

'Nobody knows but him, dear,' Ann had said helplessly. But as she grew up under Celia's thumb and became old enough to realise that there was nothing of her mother's in the farmhouse, and that her grandmother never mentioned either of her parents, Jennet began to understand more. But not all. 'Why,' she asked now as she joined her aunt in the kitchen, 'did my grandmother have such a down on my mother?'

Ann gave her a sidelong look. 'Because our Rose wasn't her choice as a daughter-in-law. Because the poor lass died young and your gran had to take over the three of you, just when she'd thought her life was getting easier, with your father running the farm and all.'

'Angus says you'd think our poor mother had died on purpose, just to be difficult.

A smile flickered across Ann's face. 'I doubt that, for I've never known anyone who loved life more than our Rose. Oh, you should have seen her and James together, Jennet, it would have warmed your heart. They were just right for each other. Like bookends, George said, and it was true enough, for poor James was never the same after Rose died.'

'He certainly didn't stop to think about what was to happen to us,' Jennet said with sudden resentment.

'Now, don't go blaming him. The man was grieving so much that he didn't know what he was doing,' Ann Logan said swiftly. 'I think he just had to get away from everything that reminded him of her. He was mebbe too gentle for his own good, James was. More interested in drawing pictures than in working the farm, and that didn't suit his mother at all.'

'Were the pictures good?'

'They were very good. He had a right talent, and I just wish he'd left some with us, so's I could show them to you. George and me offered to take the three of you and raise you along with our own two, and we'd have been happy to do it, but your gran would have none of it. She's got it into her head that we'd encouraged him, since James and my George had got so friendly when they were courting Rose and me. We used to go out in a foursome. Then, after we all married, James would come to Rothesay now and again to help George and his father with the boats; he enjoyed that. It was a sad business, right enough. Your gran's not had it easy, losing her husband just years after they wed, then seeing her only child go from her as well.'

If her father had been raised in the same disciplined, unloving way she and her brothers had known, Jennet thought, it might explain why he could not bear to go back to his mother's domination when he became a widower. But she would never really forgive him for leaving her and her brothers at the mercy of the same upbringing.

'I can tell you one thing,' Ann was saying. 'Both Rose and James would be right proud of all of you if they could see the way you've turned out.'

'Even me, after what I've done?'

'If you're talking about Jamie, he's a fine wee lad and you're making a good job of raising him,' her aunt said firmly. 'You're a loving mother and if there was one thing that could be said for both your parents, it's that they were loving folk. They'd be proud of you, and of him, you mark my words. No word about Martin coming home yet?'

'Not yet.'

'It surely won't be long now.' Ann took the boiling kettle off the gas ring and poured some water into the teapot to heat it.

'How's Alice?'

'Och, she's fine. Doing all right at the school, but she's pining for the holidays as usual. It'll be good to see all the trippers back and the place humming like a bee's nest, the way it used to be.' She poured the kettle's contents into the teapot.

'Are you going to take in holidaymakers again this year?'

'All my rooms have been booked already.' George Logan's mother had let out rooms in the three-storey house, and when he and his wife inherited it they had carried on the tradition.

'You'd not have a wee attic room to spare, would you?'

'D'you know, Jennet, we've been thinking along just the same lines. With Martin coming back home to take over the farm, and probably finding himself a wife soon and starting a family, we'd been talking about asking if you and the wee one would like to come here. You'd both be very welcome,' Ann rushed on before Jennet could say anything. 'It would be grand to have a bairn about the place, and I could do with some help when the trippers arrive. And you've still got most of your life in front of you, lassie. You could go back to nursing or whatever you might want to do, and we'd look after the wee one for you while you were studying.'

Jennet drew a deep breath. 'It's not me that I'm asking for, Aunt Ann, it's the McCabes.' She gave her aunt a brief account of Albert McCabe's unexpected arrival and the way her grandmother had sent him packing, then of Nesta's determination to stay away from the life she had suffered with her domineering husband.

'Poor woman . . . I cannae understand how these men get away with it myself, for it'd take a brave man to take his tongue to me, let alone his fist,' Ann said while her hands, big-knuckled and roughened with work, their only decoration the gold band on the third finger of her left hand, clenched slightly on the table before her.

'I thought he was going to hurt Angus. . .' Jennet shivered at the memory, 'and he might have done, if Gran hadn't seen to him.' Then the shiver gave way to a sudden giggle. 'I wish you could have seen him scrambling out of the door and into the yard with her after him and his arms all over the place, trying to protect himself from the floor brush!'

'Bullies usually have cowards sharing their skins. But your gran's being a wee bit hard on the poor woman and her bairns, ordering them out of the farm like that.' Ann poured more tea into both their cups. 'So you want us to take them in?'

'Just Aunt Nesta and Mollie and Sam. Bert's well settled at the Blaikie farm; he says he doesn't mind sleeping in their bothy if there's nowhere else for him. And Senga went back to Glasgow with her father. It's not just charity, for Aunt Nesta and Mollie are hard workers; they'd be a real help to you. To be honest, I don't know how we're going to manage without them till Martin's home. And Sam's a willing lad, he'd help about the house and run messages, and he could work with the boats now that Geordie's . . .'

She stopped abruptly, ducking her head to stare down at her tea.

'As a matter of fact, George has been thinking of taking on a lad out of the school to help when the season starts,' her aunt said. 'There's no shortage of laddies here for their holidays and desperate to help with the boats, but someone who'll be here all through the season would be a good idea. And there's two wee rooms at the top of the house that could be cleared out.'

'So you'd be willing to take them?'

'I'll need to speak to your uncle, of course,' Ann said primly, then got to her feet. 'Come and see the rooms and tell me what you think.'

During the summer months Ann and George Logan and their daughter Alice lived on the ground floor of the house, Ann and George sleeping in the wall-bed in the kitchen and Alice in a tiny adjoining room. They used the outside privy and bathed in a tin bath in the wash-house at the back of the property. The four rooms on the first floor were given over to holidaymakers, who shared the large bathroom on the landing and had the use of the front parlour. The top floor, with its slanted ceilings under the eaves, consisted of a loft where George kept some of the paraphernalia needed for his boat-hiring business and two small rooms used as storage space for unwanted pieces of furniture.

'I could give them a good clean out and there's extra chairs and beds and chests of drawers here that they could make use of.' Ann pushed open the skylight in one room to let in the fresh warm air. 'It's not very fancy.'

'It would do fine, I'm sure.'

'Anything else can be put away in the garden shed or mebbe the workshop. They'll only be sleeping here anyway, for there's enough work in the summer to keep us all busy during the day. D'you think the McCabes could manage up here?'

'I'm sure of it. They'd be so grateful, Aunt Ann.'

'Then you can tell them when you get back that I'll be expecting them whenever they're ready to move in.'

'Are you certain that Uncle George'll be in favour?'

'Why not? For all that he's the head of the family, he's gone along with everything I've decided since the day we got wed, God bless him. And he's never had cause to regret it, so there's no reason to believe he'll not go along with this. I've just met the McCabe lassie a time or two when you brought her here, but she seems decent enough, and if they're hard-working they should fit in with us. But not a word to your uncle when he comes back . . . let me have a chat when we're on our own, just to give him his rightful place as head of the household. Is that them back already?' Ann added as the front door opened. 'We'd best get down and make a fresh pot. Your Uncle George could drink the stuff all day, and Alice should be coming in soon.'

5

A big wooden box carrying all that was left of their possessions after the blitz that destroyed their home had preceded the McCabes' arrival at Westervoe Farm early in 1940. Celia, grim-faced with disapproval at having to take on evacuees, had ordered the carter to leave the box in the cottage that she had cleaned out for the newcomers.

'As if we have nothing else to do with our time,' she had sniffed as she and Jennet scrubbed floors, cleaned windows and arranged the few pieces of furniture they could spare from the farmhouse, together with some items that the Red Cross had given them. 'And no doubt they'll have it looking like a midden before the week's out. Tenement folk know nothing about cleanliness.'

That was ironic, Jennet thought a few days later, watching the lodgers arrive and noting their shocked reaction as they passed the manure pit, where the used bedding from the cow byre and the dirt from the hen houses was piled up to mature before being scattered on the fields as fertiliser. Dirt came in many forms.

City-pale and anxious, carrying shabby suitcases bound with string, hung about with various bags and parcels, the Glaswegian family had edged into the yard, huddled together for safety, bewildered by the hens and the trees and the prospect of being marooned on an island, away from the streets and tenements and trams and cinemas they knew.

Nesta, clutching an ancient cage inhabited by a mangy-looking bird, was ashen with strain and exhaustion, while Sam was already wheezing and coughing with one of the asthma attacks that, in those days, had been brought on very easily by anxiety. Senga was sullen and Bert's attempt to be the man of the family disintegrated into panic when the farm dogs, Gumrie and his elderly mother Bess, so old then that she could scarcely walk, came to investigate the newcomers.

Then fourteen-year-old Mollie stepped out of the group, skinny as a rake, her tired white face blotchy with freckles and with straggly red hair that made her look, Celia said later, like a match that had just been struck. She said, 'Call your dogs off before I give them a good kicking, missus, and tell us where my ma can sit down before she falls down. She could do with a cup of tea, too. We've had a right bugger of a day.'

And even as the air whooshed out of her grandmother's lungs in a mighty gasp of shock, Jennet knew that at last she had found a proper friend.

The two girls went to school together, discovered the joys of the local dance halls and picture houses together when they were a little older, and fell in love with the same film stars. To Jennet, it seemed as though Mollie's flaming red head lit up the farm, sparking it into new life.

It was Mollie who, on discovering that Jennet nurtured a secret ambition to study nursing in the hope of being of practical use to Angus, egged her on to fulfil her dream.

'Of course I'll miss you,' she had said, 'but you need to do something with your life, and you'll be helping the war effort, too.'

'I don't know if I could live in Glasgow all by myself,' Jennet quavered. 'I've never been away from home before.'

'You'll not be all by yourself. Glasgow's hoachin' with folk. You can't cross a street without bumping into a dozen of them crossin' the other way. You'll like it,' Mollie had insisted. 'Mebbe it'll be a wee bit frightening at first, but you'll make friends.'

'I've got a friend. I've got you.'

'I know, but you need to meet folk, Jennet. You're like a wee mouse sometimes. It would do you good to go to a bigger place.'

'What if I don't like it, or I can't do the studying? What if I fail?'

'You'll only fail if you don't try,' Mollie argued. 'If it doesnae suit, then you can come back home and tell everyone you tried it but you didnae like it. Nob'dy can call you a failure for tryin'. I'll not let them.'

It was Mollie who, when Jennet returned home only a few months later, pregnant and disgraced, had crept into the house every night for weeks, buying Gumrie's silence with saved scraps of meat, crawling up the stairs and into Jennet's bed where she held her weeping friend, not once asking anything about Jamie's father; unlike Celia, who had badgered and hectored until Angus had finally told her that, if she didn't stop it, he and his sister would both leave Westervoe. After that, Celia manufactured some story about a young serviceman tragically killed just as he and Jennet were about to marry.

Five years on, the McCabes had changed beyond recognition. They had all put on weight and the pale city look had long since given way to a country glow. The anxious lines had been largely smoothed from Nesta's face, and Sam, taller and broader, no longer suffered from chest troubles. Mollie was still as thin as a whip despite her excellent appetite, and her red hair and cocky grin were still in evidence, as were the freckles, but now her skin was creamy rather than ashen and her hair glossy.

As she put her case down by the roadside and hugged Jennet, her face was wet with tears. 'It was easier tae leave Glasgow than tae leave this farm,' she said tremulously. 'It's daft . . . I was born in Glasgow!'

'You're not going all that far away. We'll see each other often enough.'

'Mind all the good times we've had, Jen?'

'How could I ever forget them?' Together they had
yearned over Clark Gable and envied Myrna Loy, and
had walked all the way home from the pictures on a
Saturday night arm in arm, planning wonderful futures
in which they would wear satin dresses and white
furs, and smoke Russian cigarettes through ivory
holders, and be wooed by handsome men driving
beautiful motor-cars.

'Mind the Winter Gardens, and buying two tickets
for the dancing?'

'Then running upstairs and out onto the balcony to
throw them down to the rest of the crowd so that the
next two could use them to get in . . .'

The dances had been wonderful, because there had
been plenty of partners, Polish and French as well as
British. During the war commandos had trained on
Bute, and as well as the submarine base in Rothesay
Bay itself, there had been a repair depot ship off Port
Bannatyne, dealing with damaged ships that had
managed to limp as far as the Clyde.

'Mind how disgusted our Senga was when we first
came and she discovered that milk came out of cows
and eggs from hens' backsides?' Mollie's face almost
split in two with amusement.

'And when she found out that the sausages she was
enjoying came from one of our own pigs,' Jennet said,
and they were just embarking on a great rush of
memories when the bus came into view and there was
a scramble to get everything collected up.

Nesta's hug was brief, but warm. 'Thanks for

getting your auntie to take us in, pet. You'll not regret it, I promise you that. Take care of yourself, and that wee laddie of yours.'

Sam, fast approaching his fourteenth birthday, too old for hugging and too young for shaking hands, concentrated on making his most fulsome goodbyes to Gumrie, who had accompanied them along the farm lane. Now he gave the dog a final pat, snatched up a mass of bags and parcels, settled for a gruff ''Bye then' to Jennet and rushed so quickly onto the bus when it stopped that his parcels got caught up round the pole.

While the grinning bus driver and the conductor helped the lad to sort himself out and then ushered him and his mother onto the bus, Mollie spun round, pecked Jennet swiftly on the cheek and whispered, 'Don't let your gran turn Angus back into an invalid.'

Then the bus was trundling along the road and out of sight, leaving Jennet behind. The war was over and the McCabes were gone from Westervoe.

Gumrie, sitting patiently at her side, gave a little whine as though he, too, felt as if something safe and familiar had come to an end. 'Come on, then,' she told him and turned back to the farm.

Celia's father and then her husband had bred Clydesdales, the beautiful big workhorses that for centuries had been invaluable to farming communities. As a young widow, struggling to keep the farm going, she had had to give up the Clydesdales, and

now Nero was the only horse at Westervoe. Angus
was grooming him in the stable when Jennet trailed
back after seeing the McCabes off.

As she appeared in the doorway he broke off the
soft tuneless whistle he always adopted when working
with the stock to say, 'They got away all right, then?'

'You should have come with us.'

'It was only to the end of the road, and they're just
going to Rothesay.'

'I'll miss them. And so will you.'

'Things change,' Angus said tersely. 'Folk move
on.'

'You'll miss Mollie.'

'Aye . . . the way I miss the midges in the winter,'
he said sarcastically.

'After all she did for you? You're ungrateful, d'you
know that?'

'And you're sentimental and that's worse,' he shot
back at her. 'Folk come and go, there's no sense in
trying to pretend that anything good stays for ever!'
He threw the brush down, then as Nero, sensing the
tension in the air, shifted uneasily, Angus stooped
clumsily to pick up the brush, clutching at the horse's
foreleg for support. Then he turned his back on his
sister and began to whistle again as he resumed work.
Jennet, furious with him, marched off across the yard.

Twisting round as best she could to see her friend as
the bus started to gather speed, Mollie was struck by
how lonely Jennet looked, standing on the grass verge.

For a moment she wanted to stop the bus and jump off, then her mother said anxiously, 'D'you think the Logans'll like us? D'you think we'll suit?' All at once Mollie knew where her own duties lay.

Life hadn't been good to her mum . . . an unhappy childhood with parents who had been in their forties when their only, and unwanted, child was born, then marriage to a man who had turned out to be violent. Despite Celia Scott's coldness, Westervoe had been the most secure home Nesta had ever known, and now she was being pitch-forked into yet another unknown future.

Mollie wanted to put her arms round her mother, birdcage and all, and tell her that everything would be all right, always. Instead she said briskly, 'Of course. I've met the Logans before, with Jennet. They're nice. We'll be happy there. And we'll be settled, at last.'

'I'm sorry about the stairs,' Ann Logan said as she led the way upstairs, 'but you'll see for yourself by next week that we need all the rooms on the middle floor for the holiday folk.'

'We're used to stairs,' Mollie assured her, suitcase in one hand and birdcage in the other. 'We used to live three floors up.'

'You were bombed out, weren't you? It must have been terrible.'

'We managed,' Nesta said tersely. Then, as they reached the attic floor, she gasped as Ann opened one of the two doors on the tiny landing and sunlight flooded out to meet them. The room was adequate, though small and sparsely furnished; but light poured in through a large skylight, making the fresh flowers that had been arranged in a vase glow.

'There's a double bed behind here . . .' Ann drew back a curtain in the corner. 'I thought mebbe you and Mollie could share that, Mrs McCabe. And the wee room that opens from this one is for your boy.'

She opened the door and Sam shot inside, then reappeared, grinning. 'Ma, come and see this!'

The room was little more than a long cupboard holding a single bed and a chair, but once again it was well lit by a skylight.

'There's a row of hooks there for your clothes, and that wee cupboard by the bed to hold some things. And there's room for things under the bed, too.'

'And I can see the sea, Ma,' Sam carolled, his head and shoulders almost out of the open skylight.

'You'll do more than see it.' Alice Logan, who had followed them upstairs, spoke for the first time. 'My dad's expecting you to help out with the boat-hiring.'

'He'll let me work with the boats? Can I learn to row?'

'You'll have to. I'll teach you if you like,' Alice offered, then blushed scarlet.

'We'll leave you to get settled in. Come downstairs when you're ready,' Ann said, 'and I'll make a cup of tea.'

'I can make it,' Nesta said swiftly. 'We don't want

to be a nuisance. We can see to this stuff later.'

Please, Mollie prayed silently, removing the cover from the bird's cage, please let her make the tea, Mrs Logan. Don't make Ma feel like a burden.

And as though in answer to her prayer she heard Ann Logan say, 'Why not? That's the best way to find out where everything is.'

His cover removed, Cheepy blinked, stretched one leg and then the other, fluffed his feathers and began to chirp.

Everything was going to be all right.

'They're looking sonsy. You'll not be short of a good cut of bacon this winter.'

Jennet, taking a moment as she passed the low stone wall to lean over and have a word with the two pigs within the sty, jumped and whirled round. 'Struan Blaikie!'

'Ye didnae think it was one of them speakin', did ye?' Struan nodded at the animals, grinning. 'D'you often have conversations with them?'

'I wasn't talking, I was just . . . Where did you spring from? Nobody told us you were home.'

'I got through all the business of being demobbed quicker than I'd expected, so I got the first train I could, then the first ferry. I telephoned the house when I got to Rothesay and they sent someone to fetch me.' The Blaikies were one of the few families on the island to own a telephone.

'When did you get back?'

'An hour ago, just.' He hadn't even taken time to change; he was still dressed formally in his ill-fitting demob suit. It, and his short bristly Army haircut, made him look like a stranger. 'Here, I'll take that.' He took the pail she had been carrying, holding it awkwardly away from his formal clothing as he walked ahead of her, glancing about at the trees.

'Is all this greenery not grand? I've seen nothing but stone and dust and bombed buildings for months now. It's good to be back,' he said and then, as they turned into the yard, 'and this place is as bonny as ever.'

Jennet surveyed the small, solid farmhouse and the flagged courtyard, trying to see it through his eyes, but failing. She was keenly aware that the yard's flag-stones were cracked and that the walls of the outbuild-ings had not been whitewashed for years. Sprigs of grass stuck out above the guttering and the paintwork on all the doors and window frames was sadly in need of attention.

'D'you think so?'

'Oh, aye. It's just grand to be back where the River Clyde's all about you, holding you safe on the one wee lump of green land.'

She blinked, surprised. Struan Blaikie had never been so expressive before the war. 'Your mother must be pleased to see you.'

'Aye, she is,' he said and then blushed scarlet. 'She cried, Jennet. I'd never seen my mother in tears. It was hard tae take.'

Jennet, too, found it hard to imagine Lizbeth
Blaikie, deeply religious and ramrod-straight in char-
acter as well as in deportment, weeping, yet now that
she was a mother herself she could sympathise with
the woman. 'You can't blame her,' she said gently.
'After all the worry about you and Allan away fighting,
and what happened to Drew.'

'That was a bad thing for them both. For all of us.
You'd be upset yourself,' Struan said, a slight upward
inflection in his voice, a question in the eyes suddenly
fixed intently on her face. 'After all, you were the
reason he stayed on.'

'Drew stayed because he felt that someone should
go on working the farm with your father,' Jennet said
sharply.

'Jennet, he was sweet on you from the time you
went into your teens, we all knew that. And you did
walk out with him once you left the school . . . for a
wee while.'

'Yes, but there were never any promises made,
Struan. I was as sorry as anyone else when he was
killed, but we weren't sweethearts.'

Though Drew would have liked them to be sweethearts. In that way going off to Glasgow had been a
relief, for Jennet had begun to find his interest in her
more than she could cope with, especially as both his
mother and Celia Scott had made it clear that they
were in favour of a match between the two families.

Drew had died just before she returned to Bute, pregnant with Jamie, and ever since then Lizbeth Blaikie

had avoided her whenever possible, and had been cold towards her on the few occasions when they were in each other's company. Whether this was because she blamed Jennet for her son's death, or for the shame she had brought to Lizbeth's crony Celia, or even a mixture of both, Jennet had no way of knowing.

'Aye, well, what's done's done,' Struan said now. 'We cannae bring the past back.' Then, lowering his voice slightly, 'What about Angus? How's he doing?'

'Fit as a fiddle, Struan,' Angus said from behind him. 'Never better. But then, I've not been as busy as you over the last few years.'

Struan spun round, startled. 'Man, where did you spring from?'

'I've been sweeping out the byre.' Angus leaned one shoulder against the byre doorframe, taking time to adjust his crutch for balance. 'I'm useful for that sort of thing, if nothing else.'

'It's grand to see you again!' Struan's voice was over-hearty. He began to hold his hand out.

Angus cast a glance down at his right leg, twisted so that his toes only just touched the ground. 'Funny, I never think of saying that when I catch sight of myself in a mirror,' he said, and Struan's hand, ignored, fell back to his side. 'Who'd have thought six years ago that the casualties were going to be Drew and me, the two who stayed behind? And you, Martin and Allan got through the war safe and sound. It makes you laugh, doesn't it?'

'No.'

'It makes me laugh, anyway,' Angus said, with not the shadow of a smile. 'But then, I get so little to laugh about these days.'

Although the air was warm enough, Jennet hugged herself against a sudden chill. 'Have you had any word of our Martin, Struan? We've been expecting him back home any day now.'

'The conquering hero home to claim his inheritance,' Angus agreed. 'At least, that's how Gran sees him. Is he still waiting to be demobbed? We thought he'd mebbe just turn up without warning, the way he usually did when he got leave.'

'Aye, I did see him just a few weeks ago.' Struan licked his lips, glancing nervously from brother to sister, then said in a rush of words, 'That's why I came over here right away, to get the matter settled.'

'What's happened?' Jennet asked sharply. 'He's . . . he can't be wounded, surely? Not now that it's all over and done with!'

'He's fine. It's just that . . . he's not coming back to Bute. To the farm. To . . .' Struan stopped, and it was left to Angus to say, 'To us. That's what you've come to say, isn't it? He's turned his back on us.'

'He might come home later, you never know.' Struan struggled to find the right words. 'The war's unsettled a lot of the lads. Some of them were desperate to get back to normal, like me, but others . . . Life's changed too much for them to be the way they were.'

Jennet and Angus stared at each other; this was the last thing they had expected. 'What'll Grandmother say?' Jennet voiced the thought in both their minds. 'Who's going to tell her?'

'Look, I have to go. I just dropped my kitbag off at home and told them that I needed to come here before . . .' Struan stopped as Celia Scott called from the farmhouse door.

'Struan Blaikie, is that you? Come in here at once. My, you look smart.' She came striding towards the three of them. 'Did Jennet not even offer you a cup of tea and a homemade scone? What are you thinking of, lassie, keeping the man standing in the yard and him just back from fighting for his country?'

'I was just going, Mrs Scott . . . I've just arrived . . .' Struan bleated, taking a couple of steps back.

Even though she was in shock at the news he had brought, Jennet was amused by his panic. Celia no longer used the cane that had once hung on the kitchen wall and was still kept in her bedroom, but her tongue lashed and stung and her eyes poked and prodded as her forefinger had once done. Full-grown though they now were, those who had been afraid of her when they were children still felt uneasy in her presence.

When she said, 'Nonsense, you're not setting foot off this farm without some hospitality inside you,' then headed back towards the house without a backward glance, Struan could only look helplessly at Jennet and Angus before plodding across the courtyard, his shoulders slumped and his feet suddenly dragging.

Following him, with the familiar shuffle and thump of Angus's progress at her back, Jennet wondered how they were going to tell Grandmother that Martin – the apple of her eye, the saviour she had been waiting for all those long weary war years – was not after all going to come home to the farm that she had been struggling to maintain for him.

6

'You'll have a drop of whisky to celebrate your home-coming.'

'No, no, Mrs Scott, I cannae do that.' Struan, more or less forced into the most comfortable armchair in the kitchen, looked anything but relaxed. 'My mother wouldn't like it and I'm just on my way back home.'

Celia looked at him with genuine warmth in her eyes. She had always liked the three Blaikie lads. 'Would you just listen to yourself, man . . . You've been fighting for your country all over the world and now here you are, fretting about your mother smelling drink on your breath.' Then, as Struan blushed and floundered, she added, 'But that's nothing to be shamed of. You'll just have the whisky in your tea, then.' And before he could do more than squeak a protest, she had tipped the bottle up and poured a generous measure into his cup, saying over her shoulder, 'Jennet, butter some scones while Struan tells us all about his travels.'

'I'd not call them that, Mrs Scott.' Struan took a mouthful of tea and blinked at the strength of its alcoholic content. 'We . . .' he cleared his throat, then went on, 'we just went where we were taken. Half the time we'd no notion where we were. And there was little to see but mud and bits of houses.'

'Your mother said you were in Germany at the end, same as our Martin.'

'Aye, that's right.'

'That's why neither of you got home as soon as the fighting was over. Though Martin should have been, with the farm to see to and all.' Celia's voice was heavy with resentment 'Not that he should have gone at all, being a farmer.'

'He wanted to do his bit for his country,' Angus said harshly from the corner, where he leaned against the wall. 'Same as the rest of us.'

'And a fine headache that idea caused me one way and another,' his grandmother snapped. 'It's been nothing but heartbreak for me these past five or six years!'

Jennet, embarrassed, tried to smile at Struan as she handed him a buttered scone on a plate. But his gaze was on the inner door.

'Hello,' he said and, turning, Jennet saw Jamie hesitating in the doorway, still drowsy from his afternoon sleep, his light brown hair, soft and curly like her own, tousled from the pillow.

'How did he get out of his cot?' Celia asked. Then, to Jennet, 'You must have left the side down. Have I not told you time and time again that it's dangerous?'

'It was up, but he's learning to climb over it when the mood takes him.'

'Hello, my name's Struan.' The young man held out his big calloused hand. 'What's yours?'

'Speak when you're spoken to, Jamie, and shake hands with Mr Blaikie,' Celia ordered. After glancing at his mother and getting a slight nod of encouragement, Jamie crept forward and put his own small fingers into the waiting palm.

'I didnae catch your name. Are you going to tell me what it is?'

'Jamie Scott.'

'I'm pleased to meet you, Jamie Scott. You're a fine strong laddie, are you no'? Mebbe you'll come over to Gleniffer some time and help me with the farm work.'

'Aye,' Jamie agreed eagerly, and Struan laughed.

'I'll mind that promise when we next need an extra farmhand.'

'Off you go now and play outside,' Celia commanded. Jennet, catching the little boy's wistful glance at the tray of freshly baked scones, split and buttered one for him.

'There you are, that'll keep you going until dinnertime.'

'And ruin his appetite,' Celia said as the child went out into the yard. 'You spoil that bairn, Jennet.'

'He's a nice lad,' Struan volunteered.

'We've done our best by him, given the circumstances,' Celia said, and Jennet felt the colour rise to her face. Struan gave her a swift glance, then crammed the last of the scone into his mouth and washed it down with a big gulp of tea.

'So what are your plans now you're back with us?' Celia wanted to know.

'I'll be content enough to work the farm with my dad, and take over when it suits him.'

'I thought mebbe Allan would see it as his duty to come back to the island, seeing as he's the eldest now.'

'He's got no wish to go back to the farming. He's well settled at Uncle Frank's shop and he likes the butcher business well enough. And from what I've heard . . .' Struan's grin flashed out, 'he's got friendly with a Glasgow lassie.'

'Oh?' Curiosity sharpened Celia's voice. 'Lizbeth never mentioned that to me.'

'She doesnae know. Allan says she'd start going on at him to bring the lass here to meet us and name a wedding date. If anything comes of it, he'll tell her in his own good time.'

'Did you see Martin at all when the two of you were in Germany?' Celia asked.

'It's a big place, Gran,' Angus put in. 'That's like asking you if you live next door to someone in Scotland.'

She shot him an irritated look and was opening her mouth to deliver one of her stinging retorts when Struan blurted out, 'Aye, Mrs Scott, I did see him just before I left, as it happens.'

Celia's face lit up with joy; it was on these rare

occasions, Jennet thought, that she caught a glimpse of the beautiful young woman her grandmother had once been. 'Is he well? Did he say when he'll be demobbed?'

A mixture of expressions rushed across Struan's face and the tip of his tongue shot out to moisten his lips. 'As a matter of fact . . .'

'As a matter of fact, Gran, our Martin's not coming home at all,' Angus said from his corner.

Celia wheeled round on him. 'What? Don't be daft, you don't know what you're talking about,' she snapped.

'I know what Struan told me and Jennet out in the yard.' Angus eased himself from the wall and limped over to take hold of the back of the other fireside chair. 'Martin's decided that he prefers life off this island.'

'Angus!' Jennet didn't even realise that she had spoken until the word hung in the air. Her brother looked across at her, one side of his mouth curving up in a strange little smile that had only appeared since his accident. For some reason that escaped Jennet, he enjoyed riling their grandmother, and each time it happened he smirked as though he had scored a mark for himself in some secret game between the two of them.

'Of course he's coming home,' Celia said. 'He has to come home!'

'He doesn't seem to think so. He's found the big wide world, Gran, and he's going to stay in it. Who wouldn't, given the choice?'

'Leave it, Angus,' Struan Blaikie said quietly.

'But . . . he has to come home.' Celia sounded bewildered and confused. She put one hand out behind her and it found and clutched at the table for support, while the other hand flew to her mouth. 'He has to,' she said from behind it in a strange, fluttery voice. Jennet was shocked to see that her grandmother had aged ten years in a few seconds.

'Mrs Scott . . .' Struan was out of his chair in an instant, passing Jennet and taking the older woman's arm in both hands. 'Sit down for a minute.'

He guided her into the chair he had just left, while Jennet, suddenly coming to her senses, flew to refill her grandmother's cup. 'Here, Gran . . .'

'Whisky might be better,' Struan suggested over Celia's bent grey head. It lifted so suddenly that both he and Jennet took a startled step back.

'Whisky? Are you daft? Me that signed the pledge when I was six years old and had to be lifted onto a chair to do it? Whisky's for visitors, and the day one drop of the filthy stuff touches my lips is the day my soul's damned for eternity!' Celia seized the cup from Jennet, drank the hot liquid down, then slammed the cup back onto the saucer with a crash and fixed her piercing grey gaze on Struan.

'Tell me. Tell me every word that he said to you!'

'Well . . .' he swallowed hard. 'As I mind it, he just said that he wanted to see a bit of the world.'

'Has he not been doing that for the past five years, while I've been working my fingers to the bone . . .'

Celia, ignoring any contribution Jennet and Angus
had made to the farmwork, thrust her swollen hands,
the skin red and cracked, out towards Struan, 'trying
to keep his heritage intact for him? Have I not been
counting the days till I could hand it all over to him
and take a well-earned rest?' Then, suddenly, 'Is it a
woman? Is that it?'

'What?' He gaped at her, taken aback.

'Is that what's kept Martin from his duties here?
Has he found some woman that wants to keep him
from us? One of those women in the services, or
mebbe someone in Germany. Is that it? Has he met
up with a foreigner who wants him to turn his back
on his own blood kin and stay with her in her
country?'

'Not as far as I know.'

'Are you sure? We might live on a wee island,'
Celia sniffed, 'but we've heard things about our
soldiers and the women that chase after them with no
thought to the harm they might be doing. Did he not
even give you a letter for me?'

'Oh . . . aye,' he suddenly remembered, fishing in
one pocket and then changing his mind and going into
another. Finally he brought out an envelope, glancing
at the name on the front before holding it out. 'This
is for you,' he said and then, as it was snatched from
his hand, 'my father says to tell you that him and
me'll do all we can to help. He says he'll be over
later to see you.'

'Your father's been very good to us, Struan, but he

shouldn't have to go on helping out. Martin has to
come home!'

'He's a man, not a child, Gran,' Angus pointed out.
'He's been fighting for his country for the past five
years. He'll do as he wants.'

'He'll do his duty!'

'I'm sure Martin will come back . . . eventually.'
Struan stood before her like a naughty child hauled
from the safety of his desk to explain himself to the
teacher. 'Once he gets over all that's happened to him
in the past few years.'

'All that's happened to *him*?' Celia emphasised the
final word and then skirled a high-pitched derisive
laugh. 'He survived, didn't he? What more does he
want from life? Well, mebbe when his lordship decides
he wants to come back, he'll find that he's not wanted
any more. Two can play at that game!'

'Mrs Scott, you'd surely not . . .'

'It was good of you to visit and we're all pleased
to see you back, Struan,' Celia said dismissively. 'But
don't let us keep you from your parents any longer.'

Jennet followed Struan into the yard. 'I'm sorry
about . . .' She gestured towards the house.

'D'you think she means it about not letting Martin
come home?'

'I don't think she knows what she means right now.
She's upset. We'll have to give her time to calm down.'

He pulled his cap on. 'I wish I hadnae had tae be
the one tae tell her,' he said, then glanced at the kitchen

window, lowering his voice even though they had moved too far away from the house to be heard. 'Martin asked me to give these to you and Angus.' He slid a hand into the pocket he had first reached into and drew out two envelopes identical to the one he had given Celia.

Jennet, too, glanced guiltily at the window before slipping the envelopes deep into the pocket of her big apron. Struan began to turn away, then paused, his eyes on Jamie, who was running about the yard pulling his cart behind him.

'That's a fine wee laddie you've got there. My mother said his father was killed in the fighting.' It was half statement, half question.

'Yes.' Jennet had learned, over the past two and a half years, that the only way to deal with inquisitive questions was to speak in a flat monotone and meet the gaze of the questioner full on. That way she made sure that people were too embarrassed to pry any further.

'It's a shame he didnae live to see his son. You're going to raise him on your own?'

'I am.'

He hesitated and then at last he went, striding over the cracked flagstones with the square-shouldered, cocky walk he had inherited from his father.

Andra and Lizbeth Blaikie both came round that night.

'How are you, Celia?' Mrs Blaikie asked sympathetically.

'As well as can be expected, given the news your Struan brought us today.'

'Aye, he told us. It's a bad do this, Celia,' the farmer said, dropping heavily into a chair by the table.

'A bad do? It's more than that . . . it's downright ingratitude,' his wife snapped. 'What possessed him? Is it a woman, d'you think?'

'Either that or the war's done something to his brain. Jennet, make some tea and bring out that fruit-cake, will you? I don't know what I've done to deserve it all,' Celia said plaintively. 'He's turned out to be just like his father, a weak reed.'

'He wants time to himself after what he's been through,' Angus butted in.

'That's no excuse,' Mrs Blaikie told him. 'Your Martin should know where his duty lies, and it's right here, at Westervoe. Your poor grandmother can't go on for ever, and who's to run the place if he doesn't come home soon?'

'The main thing is what's to be done about the situation he's put you in, Celia,' Andra broke in. 'I'm sure you'll manage, with our help. Now Struan's back, we'll be able to help you with the harvesting and threshing and with anything else that's needed.'

'It's very kind of you, Andra, and I know you mean it, but that's not the right way to run a farm, is it?'

'Ach, don't be daft, woman! I know that you and yours would do the same for me.'

'Aye, if we were able.' Celia cast a contemptuous look at her grandchildren and added, 'But the way we are just now, I doubt if we'd be much use to a jumble sale!'

'So what did he have to say to you?' Angus, collecting eggs with Jamie's help, intercepted Jennet the following day as she returned from a small field where she had been cutting back an unruly hedge.

The ribbon that kept her hair out of her face had slipped; she pulled it off, then began to retie it. 'What did who say?'

'Our dear distant brother, of course,' Angus said impatiently.

'Not much.' Just a few scrawled lines that, in their lack of feeling, had said a lot about Martin's determination to break away from his former life and the people in it. 'That he couldn't face coming back here, that he wants to make his own way in the world.'

'Bad hen!' Jamie's muffled voice scolded from inside one of the wooden arks. There was a flurry and a squawk and then a hen rushed out of the small arched door and fled to join her sisters. Jamie, bent double, followed her out and handed a warm egg to his mother when he had straightened up. 'Here.'

'Thank you.'

'All done,' Jamie announced to his uncle and ran ahead of them as they turned towards the farmhouse.

'I wonder what Martin wrote to Grandmother?' Angus said thoughtfully.

'I doubt if she'll tell us.'

'Did he say anything about our father in your letter?'

Jennet bit her lip. She hadn't wanted to mention that part of Martin's brief letter. His pen had suddenly cut deep into the cheap paper as he wrote, 'I can understand now why our father walked out after our mother died. She must have seemed like his only escape from his sterile upbringing . . . and any life without some sort of love in it is sterile, Jen. He couldn't face going back to his past and I can't face it, either. I want to live, and the only way I can do that is by staying away until I feel strong enough to dominate Gran instead of letting her dominate me. If that day should ever come.'

'Yes,' she said. 'Yes, he did mention him.'

'Damn him!' Angus's voice was suddenly vehement. 'Damn him to hell! Does he think he's the only one who wants to escape from this place?'

'You both make it sound like a prison.'

He gave a derisive laugh. 'Aye, complete with jailer.'

'Gran's old-fashioned, just. She loves us in her own way.'

'Sometimes folk mix up love with possessiveness. I'd have been away with Martin, if it hadn't been for my accident, and you tried to get away too, as soon as you were old enough. You shouldn't have come back.'

Jennet stared at the egg cooling in the curve of her palm. Its shell was pale brown, and downy feather scraps clung to it. Seventeen years old, she had been, pregnant and terrified and alone in a big city.

'I couldn't think of anything but coming home.' She placed the egg carefully into her brother's basket.

Angus dug the end of his crutch into the ground as he swung along by her side. 'More fool you. She made you suffer as much as if you'd committed a crime, and she's been making you suffer ever since. What was there to come home to?'

You, she wanted to say, but dared not for fear of angering him even further. She had been unable to think of anything other than running back to Angus and to Mollie. The two of them had been her safety net at that terrible time.

'You were a fool,' he went on when she said nothing. 'If you'd only written to me first, I'd have told you to stay where . . .'

'That tractor's acting up again,' Jem McKenzie came to meet them as they turned into the yard.

Angus sighed. 'What's wrong with it?'

'How should I know? I'm a farm worker, no' a bloody engineer.'

Jem had worked for the Scott family for more than fifty years, and in a lifetime of knowing him Jennet had never seen the man smile. Old age and resentment at having to go on working, when he should have been enjoying a well-earned retirement, had not sweetened his disposition at all.

'If you really want tae know what I think, I'd say that it feels the way I dae,' he went on. 'It's done its bit for Britain and it's old and just wants tae be left in peace. But it never . . .'

There was a shout of pleasure from Jamie and a mad scramble of paws as Gumrie came dashing into the yard and made straight for the little boy, licking his face while Jamie hugged him.

'Stop that, ye daft animal!' Celia came round the corner, brandishing her sturdy stick at the dog. 'Jamie, how many times have I told ye not tae let him do that?'

'Likes me,' Jamie said. 'My friend.'

'He's a working dog!' his great-grandmother said, exasperated. She had done all she could to make Gumrie behave like a proper farm dog, aloof and dignified, but even though he was well trained and obedient, he still loved people. In Celia Scott's eyes that was a fatal weakness.

'Get out of it,' Jem roared as Gumrie headed towards him. The dog suddenly checked its rush, swinging round and trotting off to bully the two cats sunbathing in a corner, with a casual air that said that was what he had intended to do all along.

'It's not as if the wee soul has any other friends to play with,' Angus pointed out to his grandmother.

'You're surely not suggesting that his mother should have more bairns just to keep him company?' Celia glared at the three of them. 'So all the work's done, then, that you've got nothing else to do but stand there and gossip?'

'I'm just here tae say that the tractor's b-broke down again,' said Jem.

'Can you not fix it?'

'He's a farm worker, no' an engineer,' Angus informed his grandmother, straight-faced.

'It's a pity that wee Sam McCabe's no' here any more. He'd a way wi' gadgets,' Jem said, and Celia's mouth tightened.

'We can manage without him and his family. We'd best have a look at it.'

'No' me.' Jem tugged his cap more firmly down on his head. 'I'm away home tae my tea.'

'Already?'

'It's my usual time, and Bessie gets agitated if I'm not back at the right time. It's a long day for her on her lone. She's missin' havin' me about the place tae help with the things she cannae do any more,' Jem added meaningfully. His wife suffered badly from arthritis.

'Oh, very well, if you must. On your way past Gleniffer Farm,' Celia called after the old man as he headed for the lane and freedom, 'you can go in and ask if Andra or Struan could come and have a look at the tractor tomorrow morning.'

Jem turned and gave her what Ann Logan would have called an old-fashioned look. It was understandable, for the lane that led down to the Blaikie farm was long, and the old man's walk home would be doubled in length by the time the message was delivered.

Then he turned back a second time, his gloom lightening a little now that he had remembered more bad news. 'That dry-stane dyke down by the shore field's beginnin' tae crumble. Best see tae it afore one of the cows gets out and manages tae drown itself,' he advised and then disappeared round the corner as Celia gave a huff of exasperation.

'Angus, you'd better candle these eggs and clean them while we look at the wall.'

'I'll go with you, and Jennet can see to the eggs. She looks as if she could do with a rest.'

'We could all do with a rest, but by the time you get down there the whole wall could have crumbled. Your sister and me can manage between us,' Celia said scathingly and marched off without a backward glance.

7

Jennet, not daring to look at her brother's face, scurried in her grandmother's wake, fury boiling up inside her. She waited until they were out of the yard and into the narrow lane leading down past the two fields that lay between the farm and the Firth of Clyde before she said, 'There was no need to speak to Angus like that.'

'Like what? I said nothing but the truth and if he's not man enough to take it, that's his concern. You're too soft, Jennet. We all know that he cannae do a man's work any more.'

'He does all he can.'

'Mebbe, but it's not enough, so I'm not minded to give him a medal for it.' Celia stopped for a moment and swung round to face her granddaughter. 'We're farming folk, lassie, no' the landed gentry. And on a farm there's no room for sentiment. If an animal cannae earn its keep, it has to go.'

'So you're suggesting that we should send Angus to the slaughterhouse?'

'You're not too old to get a clout round the ear when you've earned it, madam!' Celia dealt the grass by the side of the lane a hefty swish with the stick she always carried. 'I'm saying that now that your brother's lame, he has tae accept that there's things he cannae do any more. If we waited for him to hop and shuffle around the place with that crutch of his, nothing would get done. Now stop talking and keep walking, for we've not got all day.'

There were indeed the beginnings of a break in the dry-stane wall between the lower field and the narrow strip of shore, where two or three of the top level of boulders had tumbled. Jennet clambered over the wall and the two women worked silently, one on each side, heaving the boulders back into place, then wedging them there with smaller stones until, at last, Celia was satisfied.

Before leaving she walked the length of the wall, searching for any other weak points, while Jennet followed, her own eyes straying to the view she had loved all her life, in all weathers. The Scott farm was on the west of the island, looking across the pearly waters of the Sound of Bute, a narrow section of the Firth of Clyde, to the island of Arran, its mountain range known, because of its distinctive outline, as the Sleeping Warrior.

When she turned away from the river, the inland view of fields and trees was just as beautiful. The road ran along a low hillside, and from it Westervoe, tucked into a dip in the fields, was scarcely seen. She glimpsed several cyclists at a bend in the road before they were hidden by trees, though the musical ting of a bell and the faint sound of voices and laughter rang through the air as they passed. The island was already bursting with holidaymakers, and she had heard that every steamer that arrived from the mainland carried a full complement of passengers.

Jennet loved every part of the island, but Angus was right when he said that, to them, Westervoe was more of a prison than a home. Perhaps that was how it felt to her grandmother, too. Like Jennet, Celia Scott had been born and raised there; her husband had moved there after their marriage; and when he died tragically young, Celia had worked hard to keep the place going for the sake of her son James, who had not been much older than Jamie was now.

When James grew up and married and began to raise his own family, Celia must have felt as though a load had lifted from her shoulders. But his wife's death and then his own desertion had left her with three grandchildren to tend, as well as the farm. No wonder, Jennet thought, her grandmother had become bitter. And no wonder Martin's decision not to come home had been the final straw.

'Jennet! Stop dreaming and get a move on.' Celia was already halfway up the lane, the hem of her long mackintosh swinging around the top of her wellington boots. She had two coats for farm work: the mackintosh for summer and a thick tweedy coat for the colder weather. Both were very old, but durable. A man's hat was jammed on her head throughout all the seasons.

Would it have been better if Celia had given up and let the farm go, or accepted the Logans' offer to raise her grandchildren? In some ways Jennet wished that that had happened, but in another . . .

She glanced back at the Sound of Bute and knew why her grandmother had held on through the long, hard years. She would do the same, if it were for Jamie's sake.

As the Scott family dwindled in size, so did Westervoe Farm; now it was so small that it could support only a thousand hens, the two pigs bought in each year for fattening and about fifteen cows, each of them named and with her own personality.

Today a young animal, new to milking following the birth of her first calf, got into the wrong stall by accident, and her panic when she realised her error, together with the chaos she caused among the others, reminded Jennet of a group of elderly, respectable women who had wandered into a public house in error, mistaking it for a cake shop.

'Here, Gloria, in here!' Most of the cows were named after flowers, but Mollie had insisted on calling the new cow after Gloria Swanson, the American film actress. With help from Angus, Jennet shooed her into the proper stall and untangled the others.

While his mother and uncle resolved the problem, washed the cow's udders and then settled to the milking, Jamie bustled happily up and down the line, issuing a pat here and a reprimand there.

Hand-milking had become one of Jennet's favourite pastimes. In the winter the byre was warm compared to outside, and in summer, when the farming day stretched from dawn until dusk, it gave her a chance to sit still for a while, listening to the cows chewing contentedly at the chopped turnips in their feeding troughs, and leaning against their warm flanks as she worked. Sometimes it was even possible to drowse off while her hands automatically squirted the milk into the bucket. On more than one occasion the cow had wakened her with a gentle nudge when the bucket was full, although with one of the more temperamental animals Jennet might well be roused by a sudden shifting of her support, which almost sent her crashing from the stool, or the bucket would be tipped over by a carefully aimed back hoof.

Today Gloria managed to surprise Jennet by suddenly swishing her tail, sending its tip into the creaming milk.

'Oh, Gloria, look what you've done!'

The cow, surprised at the sudden fuss, looked round at Jennet with large, naïve eyes that bore no trace of her namesake's sultry gaze, while Jamie came scurrying up to inspect the damage. 'Naughty cow, no sweeties this week!' he scolded. And Jennet, milk dripping from her dungarees, only just managed to rescue the pail before it tipped over entirely.

'It'll do for her calf,' Angus advised, rising stiffly

from his seat in the next stall. 'D'you want me to finish her? The rest are done anyway.'

'She is finished . . . She waited until the last minute.' Jennet stooped to pick up the pail. 'I'll get changed, then take this in to the calf while you and Jem take the animals back out.'

Struan Blaikie had arrived to look at the tractor, looking more like himself now that he had replaced his demob suit with heavy corduroy trousers and an open-necked shirt, though the ugly Army haircut, bristly and cropped close to the skull, still set him apart from the Struan she remembered, with his unruly tumble of blue-black hair. He grinned when Jennet emerged from the byre opposite, milk dripping from her clothes, and called across the yard, 'Throwin' yourself intae the work, eh?'

'Something like that,' she agreed, going into the house with Jamie trotting by her side. When they emerged, the cows, well able to find their way back to their field without assistance, were heading out of the yard, with Jem, Angus and Gumrie ambling along behind them.

Normally Jamie would have run to join them, but he had made a particular pet of Gloria's calf, so today he was happy to follow his mother into the calf shed. Watching him struggle to hold the pail steady while the little creature thrust her woolly head into it and sucked noisily at the milk, Jennet dreaded the day she would be taken to market. The Scotts, like most of the farming folk, had formerly sold only the bullocks and raised the heifers for their own milk herd, but a few years back Celia had decided that the calves were too time-consuming that it would be easier to sell them all on and buy in heifers when needed.

'He's going to make a fine farmer when his time comes.' Struan, rubbing oil from his hands with a rag, came to lean on the lower half of the double door to watch Jamie with the calf.

'He might not get the chance, the way things are going.'

'Is your gran still angry with Martin?'

'She'll not have his name mentioned.'

'She'll come round,' he said unconvincingly and then opened the lower part of the door and came into the shed, lowering his voice. 'I was wondering if you fancied a visit to the pictures on Friday?'

'Me?' She stared at him, taken aback. 'I don't know, Struan. I've got Jamie to see to, and I doubt if my grandmother . . .'

'I'd really like it if you'd come,' he urged. 'There's a Western picture on at the Ritz; with that Roy Rogers in it. And a scary picture with Boris Karloff at the Palace. You could choose.'

She hesitated. She hadn't been to the cinema or a dance – or even a party – since Jamie's birth. Somehow she had fallen into the habit of thinking that she had forfeited the right to pleasure or frivolity.

'There's surely plenty of girls you know that would be pleased to go with you.'

'I'd as soon go with you, and I'm sure you deserve

a wee night out every bit as much as I . . .'

He spun round guiltily as Celia said from just behind him, 'There you are, Struan. How's the tractor?'

He snapped to attention. 'I've not quite finished with it, Mrs Scott. It'll only take another five minutes.'

'Then don't let us keep you back. I hope Jennet's invited you in for a cup of tea?'

'I was going to,' Jennet said, 'but . . .'

'I was just asking if she'd like to go to the pictures with me, Mrs Scott,' Struan butted in, his face flushing. 'Friday, I thought. Would that be all right?'

'The pictures?' Celia looked from one to the other. 'Well, mebbe it's time you had a night out, Jennet. I'll see to the child for you.'

'Are you sure?'

'Just tell the man yes, before I change my mind,' her grandmother said. 'I'll make the tea.'

'So it's all right then?' Struan asked Jennet as Celia went into the house.

'I don't . . .'

'Your gran says it is.'

'Then why don't you take her?' Jennet asked, suddenly exasperated. 'What did you want to go and tell her about it for?'

'I just wanted to be sure that it was all right.'

'I'm a grown woman, Struan Blaikie. I can decide these things for myself.'

'Does that mean yes?'

She opened her mouth to argue and then decided

that it was not worth the effort. 'I suppose so,' she said ungraciously. 'Why not?'

Struan beamed. 'I'll call for you at half past six then.'

'I'll meet you at the bus stop. And Struan?'

'Aye?'

'We'll go to the Western,' Jennet said.

To Celia's annoyance, the tractor was not going to be repaired easily. It required a new part, and these days spare parts were not easy to come by.

'I might be able to find one,' Struan offered while he was having his tea. 'We've got an old machine that's not used any more and if I can't get what you need from it, I could try round the other farms. Some of them got more modern machines during the war, so they could have older tractors, like yours, sitting in their sheds. If I can't find anything, I'll have to order the part, but with shortages still making everything difficult I don't know when it'll get here. It's getting a wee bit old, too, and that might make it more difficult to get the part.'

'Well, do your best, for I'd like it to see our time out. It's not worth putting the money out on a new machine, even if we had that sort of money to throw about.'

'I'll do what I can, Mrs Scott.'

'You're a good lad,' Celia said fondly. 'Have another oatcake.'

* * *

The following day Celia surprised her grandchildren
by arriving downstairs dressed in the black costume
and ivory silk blouse that she wore for weddings,
funerals and Women's Rural Institute activities and
announcing that she had decided to pay a visit to her
sister Rachel in Largs, a coastal town on the mainland.

'I've not been to see her for a good long while and,
after all, she is my only sister.'

'Since the mountain won't come to Mahomet . . .'
Angus murmured as Jennet handed his plate to him.
She turned a giggle into a cough. Celia's younger sister,
plumper but just as strong-willed, rarely visited Bute,
for she disliked crossing the water and she loathed
animals. She had been more than happy, while still in
her teens, to marry an office worker and exchange her
island farm home for the mainland.

'What's that you said, Angus?' Celia asked from
the stove, where she was cooking, having covered her
'good' clothes with a large apron to prevent splashes.

'I was just clearing my throat. We'll manage fine,
Gran.'

'I doubt that, but there's not much to do today that
can go wrong, and Jem will be coming.'

She departed immediately after breakfast, and as
her back view disappeared down the lane leading to
the road and the bus stop, the atmosphere seemed to
undergo a change. Even Gumrie's shining eyes took
on an added sparkle and Angus went about his work
with energy and enthusiasm, deftly utilising his crutch

so that it became a natural part of his body, instead of a clumsy man-made contraption of wood, leather and padding.

If only he could be left alone to get on with things in his own way all the time, Jennet thought, watching him. Ever since the accident Celia had treated him like a helpless child, refusing to allow him to do anything that might hurt or upset him. Meanwhile, Jennet looked on helplessly, certain that Angus was being damaged both mentally and emotionally, as well as physically, but unsure what to do about it.

Then the McCabes had arrived and Mollie, heedless of Celia's silent fury, had taken it upon herself to get Angus back onto his feet. The Glasgow girl had teased, nagged and coaxed him day after day, blithely indifferent to his sullen resentment. At first he had taken refuge in silence, but once she had managed to goad him into shouting back at her, Mollie began to dare him to take control of his own life and get back on his feet. She had been like a terrier baiting a bull, dancing in close enough to sting and then darting off, deflecting all his anger and his insults with her wide grin until, finally, he had given in.

It had taken a whole year, and all the time Celia had simmered like a kettle on a low heat, saying nothing openly to Mollie but undermining her efforts as much as she could. Then came the day when Angus stumped into the kitchen on his two crutches and tossed one into a corner, then he did a lap round the big table with only the other crutch for support.

'And that one I keep,' he told Mollie, 'so that I've got something to hit you with when you get too cheeky.'

She stuck out her tongue at him. 'You'd have to catch me first.'

'Oh, I'll do that all right,' he said and flourished his free arm, like a magician who had just performed a particularly difficult trick and was inviting the audience's applause. 'What d'you think, Gran?'

Celia had turned from the range, surveyed him and then said dourly, 'You'd best sit in. Your dinner's ready.'

The day passed all too quickly. Jem worked with a will when Celia was not there to boss him around, and even the animals cooperated. When Celia arrived back early in the evening the work had been completed and Jamie was being bathed in the old tin tub in front of the kitchen range. For once the three of them had turned bath-time into a game and when Celia marched in the little boy, over-excited, screeched, 'G'eat g'an!' and waved a wet soapy arm joyfully in the air.

'Look at that . . . water all over my good rug! Sit still and behave yourself,' she admonished him.

'He's just pleased to see you,' Angus told her.

'He doesnae need to soak the place to prove it.' Celia drew three large hatpins from her hat, then removed it without ruffling one iron-grey hair. 'Make a cup of tea, Jennet, while I get changed. The steamer home was packed with folk, and their boxes and bags and cases were all over the deck. A body could scarcely move! And Rothesay's no better – bairns running about everywhere when they should be home and in their beds.'

'They're on holiday, Gran.'

'That's no excuse to let their standards go, Angus. Badly behaved bairns grow up to be badly behaved adults.'

'How was Great-Aunt Rachel?' Jennet made a fresh pot of tea while keeping an anxious eye on Jamie, praying that he wouldn't slop water over the side of the bath.

'Very well. She sends her regards to you both. I'll be back down in a minute.'

When Celia had gone, Jennet whipped a protesting Jamie out of his bath and hurried him into his pyjamas, then left Angus to give him his supper of bread and milk while she emptied and dried the bath, put it away and mopped the floor.

While Celia, back in her usual work clothes, drank her tea, Jennet put Jamie to bed and then went downstairs to dish out the supper. All through the meal Celia harangued them about idle, slatternly holidaymakers who didn't know what it was like to have to work all year round and never have time for luxuries like holidays. Afterwards she insisted on shutting up the hens herself, in order, Angus pointed out, to have the chance to check that everything had been done to her satisfaction.

'I don't care,' Jennet said from the sink where she

was washing the dishes. 'She can inspect all she wants, it's just nice not to have to do the hens for once.'

By the time Celia arrived back the kitchen was cleared and tidy for the night. Jennet took the opportunity to go out and weed the garden, leaving the other two talking about the haymaking, which was soon to start. The garden was an added chore, but she enjoyed working in it; out there she could be on her own for once, and was able to let her mind range free while her hands worked.

Haymaking should be good this year, she thought as she teased weeds from between the rows of carrots. The weather was fine and if the rain stayed away, then the hay, which had to be left lying in the field once it was cut so that it could be turned and turned and thoroughly dried, should do well.

When the midges became too much to bear she poured several scoops of water from the butt over the growing plants, then eyed the well-tended beds with satisfaction. It had been a good day all round, and now she was ready for her bed.

She had reached the living room when she heard raised voices from beyond the door leading to the kitchen. All at once the peace and tranquillity of the day ebbed away.

8

'You can't just wipe him off the map like that . . . He's your own grandson,' Angus was saying. 'You raised him!'

'Aye, I did, and if I'd known what a worthless, thankless young man he was going to become, I'd have thrashed it out of him while I still had him in my charge!'

'Mebbe you thrashed it into him,' Angus suggested as Jennet came into the kitchen.

Celia drew in her breath with an outraged hiss. 'You dare to say that to me? The belt's the only thing bairns understand, and if they grow up wrong it's because of a lack of it, not too much. As far as I'm concerned, your brother's no longer part of this family.'

Jennet, fearful that the raised voices might disturb Jamie, closed the door behind her. 'You can't pretend Martin doesn't exist, Gran. What if he needs us, or wants to come home?'

'Then want must be his master.' Celia's voice, hard

as flint, dredged up a favourite saying of hers, one
that had been dinned into her three growing grandchildren. 'I want him here right now, but he's not here,
is he? As to whether I can put him out of our lives,
I can do whatever I wish and you'd both be wise to
remember that.'

'You can do what you must, but I'll not shut my
own brother out of my life,' Angus told her.

'Then you're a fool. He's let you down as well,
leaving all of us to go off to the war when he should
have stayed here where he belonged, working this
farm. But, oh no, not Martin. All he could think of
was having a fine adventure, and never mind his duty.'

'That was more my fault than his. I was the one
who came up with the idea of us going to enlist along
with Geordie Logan.'

'And look at us now . . . you dependent on a crutch,
your cousin dead and your brother refusing to come
back home.'

Angus winced, but persisted. 'He's still our own
flesh and blood.'

'So am I, and when does anyone consider my feelings?' Celia's voice rose. 'Not one of you ever thinks
about the struggle I've had to keep the place together
so that Martin could inherit it and work it.'

'Angus's the oldest,' Jennet said, and Celia stared
at her.

'What?'

'It's not Martin who should take over the farm
anyway. Angus is the oldest.'

'Don't be daft!'

'Angus knows about farming. He won the ploughing competition two years in a row, and . . .'

'Leave it, Jen,' her brother said gruffly.

'Aye, stay out of things that don't concern you!' Celia stood with both hands clamped over the back of a kitchen chair, glaring at the two of them and breathing hard through her nose. Jennet was reminded of a carthorse she had once seen at the cattle show in Rothesay, a great fearsome creature with the same fierce stare and the same way of blowing air through its flaring nostrils.

'I'm an old woman and mebbe it's time you both minded that. I'd already decided to go and stay with my sister Rachel in Largs once your brother came back to take over the farm, and I see no reason why I should change my plans. She's been on at me to go over there for years now, so I've decided that come Martinmas I'm giving the factor six months' notice to find a new tenant.'

Now it was Jennet's turn to say 'What?' She looked at her brother and, when he just looked back at her stony-faced, continued, 'Angus, d'you hear that?'

'I've already heard it. Why else d'you think we were arguing when you came in?'

'After all these years you surely can't just walk away from this place?' Jennet asked her grandmother in disbelief.

'Everything has to come to an end. I should have moved out years ago, when your father got married, but since he saw fit to marry a lassie who knew nothing about farming, I'd to stay on to teach her the way of it. Not that she ever showed much ability for it,' Celia said. 'And the next thing I knew, they were both gone and I was left with the three of you on my hands. But now the time's come for me to let it all go to someone else.'

'We can surely manage,' Jennet protested. 'There's men coming back to the island from the war, needing work. We can hire the folk we need.'

'And what do we pay them with? This place hasnae made much money for a good while now. It's only the bigger farmers, like Andra Blaikie, that can afford to hire workers. I've been hard put to it to find the rent these past few years . . . But you'd not know anything about that, would you? It's left to me, as usual.'

'We'd have been more than willing to be involved, Grandmother, if you'd only given us the chance,' Jennet protested. Then, as Celia's nostrils flared again, she went on hurriedly, 'There must be things we can do to make more money.'

'Indeed? Mebbe you'd tell me about them, milady, since you're so smart!'

The contempt in her words whipped heat into Jennet's face, but she forged on. 'We could take in holidaymakers. There's the cottage the McCabes used.'

Celia gave a screech of contemptuous laughter. 'Trippers? Folk from Glasgow and the like? We'd just be makin' more work for ourselves.'

'We could use part of the money they'd bring in to pay a woman to do the cooking and cleaning, then you and me would be free to work outside with Angus and Jem. And there might be enough left to hire a young lad willing to learn farmwork. Quite a lot of the farms let out their spare rooms – the estate allows it.' Bute was owned by the Marquess of Bute, who lived in Mount Stuart, a splendid estate on the island. The Scotts, like almost all the other farmers on the island, were tenants.

'I'll not have strangers making free of this house!' Celia thundered.

'That'll happen anyway, if you let Westervoe go to new tenants.'

'And where do you suggest we should live when you've handed the farm over?' Angus asked swiftly as Celia rounded on Jennet. She contented herself with a narrow-eyed glare, then turned back to him.

'That's what Rachel and me were talking about today. She's got a ground-floor room you can have, Angus, and Jennet can go back to learn nursing in Glasgow.'

'I couldn't manage to take Jamie with me.'

'Of course not. He'll stay with Rachel and me while you're training.'

'But I . . .'

'Beggars can't be choosers, Jennet. He's well behaved for a child, and he can live with you once you've finished your training and you're able to support him. I hope you realise that it's very good of my sister to offer to take the three of us in.'

'So it's all been settled already, without consulting us,' Angus said.

'I'm discussing it with you now, and you can't deny that I've still got your welfare at heart. The welfare of all three of you,' Celia added.

'And Angus is expected to leave his home and the island, just like that?'

'He's not got much of a choice, have you, son? How could you manage without me to look after you?'

Angus bit his lip while Jennet watched him anxiously, willing him to tell Celia that he would have nothing to do with her plans. Instead, he lurched to his feet. 'I'm going to my bed.'

'Gran . . .' Jennet began when he had gone.

'Don't give me any more trouble than you already have, Jennet. Everything's decided and it's time we were all in our beds.' Celia got up, pausing on her way out of the room to give her granddaughter a long, level look. 'You know that your brother can't run this place on his lone, so the three of us must settle for what's best, like it or not.'

It was Celia Scott's proud boast that once her head hit the pillow she was asleep. And it was a known fact that once she fell asleep nothing roused her, until her eyes flew open on the stroke of five-thirty in the morning.

She was ignorant of the summer nights when her grandsons had gone out, first to play and later to court local girls, or when Jennet had slipped out to sit and giggle with Mollie McCabe in the warmth of the cowshed, or had tiptoed down to Angus's room, as she did that night, to talk to him.

He was still awake, reading by the light of the paraffin lamp on his bedside table.

'What are we going to do?' Jennet asked, settling on the side of the bed.

He turned a page. 'You're going back to your bed and I'm going to get on with my reading.'

'You're not. You're going to help me decide what we're going to do about Grandmother's plans.'

'The way I see it, things are already decided. The estate will find another tenant farmer. On the other hand, I don't know what's going to happen at the end of this book, so if you'll just go back to your own room and leave me in peace, I can find out before . . . Hey!' he finished indignantly as she whipped the book from his hands.

'The butler did it – so now you don't have to go all the way to the end of the book to find out.' She closed it and put it on the chest of drawers, out of his reach. 'Angus, we can't just stand by and let Grandmother give Westervoe to new tenants. It's yours by right, not hers to throw away as if it was an old coat.'

'For pity's sake, Jen, she's quite right. How can I run a farm?'

'You can manage to do a fair bit yourself, and you could get someone in . . . Bert McCabe might come back to work for you, and there's plenty of lads just out of the school and willing to learn . . .'

'And where would I find the money to pay all those workers?'

'We could find ways. We have to do something,' she challenged. Then, as he leaned back and glared at her, 'D'you really want to go and live in Great-Aunt Rachel's house?'

A shadow crossed his face, but he only said, 'Jen, when that train went off the rails at Saltcoats, I lost the right to make my own decisions. We're not strong enough to stop Grandmother once she's made up her mind. Anyway, she's done her best by us and she deserves a rest. We forget how old she is.'

'Mebbe *she* deserves to stop working so hard, but *you've* still got most of your life in front of you! I couldn't bear to see you shut away in that house in Largs,' she said passionately. 'It would drive you mad, and you know it!'

'Never mind about what's going to happen to me; just you get back to your nursing and make a living for you and Jamie. That's the important thing.'

'I'll not leave Jamie with Grandmother.' A sudden, violent shiver shook Jennet's body. 'I couldn't do that to him. I might not even get him back, Angus!'

'Of course you will. D'you think she'd want the trouble of raising another generation of this family? Think about it,' he urged, leaning towards her. 'It'll only be for a few years at most.'

'A few years? He'll have started school by then and I'll not be there to see him through that. You know what he's like, Angus, he changes and grows every day and I'll have missed all of that!'

'You can't manage to look after him and study as well. I'll be with him in Largs; I'll keep an eye on him and see to it that he knows why you're not there, and why he has to wait a wee while before you can fetch him and make a home for the two of you. I'll make sure you never lose him.'

She looked at him in despair. Angus had always been the one to see that things were all right for her. It was Angus who had stood up for her when Martin and the Blaikie lads got tired of her tagging after them and tried to keep her out of their games; Angus who had helped with her homework and taught her how to play conkers, and lifted her up to ride in front of him on the big Clydesdale horses; Angus who had carried her over the deepest streams and rubbed her nettle-stung legs with dock leaves, and scooped water from a puddle once, to cool a nasty swelling bump on her forehead after a fall.

But this time he was wrong. This time she had to do the thinking for both of them. She ground the heels of her hands into her tired eyes and forced herself to review their options carefully. And an answer came almost at once.

'If you promise to think about taking over the farm I'll ask Aunt Ann to look after Jamie for me. It would leave me free to help you take over the tenancy.'

'There's no point in even discussing it, for it's out of the question.' He started to haul pillows from behind his head, dropping them on the floor. 'It's

getting late and, since I'm to be denied my book, I
might as well go to sleep.' Only one pillow remained
now; he settled his head on it and drew the bedclothes
up to his ears, turning his back on her. 'Goodnight,
Jen,' he said, his voice muffled in the pillow. 'Put the
lamp out before you go, will you?'

In Jennet's mind, Struan Blaikie was still a childhood friend – more than that, another brother – and
it seemed daft to be going out with him, she thought
on Friday evening as she slipped on her only decent
summer dress. And if Struan hoped that there might
be more to their evening out than just a jaunt to
the pictures, she would nip that in the bud right
away.

After a hunt she found the lipstick she had carefully hoarded in those carefree days when she and
Mollie had gone together to the pictures and dancing
in Rothesay, and ran it over her mouth. A small bottle
of Evening in Paris lay beside it in the drawer; she
sniffed at it, then dabbed it behind her ears, her knees
and on her wrists. Not enough to drive Struan wild
with desire, but possibly enough to mask any farmyard smells that might be lingering about her person.

Then she gave her hair a good hard brushing in an
attempt to tame it, and went downstairs to the kitchen.

'Ooohh!' Jamie said, awed by the sight of his
mother dressed for once as a woman. Angus came out
from behind his newspaper and eyed her up and down,
then grinned.

'Very nice. You should dress like that more often.'

'I would like to, but I daren't – it would probably drive the hens wild and put them off the lay.'

'Have you not got some powder to take the shine off your nose?' Celia, always the faultfinder, wanted to know. 'I think I might have a powder puff somewhere.'

'There's no point, Gran; my face is so weather-beaten the powder would probably fall off. I've given my shoes a good rub and that should be enough.'

'You'll do, I suppose. Now then, Jamie, come here; you'll just crush your mother's nice skirt,' Celia said, and hauled at the little boy, who was clutching Jennet's knees and demanding to be lifted. As she crossed the yard Jennet heard him calling after her. How could she possibly go off to Glasgow and leave him behind for weeks, mebbe months at a time, she asked herself? It would break her heart, and goodness knows what it might do to Jamie.

Struan was waiting at the bus stop, dressed in his demob suit, with a clean white shirt and tie. His face shone, as though he had taken a scrubbing brush to it, and his hair had been well slicked down Jennet's heart sank when she saw that he had put more effort into this evening than she had.

To her embarrassment he insisted on paying her fare on the bus and on paying her into the Ritz Picture House, which was busy. If he tried to put his arm about her, Jennet thought as the lights began to dim, she would die! Fortunately he kept his hands to himself, and after the first half hour she began to relax, although she wasn't sure that she had chosen well, for the Western, with its wide-open plains and its cattle and horses, reminded her too strongly of the farm and the problems facing them all. Even Roy Rogers' bravery and his pleasant singing voice failed to lull her away from her own worries for more than five minutes at a time. She wondered, briefly, if she should have opted for the Palace Picture House and its Boris Karloff offering, but its title, *The Old Dark House*, sounded too like Westervoe as it was at the moment, with an atmosphere of gloom hanging over it.

When they left the cinema, blinking as they made the transition from dark to dusk, Struan suggested a visit to a café for a drink before catching the bus back home.

'You look different,' he said across the table.

'I'm wearing a skirt instead of britches.'

'No, it's not that. Something's bothering you. Is it to do with Martin? Have you heard from him?'

'No, and even if we did, Grandmother's decided to disown him.'

'She'd never do that!'

'Would she not? She says she's going to tell the factor next rent day to find another tenant for the place.' Rent days came twice a year, in May and November. Any farmer wishing to end his tenancy had to wait until the next rent day, then put in six months' notice of his intentions.

'But what'll you do? Where'll you go?'

'She's got it worked out that she's taking Angus and Jamie to her sister's in Largs and I'm to go back to my nursing training in Glasgow.'

Struan frowned, then asked, 'Is that what you want?'

'Of course not. For one thing, I don't want Angus to lose the farm. He loves it and all his life he's looked forward to becoming the tenant. But now Gran says he's not able.'

'I'm sure he could manage with some help. It wasnae his head that got hurt, just one leg.'

'That's what I said.' She looked at him with gratitude. 'I wish you'd speak to him, Struan. He's all set to do whatever Gran wants, and I know that it'll just make him miserable for the rest of his life if he lets her give Westervoe up.'

'I'll have a word with him,' Struan promised. 'We'd best hurry if we're to get the next bus.'

After the town, with its street and house lights, the countryside seemed very dark when they left the bus. It took a minute or two to adjust to the change, and when they did they discovered that the sky, so dark a moment before, was filled with stars.

Struan sniffed the air and gave a sigh of pleasure. 'A grand night. We might be able to start cutting the hay soon if this weather holds.'

'Mebbe. Well, goodnight, Struan, mind and talk to Angus soon, will you?'

'I'll walk you home.'

'Don't be daft, I just live down the lane.'

'Even so,' he said, putting a hand beneath her elbow.

They walked the length of the lane in silence; Jennet was happy to be left in peace to listen to the murmur of the night breeze in the trees, the muted scuffling of small animals in the long grass and the occasional mournful call of an owl, out hunting for food. Then the stables blanked out a square wedge of starlit sky, marking the entrance to the yard.

'Here we are, safe and sound.' Jennet turned and looked up at Struan, a faceless figure against the starry night. 'Thank you for this evening, Struan, I enjoyed it. I'll not ask you in, for they'll be in their beds by now.'

'Aye, it'll be the same at home.'

'Goodnight, then.'

'I was thinking, Jennet,' he said.

'Thinking about what?' If he was about to ask her to go out again, she would say no. Pleasant though the evening had been, she had neither the desire nor the time to let it become a regular event.

But it was not another outing to the pictures that Struan had in mind. 'I was thinking,' he said, 'that it would make sense for us to get wed. To each other, I mean.'

For a moment Jennet was too taken aback to say anything. When she found her voice she said the first thing that came into her mind. 'It would be a lot of nonsense, you mean!'

'You're against it, then?'

'Of course I'm against it. What on earth made you come up with the idea in the first place?'

'I've been thinking of it ever since I came home, and when you said about Mrs Scott wanting to leave Westervoe, it made even better sense for us to wed each other.' Although she couldn't see his face clearly, Jennet could tell by his voice that he was blushing. 'You want Angus to stay on here and work the farm, and she says he's not able to do it all on his own, but if we wed and I came to live at Westervoe, Angus and me could farm it between us. That way the problem would be solved.'

'But Struan, you're going to take over Gleniffer when your father decides he's had enough. He needs you there.'

'He's got plenty of farmhands, and if you married me we could work the two farms between us, and take over Gleniffer as well as Westervoe when the time came. D'ye not see what a help it would be to you and Angus?'

He was right . . . It was the answer to Angus's situation, but at the same time it only created more problems for her. 'Folk don't get married just to help their neighbours out,' she argued feebly.

'It would be more than that. I like you, Jennet; I've always liked you. I want to marry you. I'd look after you well, and Angus too, and your gran if she wanted to stay on. And Jamie too – he's a grand wee chap, and we'd be giving him brothers and sisters in a year or so.'

'Struan, your mother would never allow it.'

'That's the good thing about it,' he said. 'She's
taken our Drew's death really hard. She doesnae say
much, but she's got this wee cupboard in her bedroom
and it's full of pictures of Drew, and things he owned,
even some old receipts he signed. It's like one of those
places folk have for saints: what-d'ye-call-ems . . .'

'Shrines.'

'Aye, that's the word.'

Jennet was stunned; she would never have imag-
ined such a thing of Lizbeth Blaikie. 'How do you
know about it? She surely didn't tell you?'

'No, Helen did, the lassie that sees to the house
and helps my mother with the hens and the calves
and that. So I had a look for myself when she was at
the church with my father, and it's all there right
enough.'

'What has that got to do with us getting . . . with
you and me?'

'The thing is,' Struan said, 'if we wed, it would
bring your Jamie into our family, and that would be
a great comfort to her.'

'A comfort? Struan, your mother's scarcely spoken
to me since I came back from Glasgow. She cannae
even bear to look at me when we're in the same room.
As far as she's concerned, I'm a fallen woman with
a child that can't name his father.'

'But don't you see, once we were wed Jamie would
have a father . . . me. And he'd have the Blaikie name
intae the bargain. It would be like giving Drew back
to her!'

A suspicion began to dawn in Jennet's confused mind. 'You think that Drew fathered Jamie?'

'Of course he did. Oh, I know the word is that you met a man in Glasgow, but you werenae away all that long, were you? And ever since I came home and saw him, the wee chap's reminded me of our Drew. If my mother only knew the truth she'd welcome the two of you with open arms.'

'Struan, you're wrong. Drew isn't Jamie's father.'

'He must be!'

'He's not!

There was a pause and then he said, 'Are you sure?'

'Of course I'm sure! D'you think I've been sleeping with every man I meet?'

'No, of course not! It's just . . . I was so certain.' Disappointment weighed his voice down. 'The way he turns his head sometimes, the way he smiles . . . And I thought that was why you came back here when you knew he was on the way – to tell Drew, only he was dead by the time you got home.'

'I came back because I didn't know what else to do, where else to go.'

Struan was silent for a long moment, then he rallied. 'I still want to marry you.'

'And it's very nice of you to ask, but as I said before, it would break your mother's heart if you made me your wife.'

'Then she's a fool, for all that she's my own mother,' Struan said, his voice hard with anger. 'You're the same fine lassie you always were, and whether he's got Blaikie blood in his veins or not, that bairn of yours needs a proper father. And there's Angus to think of as well. We could make a right go of this place, the three of us, and it would be here for Jamie if he wanted to take over the tenancy when he grew up. Don't give me an answer now, just think about it.'

'I'll think about it,' she agreed, and he gave a sigh of relief and then ducked his head to deliver a hurried, clumsy kiss on the corner of her mouth.

'That's fair enough,' he said. 'But make it soon, will you? Goodnight to you, Jennet.'

9

'He did what?' Mollie yelped two days later.

'Shush, folk'll hear you!' Jennet skipped aside to avoid a small boy charging along the pavement towards them, pursued by his anxious young parents. They were walking along the Esplanade at Rothesay, battling against a sea of holidaymakers going the other way. 'These are far too big,' she went on, frowning at the loaded ice-cream cone Mollie had just bought for her.

'Ach, stop fussing, I can afford it,' Mollie said blithely. 'Anyway, you're a growing lassie, you need the nourishment, specially with the romantic life you're leading all of a sudden. Here was me, asking about your date with Struan Blaikie and expecting to hear about a goodnight kiss, not a proposal of marriage. What did you say? Did you accept him? Can I be a bridesmaid?'

'I said I'd think about it. I don't love him, Mollie.'

'Even so, it must be nice to know that someone

loves you with a hopeless, secret passion. Did you
know he loved you?'

'I'm not sure that he does . . . and if he does, it
sounded more hopeless than passionate. He said that
if we wed, the two of us and Angus could run
Westervoe and take over Gleniffer later. Mollie, I'd
just go from one lot of worries to another. Can you
see Mrs Blaikie welcoming Jamie and me into her
family? It's been hard enough living with Gran's
disappointment and disapproval. I don't want to have
to take the same thing from Struan's mother.'

'I suppose not. Are you going to tell Angus?'

'I don't know. You see, there's another problem,'
Jennet began, but just then Mollie interrupted her.

'There's our Sam.'

The boat-hirers were strung out all along the front,
each one with a queue of people waiting their turn.
Sam McCabe, a peaked cap pushed to the back
of his head, was dealing with the queue for the
Logan boats, book and pencil in hand. Down by the
water's edge Alice, who was helping a young couple
into a boat, waved a tanned arm at her cousin and
Mollie.

'Number five'll be in soon,' Sam was saying as they
arrived. 'See, that's them coming now, the boat called
Tern.' He pointed at the incoming rowing boat and
nodded to the small family at the head of the queue.
'You can go down to the slip now.'

'Hello, Mr Boatman, any chance of a row?' Mollie
asked.

'You don't know how to row a boat.'

'But you do. You could take us out.'

Sam frowned importantly. 'Can you not see I'm busy?'

'A motor-boat, then?'

'You'll have to take your turn, and there's a lot of folk waiting for them already.'

Mollie tutted. 'Och, you'd think that with me having a brother running the show we'd we able to get a wee shot whenever we wanted it.'

'Well, you can't.' Sam squiggled in the book, then stepped aside and nodded the next set of people to where Alice, having pushed one small boat off, was reaching out to help the next to dock.

'If you wait five minutes, Joe'll be bringing the launch back from its trip round the bay. I'm sure he'd be *delighted* to take you.'

He smirked and then dodged as Mollie lifted her hand to slap him.

'Don't you be so cheeky!'

'Who's Joe?'

'Just a lad who works the boats with Mr Logan,' Mollie told her airily.

'Joe Wilson, and he's sweet on our Mollie,' Sam offered, keeping out of his sister's reach.

Alice came up the beach, rosy from the sun and as placid and unruffled as ever, and took the book and pencil from Sam. 'I'm worn out hauling these boats in and shoving them out again. Time for you to use your muscles.'

'How's he doing?' Mollie asked as her brother scampered off.

'Fine. You'd think he'd been born to it. Where's the wee lad?'

'At home. I just came to bring some eggs to your mother,' Jennet said. Then, as Alice turned to the people who waited patiently in line, they left her to it.

'Our Sam's learning to row, and this morning he went out early to bring the boats round from the inner harbour. I think I'd like to learn to row, too,' Mollie confided as they went, sidestepping and dodging other pedestrians from time to time. It was the second week in July; the Greenock Fair holidays were coming to an end and the town was packed with holidaymakers.

'D'you think there's anyone left on the mainland?' Jennet asked as they paused to lean on the railings. The great sweep of Rothesay Bay was dotted with rowing boats, skiffs, small motor-boats and round-the-bay launches, while two steamers disgorged their passengers at the pier.

'Lots of 'em, and every one wishing they were here,' Mollie said through a mouthful of ice cream. 'Folk who have to live in tenements and work in shops, factories and shipyards can't wait to get to the seaside in the summer, and there's the end of the war to celebrate as well. Every room in your auntie's house is taken, right to the end of the summer, and she could have let the rooms over again. Even the Skeoch Woods are so busy there's scarce room for the trees.'

The Skeoch Woods edged the great sweep of Rothesay town at one side, and it was common for holidaymakers who could not find accommodation in one of the boarding houses to set up camp there. In summer the woods were known to the locals as the Skeoch Hotel.

'And the weather's been good, too.' Mollie finished her ice cream and began to nibble delicately round the edge of the cone. 'The boarders are out from morning to night.'

'Aunt Nesta and Aunt Ann seem to be getting on well together.'

'They are. Moving to your auntie's house has done Mam the world of good. Though we miss you all, of course,' she added hurriedly. 'You and wee Jamie and Angus. And your gran.' After all, that old crow Mrs Scott was Jennet's granny and she shouldn't be missed out.

'You don't need to be polite,' Jennet told her. 'It's much better for your mother to be here, where she's appreciated. But we miss all of you an awful lot.'

'You, mebbe. I don't know so much about your granny and Angus. Has he said anything about me?' Mollie asked casually.

'He's got a lot on his mind just now.' Jennet squinted at the blue sky, hoping that the weather would hold for the haymaking.

'If you don't hurry up with that ice cream, it'll start dripping onto those folk down below us on the beach. Are you not enjoying it?'

'I am, but there's a lot of it. The little ones would have done us fine and cost you less.'

'Ach, toffs is careless and I can afford the occasional ice cream now. Sometimes folk even leave a wee tip when they go home. Mrs Logan lets me keep the tips for myself.'

'Why not, since you've earned them.'

'There's plenty of employers would claim the lot, but not your auntie. She's awful nice, and your uncle too . . . and Alice. Would you look at that big woman paddling!' Mollie gave a trill of laughter. 'I swear the steamers at the pier lifted a good half-inch in the water when she went in.'

'Let's go down and sit on that bit of beach for a minute,' Jennet suggested. 'I'll need to get back to the farm and I've something to tell you.'

'Something bad?' Mollie asked apprehensively.

'Something worse than that,' said Jennet.

'You can't let her do that to you and Angus,' Mollie said decisively five minutes later, 'specially Angus. You might want to go back to nursing, but Westervoe's his home and it's wicked of her tae drag him away from it.'

'I can understand in a way; she's getting old and she's tired, and now Martin's let her down the same way my father did.'

Mollie tossed her long red hair back over her shoulder with an impatient whisk of the head. 'That's your trouble, Jennet Scott, you're too quick to put

yourself into other folks' shoes. It's a pity some of
them don't bother to wonder how it is for you.'

She had been the first to see Jennet on her unexpected return from Glasgow. The girl had walked into
the yard, white-faced and red-eyed, just as Mollie
stepped out of the byre. While she gaped at the appari-
tion, wondering how Jennet could possibly be in
Glasgow studying and at the same time back home
on Bute, her friend had dropped her suitcase and
rushed at her, clutching her and almost knocking her
down, sobbing, 'Oh, Mollie!'

Nesta had come running from the farmhouse
kitchen just then, white-faced and calling out, 'Jennet?
What's wrong, pet?'

And Celia Scott had looked over the stable's half
door and said in her harsh voice, 'What's usually
happened when a lassie who was brought up to know
right from wrong comes home with guilt pouring off
her face? She's brought shame on me and her brothers,
that's what's wrong! Am I right or am I wrong,
madam?'

From that day on Mollie had had to watch helplessly as her friend was made to pay over and over
again for her pregnancy out of wedlock. She had never
said a word about Jamie's father, and Mollie had never
asked. There were times when secrets had to be kept,
even from the closest of friends.

'It's Angus I'm worried about,' Jennet was saying
now, staring at the glittering bay without seeing it.
'It's as if he doesn't care any more.'

'He has tae care! It's a terrible thing tae lose the place your family's lived in for all those years, and he has tae find that out now, while there's still time, instead of later on when he's suffocating in some wee house, bein' fussed over by two old women. I'll never forget us being bombed out the first night Clydebank got blitzed,' Mollie said soberly. 'We were all in the basement with the other folk from the tenement, and afterwards my mam was determined to go back and get her insurance policies. The stairs were still there, so the ARP man said she could try to get into the flat if she was careful. I went with her.'

This was her secret, something she had never mentioned before to her friend, because for years it had been like a raw wound inside her, liable to break open and bleed if disturbed. It was dark, and with the stairs covered with rubble and the air thick with dust, it didn't feel in the least like the tenement she had known all her life. The two of them had had to feel ahead with each foot as they went, Mam first and Mollie close behind, their hands linked so tightly that afterwards Mollie's fingers ached.

'Did you get into the flat?'

'The door was still there and it was still locked. Mam had to use her key to get in. The funny thing is,' Mollie said, not feeling at all funny, 'when we got in, the house was gone.'

'What d'you mean, gone?'

'There were just a few floorboards on the other side of the door, then a big hole. The roof was gone and at least that meant that we could see better, because of the stars and the anti-aircraft searchlights slashing across the sky, but we couldn't have walked to the far wall because there was no floor to walk on. Even if there had been a floor, there was no wall – just a gap and the shape of some of the other tenements against the sky. But the wall where the mantelshelf stood was still there, and the shelf had the box on it with the insurance policies, our birth certificates and Mam and Da's marriage papers. And Cheepy was still in his cage with half his feathers gone, chirping away as if nothing had happened. It was lucky we kept his cage on the mantel. So we were able tae fetch him as well as the box.'

'I don't think I could have walked over that floor, with half of it missing.' Jennet shuddered.

'It was still our home.' It was as simple as that; although most of it, walls and furniture, had disappeared, the familiar mantelpiece and the sound of Cheepy singing meant that what was left was still home. And home – even a part of home – felt safe. Looking back, Mollie realised why some city dwellers insisted on living in the ruins of their bombed flats when possible. Where else would they want to go?

'On the way out,' she remembered, 'Mam saw her good coat still hanging on the back of the door. It was filthy with white dust and all shredded by the blast, but she took it off the hook anyway and brought it away with her. She said it had cost a lot of good money and she'd not see it left there. She'd to throw it away the next day because it could never be mended.'

A child nearby called out to his mother and the shrillness of the cry brought Mollie back to the present. 'It was only a room and kitchen, and it had dampness and it was bitter cold in the winter because the windows didn't fit, but it was still ours, and it hurts to lose the place where you grew up. I don't want that to happen to Angus and you and wee Jamie.'

'Knowing that your home had gone, seeing it like that . . . It must have been terrible for you.'

'Aye, it was.'

'I didn't realise that it had been so bad. You've never said a word about it before.' Jennet's voice was hushed, as though she was speaking in a church.

'It's not the sort of thing you want to talk about afterwards. You just want to put it away and get on with your life.'

There was more, but that wound went deeper and was still raw. Mollie might never be able to tell anyone about glancing up into the night sky during the trek to the school where they were to be given food and shelter for the night, and seeing a human leg tangled among the telegraph wires. Or the woman who, when they sheltered in her doorway for protection against the raid, opened the door and ordered them to be on their way as though they were common tinks.

She blinked, shivered in the warm sunlight, then forced her mind to dismiss her own memories as she heard Jennet say, 'So you see, Struan's proposal could

make all the difference to us. If I married him it would
solve all our problems.'

'Are ye mad? It would only make them worse!'

'With Struan to help him, Angus would be able to
take over the tenancy of the farm, and Grandmother
could move to Largs and . . .'

'And you'd be stuck with a husband you don't love.
Or are you going to tell me you've been crazy about
him for years, and the sight of him walking back into
your life made you go all weak at the knees?'

'This is real life, Mollie, not a film!'

'Even in real life I'd not consider tying myself to
a man for ever unless he made my knees go all funny
every time I thought about him. Tell me the truth,
mind . . . Do you love Struan Blaikie to bits?'

'He's a good man and a nice man, and a depend-
able one.' Jennet was sitting on the beach with her
knees drawn up and her arms linked about them. Now
Mollie put a hand on one of them.

'Not a quiver. That means you don't love him, so
don't marry him. That's my advice and you'd be a
fool to ignore it.'

'Be sensible, Mollie. It would be the right thing to
do as far as Angus's concerned.'

'No!' Mollie said the word so violently that a couple
walking by hand in hand looked at her in surprise as
they passed. She turned so that she was squatting back
on her heels, facing Jennet. 'It would be the worst
thing you could do for Angus, d'you not see that?
You'd only be looking after him and protecting him,

and that's not what Angus needs. He's had more than enough of that from your granny. If Struan Blaikie went to live on Westervoe, Angus'd just go on doing the easy jobs while Struan sees to the harder ones. He's a grown man, Jennet, he has tae learn tae make his own decisions and abide by them. If he's going to defy Mrs Scott and stay on at Westervoe, then he must do it himself, d'you not see that?' The words had flooded out in a passionate tirade and when they ended Mollie was breathless.

'I've tried to make him see that, but he won't, though I know he loves the place more than Martin ever did. If Angus had been able to go to the war, he'd have come back as soon as he was able, the way Struan has. He was a grand ploughman before his accident,' Jennet said proudly. Then, her face clouding over, 'But now it's as if he thinks he's got no right to tell Gran what he wants. He just agrees to everything she says.'

'Then make him change! Keep on at him, the way I did when your gran wanted him to spend the rest of his life in his bed or in a chair, being babied. It worked then and it could work again.'

'You're different. I don't have your cheek.'

'God almighty,' Mollie raised her eyes and her shoulders, 'now you're beginning to sound just like him. "I can't . . . I daren't",' she mimicked. 'Yes, you can, Jennet Scott, and you'd better dare before it's too late for all of you, including poor wee Jamie. How long have you got?'

'Grandmother can't give the factor six months' notice until Martinmas rent day in November.'

'November? And you're wasting valuable time sitting here on the beach blethering, when you should be at home nagging that obstinate brother of yours? Go home and start at once!'

'I need to get home anyway,' Jennet suddenly realised, scrambling to her feet. 'If I'm not back soon, I'll have Angus and Grandmother both out looking for my blood.'

'And don't forget – nag him until he can't take it any more. That's when he'll start doing what you want, just for the sake of peace,' Mollie panted as they raced along towards the bus stop.

There was indeed blood-letting when Jennet got home, but it wasn't hers. Old Jem was pacing around at the top of the lane when she stepped off the bus.

'Here ye are at last!' he greeted her, relief sweeping over his face, which was well lined and tanned like leather by a lifetime of working outdoors in all weathers. Jennet's heart seemed to stop in her chest.

'Has something happened to Jamie? Or is it Angus?' Pictures of Jamie finding his way down to the shore and drowning, or of Angus deciding that suicide was better than spending the rest of his life in Largs with Grandmother and Great-Aunt Rachel, flooded into her mind.

'No, no, it's the old yin.'

'Gran?'

'Are you comin' or are you no'?' the bus driver wanted to know, leaning across the gap between his seat and the open door.

'What are ye talkin' about, man? I'm no' wantin' tae go on yer bus. I'm just here tae fetch the lassie,' Jem barked at him, and the driver, grumbling, started up the engine.

'Come on to the house, quick!' Jem seized her arm and bustled her along the lane.

'What's happened to Gran?'

'The daft old b . . . old woman would have it that her and me should shift some of they chicken houses to another bit of the field. I told her to wait until you came, but no, she had tae have it done right away. And what happened?' Jem demanded.

'How should I know, I wasn't there!' Jennet was torn between running ahead to the farmhouse and keeping to his pace to find out what had been going on in her absence.

'She put her foot in a hole or tripped over a tussock, or somethin'. Anyway, she couped over, and the ark we were liftin' went over with her. She nearly had me over an' all. One of the carryin' poles under the ark ploughed a furrow in her leg. I'd the devil's own job tae get her tae the house,' Jem wheezed. 'We've bandaged her up, me and Angus, but I'm no good at that sort of thing and she was squawkin' and fussin' all the time, just like one of the hens. I mind when Jocky Turner lost his leg thon time when we were scythin' . . .'

They were in the yard now; Jennet took to her heels and left him behind.

Celia lay on the couch in the little-used living room, her legs covered by a blanket and a cup of strong tea on a small table by her side. Angus hovered around her uncertainly, while Jamie was wedged into a corner of the room with his thumb jammed into his mouth. As soon as he saw his mother he rushed to latch onto her skirt.

'There you are at last,' Celia greeted her granddaughter. 'I thought you'd never come home!'

'Have you sent for the doctor?'

'She wouldn't let us.' Angus was pale with shock and worry.

'I don't need a doctor, it's just a waste of money. I'm a good healer.'

'Angus, take Jamie outside and let me see to Gran,' Jennet instructed. It took a few minutes to persuade Jamie to release his grip on her, but he was finally bribed with a lollipop that Jennet had brought from Rothesay for him.

'You spoil that bairn,' Celia said sourly as the door closed behind uncle and nephew.

'I don't have time to give him the attention he deserves, let alone spoil him,' Jennet snapped back at her, too worried to care about causing offence. She lifted the blanket out of the way. 'Let me have a look.'

The wound was fairly shallow, but long and ragged. Blood still seeped from it.

'We should get the doctor out for this.'

'Don't you dare!'

'At least let me send Jem over to fetch Mrs Blaikie.'
Jennet felt round the ankle with gentle fingers. 'This
needs a cold compress.'

'I went over on my foot, just, and Lizbeth Blaikie
has enough to do without running round here every
five minutes. Put some disinfectant on the cut and
bandage my whole leg properly and it'll do. I told
you, I heal quickly.'

'Why didn't you tell Angus to disinfect it right
away? And this bandage is too loose.'

'I just wanted him to do something to stop the
blood getting onto my good sofa. Anyway, I'd no
wish to have every male in the place staring at my
naked leg. It was bad enough having to take my stocking off.' Celia indicated the surprisingly white, well-
muscled leg stretched out on the sofa. 'I'm just
grateful I've never sunk to wearing trousers, like
you. A fine pickle I'd have been in then.'

There was no arguing with her. Jennet fetched from
the kitchen the battered tin box that held the family's
supply of bandages, sticking plasters and medication,
then went back for a basin of hot water and clean
cloths and towels. Celia winced and caught her lower
lip between her teeth as the wound was cleansed and
disinfected, but rallied in time to direct the bandaging
process.

'That's better,' she finally decided and began to get
to her feet.

'Stay where you are, Gran.'

'I've got work to do.'

Jennet pushed her back down. 'You've got a badly cut leg and a twisted ankle that needs a cold compress on it. If you try to get up and go out, you'll only start the bleeding again.'

'Aye, mebbe you're right.' Celia let herself be eased against the arm of the sofa. 'My ankle could do with a bit of a rest, but just till tomorrow.'

'I'll soak a towel in cold water, then make you a fresh cup of tea,' Jennet said.

10

─────── ◆ ───────

After the three of them, with Jamie's help, did the afternoon milking, Angus undertook tasks near the house, so that he could look after Jamie and keep an eye on his grandmother, while Jennet and Jem finished shifting the arks to another part of the field. When the job was done Jennet straightened her back and wiped a hand over her perspiring face. 'I'd like to see some of them in a deep-litter house.'

'They'd be easier to look after,' Jem agreed. 'But you'd never get her to let ye do that, lassie. She doesnae like change.'

That night Celia insisted on going up to her own room, scowling at Angus when he tried to suggest that it would make more sense for her to sleep in the living room where she could more easily be looked after during the working day.

'I'll be back on my feet tomorrow,' she snapped, 'and for tonight I'd like the comfort of my own bed.'

'You'll not be back on that foot tomorrow, Gran,'

Jennet protested. 'Your ankle's still swollen.'

'A night's rest'll put it right, and I can strap it up and use one of the walking sticks, if I must. If Angus can manage, so can I. Go and turn the bed down for me, Jennet.'

'But . . .'

'Leave it, Jen,' Angus advised from the doorway. Then, when she joined him in the kitchen, he went on, 'Let her have her own way. Why shouldn't she find out for herself how hard it can be to get about with just one sound leg?'

Jennet had a struggle to get her grandmother to her bedroom. Although the woman was wiry, with not a pick of fat on her, she was difficult to manoeuvre on the narrow staircase and once or twice Jennet, her heart in her mouth, thought that the two of them were going to lose their footing and tumble back downstairs to where Angus stood at the bottom, watching and worrying. At last they managed to get along the upper corridor and into the bedroom, where Celia collapsed gratefully into the big lumpy bed she had shared with her sister and then with her husband for a few short years.

'I'll help you into your nightgown.' Jennet felt as exhausted as she had earlier when she and Jem were struggling with the arks in the field.

'You will not, I've not reached that stage yet! You can put some fresh water into that basin and bring it here, then leave me in peace so's I can wash myself.'

When Jennet took the jug of water upstairs, Celia

was still on the bed, her face drawn in the light from
the lamp, but her voice was as sharp as ever as she
said, 'Now, off you go and let me get to my bed.
Wait . . .' she added, then as Jennet turned in the
doorway 'you can mebbe bring me a cup of hot tea
in ten minutes, and two aspirin to help the pain in my
ankle.'

For once Celia wasn't first in the kitchen the following
morning, and when Jennet went back upstairs with
some tea she found her grandmother sleeping in the
middle of an uncomfortable tangle of bedclothes. The
older woman awoke with a start as the mug was placed
on her bedside table.

'What time is it?' Her voice was unusually weak
and she blinked about the room as though she didn't
quite recognise it.

'Never mind the time . . . How do you feel?'

'I didnae sleep very well,' Celia admitted, 'but I'll
be better once I'm up and on my feet.'

'You're not getting up till I see how your leg is.'
Jennet drew the bedclothes aside and then eased
Celia's nightgown just high enough to reveal the
bandaged part of her leg. To her dismay she saw that
the skin from bandage to ankle was a dark, shiny red.
She touched it gently with her fingertips and Celia
caught her breath sharply, then said, 'No need to be
so rough, girl!'

'I'm going to fetch the doctor.'

'You will not.'

'Gran, that gash is badly inflamed. I'm fetching the doctor no matter what you say.'

'You could at least help me to get tidied up first,' Celia said peevishly. 'And before you do that, you can bring a drink of water, for my throat's parched. Then you can fetch the chamber pot out from below the bed.'

She drank thirstily before allowing Jennet to wash her face and hands, brush her hair and fasten it into a neat bun at the nape of her neck, then tidy the crumpled bed. It was clear that every movement caused her pain, but she set her lips and said nothing.

When everything was done Jennet woke Jamie and carried him and his clothes downstairs. 'She's settled for the meantime, but I'll have to cycle over to the Blaikies' and ask them to telephone for the doctor.'

Angus got up from his seat at the table. 'Have your breakfast first.'

'There's no time if I want to catch the man before he goes out on his rounds. Could you see to Jamie and then let the hens out before you bring the cows in for milking? Jem should be here soon to help you.' Jennet took her jacket from its hook on the back of the outer door. 'Gran's dozing off again, so I think she'll stay that way till I get back. She must have been awake most of the night with the pain in her leg.'

Struan was coming out of house when she got to Gleniffer Farm. At the sight of her his face lit up and he came to meet her.

'Jennet? Have ye come tae . . .'

There was no time for chat. 'My grandmother's hurt herself,' she cut in, 'and I need to telephone for the doctor right away.'

'Come on in.' He led her into the kitchen, where Andra Blaikie and his wife were finishing breakfast. As soon as she heard the story Lizbeth hurried to the telephone in the big square hall while her husband said, 'I'll send young Bert to help out as soon as I can spare him.'

'I'll go,' Struan offered.

'You've got the rest of the hay to cut,' his father reminded him. Then to Jennet, 'We're nearly by with that. I was going to come over to Westervoe today to tell Celia that we'd be free tae help her with the haymakin' next week.'

'The doctor'll be over within the hour,' Lizbeth announced, bustling back into the room, followed by the maid, 'and I'll be over too, just as soon as I've got things sorted out here.'

'There's no need, Mrs Blaikie.'

'And what sort of a neighbour would I be if I didnae help poor Celia?' the woman asked impatiently, adding, 'Anyway, you and your brother could never manage on your own.'

'I'm sending young Bert over.'

'Quite right, Andra. Helen, I can trust you tae see tae the men's dinners, can't I?'

'Aye, Mrs Blaikie.' The live-in maid flushed with pleasure at being put in charge of the kitchen.

'If you're goin' to Westervoe,' Andra told his wife, 'you might as well use the wee cart and take Bert with you.'

It wasn't until she was on her way home that Jennet remembered the light in Struan's eyes when she arrived, and realised that he must have thought she was rushing over to accept his proposal of marriage.

Angus and Jem were milking the cows when Jennet got back to Westervoe.

'The hens are fed and I've put your porridge to keep warm by the range,' Angus reported. 'I thought I heard Gran calling for you, but when I sent Jem up to see what was wrong, she just pulled the sheet up to her chin and shouted at him to get out.'

Jem's wheezy chuckle floated from the next stall. 'She glared as me as if I was there tae give her a fate worse than death. Even a bull wouldnae be that brave . . . or that desperate.'

'You're making altogether too much fuss,' Celia complained when Jennet climbed the stairs. 'The doctor coming . . . and Lizbeth too, for a wee scratch.'

'A scratch that should have been looked at properly when it first happened. And I didn't ask Mrs Blaikie to come over; she insisted on calling as a friend.'

'They're good neighbours, the Blaikies. I don't know how I could have managed all these years without Andra's help.'

'Angus and me can manage between us until you're back on your feet,' Jennet argued, and her grandmother looked at her with stinging contempt.

'You two? Manage to run this farm without me?' she said. 'I doubt it.'

The leg was badly infected and at first the doctor wanted to send his patient to hospital. Jennet, banished from the room by her grandmother and listening outside the door, prayed that Celia would agree, for as well as making life easier for her and Angus, it would give her the chance to talk to him about the future. But the old woman would have none of it, and after a heated argument the doctor gave in.

'She's a very stubborn woman, your grandmother,' he said when he found Jennet in the kitchen, where she had fled on realising that he was coming out of the bedroom. 'As I mind it, she always was. Not that we've had many dealings with each other, for she's as fit as a fiddle otherwise. I've seen to the leg and put on a fresh bandage, and I'll arrange for the district nurse to come in every morning to dress it until the infection clears up.'

'How long will that take?'

'It depends on whether or not she does as she's told. A week at least, I'd say. Give her these for the pain when she needs them . . .'

He began to put the small bottle on the table, then stopped, eyeing Jamie, who had come in from the yard to take a comforting fistful of his mother's

britches. The doctor put the bottle on the high wooden
mantelshelf instead.

'You've got a healthy-looking wee fellow there.'

'He's never ill.'

'Well fed and well loved,' the middle-aged doctor
said unexpectedly. 'And lots of fresh air. That's the
way. Let me know if she gets any worse . . . the leg,
I mean,' he added with a sudden, almost mischievous
smile, and went on his way.

Lizbeth Blaikie and Bert McCabe arrived shortly
afterwards in the smart little trap that Andra always
referred to as 'the wee cart'. The Blaikies had a motor-
car, but since the beginning of the war, and the intro-
duction of rationing, the agricultural petrol doled out
to farmers had been treated with red dye to ensure
that it was only used for farm work. Some local
farmers managed to fit in the occasional jaunt by car,
but if they were caught using agricultural petrol for
their own purposes they were hauled into court and
fined. So the Blaikies, stalwart churchgoers and pillars
of the community, had brought the small carriage out
of retirement and rarely used the car.

Mrs Blaikie showed alarming signs, when she came
downstairs from visiting Celia, of wanting to take over
until her friend was fully recovered.

'Helen's been well trained, for I've had her with
me since the day after she left the school, and she
can see to things at home. I can come first thing every
morning and . . .'

'It's not necessary, Mrs Blaikie, we can manage.'

Since the doctor's visit, Jennet had rushed about the kitchen like a madwoman, tidying and dusting, polishing and cooking. Now the room was filled with tempting aromas from the meat pie in the oven and the big pot of soup simmering on top of the range. Pots of potatoes and turnips were also cooking and Jennet had even managed to start on a batch of scones.

Lizbeth Blaikie looked round the room but could find nothing to criticise. 'Westervoe's just a wee place, I know,' she said, 'but even so you'll never manage without Celia. She's held this place together since the day her man died, and if you ask me . . .' she settled her ample, well-corseted frame on one of the upright chairs at the table, 'she's worn out more than anything else. She's had a hard life, and just when she was expecting to let go of the reins and see to her own comfort for once, she was landed with your Angus an invalid and the shame of . . .'

She glanced at Jamie, playing on the hearthrug with a domesticated farm cat, and let the rest of the sentence hang in the air in letters of red fire.

Jennet's hands tightened on the rolling pin. Although Andra Blaikie was always affable, Lizbeth had found ways of making it clear that as a high-principled, strongly religious woman, she thoroughly disapproved of Jamie's presence in the world, let alone on Bute.

For two pins Jennet would have bounced the rolling pin on the woman's head; instead, with a great effort, she moved it slowly and evenly over the dough on

the table and said with icy politeness, 'It's kind of
you to offer, Mrs Blaikie, but I can see to my grandmother, and to the house.'

It did not seem possible that Mrs Blaikie, already
whalebone-rigid, could stiffen any further, but she
managed it. 'Are you saying that you've no need of
my help? Is that what you're saying?'

'I'm saying that I've got my own way of doing
things in my own house, just as you must have in
yours, and I'm best left alone to see to them,' Jennet
replied, the effort of trying not to shout putting an
edge of steel into her voice.

'Well . . .' The woman glanced again at Jamie. 'We
all know you've got your own ways, and they're
certainly not mine, or poor Celia's.'

Jennet set the rolling pin down on the table amid
a cloud of flour. 'You'll always be welcome here if
you want to visit my grandmother, Mrs Blaikie,' she
said, amazed at her own daring, 'but I'll see to the
house myself.'

The woman gave an outraged sniff, and left.

Watching her drive out of the yard, ramrod-straight
in the trap, Jennet knew that even if the sight or the
thought of Struan had made her knees go funny, as
Mollie put it, she could never become his mother's
daughter-in-law. There had to be some other way to
keep Westervoe.

'I've offended Mrs Blaikie,' she said when Angus,
Jem and Bert came in for their dinner.

'Easy done.' Her brother picked up his knife and fork. 'How did you manage it?'

'I refused to let her take over this house while Grandmother was in her bed.'

'Quite right,' Jem boomed, while Bert winked at Jennet. 'She'd have the lot of us runnin' round like school bairns and I cannae be doin' with that. Your gran's as difficult a woman as I want tae deal with.'

'Mebbe you were a bit hasty, Jen.' Angus's forehead creased with worry. 'How can you do your farm work and help with Gran's as well, and look after her and the house and the wee fellow, too?'

'Mr Blaikie says I can help out every day now the hay's nearly done,' Bert offered.

'And mebbe Mrs Blaikie's over there right now complaining about the way she was treated and getting him to change his mind about being such a good neighbour,' Angus fretted.

'He'd not do that. She doesnae rule that roost as much as she thinks she does.' Bert winked again.

'As to how I'm going to manage, I've made my own plans,' Jennet broke in. 'If you can do without me for an hour this afternoon, Angus, I'm going into Rothesay to ask if Aunt Ann could spare Mollie for a few days.'

'Gran won't like that.'

'But I would, and that's all that matters to me.' Jennet brandished the ladle at them. 'Anyone for more pie?'

* * *

When Jennet reached her aunt's gate Ann Logan was at her open front door talking to a man with the distinctive ill-fitting suit and cropped haircut of a former soldier. Behind him stood two boys of school age and a woman with a little girl in her arms.

"There's been such a rush of folk,' Jennet heard her aunt say, 'that I've not even got an empty cupboard to offer. Have you tried that house across the road?'

'Aye, and every other house in Rothesay.'

'I wish I could help, but I can't think of anyone who's got a room left to let.'

'Thanks anyway, I'm sure we'll manage. We'll just have to try somewhere outside of the town.' The man nodded, picked up the heavy case by his side and turned away, muttering an apology as he realised that Jennet was waiting to get to the door.

'I hate turning folk away,' her aunt said as they watched the little family trail along the pavement, 'specially when they've got bairns.' Then, with pleasure, 'Come in, come in, this is a nice surprise . . . two visits from you in two days?'

'I can't stop, I have to get back. Gran's had an accident and she's had to take to her bed and . . .'

'Oh, my dear! How bad is it? Come in and have a cup of tea, at least. Mollie and her mother are in the kitchen, we were having a wee rest.' Ann drew her into the house, talking all the while. 'How are you going to manage? It's Jennet again,' she added, throwing open the kitchen door. 'Mrs Scott's taken poorly.'

'She gashed her leg and it's got infected, so she'll have to stay in her bed for a week at least, the doctor says,' Jennet explained as she was ushered to a seat at the table. 'That's why I have to get back as quickly as I can. Mr Blaikie's sent Bert over to help Angus, but there's nobody in the house to see to Gran and Jamie.'

Ann clucked sympathetically. 'Is there anything I can do to help?'

'You could let me borrow Mollie for a few days, if she's willing,' Jennet said hopefully.

'Of course I'm willing!' Mollie's face lit up. 'If it's all right with you, Mrs Logan.'

'We can manage fine. With this nice weather the boarders are out most of the time, and Nesta here's been working like I don't know what, Jennet. I can't get her to slow down.'

Nesta McCabe's face glowed. 'I'm enjoyin' it,' she said, and Ann put an arm about her shoulders.

'And George says that Sam's worth his weight in gold as well, so no need to worry about us. You just see to your gran and the farm, and Mollie can stay for as long as you want. You'll have a cup of tea while you wait for her,' she added as Mollie whisked out of the kitchen.

'I've just minded,' she said to her mother when she came back downstairs, bag in hand, 'that I said I'd go to the pictures with Joe tomorrow night. Get our Sam to tell him what's happened, will you? Come on then, Jennet, we'd best go if you want to catch the next bus.'

'Mind now . . . if there's anything we can do, just send word,' Ann called after them as they set off.

'She's awful kind,' Mollie said. 'I've never seen Mam so contented, and Sam can't wait to get up and get out in the mornings. He fair loves these boats!'

'Talking about boats, is it the Joe that works with the boats that was taking you to the pictures?'

'Aye, but it's just a friendly thing.'

'It seems a shame to be leaving him in the lurch like that.'

'Ach, I'm sure he'll find someone else,' Mollie said airily. 'The lads workin' the boats are always meetin' lassies. And lassies on their holidays are always keen tae be asked out. Even by our Sam.'

'He's surely too young to think about that sort of thing.'

'That's what Mam says, but he's come back more than once with stars in his eyes. And he's started shavin'.' Mollie giggled. 'He's got as much hair on his face as I have. Listen, does your gran know I'm coming back to the farm?'

'Not yet.'

'She'll not be pleased,' Mollie predicted as they rounded the corner and caught up with the family who had been looking for accommodation. The father had put down his big suitcase and taken the little girl from her mother. The woman was hefting the case up when Jennet stopped and said on an impulse, 'Excuse me . . . I believe you were asking my aunt back there if she had any rooms to let?'

'Aye.' The man smiled at her. 'We should mebbe have thought tae write ahead and book somewhere. We'd no idea the place would be so busy, but I've just been demobbed and since the wee one . . .' he indicated the toddler hiding her face shyly in his shoulder, 'has had a bad time with the croup, we thought it would be a good idea tae give her some sea air and have a bit of a holiday intae the bargain. Someone said Port Bannatyne would be worth tryin'; it's just along the coast – is that right?'

'Would you fancy a working holiday?' Jennet asked, then as they looked at her warily, 'On a farm, I mean.'

'A farm? That would be great, Dad!' the older boy piped up. He, like his younger brother, wore his straight hair cut in a pudding-bowl style.

'I don't know about that,' the man said, exchanging doubtful looks with his wife. 'What sort of work d'ye mean?'

'We've a small farm near Stravanan Bay. The thing is, it's coming up for haymaking time and my grand-mother's ill in bed and there's a lot to do round the farm, so you and your sons could help with bringing in the hay,' Jennet gabbled, wondering at her own cheek in accosting this group of strangers. 'You'd not be expected to work all the time of course, just at the haymaking. There's nice walks around the place and we're near the shore, so the children could go down to the water. We've a cottage you could have: it's not smart but it's furnished.'

'The cottage is nice,' Mollie chipped in. 'Me and my family used tae live in it.'

'A cottage? We were thinkin' of a room, just. What sort of rent would you be askin' for a whole cottage?' the man asked cautiously.

'Hardly anything . . . nothing at all if you'd be willing to help Mollie here out with the housework and the cooking,' Jennet said to the woman. 'Folk get very hungry during haymaking. And I've a wee boy round about your daughter's age. They'd be company for each other.'

'Is there horses?' the older boy asked, wide-eyed.

'And sheeps?' his brother clamoured.

'We don't have sheep, but we've got a horse and two pigs and there's cows and hens and cats and a dog.'

'Can we go, Mammy . . . Daddy?' the boys chorused while their father turned to his wife.

'What d'ye think, Mary?' he asked, then when she nodded uncertainly he beamed at Jennet. 'When can we go?'

'Now, with us.' Mollie handed her bag to Jennet and grabbed the case. 'We're just off tae catch the bus.'

On board the bus ten minutes later she murmured to Jennet under cover of the engine's rattle, 'Your gran's goin' tae kill you!'

'I have to do what I think's best for the farm, and for her. Anyway, she'll have to catch me first, and the way her leg is just now she's not got a chance of doing that,' Jennet rapped back at her, then settled in her seat.

Part of her was scared of what her grandmother would say, of what Angus would say and of whether the unknown lodgers were going to be more of a hindrance than a help.

And part of her wanted to dance up and down the bus's narrow aisle, for at last, for the first time in her life, she was taking control of things.

11

'I will not have it!' Celia Scott stormed. 'I do not want trippers on my farm!'

'The Dicksons are a nice respectable family from Glasgow, Gran. Mr Dickson's just been demobbed and he just wants to have a wee holiday with his family. They're willing to help with the haymaking and Mrs Dickson doesn't mind giving Mollie a hand in the . . .'

'There's another one,' Celia fumed, fussing at the bedclothes. 'I thought we'd seen the last of the McCabes and now you're bringing them back again.'

'Only Mollie, and only until the haymaking's over and you're better. I can't possibly manage to look after you and see to all the outside work as well, can I?'

'Since you've finally admitted that, then why don't you ask Andra and Lizbeth Blaikie for help? They're our own sort.'

'If by "our own sort" you mean they're farming

folk, they've got enough to do on their own farm without having to help to work ours, too. By the time the haymaking's done you'll be on your feet again.'

'And then there'll be the oats to harvest.'

'We'll worry about that when the time comes.'

'You're going to ruin this place, d'you know that? Inviting God knows what sort of folk onto my farm . . .'

'It's not just your farm, Gran, it's Angus's and mine as well and we're doing our best to keep it going, given the circumstances.'

Celia glared, then said, 'Fetch Angus here at once, I want to see him.'

'He's out in the fields somewhere and anyway, he can't manage up the stairs.' Jennet made for the door. 'I've got things to do. Is there anything you want just now?'

'I want some tea, and this bed needs freshening up. And . . .'

'I'll ask Mollie to see to the tea, and she can tidy the bed when she brings it up.'

'Jennet, I will not have . . .' Celia was beginning as Jennet went out and closed the door gently behind her.

'I'm not surprised Gran was angry,' Angus said when his sister told him what she had done. 'I don't know that I'm very pleased myself.'

'Emergencies need quick action, and you're surely not angry with me for getting more folk to help with the haymaking. The Dicksons' wee girl's been bad with croup, and they need a holiday by the sea now that Mr Dickson's home at last.'

'Never mind the long sad story,' Angus snapped and went ahead of her across the yard, banging the point of his crutch onto the cobbles and ignoring the two Dickson boys, who were standing at the cottage door, staring wide-eyed at the farm yard. As Angus went into the farmhouse, Gumrie, who had been trotting at his heels, peeled away and went to investigate the strangers. The smallest boy immediately slid behind his brother, who paled but faced the dog with clenched fists and a fearsome scowl, reminding Jennet of Mollie the day she and her family first arrived at Westervoe.

'It's all right,' she called out. 'He just wants to say hello to you. Hold out your hand and let him have a sniff at it. That's how dogs decide if they like folk.'

'Mebbe he'll no' like us, but,' the lad objected, a tremor in his voice.

'Why would he not like you?' Jennet squatted down by the dog. 'His name's Gumrie. What's yours?'

'Walter. And that's Colin.'

A small face peered out from behind Walter, watching as the older boy finally stuck out his hand, holding it as far away from his body as possible, at the end of a thin, rigid arm. Gumrie sniffed the grimy fingers, then wagged his tail and licked them. Walter laughed, a surprisingly deep chuckle.

'He's got a tickly tongue. Can I clap him?'

'To tell the truth, you should never pet farm dogs because they're workers, not pets, but our Gumrie likes it, don't you, softie?' Jennet rubbed the dog's coat and he wriggled with pleasure, then wriggled again as Walter patted him. Colin emerged slowly, willing to be coaxed into introducing himself to the dog.

'Can we clap the chooky hens an' all?' he wanted to know.

Jennet shook her head. There was something very likeable about the two stolid little boys with their Glasgow speech, their masculine little faces and vulnerable, wide-eyed wonder. 'Hens don't like to be touched, and they don't like folk to rush around, either. It frightens them.'

'Who's the limpy man?' Walter asked.

'That's my brother Angus.'

'Was he hurtit in the war? Was he a sojer like my dad?'

'No, he got hurt when a train he was in ran off the rails and crashed.'

The brothers looked at her, then at each other, horrified. Then Colin said in a gruff voice very like his brother's, 'We came from Glasgow in a train, then in a boat.'

'Most trains don't run off the rails,' Jennet said reassuringly, then left them with Gumrie and tapped at the open door of the cottage. 'Is everything all right?'

'More than all right, Mrs . . . eh,' Mr Dickson

beamed at her. 'Come in, come in! Was that your
husband you were with? I'll have to thank him for
his hospitality.'

'My name's Jennet and that was my brother Angus
you saw. I'm not married. We live here with our grandmother and my wee boy Jamie.'

'Oh.' Mrs Dickson's eyes flew to Jennet's ringless
left hand. There was an awkward pause, then her
husband said, 'I'm Eric, and this is Mary. And this is
wee Marion here.' He nodded at the little girl clinging
to her mother's skirt. 'When would you like us to start
work?'

'It's just at the haymaking we'll need a hand, sometime over the next day or so. Until then you can just
please yourself and do whatever you want. Has Mollie
told you that we can sell you milk and eggs?'

'She'd a right face on her when I took her tea up,'
Mollie reported when Jennet went into the kitchen.
'She's not pleased tae see me back here.'

'She's not in a good mood with anyone just now,
poor woman. She must be suffering with that bad leg
of hers.'

'I don't think Angus is pleased to see me, either.'
Mollie's voice was bleak and her shoulders, as she
turned back to her work at the range, were slumped.
Jennet put an arm about her.

'It's me he's annoyed with, for bringing the
Dicksons to stay in the cottage. But we need their
help and Angus knows it. Where's Jamie?'

'Out in the back garden with a drink of milk and a crust to dip in it.'

'It'll be good for him to have other children around.'

Mollie raised her eyes to the ceiling to indicate the upper floor. '*She* wants her notepad and a pen and I don't know where they are.'

'I'll get them for her,' Jennet said wearily, and went upstairs.

'Fetch my notepad, my inkwell and my pen. I'm writing to Rachel,' Celia announced as soon as her granddaughter arrived, 'to ask if she'd come to look after me properly.'

'Gran, you're being looked after properly as it is, and Great-Aunt Rachel hates being on the farm. It wouldn't be fair to drag her over here!'

'The top drawer of that chest over there,' Celia directed. 'And the inkwell, pen and blotter's on top of the chest.'

'She'll not come, and in any case Mollie's staying, Grandmother, for Jamie knows her, and she can help with things like feeding the hens, too.'

Searching for the notepad, locating it and the pen and ink, then settling them all on a tray so that Celia could write her letter, Jennet marvelled at her own bravado in answering her grandmother back. But it was the only way, she realised, to keep things together. At the moment Angus was an unknown quantity; she had no way of knowing whether he was going to fight for the farm or let their grandmother decide his future for him.

'I'll leave you in peace to write your letter. But there's no point in inviting Great-Aunt Rachel here,' she added from the bedroom door. 'Even if she agreed – and she won't – I've got enough on my hands with the haymaking without having to look after her as well. Anyway, there's nowhere for her to stay. With the cottage occupied, Mollie'll have to sleep in my room, since I've not got time to turn out the room Martin and Angus used to use.'

It was like the old days, when she and Mollie used to sneak out late at night while everyone slept, to wander along the lane to the seashore, or sit in the byre or in the stable with Nero if the nights were cold, talking and giggling and making wild plans for the future.

'But this is even better,' Mollie whispered into the darkness, 'because we don't even have to get out of bed to meet up with each other.' She wriggled into a more comfortable position. 'This bed's lumpy.'

'It always was. I've slept on this mattress all my life. It's been in the family for generations.'

'Back as far as the crusades, if you ask me.' Mollie wriggled again, then settled, yawning. 'I think one of your ancestors must have left a bit of his armour in it. I thought farming folk had nice mattresses stuffed with straw or hay?'

'Only the rich ones. We need all our straw and hay for the animals.'

'At least the bed's big enough for the two of us.'

Mollie was silent for a long moment and then said sleepily, 'Does Jamie always sound like that?'

'Like what?' Jennet, alarmed, sat bolt upright in the bed, straining her eyes through the darkness of the room to see the cot in the corner of the room. 'What's wrong with the way he sounds?'

'I didn't say there was anything wrong. Does he always breathe with these wee puffy sounds?'

'Yes, it's the way children breathe.'

'It sounds nice,' Molly said, and Jennet, her alarm over, fell back against her pillow.

'What about Joe, then?'

'He's just a nice lad, that's all. I'm not going to marry him.'

'How do you know?'

'He's not the right one.'

'Does that mean you've found the right one?'

There was a pause, then Mollie said, 'Mebbe.'

'Who is it?' Jennet was wide awake again.

'That's for me to know and you to find out.'

'Tell me!'

Mollie yawned again. 'Clark Gable. Now shut up and go to sleep,' she said.

Jennet lay staring at the grey patch of window beneath the house eaves. She had thought, once, that she had found the right one. But she had been wrong.

'Mollie . . . ?' she said tentatively after a long silence and was answered by a soft snore.

*   *   *

Struan had managed to find the part he needed for the old tractor, and as soon as the Gleniffer hay was gathered in he brought it over to Westervoe, where he spent half a day in the tractor shed before emerging to announce triumphantly that the machine was once more in working order.

'Since Jem's not here, I'll take it out to let you see for yourselves,' he offered, then gaped when Jennet said, 'No, I'll do it.'

'But you don't know how to drive a tractor!'

'You're old-fashioned, Struan Blaikie. Have you never heard of the Women's Land Army? Two of them worked on your father's farm.'

'But you were never in the Land Army.'

'As good as.' Celia, reluctant to have strangers on her land, had decreed that she and Jennet could manage the farm during the war with help from Angus, Jem and the McCabes. Bert, who took to farming like a duck to water, had been a great help and Jennet, determined to play her own part, had persuaded Jem to teach her to use the tractor. Now she marched towards it with Struan saying as he followed nervously, 'I'll start it for you.'

'Don't be daft,' she snapped at him. 'What's the use of being able to drive the thing if I can't start it myself?'

'It's got a terrible kick,' he warned as she seized the starting handle.

'I know. Why don't you go into the house and teach my grandmother to suck eggs, Struan?' she suggested rudely, and swung the handle. It took three tries, but when it did roar into life she was ready for the kick-back and managed to get away with only a mild jolt from wrist to shoulder. She eased the arm surreptitiously as she marched round to the side of the tractor and clambered aboard.

'Stand out the way.' She had not driven the thing for a while and deep down she was nervous, particularly as the roar and clatter of the old tractor brought Angus, Mollie, Jamie and the entire Dickson family out to see what was going on.

Blinking as she moved from the shed's darkness to the sun-bright yard, Jennet turned the unwieldy vehicle towards the lane. The Dicksons and Mollie were cheering and clapping and Gumrie was barking; she knew that because she could see their mouths opening and Gumrie bouncing about, the way he always did when he barked. Struan was shouting something and flapping his hands at her, but she couldn't hear a thing for the noise. Angus stood back, leaning against the byre wall, his face expressionless.

Jennet had forgotten how much the tractor jolted and shook. She settled her hips firmly into the shallow curved seat and concentrated on steering a straight course up the lane to the place where it bulged out on both sides. There, she managed to turn it and then drove it back, the onlookers who had followed her from the yard scattering to right and left to let her pass and then regrouping to run after her into the yard, where she did a lap of triumph before cutting the engine outside the tractor-shed door.

'There,' she said, climbing down to applause. 'Once you learn how to drive you don't forget.'

Struan's face was a mixture of expressions; on the one hand, she knew, he resented seeing a mere woman do something that had traditionally been done only by men. On the other, he admired her.

'Not bad,' he said.

'That's what I thought.' Her body still throbbed from the tractor's vibration but at least her voice was steady. She looked past Struan to where Angus stood watching and called across to him, 'Your turn now.'

'Jennet, for pity's sake, you know the man can't do that any more,' Struan hissed at her.

'I know nothing of the kind. Come on, Angus, I'll start it for you if you like.'

He shook his head. 'I think I'll leave it to you, since you do it so well,' he said, and turned to go back into the byre. Suddenly the Dicksons were shuffling about uncomfortably. Walter, the oldest boy, began to say something and was shushed by his father. Jennet hesitated, wondering if she had gone too far, then saw Mollie, her eyes clearly signalling 'Go on!'

It had worked with the crutches; it should surely work with the tractor, Jennet thought, putting her fists on her hips. 'Angus Scott, come here and try out this thing. You were always the best driver on the farm. You're surely not going to let me beat you?'

He had turned back to the yard; now he glared as he limped towards her. 'If it'll keep you happy,' he said, then as he reached her his voice dropped, 'but I'll probably make a right fool of myself.'

'You'll be more of a fool if you don't try,' she murmured.

He brushed past her, shook his head when Struan stepped forward to help, and propped his crutch on the tractor, making sure that it was out of the starter handle's way. After starting the vehicle up with the first swing of the handle, he used the crutch to get round to the side and then propped it up again and hauled himself up and into the seat, leaning down to lift the crutch and wedge it securely by his side. Then he swung the tractor round in a wide arc before taking it out into the lane with everyone following.

At the widest part of the lane, where Jennet had used the space to turn the machine in a circle, Angus operated the controls deftly to swing the tractor round, then reverse it so that he could turn it back towards the yard, where he reversed it into its shed before sliding to the ground.

When he emerged, crutch snugly tucked beneath his arm, there was an excited scatter of applause. Mollie, Jennet noticed, had put Jamie down in order to clap wildly, her freckled face beaming from ear to ear.

Angus acknowledged the cheers with a faint ducking of the head. 'All right?' he asked his sister. 'Can I get on with my work now?'

'You've been practising, haven't you?' she asked, her voice too low for anyone else to hear.

'You don't think I'd have touched the thing in front

of all those folk if I'd not been sure of myself, do you?'

'You . . . !' She punched him lightly on the arm. 'Why haven't you been driving it in the fields instead of leaving it all to Jem?'

'I couldnae bear the thought of Gran making a fuss and fretting in case I managed to turn the thing over with me underneath. Mebbe I would have, too; mebbe I've lost the right way of working it.'

'I doubt that,' Jennet said, and if it hadn't been for the onlookers she would have hugged him, even though their grandmother disapproved of unseemly demonstrations.

When she went into the kitchen Celia's walking stick was beating a steady tattoo on the bedroom floor above.

'Where have you been, and what in the name's going on out there?' she burst out as soon as her grand-daughter appeared. She was sitting up in bed, her hair in stiff spikes around her head. 'It sounds as if the world's gone mad!'

'Struan's fixed the tractor, that's all, and I took it up the lane to try it out.'

'It sounded like more than that,' her grandmother said suspiciously. 'Who was doing all the clapping and cheering?'

'Just Mollie and the folk renting the cottage.'

'I knew they'd be a mistake. How's a body to get any rest with rabble like that carousing about the place day and night?'

Jennet began to smooth the blankets and shake out the pillows. 'They're not going to be carousing about the place at all,' she said. Then, realising that she might as well tell the truth now, rather than be caught out later, she continued, 'They just clapped when Angus took a shot as well.'

'Angus?' the old lady squawked. 'You let your brother drive the tractor? D'you want to kill him altogether?'

'He's perfectly able, Gran.'

'Of course he's not able, you stupid lassie, he's only got the use of one good leg. And how did he get into the seat? If Struan helped him up, I'll have something to say to that young man.'

'He climbed up himself, and he took the tractor into the lane, then brought it back and put it in the shed and climbed down again. He's as good with it as ever he was, Gran.'

'How can he be? Look at what happened to poor Drew Blaikie. What were you thinking of?'

'I was thinking that it's good for Angus to do more about this place. He's got the sense to know what he can and can't do.'

'Neither of you,' Celia said darkly, 'has the sense you were born with. Sometimes I think Rachel's right when she says I should wash my hands of you both, and Martin, too!'

The tirade flowed on, while Jennet tidied the bed and combed Celia's hair and wished, silently, that she would follow Great-Aunt Rachel's advice. There was

nothing Jennet would like more than to be washed off
her grandmother's hands.

With Mollie and Mary Dickson running the kitchen
and looking after the two children and Celia, who was
still confined to her bed, Jennet was free to work out
in the field with the menfolk.

Angus and Jem had scythed the hay and, as tradition
dictated, it had been left lying in the field for three
weeks, 'hearing the church bells ring three times' and
being turned regularly to ensure that it was thoroughly
dried. Had there been much rain during the drying
process, it would have had to be gone through again,
but this year Nature had been kind.

It was a long tiring job, working from early morning
until well into the evening, gathering up the dried hay
and tying it by hand into bales that were then taken
by cart to the hayloft. Eric Dickson proved to be an
asset, cheerfully following orders without question or
complaint, while his sons, brown as berries now,
played in a corner of the field, out of the way but
within calling distance so that they could be
summoned to help where and when they were needed.

When their father sent them off to the farm to tell
their mother that the workers were ready for some
food, the two of them scampered off at once, to reap-
pear half an hour later, each hauling on a shaft of the
old red wooden dog cart that had once been harnessed
to a pony and used to transport the Scott women and
children.

Jamie was perched on the cart, giggling as it jolted from rut to hummock, while little Marion Dickson sat beside him, smiling nervously and clinging to the raised sides. Baskets filled with food and drink were packed around them, and Mollie and Mary Dickson walked on each side of the cart, keeping an eye on the children.

They were cheered into the field and almost knocked off their feet by the workers, hot and parched and starving. 'You don't mind, do you?' Mollie asked Jennet as she lifted Jamie down from the dog cart, then began unpacking the food. 'I remembered seeing this when we lived in the cottage, and it saved us havin' tae carry the wee ones as well as all the food.'

'It's nice to see it out and about again. Is Gran . . .'

'She's been fed and the nurse has dressed her leg. She thinks it's looking much better today. In fact, she thinks your gran could come downstairs for a wee while in a day or so, but she wants tae arrange for the doctor to visit first,' Mollie said while Jamie and Marion, who had become firm friends, scampered off across the field hand in hand, returning later to claim their share of the picnic.

Jennet sank down thankfully on the field's grassy fringe and mopped her face with a corner of her sacking apron. Across the Sound of Bute, glittering in the sunshine, Arran was mistily tranquil beneath a blue sky. Passenger steamers on the Tighnabruaich run churned along the Firth now and again, and the white sails of yachts slid past.

'It's grand, isn't it?' Struan came to sit by her side, nodding at the field, the shore beyond, the water and the hills that seemed, with the heat haze about them, to float on the water. 'I keep wondering if I'm going to wake up and discover that I've just been dreaming and I'm still far away from home.'

'D'you want me to pinch you just to make sure?' she asked, and he grinned.

'It would be better than a nip from a louse. That's what usually woke me when I was away.'

'You never had lice!'

'Of course I did, and so would you if you'd been days and nights without even the chance to take your uniform off or have a wash.'

'That's the sort of thing we didn't even think about, back here where things were much the same as usual.'

'Best not to think about them. And don't ever mention them to my mother, she'd not like the idea at all,' he said. Then, 'You've got bits of hay in your hair. Sit still a minute.'

His breath touched her cheek as his hands gently teased the dried grasses from the mane of hair she had tied back with a scarf. 'That's better,' he said, and then, his voice suddenly husky, 'Jennet, I swore tae myself that I'd not pester ye for an answer, but ye look that bonny today with the sun in your hair that I cannae wait any longer. Have ye thought about what I asked?'

Her heart sank. She looked round for Mollie in the hope that she could signal her friend to come to the

rescue, but she, and the others, were watching the
children playing among the hayricks. 'Struan,' she
began carefully, 'I still don't think it would be the
right thing for us to marry.'

'If it's my mother you're thinkin' on . . .'

'It's not . . . well, not just her. It's me, I don't want
to get married to anyone.'

'Is it because ye're still pinin' after the wee lad's
father?'

Surprised, she turned to look into his sun-warmed
face. 'Of course not, that's all in the past.'

'Then I suppose I'll have tae accept what ye say.'
He got to his feet, then stood for a moment, looking
down at her. 'But I'll ask ye again, because you're
the one I want, Jennet.'

12

As Struan went off to play with the children, Jennet, unable to face the others just then, began to pile loose hay on the dog cart to make a soft bed for the children's return journey. As she finished she saw that Angus, sitting with Andra Blaikie, Eric Dickson, Jem and Bert McCabe, was watching Struan and the children, his mouth tight and his fingers shredding a grass stem.

For a moment she thought that he disapproved of the way his friend was gambolling about like a child himself, then she realised that he was envious of Struan's ability to tumble about with the youngsters when he himself could not.

He met her gaze and grabbed his crutch, using it to lever himself up from the ground. 'Back to work,' he bellowed, brushing away Eric's attempt to help him to his feet. Mollie and Mary, who like the rest of her family had blossomed in the few days they had been staying in the farm cottage, scooped up the exhausted toddlers and sat them in their nest of hay, then they each took a shaft and began to haul the cart back to Westervoe while the others returned to their back-breaking work. Jennet and Struan were using long-handled pitchforks to pass hay up to Andra and Eric, who stood on the bed of the cart.

By mid-afternoon the Dickson boys had begun to weary of the field. Their father lifted them onto the back of the loaded cart, where they were able to swing their legs over the tail.

'I just hope they don't get any ideas when we go back home,' he said as his sons went off, grinning. 'Cadgin' a ride in the country's one thing, but it's not the same in a city street.'

'Did you never run after a cart and jump onto the back of it for a wee hurl, man?' Angus challenged, and the man laughed.

'Of course I did, but my father and mother never liked it any more than I do now it's my own bairns.'

It was a relief when milking time came. Jennet rested the butt of her fork on the ground so that she could straighten her stiff back gradually, and pushed back her hair, damp with sweat, with a swipe of her hand. Eric jumped down from the cart to take over from her, nudged on by Andra's 'Come on, man, the hay'll no' float up here on its own!'

She and Angus hobbled rather than walked to the field where the cows, waiting patiently by the gate to be taken to the byre, blinked at them in gentle-eyed surprise.

'They think we've aged years since the last milking,' Jennet said as she swung the gate open.

'And they're right,' Angus answered as the two of them trailed after the animals like tired children tagging along after their parents. At one point Jennet dozed off in the byre, slumped against a round warm flank, not realising that she was asleep until Mollie said from above her head, 'Are you really going to dive into that pail of milk, or would you settle for a cup of tea instead?'

Jennet sat hurriedly upright. 'I wasn't sleeping . . .'

'Only thinking; I know, your brother's tried that one on me already. Here,' Mollie thrust the steaming mug at her. 'Get that down your throat before you go back. And you can take this with you.' She indicated the bottle-filled basket at her feet. 'They must be parched out in that field.'

Some farmers made use of a wooden-toothed, horse-drawn hay gatherer known as a 'Tumblin' Tam', which left the hay in piles to be built into haystacks out in the yard, but at Westervoe the hay was carted from the field to the hayloft.

'And a good thing too, since we'd have to hire someone to thatch it properly,' Jennet explained to Eric Dickson as they perched on the tailgate of the cart, swinging their legs. 'It takes a master craftsman to do that job well enough to leave the hay weatherproof.'

'It's good to see the field cleared and know the job's been done right.' He indicated the cleared area as the cart jolted out of the gate. Dusk was falling and the midges had begun to bite; he leaned forward, holding on with one hand and using the other to scratch at the calf of his leg. 'It's amazin' how much there is to know about the country. I've learned more in the past few days than I learned in a year before.'

'And you've had to work hard. This is supposed to be your holiday.'

'It's been the best ever, for all of us,' he assured her.

The light spilling from the kitchen's open windows was welcoming, but Andra scorned Jennet's offer of supper before going home.

'We'll have the supper, but we've got the last load of hay to stow away before then.'

'But it's nearly eleven o'clock!' groaned Jem.

'If a job's worth doing, it's worth doing well. You go in and help with the food, Jennet . . . Angus, you can tend tae your horse. The rest of you . . . get on with it.'

'They're working on and Jem's not best pleased,' Jennet reported when she went into the kitchen, blinking and putting a hand up to shade her face. Soft though the lamplight was, it seemed over-bright after the darkness outside. 'I doubt we'll see him at the early milking tomorrow.'

'He'll look happier when he's got a good supper in his belly,' Mollie predicted confidently from the range, where she and Mary Dickson were hard at work.

'We'll all feel happier.' The smell of cooking made Jennet's mouth water. 'How's . . .'

'She's fed and watered and the same goes for the pigs,' Mollie said blandly, but with a gleam in her eyes. 'And all three of them are comfortable. The hens have been shut up and the cats fed, and I'm just about to put Gumrie's dinner out for him. And the byre's ready for the morning.'

'Mollie, you're an angel.'

'I know I am, but it's thanks to Mary here that I was able to get out and get the work done. I nearly fed the calf, before I remembered that the wee thing's not here any more.'

'We'd a bad time with Jamie when she was taken away. He looked high and low for her for days. I don't know what he'll be like when the pigs have to go in the autumn. Did he go to his bed all right?'

'He's not exactly in his bed,' Mollie said. 'He's in yours. They were all asleep on their feet, even the big lads, so we tucked the lot of them into the same bed. It was the best way, since Mary's working here with me.'

'I hope you don't mind,' Mary added anxiously. She and her pretty little daughter had never quite lost their shyness, though their menfolk had made themselves at home in and around the farm within the first twenty-four hours.

'Of course not, it's a good idea. I'll just look in on Grandmother.'

'Not until you've stopped being a scarecrow.'

Mollie nodded at the grasses that had drifted to the floor around Jennet's feet. Hurriedly she retreated to the yard, where she took off her big apron and her headscarf and shook them hard to get rid of most of the hay caught in their folds. Then she brushed herself down and ran her fingers through her hair before tying it back again. The men were still bustling round the cart in the last of the day's light, hefting bales of hay between it and the shed that housed the hay-loft.

'How's the hay doing?' Celia said as soon as Jennet put her head round the door.

'I thought you'd be asleep by now.'

'How can I sleep when it's haymaking? What's happening?'

'The field's cleared and the men are just putting the last of it into the loft.'

'Mind and give them a good supper. They deserve it and Westervoe's always been known for its hospitality.'

'Mollie and Mary are setting out a banquet fit for a king. Would you like me to bring something up for you?'

'I've got no appetite, stuck here day after day,' Celia grumbled. 'But since you're here at last, you could fetch the bedpan. I could fairly do with it.'

'You should have got someone up before this.'

'I don't care to be beholden to strangers,' Celia said stiffly.

'Mollie's not a stranger . . . and Mary's a very nice

woman. She'd be pleased to do anything she could for you. Hold onto my arm and I'll ease you up.'

'You smell like a hayfield,' her grandmother said as she was settled on the chamber pot. 'It's a good smell.' The longing in her voice was so strong that Jennet wished she could lift the old woman up in her arms and carry her downstairs and out into the fresh air, away from the claustrophobic room, which must be like a prison cell to someone so used to being out and about all the time.

But she had to settle for saying, 'It's a good crop. We'll be all right for the winter feeding.'

'Someone else will, you mean,' Celia said harshly. 'I've decided that we'll move out as soon as the factor finds a new tenant. No sense in waiting until the spring if we can go before winter. Don't just stand there, lassie. How can I do my business with you staring at me? Come back in a minute or two.'

Jennet moved on to her own room. In the dim light from the window the four children sleeping in her bed were just a smudgy row of heads on the pillows. The air was filled with the sound of breathing, some of it snuffly, some of it light and even. Jennet tiptoed out again and waited in the dark corridor, leaning against the wall, until the muffled sound of Celia's bladder being emptied ended, and it was safe to go into the room and help her back to bed.

Despite the exhaustion of a long, hard day's work, elation at knowing that yet another task had been successfully completed turned the late supper into a party. The mountain of food prepared by Mollie and Mary vanished with surprising speed and the big teapot was refilled again and again.

Finally Andra pushed back his chair, slapping both hands on his generous belly. 'By jings, that was good! I'm that set up I could go out and do another day's work.'

'You'll have to in just a few hours,' Angus reminded him wryly.

'Ach, well, we can catch up on our sleep during the long winter nights. That's the way it is in farming. Come on then,' Andra ordered his son and Bert McCabe, 'time we werenae here.'

Even the business of removing the Dickson children from the bed had not roused Jamie fully. He murmured irritably when Jennet eased him into her arms, swatting at her with a limp hand; then, as she shushed him, he fell back into sleep, his soft breath stirring against her neck.

For a long and precious moment she stood by the window, holding him close and looking out at the night. She would have remained like that for much longer if Mollie hadn't come in with a lamp, yawning and knuckling her sleepy eyes.

'What a day! It's a lot easier looking after lodgers.'

'I'm sure it is.' Reluctantly Jennet laid Jamie down in his own little cot and drew the blanket over him. Behind her Mollie busied herself with the bed,

plumping up the two pillows and smoothing the lower
sheet.

'At least none of them have peed in it. I wondered
when Mary suggested putting them all in here together
if it would be all right, but I didnae like to say
anything.' She began to undress.

'Struan asked me again, today.'

'When did he manage to find the time?'

'When you were all watching the children playing.
I turned him down, Mollie.'

'Quite right, and better to do it now than keep the
poor man waiting and hoping. Was he all right about
it?'

'He says he'll ask me again, later.'

'How is it,' Mollie asked, irritated, 'that men cannae
just take no for an answer when they never seem to
have any trouble with "yes"?' She buttoned her
pyjama jacket and picked up her hairbrush. 'He must
be really sweet on you.'

'I wish he wasn't. Now I know I've got it all to go
through again.'

'Best leave what happens next till it happens,' Mollie
said philosophically, her hair crackling and glowing
like flames in the lamplight as she brushed it.

A bicycle spun into the yard the following evening,
its rider ringing the tinny little bell on the handlebars
to announce his arrival and setting the hens
squawking, and Gumrie barking, while the cats arched
their backs and spat.

Mollie, giving Jamie his bath while Jennet made his supper, jumped up and looked out of the window. 'It's that Joe Wilson!'

'The lad that works with Uncle George?' Jennet joined her at the window. 'So it is. He's come to call on you, Mollie.'

'The cheek of him, just turning up without as much as a by your leave!'

'Since when did folk have to make an appointment to see your ladyship?' Angus asked from the table, where he had taken the chance to have a quick look at the newspaper.

'Well, I mean . . . He's got no right to come chasing after me like that!' Mollie, flustered and pink-cheeked, made for the door. 'I'll find out what he wants and send him off home.'

'You will not, you'll ask him in, since he's cycled all this way just to see you,' Jennet called after her. Then to Jamie, who had taken advantage of the sudden inattention to lift a soapy arm high above his head and was preparing to smack the flat of his hand down hard on the water, thus creating a tidal wave, 'No you don't, young man. I've got enough to do without mopping up the floor after you.'

She snatched up a towel and scooped him out of the bath, then carried him to the big wingback chair that was usually her grandmother's property. Secretly she was glad of the chance to dry her son's wriggling little body and tuck him into his pyjamas. She loved the weight of him in her lap and the freshly bathed smell of him, and the way his damp, fairish brown hair stuck up in little spikes about his neat skull. Since Mollie had come back to Westervoe to help out, Jennet had missed her time with Jamie.

Mollie came stamping back into the kitchen followed by Joe, a young man no taller than she was, his fair hair rumpled from his bike ride. He shook hands shyly with Angus and Jennet, chucked Jamie under the chin and refused the offer of some tea.

'You'll take it,' Mollie snapped. 'It's not polite to refuse.'

'Mebbe you'd prefer a glass of lemonade,' Jennet suggested. 'It's a warm evening.'

'Aye, that would go down well,' he agreed, and allowed Mollie to push him down into a chair by the table. Angus, who before his accident had been the most social member of the Scott family, folded the newspaper, cleared his throat and announced that he was going to start putting the hens in for the night.

While Mollie fetched the lemonade, Jennet began to supervise Jamie's supper, a bowl of bread and milk. 'You'll be keeping busy with the holidaymakers?' she asked their visitor, wiping a dribble of milk from Jamie's chin.

'It never stops. As fast as a boat comes in it's out again.'

'You'd think with all the hirers round the bay, and at Port Bannatyne too, that there might not be enough customers to go round.'

Joe grinned, more relaxed now that he was on a

subject he knew. 'Not a bit of it. Ye can see the folk dashin' off the steamers as soon as they come in tae get tae the wee boats. It's like watchin' ants round an anthill, so it is. Some of them come to the island every year, and they have their favourite hirer and their favourite boat. They get right irritated if someone else's got it out when they come lookin' for it.'

'You'll be glad of Sam's help then.'

'He's a nice lad and he fairly likes workin' with the boats. I'm teachin' him to row,' Joe said proudly. 'He's comin' along well.' Then, his grin widening, 'The other day . . .'

'Now don't you start on any of your boring stories, Joe Wilson,' Mollie broke in. 'Jennet's got more to do than sit and listen to you goin' on about these blessed boats of yours.'

'I do want to hear about them, and I'm not doing anything else, because it'll take Jamie a while to work his way through this bowlful.' Jennet frowned at her friend, who frowned back. 'What were you saying about Sam?'

Joe had just taken a mouthful of lemonade. He choked slightly, then managed to swallow it down despite the way Mollie thumped his back. 'He came with me the other mornin' tae fetch the boats round from the inner harbour. They're all linked together, see, with a motor-boat at the front so's they can be towed round to the bay fast before the holiday folk get down there. They have to be washed out first, see, and I'd done my lot and got back into the motor-boat

and started the engine ready to go. Sam was climbin'
intae the punt at the back tae wash it, only he slipped
and fell, didn't he?'

'Into the water? Can he swim?'

'After a fashion – we all have to be able tae do that,
the number of times we go in. Anyway, he managed
to catch hold of the side of the punt, so I knew he was
all right. I'd started up and I could see one of the other
hirers on his way to fetch his boats, so I just kept
going, out of the harbour and round in front of the
pier to our berth, with Sam bein' pulled along behind
me.' He gurgled with laughter, slapping his knee.
Jamie, who had been following the story closely
without understanding it, burst out laughing too,
spraying the table with bread and milk.

'And when did he get out of the water?' Jennet
asked, mopping the table and Joe's arm, both speckled
with her son's supper.

'That was the laugh; by the time I got round, folk
were already beginnin' tae queue, so I was too busy
tae do anythin' about Sam. One lady says tae me,
"Boatman, d'you know there's someone out there in
the water, holding on to one of your boats?" and I
says, "It's all right, ma'am, that's just our Sam, he'll
keep."'

'Was he all right?' Despite her irritation, Mollie
had been following the story closely.

'Right as rain. Looked a bit like a wet day by the
time I got round to haulin' him out, though,' Joe added.
'He'd to go sloppin' off tae the house tae get changed.'

Though Jamie wanted to stay with their visitor, Jennet took him up to his bed as soon as he had finished his supper. 'Who's that downstairs?' her grandmother called out to her as she passed her bedroom door.

'Just a friend of Mollie's.'

'A friend? A man by the sound of it.'

'A very nice young man. Be still for a minute,' Jennet told her son, who was wriggling about in her arms.

'We've got more to do than entertain her callers!'

'He'll not be staying long. Mollie didn't know he was coming here and she's not pleased about it. I'm just putting Jamie to bed,' Jennet said, and escaped to her room.

When she returned to the kitchen, tiptoeing along the corridor so that her grandmother would not hear her and summon her to an interrogation, Joe got to his feet. 'I'd best be gettin' back.'

'You don't need to rush away,' Jennet assured him. 'Stay as long as you like.'

'I was wonderin' if Mollie would like to come out for a wee run with me, seein' as it's such a nice night.'

'A good idea, she's been working too hard and she needs some fresh air, don't you, Mollie?' Jennet smiled into the other girl's angry eyes. 'Just give me some time to help my brother with the hens, then you can be off.'

'He seems nice enough, Mollie's young man,' Jennet said as she joined Angus at the hen houses.

He grunted, shooing in the last hen, which had stopped for a final peck at the ground, then slamming the door down behind it.

'Gran wasn't pleased. She seems to think that Mollie's got no right to have followers.'

'If she had her way, the world would come to an end because nobody'd be allowed to have followers,' he said over his shoulder as he made for the next ark.

'It depends who they are,' Jennet said. 'Gran and Mrs Blaikie did all they could to push Drew and me together. And we weren't even all that bothered about each other.'

'It was always Allan Blaikie you were keen on, wasn't it?'

Jennet, about to close an ark door, stopped and straightened, staring at him. 'What makes you think that?'

'Oh, wee things. Like the way you always made sure your hair-ribbons were neatly tied when you knew he was coming over.' A teasing note crept into his voice. 'And your sudden interest in baking when you discovered how fond he was of gingerbread. Martin and me weren't, but we'd to eat it anyway. And the way you went all pink whenever Allan walked into the kitchen. Just as Mollie did when her friend Joe arrived a wee while ago.'

'I was only a schoolgirl then,' Jennet told him sharply. 'Schoolgirls always need to have a crush on someone. And you don't know as much about women as you think, Angus Scott, for Mollie was flushed because she was angry with Joe for arriving out of the blue, not because she fancies him.'

'Aye, that'll be right,' he said sarcastically, and swung himself towards the next row of arks.

13

'Joe had no right to embarrass me in front of you and Angus,' Mollie said that night when Angus had gone to bed.

'How did he embarrass you? He's a nice lad, there was nothing wrong with him calling on you.'

'It's not my house, though. What did Angus say? Was he angry about Joe?'

'No, why should he be angry?'

'The way he went out not long after Joe arrived . .'

'You know Angus, he's not good with strangers since his accident. And he'd have gone out anyway because the hens had to be shut in for the night.'

'And I don't know what got into you, making me go out with Joe.'

'You needed some time off; he's a nice lad and he'd come all that way just to see you.'

'He's asked me to go to the dancing with him tomorrow night, at the Winter Gardens.'

'I hope you said you would. You love dancing.'

'So do you. Why don't you come, too?'

'Have you never heard that two's company and three's a crowd?'

'I'm serious, Jennet. You need time off more than I do. I'm sure Joe could find someone for you.'

'No, thanks.'

'Och, go on! It could be like the old days.'

'I couldn't leave Angus on his own with Jamie and Gran to see to.'

'I'm sure Mary Dickson would help out. She's a nice woman, when you get past her shyness, and she's good with Jamie. He's loving it, having wee Marion to play with.'

'The Dicksons are going home the next day and it wouldn't be right to expect Mary to help out on her last night here. Anyway, I don't really want to go dancing any more,' Jennet said stubbornly, and nothing Mollie said could change her mind.

Dancing belonged to another time, another Jennet. The past could never be brought back.

'You're squiggling it, I can feel you squiggling it!'

'I am not,' Jennet retorted, 'it's your legs, they're all bandy.'

'Cheeky b . . .' Mollie, standing on a chair in the kitchen, remembered just in time that Jamie was an interested observer, and changed it to 'Cheeky thing. I've got lovely legs, haven't I, Jamie?'

'Got tea on them,' he said, giggling.

'Only because your Auntie Mollie can't afford to buy stockings. And she's too respectable to get them from a Yank.'

'There aren't any American soldiers on Bute, you mean.' Jennet paused to lick the stubby eyebrow pencil that Mollie had managed to keep all through the war years, then returned to the task of drawing a straight line down the calf of her friend's left leg, to simulate the seam of a stocking. Mollie had already rubbed strong tea into both legs to create an instant tan.

'Now if I was our Senga, I could have all the silk stockings I wanted, on the black market,' Mollie said. 'Did I tell you her boyfriend's one of those spivs that can get you anything you want?'

'For a price.'

'From what I know of our Senga, she'll be payin' in kind.' Mollie's voice was heavy with disapproval. 'I don't know what Da's thinking of, letting her behave like a . . .' Again Mollie paused, remembering Jamie, then she went on, 'like that. Too busy with his own fancy woman, I suppose.'

'Stop chattering, you're putting me off. Can you go over there for a minute, pet?' Jennet added to Jamie, who was watching her work so closely that his head was pressed against hers. His tongue, like hers, was sticking out; now he drew it in to say, 'I'm helping!' and then it appeared again and his eyes, close to Mollie's tea-stained legs, concentrated so hard that they went into a squint. Jennet had to swallow down her amusement in order to focus all her attention on getting the line straight.

She had reached Mollie's heel when Angus walked in from the yard. Mollie immediately shot off the chair, pushing down the skirt she had been holding up round her thighs. The chair rocked back on two legs and Jennet had to catch and steady it as Mollie hurriedly put her shoes on.

Angus looked in surprise at the three startled faces. 'What's amiss?'

'Drawing on Mollie's legs,' Jamie explained helpfully, and the girl swooped on him, tickling him until he was helpless.

'See you, you've got a big mouth, Jamie Scott.'

'So have you. It's red,' he said between shrieks of laughter. 'And you smell.'

'That's perfume! Say you like it . . . say it or I'll tickle you to bits!'

'I like it, I like it!' Jamie shrieked.

'Joe's taking Mollie dancing tonight,' Jennet explained to her brother. 'Doesn't she look lovely? Let him have a look at you, Mollie.'

The girl released Jamie and stood awkwardly before Angus, looking for all the world, Jennet thought, as though she were a naughty child who had been sent to the headmaster for punishment.

Mollie's eyes were bright with embarrassment under Angus's scrutiny and her hair curled round her flushed face. She was wearing a floral-patterned skirt and a short-sleeved peasant-style blouse that she had embroidered herself with poppies and cornflowers along the low elasticised neckline. It had slipped at one side, revealing the curve of a shoulder, and now she pushed it back into place, her flush deepening.

'Very nice,' Angus said, his voice flat, and went over to the sink. 'The byre's swept out and ready for the morning.'

'Is that all you can s—'

'I'd best go,' Mollie cut in, snatching up her jacket and her bag. 'I said I'd meet Joe at seven, to make sure we got in all right.'

'Mind now, you don't have to hurry back tomorrow morning. We can see to things,' Jennet instructed as she and Jamie followed the girl out into the yard, where Jennet's battered bicycle was propped against the wall. 'It'll be nice for you to spend a night with your mother and Sam. Tell them all that we're asking after them. And have a lovely time.'

'I'll have a great time. It'll be good to be dancing again.' Mollie finished tying a scarf over her hair to keep it from being blown to bits, slung her bag into the basket and seized the handlebars. 'I'll tell you all about it when I get back,' she called as she pushed off. Then, with a cheerful trill on the bell, she headed across the courtyard and into the lane.

As she cycled along the road to Rothesay, where Joe was waiting for her, Mollie blinked hard to hold back the tears that threatened to ruin her carefully applied mascara.

'Very nice,' he had said, in that flat voice that he always used when he was angry, or bored. He hadn't even looked at her properly. He never did, because as far as he was concerned she was nothing more than a nuisance, an evacuee from Glasgow, a pest who had nagged him out of his chair and onto a crutch. He had been glad when she and her family left Westervoe, and dismayed when his sister brought her back to help out after Mrs Scott's accident. She knew it.

She sniffed hard and told herself that he didn't matter a jot. If that was the way Angus wanted it, it was all right with her. Mollie McCabe had her whole life in front of her; she was going places, and one day he might realise that there was more to her than just a Glasgow lassie who got in the way of his precious life. But his discovery would come too late, because by then, she vowed to herself, she would have found someone else who could make her knees go weak and her heart flutter by being in the same room.

She rang the bell for no reason at all, just as an exclamation mark to her decision. She was going dancing and it was going to be a great evening, and Joe was waiting for her. Joe liked her. It was good to have a lad who liked you.

She came to the top of a hill and stuck her feet out to the sides, freewheeling down, forging through the rush of air that sought to hold her back. 'Look out, world, Mollie McCabe's coming,' she shouted into the wind.

But deep inside she couldn't forget that flat voice

saying, 'Very nice', and the way he had immediately
turned away and started talking about his precious
byre.

'You might have been more enthusiastic,' Jennet said
when she returned to the kitchen. 'Mollie looked
lovely, and you know it.'

'I said she looked very nice, didn't I?'

'I've heard you compliment one of the cows with
more enthusiasm. You disappointed her.'

'Don't be daft, she doesn't give a damn about my
opinions.'

'Of course she does. You're a man, aren't you?'

'I doubt if that's the way Mollie McCabe sees me,'
Angus said. He had washed and rinsed his hands; now
he reached for the soap and started again. Anything
to keep his back turned to Jennet and her nagging, he
thought sourly.

He looked at the water gushing from the tap, and
the soap bubbles foaming over the backs of his
hands, and thought about the flush on Mollie's pretty
face, the way her eyes had been sparkling with
excitement at meeting her lad. He recalled the
glimpse of the hollow between the tops of her soft
full breasts as she stooped to put on her shoes, and
the way her pretty blouse had slipped, revealing the
smooth creamy curve of her shoulder.

Angus swallowed hard in an attempt to rid himself
of such thoughts and seized the small stiff-bristled
brush, scrubbing at his nails until the skin immediately

below them stung. Then he rinsed again and again before straightening and reaching for the towel.

He dried each finger meticulously, then picked up the crutch that came between him and everything he wanted most in the world and made his way through the kitchen to his room.

Celia Scott managed to get downstairs the next morning with help from Jennet and the nurse, who warned as she settled her patient in the wingback chair, 'Mind now, no walking around. You'll only make the wound worse again.'

'I'm not a daft bairn, or a silly-headed lassie,' Celia snapped. 'I know how to look after myself!'

'If you knew that, then why did you hurt yourself so badly in the first place?' asked the nurse, who had known her for years and was in a position to take certain liberties.

Any rebellious plans the invalid might have had soon disappeared. Since Jennet and Angus were busy and Mollie was not yet back from Rothesay, Celia was left in charge of Jamie, who was under strict instructions to be a good boy, fetch anything Great-Gran needed and make sure that he didn't go too close to her bad leg. He followed every instruction to the letter, but even so Celia was exhausted and longing for her bed by the time Jennet came in to make a cup of tea in the middle of the morning.

She helped the older woman upstairs and came back down to find Jem sitting at the kitchen table eating biscuits while Angus made the tea. 'She's not nearly as able as she thought she was, and I had the devil's own job getting her upstairs on my own. I don't know when she'll be able to get back to working the farm, if ever.'

'She'll manage it,' Jem predicted. 'I know that woman. I came tae this farm as a lad, not long after she got wed. I was here when yer father was born, and I mind that she dropped him as easy as winkin' and got back tae her farm work within days. A wee cut on the leg won't hold her still for long.'

'It was more than a wee cut, Jem, it was a right bad gash and it went septic. She's not as young as she used to be, remember.'

'None of us are, lassie,' the old man said, his eyes suddenly bleak. 'None of us are.'

Just then there was a sudden flurry in the yard, and the brisk tinging of an old bicycle bell. Angus, slumped at the table with a mug of tea between his two hands, groaned. 'She's back again.'

'Just in time for her tea,' Jennet said as Jamie tumbled out through the door to welcome Mollie. She swept into the kitchen, beaming round at all and sundry, with the little boy clamouring at her heels, 'Present?'

'Jamie! Mind your manners.'

'Ach, leave him alone, Jen. Yes, I did bring you somethin', Mr Nosy, but you'll have tae wait till later, when I've had a nice cup of tea. I'm parched!'

'Did you enjoy the dancing?'

'It was grand,' Mollie said enthusiastically. 'We danced every dance and your auntie said to invite Joe back for his supper after, so we'd a nice time at the house as well.'

'Come on, Jem, time we were back at work.' Angus planted his hands flat on the table and heaved himself to his feet.

'I don't know what's wrong with Angus,' Jennet said as the men went out with Jamie trailing behind them. 'He's been out of sorts all day. Mebbe it's because Grandmother was downstairs earlier.'

'Ach, it's just his way,' Mollie said airily. 'Anyway, about the dancing . . .'

The Dicksons left the following morning, tanned and happy after their holiday.

'The best yet,' Eric said enthusiastically, pumping Jennet's hand, then Mollie's, vigorously.

'Eric's right, the bairns had a wonderful time, and so did we, didn't we, Eric?' Mary's face, wan and creased with worry when Jennet had first met her, was wreathed in smiles now.

'I'm goin' tae be a farmer when I grow up,' Walter announced, and his brother, not to be outdone, chimed in, 'An' I'm goin' tae be a tractor man an' all!'

'This is for you . . .' Mary handed an envelope over. 'It's the rent we agreed on.'

'But that was before you all put so much work into the haymaking,' Jennet protested. 'You earned the cottage.'

'Then call it a thank you for your kindness in taking us in,' Mary urged, while Eric chimed in with, 'We just want to show our appreciation.'

'Me and Mam and the rest of us were just the same as them, all peely-wally when we arrived, and fit and brown when we left,' Mollie mused as they waved goodbye to the Glasgow family. 'There's somethin' about this place that's good for folk.'

'Unless you grow up here,' Jennet said wryly, and then, opening the envelope, 'This is too much, I'll have to make them take it back!'

'Hold on . . .' Mollie put a hand on her arm as she was about to set off across the yard. 'Let's see.' She took the envelope and tipped its contents into her hand, skimming deftly through the notes and coins. 'No, it's fine. Less than your auntie charges, but she provides breakfast as well. And don't even think about giving it back, it'll be the money they put aside for this holiday, and decent working folk like them don't like to feel beholden.'

'If you're sure that it's what they want . . . It'll help to pay for the hire of the threshing mill in November,' Jennet said as Mollie nodded vigorously. 'Or it could pay for an extra farmhand to help out with the oat harvest.'

'When I was staying in Rothesay the other night after the dance,' Mollie mentioned casually, 'your auntie was saying that the place is still full to bursting. She wondered if you'd be willing to take in some more trippers.'

'Gran would never agree to it. She only let the Dicksons stay because they were here by the time she knew about them.'

'Jennet, you're a grown woman with a child of your own and a mind of your own, too. And Angus is older than you are. Is it not time the two of you stopped fretting about what your gran wants? Surely the farm belongs to you just as much as to her, now.'

'You're right, and if renting the cottage out brings in some money, it would be worth doing. And it's only until the holiday season's over. I'll speak to Angus,' Jennet said.

'It's not worth the fuss Gran would make,' Angus said decisively the next morning as he and Jennet went to bring the cows in.

'But we need the money, and surely this is our chance to show her that we can bring in extra money and run the place perfectly well between us. She's still determined to let it go back to the estate, come Martinmas. We don't have all that much time to take matters into our own hands.'

They had reached the gate; Angus unfastened it and gave it a push so that it swung wide. The cows began to amble out, supervised by Gumrie, and when they were all clear of the gate Jennet gave it a hefty push, then managed to slip through the narrowing opening before the big gate hit against its post.

'We're not bairns playing pretend games now,'

Angus said irritably as he latched the gate. 'This is real life.'

'And it's the only one we've got, so we should make the most of it. You surely don't want to leave this place?' She indicated the fields, the great blue arch of sky above, the familiar rutted lane and the cows themselves, their great backsides swinging rhythmically and their tails swishing at the occasional fly.

'I tried making the most of my life once, and look where it got me. Come on,' Angus added impatiently to a cow lagging behind the others. She gave him a surprised look from her large gentle eyes and then hastened her pace slightly. 'How could the two of us run this place?'

'Gran managed when we were growing up.'

'Only by making the three of us work here every minute we were out of school. D'you not remember having to get up at the crack of dawn and work till it was time to go to the classroom, then starting again when we came home, until it got dark? D'you really want that for Jamie?'

'It doesn't have to be like that for him. I'm sure that you and I could think of a better system. Anyway, we had good times, too,' Jennet argued.

'Not many, and there was no chance of us choosing what we wanted to do with our lives; Martin and me had it dinned into us from the time we could walk that we were going to be farmers, and the three of us were taken out of school as soon as we were old enough to work here full time. Not that we had much in the way of brains, but you could have stayed on in school, Jennet, if she'd let you. You could have made something of yourself.'

'I got to Glasgow, remember? And it wasn't Gran that spoiled my chances there – I did it myself. We could make a go of Westervoe between us, Angus, with help from Jem and Mollie.'

'Mollie's a city lassie,' Angus said scathingly. 'She can't run a farm any more than I can.'

His apparent determination to look on the black side began to anger Jennet. 'She can look after the house and the garden and Jamie, so's I can get on with the work. She can feed the hens, the pigs and any calves we might have. She can look after the holidaymakers who'd rent the cottage.'

'Jen . . . !' he began, then shrugged and let the matter drop as they turned in at the farmyard.

Jennet picked it up again later, once the cows were back in their field and the milk had been cooled and poured into large churns that Mollie, Jennet and Jem manhandled between them to the lane, to wait for the cart that would take them to the boat. Angus had been brushing out the byre; now Jennet joined him, picking up a wide shovel and hefting straw and dung into a barrow.

'You saw how much the Dicksons enjoyed helping out on the farm, Angus, and other folk would enjoy that sort of thing, too. They see it as something different. It's not like work to them; it's pleasure because they're only doing it for a week or mebbe two. And Aunt Ann says she can send folk to us.'

'You think Grandmother would agree to that?' Angus asked.

'You're the oldest and the farm's really yours now, specially since Martin's not coming back. It's you who should decide these things, not her.'

He stopped work and leaned on the brush. 'Do as she says, Jen, go back to Glasgow, get on with that training and think of your own future, and Jamie's.'

'And what about yours?'

'This,' said Angus, slapping his crippled leg with the flat of his hand, 'is the rest of my life. And whether I spend it in Largs or Outer Mongolia doesn't matter.'

'For God's sake, man, you've got a bad leg and that's all that's wrong with you! The rest of you works fine, so why shouldn't you be a farmer like you've always wanted?'

'Mebbe what I want now is peace from your naggin'. Mebbe all I want to do is get out of this . . . this prison and go and live in a place like Largs, where I might meet folk and enjoy myself!'

'All right then, you go and have a good time with Grandmother and Great-Aunt Rachel. I'm staying on here, Angus, and I'm keeping this farm going for me and Jamie, and if you won't help me I'll find some other way.'

'Supposing he grows up like his Uncle Martin and throws it all back in your face?'

'So that's what's been gnawing away at you?' Jennet picked up the handles of the loaded barrow, taking a moment to steady herself against the weight. 'You were counting on Martin coming back so that you could work the farm between you. And now you think you're going to lose it. But you don't need to. Martin might not be here, but I am,' she stormed, and when he turned his back on her and said nothing, she flounced out of the byre – or as close to flouncing as she could get, weighted down as she was by a barrowful of dung.

14

'I'm going to my sister Rachel's,' Celia Scott announced as the midday meal ended. 'She's willing to have me and there's a nice garden at the back where I can sit out and rest this daft leg of mine.'

She glared from face to face as though waiting for a comment, but both her grandchildren were so surprised by the unexpected news that it fell to Jem to say, as he pushed his chair back, 'Aye, well, that's the sensible thing tae do. Ye're of no use tae anyone here as ye are. I'm off back tae the end field tae have a look at the hedgin',' he added to Angus, and stumped out.

'He's right of course, I'm useless round here until my leg mends, so I might as well get out of the way. And it'll give me and Rachel the chance to sort out what's to happen once this place is off our hands.'

'When are you going?' Angus asked.

'Rachel's coming over today to help me with the travelling.'

'Great-Aunt Rachel's coming here? Today?' Jennet rose in a panic, looking round the kitchen. Great-Aunt Rachel, like Mrs Blaikie, disapproved of untidiness.

Celia glanced at the clock. 'She'll be on the boat now. She'll get the bus out here, and Andra Blaikie's kindly offered to take us back to the pier so's you can both get on with seeing to this place.'

'When did you arrange this? Why did you not tell me sooner, so that I could have got things ready for Great-Aunt Rachel?'

'You've been too wrapped up in your work to pay any attention to what a poor old body like me has to say,' Celia said spitefully.

'Gran, you know I'd have listened!'

'Well, it was only arranged yesterday. The nurse called in at Gleniffer to ask Lizbeth if she'd telephone Rachel, and as it turned out Rachel wasnae doing anything today, so she was willing to come and fetch me. Lizbeth brought word when she called in yesterday to see me.'

'There's your clothes to pack, arrangements to be made . . .'

'I'll only need clothes for a week or two. Mebbe it'll not be a bad thing for you two to be left to manage on your own for once, without me there to keep an eye on the place.'

'Of course we can manage,' Jennet said sharply. 'Angus's more than capable of running the place.'

'I doubt that,' Celia said, then added pointedly, looking at Mollie, who was working at the sink, 'but

whatever the truth of it, I don't think that this is a
matter to be discussed before outsiders.'

'Mollie is not an . . .'

'Come on, Jamie pet,' Mollie said, reaching for the
towel. 'We'll go and give the pigs their breakfast, will
we?'

'Mollie,' Jennet said quietly when she and Angus
were alone with their grandmother, 'is not a stranger.
She's part of this family.'

'She is not, and never will be, part of my family,'
Celia rapped out, fisting her hands on the table and
easing herself slowly and painfully to her feet. 'And
I'll expect her to be back where she belongs by the
time I come home. Now . . . help me upstairs so's I
can be ready when Rachel arrives.'

As Jennet helped her grandmother to the door she
looked at Angus over her shoulder, trying to signal
with her eyes; but he stayed where he was at the table,
staring down at his hands.

Celia's packing took up most of Jennet's morning.
Since Celia wore work clothes most of the time and
had only two sets of 'good' clothes – one for church
and the Women's Rural Institute meetings, the other
for more special occasions – there was little to be
done as far as her clothes were concerned, but even
so the suitcase kept having to be repacked to make
room for items that Celia suddenly remembered . . .
her Bible, a book of poetry she liked, the small
jewellery box containing a few items that had been

handed down from her mother, a little photograph album.

Then Jennet had to help her to dress and do her hair and choose a suitable pair of gloves . . . which led to more repacking, because they had both forgotten about gloves.

'I despair of you, Jennet, I really do,' Celia said at that point, completely ignoring the fact that she herself was equally guilty. 'You're turning into nothing more than a farmhand these days. You know that respectable women should always wear gloves!'

'As far as I'm concerned, they'd get in the way of milking and mucking out the byre,' Jennet retorted, almost at her wits' end. Although the flash of impertinence soothed her for a few seconds, it had to be paid for by putting up with a time-wasting lecture on manners to one's elders.

When she finally went downstairs Mollie and Jamie were in the kitchen; the table had been cleared and the dishes washed, and a pot of soup was simmering on the range. Jennet snatched her jacket from the nail behind the door. 'See to Grandmother if she calls, will you?'

'She'll not want me, she'll want you.'

'Then she'll just have to want, for I've never been as close to throwing her down the stairs,' Jennet said and fled to the comfort and security of the farmyard.

Mollie would have given all she had to run out after her friend, but she knew by the look on Jennet's face that she really was close to breaking point. Why did Mrs Scott have to be so difficult about everything, she wondered, as she washed Jamie's hands and face and combed his hair, much to his annoyance.

'Now you sit down there and play nicely,' she ordered, giving him his building bricks; then, deciding that they might look too untidy when Mrs Scott's sister arrived, she took them away from him and replaced them with a battered toy pony on wheels. Once he was settled she set to and cleaned the entire kitchen, rearranging the dishes on the dresser and even, when there was nothing else to do, brushing the toy pony's mane. Jamie, intrigued, insisted on taking over the task just as his great-grandmother called 'Jennet!' from upstairs.

Celia was sitting on the edge of her bed fully dressed, even to her hat and gloves. As soon as she saw Mollie, her face tightened in disapproval; as though, Mollie thought, she had been sucking one of those round green sweeties known to children throughout the west of Scotland as soor plooms.

'I called for my granddaughter,' she said haughtily.

Hoity-toity, Mollie thought, while aloud she said politely, 'Jennet's working outside, Mrs Scott. Are you wanting to be helped downstairs?' When the old woman hesitated, then gave a cool, reluctant nod, Mollie stepped forward. 'Take your stick in that hand and take my hand with the other,' she instructed, slipping her arm about Celia Scott and easing her up from the bed. 'And don't try to help yourself, just let me worry about that. I'll come back for your case after.'

Under her calm but precise directions they were in the kitchen in no time at all.

'Your sister won't be long now so I'll start the tea,' Mollie said as she settled the old woman into her wingback chair. She nodded to where the kettle gave out a plume of steam on the range. 'You'll be ready for a hot drink after the effort of getting yourself ready for the journey.'

'Where did you learn how to help folk like that?' Celia asked, impressed despite herself.

'There was an old lady in our tenement in Glasgow. She lived alone, but she was a right independent soul and she'd not move to a ground-floor flat,' Mollie explained as she set out the best cups and a plate of scones she had buttered earlier. 'She'd lived there for over fifty years and was determined that she was going to die there. And, poor old soul, she did, but luckily it was in her sleep just a week before the bomb hit the place, so that was a blessing. All the weans in the close called her Granny Adam.'

'I don't want any scones,' Celia said.

'Your sister'll be ready for something to eat when she arrives. Anyway, Granny Adam always needed help on the stairs and my mam showed me how to do it properly. She worked in a hospital before she got married to my da,' Mollie said proudly.

Nesta had been a ward maid, not a nurse, but by keeping her eyes and ears open she had learned a lot. The only thing she had not learned was how to judge a man. Mollie was convinced that if it had not been for her da, her mam would have done well for herself.

She finished laying the tea-things out and turned to the chair, a hopeful smile dying on her face as she encountered Celia Scott's scowl. Best not to put the milk out just yet, she thought, for that face'll just sour it before it's needed. Aloud she said, 'I'll just fetch your things down, then.'

'Andra Blaikie can do that when he comes over.'

'I'll save him the trouble,' Mollie said, and escaped through the inner door.

Estimating that the boat bringing Celia's sister over must have been in for a good half hour by now, she took refuge in the room she shared with Jennet and watched from the window. After five minutes a portly, smartly dressed woman walked gingerly into the yard, flapping her handbag at any hens who ventured too close.

Mollie bolted into Celia's room, snatched up the suitcase and the shabby little travelling bag beside it and arrived back in the kitchen just as Celia's sister reached the outer door.

The woman gave Mollie one swift glance, then swept past her into the room as though she did not exist. The gauzy scarf looped about her throat wafted along behind her like the wake of a large, perfumed ship. 'Celia, for goodness sake will you look at yourself!' she trumpeted. 'You're in sore need of some proper care and attention!'

Suddenly Celia Scott seemed to shrink and age.

She reached up to clutch her sister's hand. 'Rachel, it's so good to see you!'

'Where's Jennet? And Angus?'

'Working. Where else would they be?'

'They should be here with you!'

'I'll fetch them,' Mollie said, 'when I've poured the tea.'

'I'll see to that.' Rachel took control, almost barging Mollie out of the way. 'I can attend to my sister, thank you, while you fetch her grandchildren.'

Jamie, who had been ignored by both women, jumped up and scurried after Mollie, locking his hand in hers so that they left the house together.

'Don't you see that this is going to be our best chance?' Jennet said hotly to her brother. Then as Angus, leaning on the wall of the piggery and scratching the occupants' backs with a stick, remained silent, 'She'll be away for a good two weeks . . . a month mebbe. We have to do more than just keep the place going until she comes back. We have to prove that we can run it our way.'

'And just what is "our way"?'

'Bring in more lodgers so's we can earn a bit of money, and change anything we need to change. This farm's not moved on since we were born . . . since before we were born,' Jennet said passionately. 'There are probably easier ways of doing things.'

'Such as telling the estate in November that we're leaving.'

'And until then? We have to try, Angus!'

'If you want to try something new, then go ahead. I'll not stand in your way.'

'But we can't go behind Gran's back. I'll not have her coming home and changing things back to the way they were before. We have to tell her what we're going to do, and we have to tell her together . . . and mean it. Please, Angus!'

He heaved himself away from the wall and snatched up the crutch that had been propped by his side. 'If you're going to go on like this all the time Gran's away,' he said over his shoulder as he made for the yard, 'I think I'd rather go with her today and be done with it.'

'Will you stop feeling so sorry for yourself and start being the farmer you really are?' She followed him into the yard just as Mollie and Jamie emerged from the house.

'She's arrived and she's terrible, and I don't care if she is your blood kin,' Mollie said breathlessly. 'Your gran's ready to go and she's looking for the two of you.'

'We were just going in anyway. Come on, Angus.'

'Not me. I'll come and see her off when Mr Blaikie arrives.'

A loud rapping on the kitchen window brought their heads round to see that Rachel was signalling at them.

'We have to go in. Angus, we need to talk to Gran together!' Jennet said desperately, and he looked at her as if she were a stranger.

'You're the one with all the high ideas, so you can tell her yourself. I'll not get involved,' he said, and went into the stable. Jennet took a deep breath and rubbed her hands down the legs of her britches.

'All right, if I must, I must. Mollie, keep Jamie out here with you,' she said and marched into the house.

Mollie looked from her friend's retreating back to the open stable door. Then, drawing a breath every bit as deep as Jennet's, she went into the stable, with Jamie trailing along behind her. Angus, his back to her, was sorting through some of the tack.

'You might have gone in with her instead of leaving her to face them on her own.'

'Keep your nose out of our business, Mollie McCabe,' he said without turning round.

'Jennet is my business. She's my best friend, and you might think that I'm an ignorant Glasgow lassie and not worth bothering about, but I love this place and it's done a lot for me and my family. I can see why she cares about it. I just wish you did.'

'You don't know what you're talking about.'

'I didnae come down the Clyde in a banana boat, Angus Scott. I've got eyes, and I've got a brain between my ears and all. Jennet's right when she says this place should be yours. If it comes to that, it *is* yours.'

'If it was, the first thing I'd do is run you off it.'

'Mebbe you would, for you've never liked hearing the truth from the likes of me.' Mollie's temper boiled over. 'D'you know what you are, Angus Scott? You're a snob, just like your old witch of a grandmother. Mebbe you should do what you said – go with her today and rot in Largs with her and her snobby sister, for it seems to me that you all deserve each other. I feel sorry for Jennet, havin' you two as kin. She deserves . . .'

A small hand crept into hers. 'Where's the witch, Mollie?' Jamie enquired nervously, his eyes darting round the dark corners of the stable. She bent and swept him up into her arms.

'Not a real one, silly, there aren't any real witches. Angus and me are just playing a game. Come on, let's go for a nice wee walk, just the two of us.'

At the stable door she turned, the anger suddenly draining out of her. 'I'm sorry for what I said. Jennet's not the only reason I love this place,' she said, and then as he remained silent, 'You know that, don't you?'

'Go away.'

'Angus . . .' She took a few steps towards him.

'Just go away,' he said between gritted teeth, his back so rigid that much as she wanted to touch it, she was afraid in case she discovered that it was made of flint instead of flesh and skin and bone.

'I might as well,' she said, and carried Jamie out into the sunshine.

'You're all set, then?' Jennet was saying in the kitchen.

'Where's Angus?' Celia asked in reply. 'He should be here to greet his aunt and see me off.'

'He's on his way.'

'Janet, do you always come into the house with those big heavy boots on?' her Great-Aunt Rachel wanted to know, wafting a handkerchief before her nose. She always insisted on using the more refined version of Jennet's name and had never accepted the fact that her sister's granddaughter had been christened with the Scottish pronunciation.

Jennet glanced down at the offending boots. 'This is the working kitchen, Aunt Rachel. We don't wear our farm boots and shoes beyond that door, but if we took them off every time we came in and out of this room we'd never have time to catch up with all we have to do.'

'I'm sure it's unhygienic, bringing dirty clothing like that into the room where you cook and eat your food.'

'A peck of dirt never hurt anyone, Rachel,' Celia broke in. 'If you want another cup of tea take it now, for Andra'll be here any minute.'

'I'll wait until I get home before I have more tea,' her sister said in a voice that damned the Westervoe Farm version for ever.

'Gran, about me and Angus looking after the farm . . .'

'If there are any worries, just go to Andra for advice. He's promised to keep an eye on you.'

'Nobody needs to keep an eye on us,' Jennet said. 'We're grown adults and we know about farming. What I was going to say is, if we feel that changes need to be made while you're away, we'll go ahead and make them.'

'Changes?' Celia, who had been slumped back in her chair, looking like a stranger in her good black coat and hat, suddenly snapped upright. 'What sort of changes?'

'Anything that we think might make the work easier. Taking on another farmhand, for instance.'

'And where would you find the money to pay someone else?'

Jennet fisted her hands by her sides, digging her nails deep into her palms. 'I'm going to rent the cottage out again.'

'To trippers?' Celia asked, then as Jennet nodded, 'Over my dead body!'

'You'll not be here, Gran, dead or alive, so it'll not make any difference to you.'

'Don't be impertinent!' Great-Aunt Rachel said, outraged.

'I'm not, I'm just saying that since it's Angus's right to inherit this farm, it's his right to make whatever changes he thinks it needs.'

'And where is Angus?' Rachel demanded to know. 'I don't see him here, speaking out for himself. If you ask me, Celia, it's this little madam who's going to be making all the decisions behind your back.'

'I'm not going behind her back, I'm making things clear before she leaves. Not that it's any of your affair, Great-Aunt Rachel.'

'That's enough, young woman!' Celia rapped at her,

while her sister gasped. 'Have you not listened to what I've told you over and over again? We'll all be out of here by next April and you'll be doing your nurse training in Glasgow by September next, so there's no need for any changes. They'll be up to the new tenant at Westervoe.'

'But Angus needs to stay here and run his own life.'

'I'll look out for Angus.'

'By that, you mean that you'll turn him into an invalid between you.'

'He *is* an invalid, and closing your eyes to the truth won't change anything.'

'Plenty of folk manage fine with worse disabilities than Angus. What about Douglas Bader?'

'That's different!'

'How is it different?' Jennet persisted. Then, as her grandmother said nothing, 'Gran, I'm only asking for the chance to show you that me and Angus can take over Westervoe and run it together.'

'You're havering!'

'Give us a year . . . please. You've done more for us than any woman should have had to do and you deserve your rest. Stay with Great-Aunt Rachel, if that's what you want to do, and leave the farm to Angus.'

'What has Angus got to say about this daft notion of yours?' Celia asked. Then, when Jennet said nothing, she swept on triumphantly, 'I'll tell you what he said, Rachel . . . the same as me. That's why he's not in here standing by the girl. He knows he's not able.'

'He is able, and if he finds that he can't manage the place I'll take it on.'

'You? Don't be daft!'

'I've got Jamie's future to consider. Westervoe's his birthright too, and plenty of farms here on Bute have been run by women. You did it yourself.'

'I was looking out for my son and then for his bairns, every one of them born in wedlock,' Celia rasped. 'If you want to do the right thing by that lad ye birthed, ye'll let him get off this island to a place where nob'dy knows the shame he's brought on us.'

Each word was like a slap in the face, but Jennet rallied. She had too much at stake to let her grandmother's cruelty touch her.

'Let you have him, you mean? You'd never stop reminding him that he doesn't have a father. You'd hammer that shame into him with every breath he took.'

'I'd certainly teach him how to accept and overcome his bad start in life. As for keeping on Westervoe for his sake . . . he's got no right to it.'

'He's got every right. I'm a Scott and I'm his mother.'

'And who's the father, that's what I'd like to know.'

'The lassie mebbe doesn't know that herself, Celia,' Rachel said, her round, carefully made-up face pink with indignation and excitement. 'Since the war this country's fair littered with by-blows fathered by men from all over the world on lassies with no more sense than to let themselves be treated like . . . like . . .'

'Like common whores,' Celia ended the sentence coldly. Then her head whipped round as Angus said from the doorway, 'My sister is not a whore, Grandmother, and I won't have you miscalling her.'

'So she's told you who fathered the bairn, has she?'

'She has not and I've never asked, for it's her business, not mine. But I know Jennet, and you should know her too, since you raised her.'

Celia had the grace to drop her eyes from his gaze, but Rachel spoke up in her stead. 'Aye, she raised the pack of you and look how she's been repaid . . . Your brother running off, just like his father before him, and Janet bringing home a bastard to shame my sister in the eyes of all the folk on this island!'

'It seems to me,' Angus said coldly, moving further into the kitchen, 'that the rest of the island's not nearly as bothered about that as you two are. And since you don't even live here, Great-Aunt Rachel, I'll thank you to keep your neb out of this family discussion.'

'What? Are you going to allow him to speak to me like that?' Rachel rounded on her sister. 'And me opening my own house to him, too!'

'Just a minute, Rachel. About this nonsense Jennet's been talking, Angus . . .'

'I know what Jennet has in mind for this place.'

'And you've told her no, haven't you?'

'I did, more than once. I thought the same as you, Grandmother, but now that I've had time to think about it,' Angus said calmly, setting his crutch aside and leaning back against the wall, arms folded, 'I think some of her ideas might be worth trying.'

'What?'

'Why don't you just enjoy your wee holiday in Largs and let me and Jennet have a try at running the farm? Forget about handing in our notice at Martinmas and leave it until next May, when the Whitsun rent's due. That should give us time enough to test ourselves. After all, as Jennet keeps reminding me, it's my birthright.'

'But you're a cripple,' Rachel burst out, unable to hold her tongue any longer. 'You're not able!'

Angus's face had darkened at her use of the hated word. Now he looked her up and down before saying, 'There are different ways of being crippled. Mine's a bad leg, but some folk are worse off. They think they can see and hear, yet they cannae understand what they're seeing and hearing. Other folk are locked so tightly into their own minds that they cannae understand what they're being told. For myself, I'd as soon settle for havin' a bad leg.'

His grandmother gaped at him, her mouth opening and closing, but no words coming out. Even Rachel could not find any words. Then the silence gripping the kitchen was broken by the chug of an engine as Andra Blaikie's small saloon car turned in at the yard.

'Ready, Gran?' Angus said pleasantly. 'You'll have to go or you'll miss your boat.'

* * *

'God help us,' he said as they waved the car off, with Celia and her sister sitting erect in the back seat. 'What have you done to me, Jennet?'

'Did you mean what you said?'

'Scarcely a word of it, but they got me angry, the way the two of them were going on as if they were the only folk with the right idea of things. I think you've lost your reason, but even so you're my sister and I couldnae let the two of them speak to you like that.'

'Are they gone?' Mollie came round the end of the old stable, Jamie by her side. 'Have we missed them?'

'Aye. Lucky, aren't you?' Angus said. Then, turning back to Jennet, 'We're both going to regret this, you know.'

'At least we'll have tried.'

'I suppose so. But it's only until next May at the latest, mind.' Then when she nodded, 'So . . . where do we start?'

'By getting some lodgers in, and turning that old stable into a deep-litter house,' she said, feeling as if a load had been lifted from her shoulders. 'I'm sick of those old arks!'

15

In Rothesay local folk and holidaymakers flocked to the town's annual August Carnival, while at Westervoe Jennet and Mollie slaved to turn the old stables, once inhabited by the fine Clydesdales bred by Jennet's great-grandfather, into a deep-litter hen house.

'You're every bit as much of a slave driver as your gran,' Mollie complained, slapping whitewash on the stone walls. 'She's not been gone a fortnight and you've already got me working myself into a puddle of sweat.'

'If you want to go to Rothesay, then off you go.' Jennet, perched precariously on the top step of the old folding ladders, reached up as high as she could in order to get her brush into a difficult angle between wall and roof. 'You're not a prisoner.'

'No, just a fool. And watch what you're doing,' Molly squawked as whitewash from Jennet's brush dripped down on her. 'Anyway, how could I go and enjoy myself when I know you're half killing yourself in here?'

'We've got to get the hens out of the oldest arks and in here before winter comes. I can't face having to move all those arks about in the rain and cold, and some of them are just about ready to come apart in our hands. And it all has to be done before the harvesting starts.'

'And before your gran comes back, so's she can't put a stop to it.'

'How did you know?' Jennet peered down through the ladder's rungs at the top of her friend's red head.

'Because it's what I would do myself in your shoes.'

Since leaving for Largs, Celia had only written two short letters to her grandchildren, reporting on her own improving health and her sister's kindness and assistance, and asking about the farm work. She had not as yet mentioned her return. Although her letters were addressed to Angus alone, Jennet had replied with similarly brief and factual letters. She had made a point of mentioning the holidaymakers in the cottage and the progress of the deep-litter house, but Celia did not refer to them, or to the quarrel they had had just before she left Westervoe.

'D'you not think that Angus's looking a lot better these days?' Mollie's voice floated up from below.

'You're right.' Jennet had noticed that Angus seemed to be taller, easier in his movements and more relaxed these days, despite the hard work and the long hours.

'It's because *she's* not here,' Mollie said. 'The man never knew where he was with her – one minute she was telling him he shouldn't do this and that, then the next she was criticising him for not doing more. If you ask me, he's better off without her. You both are.'

'It's not as easy as that,' Jennet said glumly. 'She'll be back soon.'

A groan floated to her ears from ground level. 'Don't spoil a nice day,' Mollie implored her.

It had taken them a week of hard work to clear the stables of all the rubbish that had accumulated over the years and then shovel piles of dirt from the floor, before sluicing the place with water and disinfectant. Jamie had gone off to stay with the Logans in Rothesay so that his mother and Mollie could get on with the new hen house. To Jennet's relief and, at the same time, her distress, he had gone off eagerly on his new adventure without a backward glance.

'I wonder how Jamie's getting on?' she said now.

'He must be having a better time than we are. You're missing him, aren't you?'

'It's the first time he's been away from me. You don't think he'll be homesick? He doesn't know Aunt Ann and Uncle George all that well.'

'You'd be told if he was miserable. And he knows Mam well enough; she's looked after him loads of times when you were working. He'll be having a great time,' Mollie said robustly. 'Your auntie and my mam will be spoiling him, and your uncle and Sam will have him out in the boats all day.'

That only brought more worry for Jennet. 'What if he falls into the sea?'

'Don't be daft, they wouldn't let anything happen to him.'

The new cottage people, a young couple, stopped to exchange pleasantries on the weather as they left on one of their long walks. It would have been useful, Jennet thought, attacking a dark corner, if they had been as helpful as the Dicksons, but friendly though they were, the new lodgers had no interest in anything but each other. On their honeymoon, Jennet thought, but Mollie reckoned they hadn't got as far as the altar.

'Off walking . . . I told you, they're too keen to keep out of other folks' way,' she said now.

'That might just be shyness. And she's wearing a wedding ring.'

'For all you know, someone else might have put it on her finger.'

'You're terrible, Mollie, thinking the worst of them.'

'Folk arenae always the way they seem,' Mollie said darkly, then gave a sudden yelp and danced back, her brush thumping to the ground. Jennet jumped and had to clutch at the ladder to save herself from falling off.

'A spider!' Mollie whimpered from below.

'For goodness sake . . . you nearly had me off this ladder over a spider? The place is full of them; you should know that by now. Don't be such a baby!'

'But this one was the size of a dinner plate!' Mollie snatched up a spade and advanced cautiously, her eyes darting over the ground before her.

'Don't kill it, you might bring the rain,' Jennet

advised from above. 'We can't have that, not with the harvest due to start soon.'

'I'm certainly not going to invite it to stay for tea. And you're late in starting to fret about the harvest, for we must have killed hundreds of the creepy-crawly things since we started work in here. It's gone,' Mollie announced with relief, 'it must have run out.'

'Sensible creature.'

They worked in silence for another five minutes, then Mollie said, 'Did Mam tell you that our Sam's courting?'

'What? He's a child, just out of school!'

'Mebbe not courting exactly, but he's got pally with a wee lassie who was in his class at the school. Mr Logan told my ma that she's been down at the boats every day during the summer and Sam takes her out in one of the wee boats most evenings after they've closed down.' She coughed, spat and then asked, 'D'you not fancy a drink of water? My throat's full of dust.'

'I fancy a cup of tea. Hold the ladder steady while I come down.' Jennet descended cautiously and when she reached the ground she dragged the scarf she had been wearing turban-fashion from her head and shook it, releasing a shower of dust and grit. Bending from the waist, she ran her hands again and again through her long hair and then stood up, shaking it back over her shoulders. 'That's better; my scalp was beginning to feel all itchy. Think of the state Jamie could get into if he was trying to help us in here.'

She glanced around the big enclosure. Once the walls were painted they would put in laying boxes and cover the floor with a deep layer of straw. In winter the hens would stay indoors, snug and safe and easy to care for, and in summer they would be free to roam outside. 'It's beginning to look much better, don't you think?'

'Aye . . . as long as the hens aren't too particular.'

'It's a sight better than those old arks they've been living in. Come on, the men'll be coming in for a drink soon, so we might as well have ours first.'

'So that's Senga in Glasgow with a lad,' Jennet said as they crossed the yard, 'and Sam with a lass, and you with Joe . . . all of you courting. It must be the summer weather.'

'Joe and me aren't courting. I've told you time and again that he's just a friend.'

'The way I thought Struan was just a friend to me before he proposed out of the blue?'

'Joe's got more sense than to propose. He knows that he'd be sent off with a flea in his ear if he tried any nonsense like that.'

'I wish I'd been able to send Struan off with a flea in his ear,' Jennet said. The young farmer kept eyeing her wistfully when he was in her company and although he had not raised the question of marriage again, Jennet could not forget his declaration that he would ask her again 'later'.

'Joe likes you,' she said, pushing Struan from her

mind as they went into the kitchen, 'and he's a nice lad.' Joe had become a regular visitor to the farm.

'I like him too, but it would be a queer old world if we married folk just because we liked them.' Mollie threw a handful of tea leaves into the pot and filled it from the ever-ready kettle. 'And if he's good to me it's his own choice, for I'm not like our Senga, I'd never expect anything from a man.' She refilled the kettle at the sink, turning the tap on so hard that water sprayed everywhere.

'Stupid tap!' she roared, clashing the kettle down on the hob. Her face was filthy and splattered with whitewash, while rivulets of sweat had cut clean streaks down her cheeks. Poor Mollie, Jennet thought, running an arm over her own face, which she knew must look just as bad; if she hadn't been called back to help out at the farm she would be in Rothesay right now, enjoying the good weather instead of being stuck in the old stables.

'Jen, can I ask you somethin' very personal?'

'What is it?'

'Did you love Jamie's father?'

Jennet felt her insides shrink together, as though for protection. It was the first time anyone had asked such a personal question, other than her grandmother's angry demands to be told the truth at once. It had been easier, in the face of that cold, hard anger, to refuse to answer.

'Just say if I'm being cheeky and I'll shut up and never mention it again,' Mollie was stumbling on.

'No, you're not being cheeky at all.' Mollie was a friend, her dearest friend, and she deserved an answer. Besides, it was all in the past now. 'I really thought I did love him at the time.' Jennet sat down at the table. 'Of course I did, or I'd not have . . .' She bit her lower lip, then grimaced at the taste of dust and whitewash on her tongue. 'It was all so . . . He was on leave and he'd discovered that war wasn't the adventure he thought it was going to be. He was scared, and I suppose I wanted to make him feel that someone cared. And that was the only way I could . . .'

'Did he ever know about Jamie?'

'Yes, he did.' The bitterness that had ebbed away over the years came flooding back as Jennet recalled the way he had reacted; the colour draining from his young face, the panic in his voice. 'He didn't want to know,' she said, and Mollie reached across the table to put a hand on her arm.

'He sounds like a right sod, leavin' you in the lurch like that.'

'He couldn't take the extra worry. He thought the best thing would be for me to . . . you know.'

'Get rid of Jamie?' Mollie asked, horrified.

'He wasn't Jamie then, he was just . . . nothing, really. Just a problem that made me feel sick in the morning. Just something that wouldn't go away.'

'But you wouldnae do it.'

'I was going to . . . What else could I do? One of the girls I was training with got me the address of a woman who helped girls in my condition, but when it came down to it I couldn't.'

'I should think not! Imagine if wee Jamie had never been born!' Mollie said, shocked, while Jennet stared down at the scrubbed wooden table, remembering the side street with its high tenements, the children with runny noses playing on the pavement, the close with its smell of dirt and defeat, the scarred door behind which the illegal abortionist plied her trade. She had lifted a hand to knock on the panels and then lost her nerve completely and run back to the street.

'To tell the truth, Mollie, I was just like . . . like him.' She stopped herself just in time from saying his name. 'I was scared of being hurt and mebbe dying, so instead of going to the woman I came home to Angus. And to Gran.'

'And the man got away with it. D'you not hate him for the trouble he caused you?'

'Where's the sense in that? I've got Jamie, haven't I?'

'Aye, but you paid a hard price at the time. I'd still hate him if I was in your shoes. No matter how frightened he was with the war and all that, it wasn't fair to leave you to face things on your lone. You're too understanding at times, Jennet Scott. He was a bastard and it's time you came out and said it.'

'I've never said that about anyone in my life!'

'D'you still love him?'

'Of course not, but . . .'

'Then I dare you.' Mollie leaned across the table,

her eyes bright now with amusement. 'You've managed fine without him and you'll go on managing fine, but mebbe it's time you said what you really think. Letting yourself be angry's like vomitin', it gets rid of all the badness and makes you feel better.'

'How do you know about these things?'

'I've lived in a city,' Mollie said calmly. 'I've seen and heard all sorts. And my mam always said I'm like a sponge. I take everything in and forget nothing.'

'Are you sure she didn't mean the fluffy kind that's all jam in the middle?' Jennet was beginning as Angus, Jem and Norrie, the lad they had taken on and were paying with the last of the money earned from selling that year's early potato crop, came in from the fields looking tired, dusty and parched.

'You see to them,' Mollie jumped to her feet, snatching up her mug, 'and I'll take this with me and get back to the whitewashing.'

'You're supposed to put it on the walls, not your face,' Angus said as she passed him.

'This isnae whitewash, this is a very expensive mud pack, the sort that Claudette Colbert swears by,' she retorted, and went out.

Jennet opened her mouth to ask her brother, as he slumped down at the table, rubbing sweat and grime from his face, if he was all right, then she closed it again. Mollie was right when she said that his grandmother had smothered him, and Jennet was determined not to do the same.

She had forced them both to take a hard road, and

it wouldn't get any easier over the next few months,
but they had to keep going until November was behind
them and the twice-yearly rent paid. Then the farm
would be theirs – hers and Angus's – for another six
months at least. And during the winter – short days
and long nights, the cows in the shed and most of the
hens in the big new hen house – they would have time
to take a rest and plan out the next year together.

'You look worn out,' Ann Logan said flatly when her
niece arrived to claim her son back.

'It's been hard work, but we've finished the new
deep-litter house, thanks to you looking after Jamie.'

'It's a pleasure to have him here. You've brought
him up well, Jennet. Are you sure you don't want to
leave him with us for a wee while longer, till you and
Angus get on your feet?'

Kind though the offer was, it made Jennet feel
uneasy. No matter how hard life at Westervoe became,
she needed to have Jamie with her. He was her reason
for living.

'No, you've got a full house as it is and I can
manage fine, as long as you don't mind us keeping
Mollie for a bit longer.'

'It's up to her. Nesta's a treasure and the two of us
can manage well enough with some help from Alice.
She's got Jamie down at the boats, but she'll be
bringing him back in a wee while for his dinner.'

After a week, a wee while was too long to wait.
'I'll go down to the bay and walk back with them.

It'll give me a chance to see a bit of Rothesay for once.'

The town was still as busy as ever and Rothesay Bay still thronged with boats. Queues waited at every one of the boat-hirers, and Alice was on duty with the book while her father helped people in and out of the boats. There was no sign of Jamie.

'Come for the wee lad?' Alice greeted her cousin. 'Joe's taken him out on the launch.' She pointed a brown, freckled arm. 'See? They're coming back in now.'

As the boat came smoothly into the shallows, Jennet saw her son sitting aft beside Joe. The young man had given him his cap and Jamie had pulled it down until his small face was almost hidden by the long peak. When the trippers had left the launch Joe swung the little boy up into the air and across to George Logan, who jiggled him about, making him laugh, before setting him safely down on the shingle.

'Now then, me lad, who's this come to see you?'

He took the cap off and Jamie glanced at Jennet, looked away and then glanced back. For a heart-stopping moment she thought he had forgotten her, then a huge grin split his face in two, and with a screech of 'Mum!' he launched himself at her.

She scooped him up, holding tightly to the compact, wiry bundle of flesh and skin, bone and sinew. His hair and skin smelled of salt air and the indefinable scent that was – and always had been – Jamie's own. She had thought, before his birth, that only animals could recognise their young by smell alone, but she had been wrong.

'Did you have a good time? Did you miss me?'

'Mmm,' he said enigmatically. 'I was on the boats. I had ice cream and I digged a big hole in the sand and . . .'

He talked all the way back to the house, marching along between Alice and Jennet, holding both hands but occasionally releasing one or another to point something out.

'So he wasn't homesick?' Jennet asked her cousin over his head.

'Not a bit of it. He had a wee cot up in Sam's room and the two of them got on fine. It's done Dad and Mum the world of good, having him here,' Alice said warmly. 'I think it's helped them to get over losing Geordie. Jamie made such a fuss of Dad right from the start and he loves Sam and Joe. He scarcely bothered with the womenfolk. For all his age, I think he likes being one of the men. I suppose that's natural for wee laddies – they need their fa . . .'

Then, realising what she was saying, the girl stopped short, flushed bright red and changed the subject.

In mid-September Struan Blaikie and Bert McCabe helped bring in Westervoe's oat crop. Angus used the tractor to do the cutting, while the others – Jennet and some of the older youngsters from the local schools included – followed along behind, gathering up the oats, binding them into bundles by hand, then stacking them in stooks of six, three on one side, three on the other, carefully angled so that they leaned into each other.

'Just looking at these stooks makes the insides of my legs sting,' Angus said unexpectedly as he and Jennet walked out that evening to survey the stubbled field with its neat stooks.

'You mean the way we used to pretend they were horses and we were cowboys?' she asked, and he laughed.

'It was great, wasn't it?'

'We'd have got a right leathering if Grandmother had known what we were doing to the crop.'

'That was part of the pleasure,' Angus said. 'We didn't get much of a chance to be rebellious . . . but we paid a price in our own way.'

They had indeed. Every year the stiff stalks had taken their toll on the tender skin of their inner thighs and calves. After galloping to the end of the earth on their oat steeds, Jennet in her summer frocks and her brothers with their shorts on, they had all suffered agonies from hundreds of tiny scratches, especially in bed at night. But every year, until they got too old for such nonsense, they had gone back to play on the stooks.

'I mind once when you managed to sneak into Grandmother's bedroom while she was still down-stairs,' Angus said, 'and you found some cold cream to ease the stinging.'

Jennet had forgotten, but now that he had triggered the memory she recalled skimming a lump of cream from the tin that Celia kept in a drawer by her bed and running like a scared rabbit back into the boys' bedroom, where the cream was doled out between them. 'It made the burning sting even more at first.'

'But it helped in the end. By God,' Angus said with a final backward glance at the field as they headed for home, and bed, 'if I caught any youngsters messing about with the stooks now, I'd tan their hides for them.' Then he said with a sudden change of subject, 'Is Struan not awful quiet, these days?'

'I never noticed,' she lied.

'You didn't fall out with him that night he took you out, did you?'

'It was just a night at the pictures, that was all.'

'Ach well, whatever's ailing him, he'll get over it,' Angus said and whistled to Gumrie, who was off investigating a rabbit hole. The dog came running, his plumed tail lashing from side to side, his long-muzzled face grinning.

'Daft animal,' Angus growled affectionately. 'Your mother must have been seeing a poodle without us knowing it. You've no idea how farm dogs are supposed to behave, have you?'

And Gumrie, who was an excellent farm dog when he wanted to be, widened his grin before falling sedately in at his master's heel.

16

The new deep-litter house looked quite magnificent. Snug and clean, with the walls whitewashed and the laying boxes, food troughs and water dishes installed and the floor covered with a thick layer of clean straw, it was, Mollie said, as good as Buckingham Palace, as far as hens were concerned.

Jem and Norrie had cut doorways and installed sliding doors so that in good weather the hens could be let out to forage in the yard and the small field adjacent to the old stables; in the winter, when they stayed inside, the daylight hours could be falsely extended by the use of lamps hung from the rafters.

They all gathered to see the chosen hens introduced to their new home, with Jem and Norrie staying on late for the occasion. Since hens were creatures of habit, they waited until dark before moving them, when most of the birds began to find their way to their own arks for the night.

One by one the arks that were being kept were

filled and closed, while the inhabitants of the old, rotting hen houses, on finding themselves shut out, huddled together miserably round the entrances, ready, Jennet hoped, to be gathered up and conveyed to their lovely, snug new palace.

But as always tended to happen with poultry, the sleepy birds roused themselves as soon as Jennet and Mollie attempted to carry them to their new home, squawking and panicking and fleeing in all directions. Those that went inside took one look at the huge interior, so different from the small crowded arks they were used to, and promptly rushed out again.

'If they'd just take a minute tae look at the place, they'd not want tae leave,' Mollie panted, heading for the deep-litter house with a hen tucked under each arm.

'Hens don't think like that. Hold them by the feet,' Jennet advised, 'you can carry more that way.'

'I cannae bring myself tae do that, but I'm gettin' tae the stage where I could wring their necks without lettin' it bother me,' Mollie added as one of the hens managed to flutter free and make a noisy escape, its wings and neck outstretched. 'Now I'll have tae catch it all over again!'

'I swear that I've carried the same hen in three times already,' Jennet said, resignedly. 'How many does that make now, Angus?'

'I don't know.' He dried his eyes, wet from laughter.

'What d'you mean, you don't know?' Mollie doubled her fists on her hips and glared at him.

'Every time I laugh I lose count again.'

'You're not supposed tae laugh, you're just supposed tae count. I thought you were clever?'

'You've got a feather on your chin and every time you speak it waggles,' Angus said, and began to laugh again.

'I suppose it's grand tae see him laughin' for a change,' Mollie said as she and Jennet plodded back to the arks to gather more hens. 'It suits him.'

'He used to do it a lot,' Jennet said, remembering. 'A long time ago.'

Celia Scott's weekly letter arrived the next morning, two days earlier than usual. Jennet, finding it on the kitchen table where Mollie had left it, stared down at the black, angular lettering on the envelope. There was something different about this one, she knew it. It must be the letter she had been expecting and dreading, the one that carried details of their grand-mother's return. At least, she thought bleakly, the deep-litter house was completed and occupied; Grandmother couldn't put a stop to that new venture when she returned.

It was only when she picked the letter up to put it behind the clock for safe-keeping that she discovered another envelope, this one addressed to both Angus and herself. Letters were rare events at Westervoe Farm; usually only bills and reminders were delivered, and it was very unusual to receive two letters in a month, let alone two sharing the same post.

She turned the second letter, the one addressed to them both, over in her hands. The clumsy handwriting that sloped instead of keeping to neat lines was vaguely familiar; it took a full minute before she knew where she had seen it before – on the infrequent letters that Martin had sent home during the war.

Her first instinct was to rip it open; then, realising that she must wait until Angus was there, she settled for turning it over and over in her hands, feeling the weight of it. It was quite bulky, which meant that there must be more than one sheet of paper inside.

'Give them to me.' Jamie was clamouring about her, reaching up to the envelopes. He loved opening letters, and sometimes when Jennet or Mollie had time they wrote letters to him and posted them through the door. He cherished them, reading and rereading them and making up different interpretations of the scribbles on the page.

'They're for Angus.' Jennet put both envelopes behind the clock on the mantelshelf and tried to turn her mind to the day's work.

There was no opportunity to mention the letters to Angus, for they were both busy all day and when they met in the kitchen to eat, Mollie and Jem and Norrie were with them. The day seemed to drag by, and with every hour that passed Jennet felt as though the envelopes stuffed behind the clock were sending out urgent signals in her direction.

Angus, tired out after a hard day's work, went to his bed immediately after they ate that evening; Jennet made herself wait until Mollie went upstairs before taking the envelopes to his room, where he was reading in bed. No matter how tired he was, Angus always ended the day with a book.

'It's early,' he commented when she laid their grandmother's letter on the bed.

'Mebbe it's brought news,' she said, and saw her own apprehension mirrored in her brother's eyes for a second before he blinked it away.

'It was bound to happen sooner or later.'

'This came as well.' She laid the other letter beside the first.

'Martin!' He put his book aside after carefully marking his place, then picked the envelopes up, one in each hand, and raised his eyebrows at her. 'Which one first?'

'Martin's. No, Gran's. No,' she said swiftly, 'Martin's. I think we know what Gran's got to say.'

'Martin's it is.' He put the other letter aside, then opened the chosen envelope. 'D'you want to read it?' he asked. Then as she hesitated, 'I'll take it out and you read it aloud. I'd as soon hear it as see it.'

There were two sheets of paper, closely written. She glanced at the first few lines and blurted, 'He's out of . . .'

'Just read what he says, dammit!' Angus's eyes were like hot coals on her face, his hands tense on the quilt. Jennet licked her lips, shifted position slightly in order to bring the letter nearer to the lamp, then began to read.

Martin was out of the Army, and back in Britain. A mate from his platoon had found him a place where he himself worked, on a farm in the south of England.

'A farm, by God!' Angus interrupted. He barked a strangled, mirthless laugh. 'Here we are, struggling to keep this place going without him, and he's working on someone else's farm!' Then, as she glanced up, 'Go on!'

It was a big farm, Martin wrote, and he was working with the horses and lodging with his mate's family. 'I wrote to Struan Blaikie, and he told me that Grandmother's in Largs just now, so I knew it was safe to write to you without her getting the letter first. Don't be angry with Struan. I made him promise to keep quiet. I've been wanting to make things right with you two,' Jennet read on, then stopped when Angus snorted and made a sudden movement in the bed.

'Go on!' he snapped, and she returned to the letter.

'I'm not going back to Bute. I suppose I knew that the day I left to join the Army. I think it's what I had been waiting for all my life . . . getting the chance to leave Westervoe. I didn't know if I was going to make it through the war, but when it was over and I found myself still in one piece I knew that I would have to make a new life for myself somewhere else. Reg and me became pals because we were both farm lads, and that turned out to be lucky for me. I like working with the horses – I always liked animals and mebbe if things had been the way they used to be and

Clydesdales were still being bred at Westervoe, I'd have been okay about going back there.

'Or mebbe if our mother hadn't died and our father had stayed on I'd have been fonder of the place. I don't know, and there's no sense in wondering now about these things. Being brought up by Grandmother was like being locked in a dark cupboard, and I know war's a terrible thing, but for me it was like being set free into the fresh air and sunlight and being able to breathe for the first time in my life. Even if I had been killed or wounded, it would have been because of my choice, not hers. And that's why I could never go back into that wee dark cupboard.

'There's something else . . . someone else, I should say. I am courting Reg's sister Nancy, and if I am lucky she might agree to marry me when the time is right. She's a nice lassie; I hope that one day I will be able to take her to Bute to meet the two of you, but not while Grandmother's running the place. If it sounds as if I am afraid of her, then I suppose that is the truth.

'I just wish that you had been able to break free along with me, Angus, and I am sorry to have let the two of you down, for I know you must think that that is what I have done. I just wanted you to know that I am all right, and that I will not be back or looking for a share of Westervoe, or expecting anything from you.

'I am trusting you not to tell Grandmother where I am. If you think it best, you can give her my regards, but don't tell her too much. I hope you are both well and I hope, Jennet, that your wee boy is thriving. I would like to see him sometime. Reg and Nancy have a wee nephew and when I see him I think about your lad, who would be much the same age. I will write again sometime. Your affectionate brother, Martin.'

Angus uncurled his fingers, straightening them carefully, and leaned back, hands behind his head.

'So now we know that he's well, and that there's no sense in wondering if he's going to come back,' Jennet ventured after a long pause.

'Aye.' He stared up at the ceiling for a while and then said, 'I know what he means about the wee dark cupboard. Did you feel like that when you went to Glasgow? As if you'd been set free?'

Jennet had never thought of it in that way, but now she remembered the pleasure of meeting new people, walking Glasgow's streets in her spare time, wandering in and out of shops and deciding what she wanted to eat and when she wanted to eat it.

'Yes,' she said slowly. 'I suppose I did.'

'I wish I could feel like that,' Angus said wistfully. 'He always did like horses, our Martin. D'ye mind how he used to go across to Gleniffer whenever he got the chance to help with their horses?'

'Of course I remember. I was the one that was always being sent round on my bicycle to fetch him back. What are we going to tell Gran about this?' Jennet tapped the letter.

'Best to say nothing.'

'But surely she should know that he's not coming back. And that he's all right.'

'Fair enough, if she'd accept that and let it be. But you know her . . . She'll go on and on at us to tell her everything, the way she did with you when you . . .' Angus stopped, then said, 'when you came home from Glasgow. And she'll not be happy until she forces us to hand the letter over. D'you really want her to read what Martin says about her?'

'No!'

'Neither do I, though part of me says she deserves to see it. We'll leave things as they are for the time being,' Angus decided, then sat upright and leaned over to pick up the second letter. 'My turn to read it.'

He ripped the envelope open, scanned the single sheet of paper in one glance and then said, 'Good God.'

'What is it? Is her leg bad again?'

'She's fine,' Angus said slowly, rereading the letter. 'But she's mebbe not coming back.'

'Not coming home? But . . .'

'Read it for yourself.' He handed the page over and she was aware of him studying her face closely as she read.

Celia's letter was, as always, a single page, brusque and to the point. Rachel had looked after her well and, thanks to her sister, Celia had made a full recovery and was now well enough to return to Bute.

'However,' she continued – her writing, unlike Martin's, so spiky and black and so deeply scored into the paper that it almost spoke aloud – 'we are now approaching rent day and, as you know, I wish to hand Westervoe Farm back to the estate so that it can go to another tenant. I have settled well enough in Largs and I have fully made up my mind that when I return to Bute it will only be to arrange the farm's affairs and collect the rest of my personal belongings.

'Should you decide, or be persuaded against your better judgement, that it is in your own interests to continue trying to farm Westervoe, Angus, then you must do so without the benefit of my assistance and knowledge, for I have fully determined to spend the rest of my life here in comfort with my sister, my closest blood kin.

'You will still be made welcome, should you decide to join us here. Rachel is also prepared to take the child until such time as your sister completes her nursing studies and is in a position to care for him herself.

'Please let me know of your decision soon. Rachel sends her best wishes and her prayers that you will be guided to make the right choice. Your affectionate grandmother, Celia Scott.'

Jennet handed the page back and watched as Angus folded it neatly and tucked it back into its envelope.

'What are you going to do?' she asked at last, her voice husky.

'It's a big step, Jen, the two of us taking on this place.'

'We've been doing well enough since she left.'

'Aye, but that was different. I thought she was coming back and I was trying to keep the place for the three of us.'

'It's still the three of us, if you count Jamie.'

'That's another thing . . . You cannae go on trying to work the farm and look after the house and the bairn at the same time.'

'Plenty of women have done that.'

'Because they had to. Because they were widowed with growing families and nowhere else to go. If I was as able as I used to be . . . as able as our Martin,' he added with a return of the old bitterness, 'I'd say stay, and welcome, and I'll look out for the two of you. But I'll not feel beholden to you in that way.'

'This place is as much my right as yours and I'm sure that Mollie wouldn't mind staying on for as long as she's needed.'

'Mollie has her own life to think of,' Angus broke in sharply. 'We can't go on making use of her the way Grandmother made use of us. And Jem's not getting any younger. He's got his wife to look out for, the same as you've got Jamie, and I know that he doesn't want to go on working all his life. Norrie's willing enough, but he's still learning. Then there's your own future to think of.'

'Will you stop making excuses and finding reasons for us to do as Grandmother wants?' Jennet snapped, suddenly furious with him.

'I'm only being sensible. One of us has to be.'

'No, Angus, you're being difficult. Why don't you

stop finding reasons for leaving and start finding reasons for staying? This place could be the future for both of us!'

'Aye, if we're willing to work every minute of daylight that God sends. What if Jamie grows up to hate the place? Then you'll have sacrificed your life for nothing.'

'As long as it worked for you and me it wouldn't be for nothing. And Jamie won't have . . .' Jennet stopped and Angus finished the sentence for her.

'He won't have Grandmother to contend with? I suppose you're right. That woman's caused a lot of misery one way and another, Jen.'

'She meant it for the best.'

'Meaning things for the best can cause the most trouble,' Angus said drily.

'If it makes you feel any better I'll agree to stay for one year. If we can't make a go of the farm by rent day next November, I promise that I'll go back to nursing. Jamie'll be a bit older then, and mebbe you'll be managing so well that you won't need me.'

'I doubt that.'

'Will you try it?'

'I'll think about it.' He put both letters on the bedside cabinet. 'We've got weeks to go before Martinmas – no sense in rushing into decisions tonight.'

'Gran'll be waiting for an answer.'

'Let her wait,' Angus said.

* * *

The next day Jennet took an axe and set about the old arks, systematically reducing them to pieces one by one.

'You're goin' about these poor old things as if they were your mortal enemies,' Mollie said when she and Jamie came out to look for her.

'I never realised how satisfying chopping wood is.' Jennet, breathless, lowered the axe and pushed back the hair that had fallen about her hot face. 'It's a great way of working out your frustration. I should have gone into forestry work.'

'Here, we brought you something to drink.' Mollie held out a bottle of cold tea. 'What's bothering you this time?'

Jennet wiped her hands on her britches and unstoppered the bottle. After a good long drink she said, 'You might as well know . . . it's Gran again.' She ran through the letter's contents briefly, ending with, 'So now I've got to make him agree to take on the tenancy and make a go of this place.'

'For a start, you're never goin' tae make Angus Scott do anythin' he doesnae want tae do. You need to let him decide for himself . . . or let him think that he's decided for himself. And he's right, Jennet, it's a big decision and you both need to take time to think about it.'

'Whose side are you on? I thought you were keen on Angus and me staying here.'

'I am, but until now Angus has had his grandmother telling him what to do . . . and making him feel slow and useless most of the time,' Mollie added, scowling. 'The last thing he needs is for you to start taking her place. I know you'd not do that deliberately,' she added as Jennet gaped at her, 'but you have to stop pushing him to do what you want. He needs time.'

'We don't have much time left. Out of the way, Jamie.' Jennet picked up the axe and renewed her attack on a half-demolished ark. 'Whatever happens, Mollie, I'll not let him go to Largs. I'll not have him raised the way we were.'

'I'm sure your auntie would take him if it came to that, but it might not. Just be patient with Angus. Give him more time and when he comes to a decision, let it be his. Men need to feel as if they're in charge even when they're not.'

Jennet paused, the axe raised for a hefty blow. 'How do you know so much all of a sudden?'

'I've got a difficult father, and two brothers. I know about men.'

'I wasn't talking about men. I meant, how do you know so much about what works with Angus?'

'One man's much the same as another. And now I'm going to take Jamie out of your way,' Mollie said, 'so's you can pretend these old arks are your gran or me, or anyone else who's annoying you, and smash the life out of them.'

17

―――――◆―――――

Time passed and still Angus said nothing about his plans for Westervoe, or his own future. In her next weekly letter Celia Scott made no mention of her ultimatum – seemingly she was prepared to wait for an answer, but Jennet found the waiting almost unbearable. Much as she hated it, she took Mollie's advice to bide her time and bite her tongue until her brother was ready to share his thoughts with her.

Every one of the old arks had been smashed to kindling wood and now she was getting some satisfaction from making sure that those being kept were wind-, snow- and water-tight for the winter. The cows would be brought in for the worst of the winter months, and the pigs, cosy enough in their stone-built pigsty with its high walled yard, would be taken away by the butcher early in November. However, the hens would have to stay out in the fields with the arks as their only shelter.

She was still waiting for an announcement from her brother when Bert McCabe called at Westervoe one night after work, tapping on the door and asking nervously if he might have a wee word with 'the master'.

'Of course you can, any time. Come in and sit your-self down, man.' Angus indicated a chair, but Bert shook his head.

'I'm fine as I am.' He stood in the middle of the kitchen, twisting his cap between his big, capable hands. 'In p-private would be best,' he went on awkwardly.

'You can't say what it is in front of Jennet and Mollie?' Angus asked, surprised, and the young man's face went beet-red.

'It's difficult.'

'For goodness sake, Bert, we surely know each other better than that by now,' Jennet snapped. Angus's silence was fraying her nerves as it was, and she didn't want any of Bert's nonsense. 'I'm not a delicate young lady with white hands and nothing but air between my ears!'

He took a step back, away from her anger. 'It's . . . it's personal, like.'

'Personal my foot,' Mollie broke in from the sink, where she was washing the dishes while Jennet dried them. 'Why don't you just spit it out and get it over with?' Then, as her brother glared at her and started stumbling over his words again, she went to stand beside him, drying her hands on her apron. 'The thing is, he's here because he's got himself into a right pickle, haven't you, you daft lump?'

'Will you just mind yer own business?' Bert appealed, crimson to the tips of his ears. 'D'ye have tae tell the whole world my business?'

'You're here tae tell them, aren't you? And it's not as if you've done anythin' terrible. It happens all the time,' she said flatly. Then, to the Scotts, 'This brother of mine's got the Blaikies' wee servant lassie intae trouble and Mrs Blaikie's livid about it. She wants the two of them off her farm and they've nowhere to go.'

'Mollie, for pity's sake!' Bert was so mortified that he was almost in tears.

'You were going tae take all night about it, and some of us would like tae go tae our beds. It's the cottage,' Mollie swept on, 'Bert and the lassie want tae get married, but they've nowhere tae live. And Mr Blaikie cannae let them have a cottage on his farm because Mrs Blaikie wouldn't allow that, the state she's in just now.'

'Is that right about you getting married?' Angus asked Bert, and when the younger man nodded, 'What does the girl's family say about it?'

'That's the thing, she doesnae have nob'dy but me. She's an orphan with nob'dy tae look out for her,' Bert blurted. 'And I was wonderin' . . . your wee cottage . . . Now the holidays are over . . .'

'Are you still working for Mr Blaikie?' Jennet asked.

'Till the end of the month just, because the missus is in such a takin' about havin' tae find another lassie and train her up that she says she doesnae want tae see sight nor sound of either of us. Mr Blaikie says that with the winter comin' in and Struan back home, he could let me go like she wants, but he'd mebbe find work for me in the spring once the missus has got over it.'

'That means that you could work for us instead,' Jennet realised aloud.

Bert's face lit up. 'That would be grand, if ye'd have me. And Helen's a fine wee worker, and good with the poultry, too. Mrs Blaikie trained her up well.'

Jennet opened her mouth to say something, caught the warning in Mollie's eye and left it to Angus.

He hesitated, pulling at his lower lip, then said finally, 'I'd not want to see you and the lassie homeless, Bert, and we could use a man like you around the place.'

'And if you both worked for us, you and the girl could have the cottage rent-free,' Jennet chimed in.

'Rent-free?' Angus asked when Mollie had escorted her brother outside, shutting the door on his gabbled thanks.

'If he's going to work for us and she's willing to help in the house, it seems only fair. We couldn't refuse, not with the way things are between them,' Jennet said. Then, with a sudden giggle, 'Imagine me with a lassie well trained by Mrs Blaikie, while she has to start all over again with someone else.'

'That'll be another black mark against you, as far as she's concerned.'

'At least we're being more Christian about the matter than she is. The thing is . . .' Jennet went on tentatively, 'if we leave the farm now, the new tenants might put Bert and his wife out of the cottage.'

'So we're stuck with this place, are we?' Angus asked. 'That's a pity.'

Something in his tone made Jennet suspicious. 'You were going to say yes all along, weren't you?'

'Mebbe I was and mebbe I wasn't.'

'Angus Scott, you're a right pig! Keeping me waiting and waiting, and worrying about what was going to happen to all of us, and all the time . . .' She picked up a cushion from the smaller fireside chair and shied it at him. He dodged sideways and it flew past him and into the sink, with Jennet in hot pursuit.

'It's gone into the washing-up water . . . It's all wet now!'

'You can explain it to Mollie,' Angus said, 'for I'll not. And I kept quiet about staying on to teach you not to nag at me in the future.'

'I'll never nag you again, and that's a promise. Oh, Angus!' The Scotts were not used to hugging and kissing, but even so she threw her arms about him and kissed him on the cheek.

'I'll write to Grandmother tonight before I go to sleep,' he said, disentangling himself from her arms. Then he added, with the ghost of a smile tugging at his wide mouth, 'She'll not be pleased.'

'Write to her tomorrow,' Jennet said on an impulse. 'Tonight we're going to have a bonfire.'

'A what?'

'A celebration bonfire, like the ones they had when the war ended.' Jennet suddenly felt as though her own war – hers and Angus's – had ended that night. 'And we can roast potatoes in the ashes.'

'And burn a guy?' Angus asked drily.

'I know we're too early for November the fifth, but we've got all that rotten wood from the old arks piled up and ready to light, and it's as dry as anything. I'm going to fetch Jamie out of his bed,' Jennet said. 'It's a family celebration and he needs to be with us.'

It was a splendid bonfire, and as it roared and crackled and tossed great handfuls of sparks up into the night sky, Jennet hugged Jamie, warmly wrapped in a blanket, and watched the awe and pleasure in his eyes.

'One day when you're a very old man,' she said, 'you'll tell your grandchildren about this and say it was the first night of the rest of your life!'

Later, snuggled into the bole of a tree, feeding him pieces of hot roasted potato, her fingers charred black from the burned skins, she murmured to Mollie, 'It was you that put your Bert up to it, wasn't it?'

'Me?' The other girl's eyes widened. 'How can you say such a thing? Him and that Helen did it all by themselves, with no help from me or anyone else!'

'I'm talking about the cottage, not the baby! You suggested it to him, didn't you?'

'Mebbe I did and mebbe I didn't. It's a good idea, though. Bert's just the man you need around this farm, and now everyone's well suited. Come on, you,' she scrambled up and plucked Jamie from his mother's arms, 'let's do what the Red Indians do and dance around the fire!'

Angus Scott watched from the shadows as she whirled in and out of the fire's glow, the laughing child in her arms, her red hair lifting about her face and the glow from the flames turning her green eyes to emeralds. He thought that he had never seen anything so beautiful, so desirable and so unattainable.

In Celia Scott's day the food-pig had always been slaughtered on the farm, making Martinmas an ordeal for Jennet, who had been put in charge of the pigsty and its occupants before her tenth birthday. Despite her grandmother's disapproval, she could not resist becoming attached to the pigs in her charge and she dreaded and hated the butcher's annual visit. She could still hear the shrill screams of her friends as they sensed their fate and could still see their lifeless bodies hung up in one of the sheds to be scalded and bled. She didn't want Jamie to go through that misery.

Like his mother, Jamie was fond of the pigs, and today, knowing the butcher was coming to have a preliminary look at the animals, Jennet had instructed Mollie to keep him well away from the yard until after the man had been and gone, just in case his sharp little ears picked up the wrong comment.

She herself had opted to start on one of her most hated jobs, cleaning out the arks. Ousted hens were clucking and scuffling and fussing outside, while Jennet, inside the confined and smelly space, chipped grimly at droppings that had accumulated on the floor and then been stamped into a solid mass by clawed feet.

It was a beautiful sunny early-autumn day, but within the ark, barely large enough for her to turn round in, it was dark and hot. She had pulled an old cap of Angus's over her head to protect her hair, and now she could feel sweat trickling from beneath it to run over her hot face, before dripping from the end of her nose onto the wooden floor. Every now and again she had to stop to wipe moisture from her eyes and forehead, and she was convinced that, if she really wanted to, she could wring out her eyebrows. Although she was only wearing light trousers and a blouse with the sleeves rolled up the heat made her body itch all over.

'Jennet!' Angus's voice was muffled by the wooden walls about her.

'What?' she yelled back irritably, her own voice echoing within the ark, and went back to attacking a particularly difficult section of dirt in a dark corner. At last it gave way beneath the onslaught from her scraper and she scooped it up and tossed it into the nearly full bucket by her side. That would do, she decided. A quick brush out, an armful of clean straw and one more ark would be done.

Carefully, lest some daft and vulnerable hen was behind her, she edged backwards through the small door of the ark, pulling the bucket after her, until with a sign of relief she was out in the fresh air and able to stand up.

'Jennet, did you not hear me?' Angus asked from the field gate.

'Yes, I heard you.' She stretched, easing her cramped limbs, 'but I wasn't going to crawl out just to find out what you . . .' She turned, then stopped short as she saw the man walking down the lane to the gate, head up and feet landing solidly and confidently on the ground, heel to toe. The Blaikie strut, Angus had always called it.

'Look who's come to see us!' Angus said triumphantly, as though he had pulled the newcomer from a magician's top hat.

'Hello, Jennet.'

'Allan Blaikie.' She approached the gate slowly, well aware of the fright she must look. 'What are you doing here?'

'He's come back to the island!'

Jennet's mouth went dry and a cold shiver ran from the top of her head to the soles of her feet. 'You've gone back to farming?'

'I'm staying at Gleniffer, but just until I get a place of my own,' Allan said, his clear blue eyes looking her up and down. 'My uncle's bought over Matt

McGuire's butcher's shop in Rothesay, and I've been sent to run it for him, since I know the island. Did my father not tell you?'

'Not a word.'

Allan opened the gate for her, then reached out to take the bucket from her hand. 'Mebbe he didnae see the news as important,' he said as the three of them began to walk back to the farm. 'You're looking well, Jennet.'

'How can you tell?' she asked tartly, well aware of the sight she must look, covered with muck and with her face red from the heat and no doubt streaked with dirt. When she hauled the cap off to let her hair fall free, it landed in a tangled mass against her neck, heavy and damp, and she had to fight the urge to give her scalp a good scratch.

'Angus's been telling me that the two of you have taken over the place.'

'That's right.'

'And you've got a couple of pigs you'll want rid of, come Martinmas. I thought I'd take a look at them while I was here.'

At the pigsty he opened the wooden door and went inside. Jack and Jill, rooting contentedly about their little yard, nosed at him in the hope that he might have brought some titbits. The sty had been cleaned only that morning and the pigs, Jennet thought, looked more respectable than she did at that moment. She leaned her folded arms on the wall and watched as Allan went into the sty.

The meat from one pig would keep them going over the winter, and the money they got from Allan for the other would go towards the farm rent and the cost of buying in winter feed for the cows to augment the hay and bruised oats they had grown during the summer. Renting the cottage to holiday visitors had helped a little, but as always the pigs were an important source of income.

'You've looked after them well,' Allan said.

'Oh, we still know how to farm,' Jennet told him sharply, 'even though my grandmother's not here to tell us what to do every minute of the day.'

As soon as the words were out she realised how childish and petty they sounded, but he merely raised an eyebrow and then said, 'Will ye want me to tend to your own animal here?'

'No!'

'Jennet wants them to be taken away this time,' Angus began to explain, 'because the wee . . .'

'Because I hate having them killed here,' Jennet interrupted. 'I never liked it and it's not going to happen here again.'

'I mind how much you hated it,' Allan said. 'Remember the day I found you hiding in the hayloft with your hands over your ears, saying prayers and multiplication tables and God knows what to keep the noise out?'

It was just as well, Jennet thought, that there was enough dirt on her face to hide the blush. 'I mind you laughing at me for being such a baby.'

'Did I? I was a right bully in those days, according to our Struan. When the time comes, I'll take your two over to Gleniffer and see to them along with my dad's pigs,' Allan assured her. 'Right, then, I'd best be getting back to the shop.'

To Jennet's horror her brother said, 'Come in and have something to drink first, man.'

Allan's eyes brightened and he opened his mouth to accept, then closed it again as Jennet said swiftly, 'Mollie's busy bottling brambles and redcurrants, so the kitchen's all upside down, and I'm not in a fit state to entertain you.'

'I'd best get back to the shop anyway.'

'Another time, though . . . What about Friday night?' Angus suggested. 'We could have a good talk then.'

'Would that be all right with you, Jennet?'

'Of course it is,' Angus said heartily. 'You're as eager to hear what he's been up to as I am, aren't you?' he asked his sister, who could have slapped the pleasure off his face. Instead she had to force a polite smile and say, 'Yes of course, Allan. Friday night.'

'Fine, we'll see you then,' Allan said, and he turned towards the van standing in the lane . . . then spun back to face the yard as a high, clear, unmistakably childish voice said sweetly, 'Come on, ye wee bugger . . .' And Jamie walked round the corner of the deep-litter house, trailing Gumrie behind him on a long string.

'Come on, ye wee bugger,' the little boy said again,

too intent on the dog at his heels to notice his mother until she said, 'Jamie, what d'you think you're doing?'

He beamed at her. 'Taking Gumrie for a walk 'cos he's . . .' He stopped short as he noticed the stranger.

For his part, Allan Blaikie stared at the little boy as though he had seen a ghost. He moistened his lips, then said, 'Is this . . . ?'

'Jennet's wee laddie,' Angus said. 'Your mother surely told you about him.'

'Aye.' Allan said as Jennet reached out to draw her son to her side. 'Aye, she did, but I never realised . . .' He stopped, then said, 'I thought he was a wee thing in a pram . . .'

'He was once, but that was a good year or two past. This is our Jamie,' Angus said proudly.

Jennet would have clung to Jamie, but he pulled free and marched forward, his hand held out as Celia had taught him from babyhood.

'Hello,' he said. It was a moment, Jennet knew, that she would never forget, a moment she had never wanted to see. Her son, her baby – and nobody else's, ever – walking away from her and towards the father he had never seen. The father who had denied him even before he was born.

She watched as Allan put his own hand out to take the child's small fingers, holding them carefully. 'How d'ye . . . how d'ye do, Jamie?'

'What's your name?' Jamie had to tilt his head right back to take in the height of the man towering over him.

'I'm Allan. I live at Gleniffer.'

'No you don't,' Jamie said flatly.

'I'm Mrs Blaikie's other wee boy, just the same as you're your mummy's wee boy, and I've been away. But now,' said Allan, 'I've come back home.'

The words sent a shiver down Jennet's spine, but Jamie gave a snort of laughter. 'Not a wee boy. Big old man!'

'Jamie Scott!'

'Leave him be, Jennet, mebbe he's got the right view of things, the way I feel sometimes.' Allan gave a wry smile that twisted one side of his mouth and raised one eyebrow in a way she had once found heart-stoppingly attractive.

'I like Struan,' Jamie said.

'And I hope you'll like me as well, once we get to know each other,' Allan replied.

'Here.' Jamie, still holding Allan's fingers, towed him back to the sty, where he picked up a stick leaning against the wall. 'Lift me up,' he commanded, and Allan did as he was told, setting the small booted feet on the rounded top of the wall and holding Jamie firmly about the waist.

'Mind now,' he cautioned as Jamie, putting all his trust in the hands supporting him, leaned his entire body forward to scratch the pigs' backs with his stick.

'Jack and Jill,' he said. 'My friends.'

'I mind someone else who had friends like that and they were called Jack and Jill, too.'

'Do they live near here?' Jamie waggled the stick

industriously. 'See, they like this' and he tickled them
with the stick.

Jennet could not bear it any longer. 'Jamie, Mollie'll
be wondering where you've got to. You know you
were told to stay with her today.' She moved forward
and took the child away from Allan, lifting him into
her arms.

'Gumrie go for walk.'

'I'd best be going,' Allan said, his gaze still on
Jamie. 'I'll see you on Friday.'

Jamie wanted to watch the van move off along the
lane, but Jennet carried him back to the safety of the
yard.

'You smell,' he remarked as they went.

'So would you if you'd been cleaning out the hen
coops, you cheeky wee monkey.'

The house door flew open as they neared it, and
Mollie erupted into the yard, coming to a halt as she
saw them.

'There you are! I'm sorry, Jennet, I took him into
the garden to get some kale for the dinner and the
next thing I knew he'd gone.'

'It's fine. Everything's fine,' Jennet lied, while
Jamie explained, 'Gumrie wanted walk.'

'He's a farm dog,' Jennet argued, lowering him to
the ground, 'and farm dogs don't get taken for walks.'

'Gumrie does,' Jamie insisted. Then, to the dog,
'Come on, ye wee bugger.'

Mollie's hands flew to her mouth as boy and dog

trotted into the house. 'What did he say? And where did he learn it?'

'Probably from Jem.'

'I'm going to have a word with that old man. He should mind his tongue when the bairn's near!'

'You might as well order him not to open his mouth at all,' Jennet said.

18

Andra Blaikie walked into the kitchen when they were at their breakfast the next morning.

'Young McCabe tells me that ye've offered your wee cottage tae him and the lassie.'

'There's no reason not to, since it's lying empty,' Angus said shortly. Since Celia had gone, relations between him and the bluff farmer had become fragile, mainly because Angus mistrusted his neighbour, seeing Blaikie as his grandmother's ally.

'Ach well, if they've made up their minds tae wed I suppose they have tae find somewhere.' Andra drew out a chair and sat down without waiting for an invitation, which was as well since Angus did not seem disposed to issue one and Jennet was busy with Jamie. 'He says ye're willin' tae take him on over the winter, too.'

'Since he'll be right here on the farm anyway, and since you're letting him go, it makes sense.'

'He's a good worker, but I've got enough help with Struan back home, and there's not so much to do during the winter months. Thanks, lassie,' Andra said as Mollie put a plate of food before him. He forked a fried egg and a large lump of sausage into his mouth and said through it, 'I'd have kept him on, and mebbe found somewhere on Gleniffer for the two of them tae bide until they got themselves sorted out, but Lizbeth's taken a right scunner tae the lad.'

'That's my brother you're talking about, Mr Blaikie,' Mollie reminded him sharply, splashing some tea into a huge mug for him.

'Eh? Oh aye, so it is. But I don't mean anythin' against the laddie; you've just heard me say I was for keepin' him on. It's the wife; she took that lassie from an orphanage and trained her up to be a braw wee servant and good with the hens forbye. And with her bein' so keen on the church and its teachings, she's taken it hard that the girl's fallen just when she was doin' so well.'

He took a mouthful of tea and then changed the subject. 'Allan was sayin' he called in yesterday tae see the pigs. Ye'd be surprised tae see him back on the island.'

'We were.' Jennet kept a wary eye on Jamie, who was trying to stuff an entire egg into his mouth in imitation of their visitor.

'It seems that my brother's done so well for himself in Glasgow that he's bought over Matt McGuire's shop in Rothesay and set Allan up to run it. His mother's right pleased to see him back on the island. You and him were aye good friends when ye were growin' up, Angus.' Blaikie mopped his plate with a slice of bread. 'Any word from Celia?'

'We heard the other day. She's not coming back.'

'D'ye tell me?' Andra said in amazement, his jaw falling to reveal the last of his breakfast. 'How's that, then?'

'She wanted the farm to go to new tenants, but we've decided to keep it on.'

'Just the two of ye?' Blaikie looked from brother to sister and back again. 'Celia's not said a word about this in her letters tae Lizbeth.'

'I've no doubt she will; it's just been decided.'

'Ye think ye'll manage?'

'We'd not take it on if we thought otherwise, Mr Blaikie.' Jennet put a finger beneath Jamie's chin to close his mouth, which had also been hanging open.

'Well, ye've got big hearts; I'll say that for ye. And I'm just along the road when ye need help.'

'We'll try not to trouble you. After all,' Angus said, 'we'll have Bert McCabe here from Martinmas, and you've said yourself what a good farmhand he is.'

'Aye, he is. Well, good luck tae ye.' The farmer pushed his chair back and got to his feet, patting his stomach. 'That was a nice bit of food, lassie.'

'I'm glad you liked it.' Mollie, clearly still annoyed over the remarks about her brother and his future wife, sounded as stiff as Angus.

'You know that Mrs Blaikie'll be reporting on us

with every letter she writes to Gran?' Jennet said when Andra had gone.

'There's nothing we can do about that, except try to make sure that she can't say anything bad.'

'Jamie, don't you dare do that unless you're going to eat every bit of it,' Jennet said sharply to the little boy, who was gleefully wiping a slice of bread round his plate in imitation of their visitor. 'I'll not have you wasting food like that.'

'Talking of waste, you're very free with our food,' Angus told Mollie as he hoisted himself to his feet. 'You never heard me inviting him to sit at our table and eat with us, did you?'

'But your grandmother always made sure he was fed if he came in while we were at the table.'

'Mebbe so, but it's not my grandmother who's in charge now. I can't afford to throw good food away on a man who's on his way home right now for another breakfast!'

'What is the matter with this place this morning?' Mollie asked as the door closed behind Angus. 'He's beginning to sound just like old Mrs Scott . . . and you were in a right thrawn mood last night.'

'Of course I'm thrawn,' Jennet snapped, watching Jamie sauntering out to feed the hens with the unwanted slice of bread he had hidden up the front of his jumper. 'I always was. I'm a Scott of Westervoe, God help me!'

'For goodness sake, away you go and get on with some work and leave me to do mine in peace.'

'Mebbe this place is getting to be too much for us already,' Jennet said as she dragged on her jacket and tied a scarf about her hair. 'Mebbe Grandmother was right, and I should have gone back to Glasgow.'

'And left Jamie with her? Don't be daft. And when you come back for your dinner,' Mollie called after her as she left, 'see and have a smile on your face.'

That, Jennet thought, was highly unlikely. At that moment she felt as though she might never smile again. Not, at least, while Allan Blaikie remained on Bute.

Despite his protests Jamie was bathed and put to bed earlier than usual on Friday evening. When she had tucked him into his cot Jennet stayed with him for a while, reading story after story to him, partly as compensation for the earlier bedtime and partly as an excuse to be out of the way when Allan arrived.

Jamie was almost asleep when she heard Angus greeting their visitor, but even so his eyes flickered open.

'Who's that?' he mumbled round the thumb he had stuck into his mouth.

'The Sandman coming to take you to Beddy-byeland.'

'Can I go and see him?'

'Stay here and close your eyes. That's the best way to see the Sandman. I'll go on reading and we'll pretend we don't know he's here. That'll bring him upstairs as quick as a blink.'

She read on long after he had fallen asleep, but at last she had to close the book and go downstairs to where the men were talking at the kitchen table.

Allan, dressed in his good suit, got to his feet when she went into the kitchen and, to her surprise, shook her by the hand.

'D'you not want to take Allan in by, Angus?' she asked her brother.

'I'd as soon be here as in the parlour. I'm surely not a visitor in this house, Jennet.'

'I suppose not.' She fetched her mending bag and sat down on the smaller of the fireside chairs.

'Do we have any beer in?' Angus wanted to know.

'There's some in the press in the other room.' She began to get up again, but Angus waved her back into her chair.

'I'll get it.'

'When can I see you?' Allan asked low-voiced when they were alone.

'You're seeing me now.'

'Alone, I mean. I want to talk to you.'

'We did our talking, years ago, and there's nothing left to say. Nothing,' she added sharply as he opened his mouth again. For a long moment they locked eyes, then Allan Blaikie shrugged.

'Jennet, I only live a quarter of a mile away now. We're going to have to face each other sometime,' he said, then Angus was back in the room, fetching glasses and pouring beer.

* * *

'So how are things?' Allan wanted to know when Angus had settled down again.

'Not too bad, considering. Better now that we've got Westervoe to ourselves, eh, Jennet?'

Allan laughed. 'To hear my mother tell it, anyone would think the two of you had thrown the old woman off the farm and told her not to come back.'

'It was her own choice entirely, but she wasnae pleased when we said we'd try for running the place between us.'

'It is a shame Martin didn't come back.'

'That's up to him,' Jennet said levelly. 'We don't need him any more than we need Grandmother.'

'I'm sure you're right.' Allan's gaze slid from her to a spot by the leg of her chair. Glancing down, she saw a discarded ball on the floor. 'The wee fellow'll be in his bed by now?'

'Long since.' Jennet scooped up the ball and pushed it into her apron pocket while Angus asked, 'But what about you? Struan said something about a young woman a while back. Someone in Glasgow.'

'Oh, that.' Allan sounded uncomfortable. 'We parted a while since. She was wanting to settle down and I didnae see myself as her husband. What about you, Angus, and that lassie in Saltcoats?'

'It turned out that the thing she liked best about me was the way I could walk about on my own two legs,' Angus said harshly. 'Once I stopped doing that she lost interest.' Then, into the sudden awkward silence, 'So tell us what sort of war you had.'

'Much the same as Struan, and I suppose you'll have heard it all from him. We were both lucky to get through the fighting in one piece.'

'That must have come as a surprise to you,' Jennet put in. Then, when both men stared at her, 'Did you not say once that you were sure you'd be killed?'

For a moment he looked at her, his eyes blank, then he coloured as memory flooded back. 'Aye,' he said, the life suddenly gone from his voice. 'I mind that time. I mind it well.'

'I'm sure everyone caught up in a war must wonder if he's going to survive,' Angus said. 'Though I'd not have thought you'd have any doubts, Allan. You're not the sort to doubt.'

'Oh, I had them all right, a lot of them,' Allan said, still in the same flat voice. It took some coaxing from Angus, but finally he began to talk about his war. Jennet glanced at the clock; Allan would surely take himself off once he had had some supper, but it was still too early for that. She must endure another hour of his company first.

She kept her head bent over her work, trying to shut out his voice, then she found herself listening almost against her will, caught up in the vivid word pictures he painted of men who had been plunged by war into a half life, where they were no longer people in their own right, but single units forged into one war machine with no thoughts of the future because, for them, it might not last beyond the next day, or the next hour, or even the next minute.

A muffled cry from above brought them all back to the present, and when Jennet looked at the clock she was astonished to see that more than two hours had passed.

'Is that the time already? You'll be ready for your supper.' She jumped up, almost scattering her sewing over the rug, and picked up the kettle. 'I'll get this going, then I'll have to see to the wee one . . .'

'I'll do that, you tend to the bairn.' Allan got up from the table and took the kettle from her hand.

Normally Jamie, who rarely woke once he was down for the night, could be soothed back to sleep if anything roused him, but this time he must have had a bad dream. When Jennet got to him he was clawing his way out of the cot, his face red with panic and wet with tears. When she picked him up he clung to her, and squealed when she tried to put him back in the cot.

'Not tonight of all nights, Jamie!' she begged him, but it was no use. He was determined to be with her, and downstairs the two men were waiting, no doubt with growing impatience, for their food. She had no option but to wrap him in a blanket and carry him down to the kitchen, where Angus was setting the table while Allan, who had made tea, buttered some homemade scones.

'Angus showed me where they were. I hope it's all right to . . .' He stopped, his eyes on the child in her arms, then went on, 'to put them out.'

'Of course, they're meant for visitors.'

'There you go again. When has Allan ever been a

visitor in this house?' Angus wanted to know. 'There's new-made bramble jelly too, Allan, fetch it from that press.' He sat down and held his arms out to his nephew. 'Come on, wee man, come and tell your Uncle Angus what wakened you.'

Jennet would have preferred to keep Jamie on her lap, but to her annoyance he held his arms out to Angus and she had no alternative but to hand him over. Allan seated himself opposite.

'Remember me, Jamie?'

Jamie blinked sleep from his eyes. 'Mrs Blaikie's wee boy.'

'That's right.' Allan dipped a hand into his pocket. 'See what I've got?'

He drew a small mouth organ from his pocket and handed it over. The child turned it over in his hands, frowning.

'What's it for?'

'Give it back and I'll show you,' Allan offered, and when the instrument was returned he blew softly into it, producing a trill of notes.

Jamie squealed with excitement. 'Look, Mummy! Do it again!'

'So you've not forgotten how to play a good tune?' Angus asked, grinning.

'Try it for yourself.' Allan wiped the instrument on the heel of his hand and gave it to Jamie. 'It's been everywhere with me, and it's cheered up many a sorry night when we were all homesick. You blow into it, Jamie, like this . . .'

He pursed his mouth and blew gently, and Jamie did his best to copy him, but without success. 'You,' he demanded, handing the mouth organ back.

Allan cradled it in his two hands and lifted them to his lips. He took a breath, then filled the kitchen with the strains of 'Lili Marlene', swinging as soon as he had finished into 'Danny Boy'. Then he stopped and jumped to his feet as Mollie came in, her red hair tousled and her cheeks glowing from the cycle ride back to the farm after a night out with Joe.

After Mollie had fallen asleep that night Jennet slid out of bed and went to sit in the old nursing chair that stood by Jamie's cot. It was too dark to make out the details of the little boy's sleeping face, but her mind's eye knew every line of it, from the silky eyebrows down over the snub little nose to the mouth, now pursed in sleep, and the neat chin.

Once or twice during the first few days of Jamie's life she had detected something of his father in his tiny face, but now he was just Jamie, a person in his own right.

One of his hands lay outside the blanket, palm up and with the fingers curled like the petals of a half-opened flower. Jennet touched her own forefinger gently against his palm and he gripped at it, stirring and mumbling something before slipping back into slumber. She leaned forward, comforted by the contact, and laid her face against the bars of the cot, wishing that she could pick him up and hold him close for comfort and reassurance.

Home on leave before going overseas, Allan Blaikie had come to Westervoe to visit Angus, who was still experiencing pain in his crippled leg in the wake of his accident. As he was leaving, Allan had asked Jennet to walk down by the shore with him. It had been a mild autumn night, half dark and with the waves shushing gently a few feet from where they walked. Allan was off to rejoin his regiment the following day, and Jennet was leaving in two days' time for Glasgow.

'You'll be looking forward to it,' he said.

'I'm not sure. Glasgow's a big city and I've never been away from home before.'

'Och, it'll be grand. You'll meet new folk and you're learning a new trade. Anyway, it's time you were spreading your wings. If you stay here you'll marry into another farm and have a parcel of bairns, with no chance to see a bit of the world first.'

'That's what Martin said in his last letter.'

'He's right. Make the most of your youth while you can, Jennet. There's thousands of lads that'll not get that chance,' he said, a new, bleak note coming into his voice.

'I'll be coming back here often to see how Angus's getting on. Mebbe you could write to him while you're away, Allan, and tell him what's happening with you. He needs to keep in touch with other folk, and Martin's not much of a letter-writer.'

'Neither am I, but I'll try.' Allan paused to pick up a stone and throw it, with a powerful swing of his arm, far out to sea. It was too dark for them to see where it landed, but they heard the splash. He walked on quickly, making her hurry to keep up with him, then suddenly he said over his shoulder, 'I scarcely recognised him when I went into that room tonight. He's away to skin and bone and he looks so old, Jennet. He's not Angus any more!'

'Of course he is! He was in terrible pain at first, but it's getting better. And he's still the same laddie he always was.' It had been Jennet's fear, too, that the rail accident might have changed Angus in more ways than just physically.

'How can anyone get over what's happened to him?' Allan demanded.

'When I went to Glasgow for my interview I saw more than one man who'd lost limbs or eyes in the fighting, but they're learning to deal with it and get on with their lives. You must have seen folk like that yourself, for there are a lot of them about these days.'

'Aye, I've seen them, but I know that I could never be like them, or like Angus,' he said; then, low-voiced, 'Jennet, I couldnae bear it.'

'Of course you could, if you had to.'

'Allan Blaikie's able for anything and afraid of nothing,' Celia Scott used to say when Jennet and her brothers arrived home late and soaked through from damming a burn under Allan's supervision, or bruised and bloody and with their clothes torn because he had led them on some perilous expedition involving tree-climbing and rock-scaling. Although Drew was the older brother, it was always Allan who planned their games and set the dares. And it was usually Allan who triumphed, jeering at the others from the very top of the tallest tree or standing high above them on a sheer sheet of rock with scarcely a handhold to it. Allan, tall and strong, confident, sure of himself and fearless.

'When we were all growing up, you were the one who was never afraid of anything,' Jennet said now, remembering.

'That was when I was just a daft laddie,' he told her impatiently. 'All youngsters think they can handle whatever life throws at them. It's not till you get older and go out into the world, and see the sort of things folk can do to other folk, that ye realise what's real.'

'But even so . . .'

'Will ye listen tae what I'm sayin'?' Allan said, his voice suddenly rough and hard. 'If all I wanted was someone tae tell me nothing'll happen to me, I'd be home right now talkin' to my mother; and if I wanted someone tae tell me tae stop bein' a daft, imaginin' fool, I'd go tae my father. But right now I just need someone tae let me say what I think inside, and Angus's in no fit state for that, not with what's happened to him.'

He had begun to walk faster along the shoreline; now he stopped and turned to face her. 'We're not bairns any more, Jennet. Nob'dy's able tae put a bandage or a plaster on the bit that hurts and make it better, because it hurts here . . .' He slapped the heel of his hand against his head . . . 'and here.' He made a fist and punched himself hard in the chest. 'And it won't go away as long as I'm wearin' that damned uniform and carryin' a gun, and knowin' that somewhere over the hill there's a poor bastard like me, mebbe even a laddie from a German farm, with a uniform and a gun. And when the two of us meet, Jennet, one of us is goin' tae have tae kill the other. And d'you know what frightens me even more than that?'

'What?'

'Mebbe he'll be a bad shot,' he said thickly, 'and I'll end up a cripple for the rest of my life, like poor Angus back there!'

'Allan . . .' she began, then stopped because she didn't know what else to say. Words were an inadequate response to the anguish in his voice.

'D'you think I could say any of that tae my parents, or to your gran? They'd be shocked if they knew what a coward I am!'

'You're not a coward. All the other soldiers must be thinking the same as you.'

'If they are, then they're makin' a damned good job of not lettin' on. Some of them even seem tae be enjoyin' themselves, and all I can think of is whether I'm goin' to make a fool of myself when the time comes, and run away or pee myself, or . . .'

His voice broke and he turned away slightly, a hand

at his mouth. Jennet tentatively touched his shoulder
and discovered that it was shaking. She gripped it,
thinking that the contact might help, and then
suddenly he turned and went into her arms, clutching
at her, his face wet against her neck. 'Tell me, Jennet
. . .' His voice was muffled, 'tell me it's goin' tae be
all right. Make me believe it'll be all right!'

'It will.' She stroked his hair, which was free of
grease and surprisingly soft, and when he straightened she wiped the tears from his cheek with the ball
of her thumb. 'It'll be all right,' she told him fiercely.
'Nothing's going to happen to you. I'd not let anything
bad happen to you, ever!'

He gave a choked laugh. 'How are you going to
manage that, Jennet Scott?'

'Because I love you.' It was the first time she had
admitted it to anyone other than herself. She had never
dreamed that one day she would say it to the man
himself. 'I love you,' she said again. 'I always have.
And I'll never let anything happen to you!'

Looking back, she could not remember who kissed
whom first, or when they moved to sit and then lie
on a patch of grass beneath the dry-stane dyke that
bordered one of Westervoe's fields. She only remembered their kisses, his hands and his skin and the smell
of him, and the urgency of their lovemaking. She
remembered the sudden pain as he entered her, dulled
almost at once by the need to be close to him, to ease
his misery and help him in whatever way she could.

They had scarcely said a word to each other later,

as they tidied themselves and walked back quickly to
Westervoe, where Allan had said a hurried goodbye
in the lane, then turned away in the direction of his
own home.

'You shouldn't be out walking at night just now,'
Celia had scolded her when she went indoors. 'The
island's full of men we know nothing about these
days, not to mention mines and all sorts. Still, as long
as Allan was with you, I suppose you were all right.'

If only her grandmother had known, Jennet thought,
with a wry twist of the lips as she eased her finger
from Jamie's fist and crept back to bed. Because she
had been in Glasgow for a full three months before
it dawned on her that she was pregnant, and because
she then waited another two months, not knowing
what to do for the best, before returning home,
everyone had assumed that Jamie's father was some
unknown serviceman whom Jennet had met in the
city. What would her grandmother think if she knew
that Jamie had been fathered below one of her own
dry-stane dykes by her best friend's son?

Mollie turned over as Jennet crept into bed beside
her. 'What's the matter?' she mumbled.

'It's all right, I just thought I heard Jamie,' Jennet
whispered, and almost at once Mollie was asleep
again.

19

Nesta McCabe insisted on a proper wedding for her son and his intended bride.

'Just because there's a bairn on the way that's no excuse for the two of them to make a quick wee promise before the minister, then go on as if nothing's happened,' she said, and Ann Logan agreed with her.

'We'll have a party in our house after the church ceremony. Now the holidaymakers are gone, we can use the front room. And since the lassie has no family of her own it'll be nice for her to know that there's folk who care.'

She brought out her sewing machine, and between them she and Nesta made a dress and matching jacket for Helen, a shy, dark-haired girl who stayed close to Bert's side when he took her to meet his family and the Logans.

With Alice's help the two women cooked and baked for the occasion, using precious rations and bringing out hoarded tins, while at Westervoe Mollie and

Jennet, when she managed to find the time from her farm work, got the cottage ready.

To Mollie's dismay, her sister Senga accepted the wedding invitation sent by their mother.

'What made you tell our Senga about it?' she wanted to know.

'It's a family occasion, it's only right that she should be asked.'

'And did you send one tae my father an' all?'

'I did not. D'you think I want him spoiling things for Bert and mebbe bringing his woman friend to embarrass us all in front of the good friends we've made here? Oh, I know all about her,' Nesta added as Mollie gaped.

'How . . . ? Senga told you! That one couldnae keep her mouth shut tae save her own life!'

'I'd a right to be told. Oh, I know you kept quiet to spare my feelings . . .' Nesta put a hand on her daughter's arm. 'You're a good lassie, but it's as well for me to know the truth. Anyway, it's not bothered me one bit. To be honest with ye, Mollie, it's a relief to know he's got someone else tae keep him busy. That way, he'll leave us in peace.'

'Is Senga's boyfriend coming with her?'

'I don't think so. She never mentioned him. Mrs Logan says she can stay here . . . for nothing, she says, since she's my daughter.'

'Well, you can just tell her to charge Senga what she'd charge anyone else. From what she says in her letters she's not short of a shilling or two, and that

boyfriend of hers seems to be very well off, thanks
to the black market.'

'Now you don't know that for sure, Mollie. And
even if he is,' Nesta added, 'I'd as soon not know
anything about it. All I'm asking is that you and your
sister get on well while she's here. This wedding's a
family occasion and it means I'll have all my children round me again. I want to enjoy every minute
of it.'

For her mother's sake Mollie bit her tongue and set
out to be nice to her sister, who was wearing such
high heels when she arrived that she had a terrible
job getting down the gangway between steamer and
pier. She tittuped towards the waiting reception party
for all the world, Mollie thought, like a newborn calf
staggering about a byre. A small hat, mostly flowers
and veiling, was perched above one eyebrow and her
costume clung to her plump body as tightly as she
herself clung to the gangway railing.

'Has she got no luggage?' Mollie wondered, for her
sister carried nothing but a shiny new-looking
handbag. The question was answered when an elderly
man, who had trotted off the boat behind Senga
clutching a large suitcase, followed her over to where
her mother, sister and brother waited, and put the case
down with an audible sigh of relief.

'Thank you so much,' Senga crooned, fluttering her
eyelashes – easy enough to flutter, Mollie realised,
since they were artificial. 'You're so kind!'

He blushed, muttered something about it being a

pleasure, and tipped his hat to her and then to Nesta and Mollie, before disappearing back into the crowd.

'Who was that?' Nesta asked, and her daughter gave an elegant little shrug of the shoulders.

'I don't know. Just some old man that was on the boat.'

'It was kind of him to help you. D'you think we should have offered him a cup of tea?'

'What for?' Senga asked in amazement. 'He wanted tae carry my case, I didnae ask him to.'

'How long are you staying?' Mollie eyed the case.

Again, Senga twitched her shoulders elegantly. 'A few days, mebbe a week. It depends.'

'On what?' Sam, who had developed muscles as well as confidence after a few months of working with the boats, lifted the case as though it weighed no more than the bag.

On whoever she gets her claws into, Mollie thought, trailing after the others. All her life Senga had spoiled things for her. While working in a Rothesay shop after she left school, Mollie had gone out dancing once or twice with the shop's delivery lad. She had enjoyed his company, and he was a good dancer, but then came the wet, cold night when he had insisted on escorting her home on the bus. She had invited him in for a cup of tea, and by the time he left an hour later he was Senga's.

She had dropped him within a month, for he was not her type. With Senga, it was the chase that mattered, and the pleasure of taking someone else's property.

There were some things, Mollie thought, that you could never forget.

A gratifying number of guests crowded into the Logans' parlour after the church ceremony. Alice's young man was there, and the girl with whom Sam McCabe was walking out. Joe had been invited, and so had Jem and his wife. To his delight Jem, who had been friendly with Helen's uncle, had been asked to give her away at her wedding since she had no male relations of her own.

Dressed in his best clothes, without the filthy cap he always wore when he was working, and with his thick white hair and beard washed and trimmed, Jem was beaming with pride at being given a position of honour, scarcely recognisable as the gruff, irritable farm worker Jennet had known all her life. His wife, a shy little woman, could only walk with the aid of a stout stick, and it was touching to see how attentive Jem was to her.

The wedding presents had been set out in the parlour, with a large cut-glass bowl, Senga's gift, as the centrepiece. 'Goodness knows what use they'll have for it, but it's certainly bonny,' Mollie said low-voiced as she and Jennet surveyed the collection. 'You should have seen Helen's face when she took it out of its fancy box. She was like Cinderella bein' told that she could go to the ball, the wee soul. Trust our Senga!'

In a smart silky dress, the threads woven in such a

way that with every movement the colours seemed to shift and merge into each other, Senga moved about the Logans' front room like an exotic butterfly, her long-lashed eyes missing nothing, a slight smile curving her red lips as she watched and listened.

When Mollie went into the kitchen to make some more sandwiches, Senga followed, leaning against the dresser and taking a little enamelled compact out of her bag.

'She's a right wee mouse, that lassie our Bert's got into trouble,' she said, staring at herself in the compact's mirror, then licking the tip of a finger before smoothing a pencilled eyebrow carefully. 'You'd wonder how he managed it.'

'You should ask him if you're so interested. I wouldnae know anythin' about that sort of thing.' Mollie cut viciously into a loaf of bread.

'You mean you've never . . . ?'

'I leave these goings-on to you and our Bert.'

'You always were a prude, weren't you? So nothing happened between you and that Angus Scott?' Senga asked, and Mollie's knife plunged deep into the butter.

'What d'you mean?'

Senga prodded at a curl with a crimson-tipped fingernail, then slid the mirror into her bag and leaned back against the dresser, crossing slim nylon-clad legs. 'You used to have a right crush on him. Did you never do anything about it?'

'I never had a crush on him, I was just tryin' tae make him get out of that chair, because Jennet hated the way his gran kept wantin' tae turn him into an invalid.'

'A right wee Florence Nightingale you were,' Senga recalled. 'You mean to say he never thanked you properly for it?'

'You watch too many films. We're not all looking for romance.'

'Most of us are. Most of us like to enjoy ourselves while we're still young, though some of us are born middle-aged and dreary.' Senga's voice was spiteful. Then, as Mollie refused to rise to the bait, she lounged where she was, studying her sister closely. 'You sure there's nothing going on between the two of you? 'Cos he's different from the way he used to be,' she rambled on when Mollie said nothing. 'I mind being quite scared of him when we all lived at the farm, because he was so sour-faced and angry-looking all the time, as if he wanted to punch someone. But now he's quite good-looking really. Mebbe he's got himself a girlfriend. Well, has he? Cat got your tongue?'

'Sorry, I didn't realise you were waiting for an answer; I thought you were quite happy just babblin' away there and watchin' me workin'. No, Angus Scott's not got a girlfriend as far as I know. He's too busy workin' the farm tae think about that sort of thing.'

'Mmm. I've never had a boyfriend who's a cripple,' Senga said thoughtfully. She smoothed both hands down her skirt from waist to thigh, almost as though she was caressing her own rounded hips, and then said, her voice soft and creamy, 'I wonder what it's like tae make love tae a bloke with a gammy leg? I wonder if it's different?'

A chill flickered through Mollie. Not Angus, she thought, suddenly visualising him falling under Senga's spell, only to be thrown aside like all the others.

'I thought you already had a boyfriend in Glasgow. Or have you dumped him, the way you always do?' She tried to keep her tone casual.

'You don't dump Kenny.' The creaminess left Senga's voice; it took on a thin sound as she added, 'It's not somethin' he'd stand for.' Then, her confidence returning, 'But Kenny's not here, is he? And if Angus Scott doesnae have a girlfriend . . .'

'He might have, for all I know. The only man I'm interested in is my Joe,' Mollie said, her back to her sister. Even so, she could feel Senga's sudden change of mood so strongly that it was like a clap of thunder.

'He's quite a nice-looking chap.'

'I think so.'

'But you've not . . . gone all the way with him?'

'Not yet. I believe in taking my time.'

'You must be sure of him, then,' Senga said thoughtfully.

'Of course I am. He's not interested in anyone but me. Listen, they'll all be starvin' in the front room. Are you going tae stop behavin' like Cleopatra on her barge and help me with these sandwiches?'

Senga gave the practised twitch of the shoulders

that passed for a shrug and eased her backside away from the dresser.

'All right,' she said and, picking up the plate, half full of sandwiches, she sauntered back to the front room.

When Mollie took in a second plate five minutes later her sister was listening with wide-eyed fascination as Joe talked, his face alight.

'She's making a right fuss of your Joe,' Jennet hissed, taking the plate from Mollie. 'You'd better go over there and get him away from her!'

Mollie glanced across the room to where Angus was talking to George Logan, and twitched her shoulders in imitation of her sister's delicate shrug. 'Ach, she'll not be staying on the island for long,' she said. 'And anyway, I'm not bothered.'

Helen and Bert McCabe moved into the cottage on the night of their marriage, and the next morning, after Bert had gone to work, his bride presented herself at the kitchen door, waiting for her orders.

All the girl knew was work, and it seemed to be all she wanted to do. She scrubbed and polished, washed dishes and laundered clothes, baked and cooked, and scarcely said a word to anyone other than Jamie. On a few occasions when she believed she was alone with the little boy, Jennet heard them chattering to each other, but as soon as she or anyone else appeared Helen retreated into silence.

'I wish she'd just relax and be happy,' Jennet fretted to Mollie.

'She is happy, in her own way. Best to let her be. You'd not think any man would have a chance to get up to mischief with such a wee shy thing, would you?' Mollie echoed her sister's words on the day of the wedding.

'She reminds me of myself,' Jennet said drily, 'and look what happened there.'

Helen even made butter for the household, scrubbing and scalding the small hand-churn and slipping into the byre after milking time to skim cream from the top of the milk. In Jennet's childhood she had helped her grandmother to churn the farm's butter supply, but there had been no time for such luxuries once the war came. Jennet had forgotten how good the rich yellow stuff tasted on homemade bread, and Helen kept back the buttermilk from the process for herself and Jamie. 'It's good for both of us,' she said. Jamie loved the new drink and went about most mornings, until he was caught and wiped by one of the adults, sporting a creamy moustache.

Helen's hard work in the kitchen meant that Mollie was free to help Jennet clean out the big cowshed in readiness for the winter, when the cows would be brought in from the field. Angus, Jem and Norrie were busy ditching and checking the dry-stane walls and cutting back trees and hedges. The days were growing shorter and the evenings darker, and the smoky smell of bonfires made from dead tree branches and hedge cuttings hung in the air and lingered on Angus's clothing when he came into the kitchen.

Senga was right, Mollie thought, watching him; he
had changed since he and Jennet had taken over the
farm. His movements were more confident now and,
although he was still quiet, the bitterness that had
tightened his mouth and hooded his eyes had given
way to determination and self-belief. She was grateful
that Senga had left the island, for if her sister had had
even the slightest suspicion of Mollie's true feelings
for Angus Scott, she would have gone after him like
a ferret after a rabbit.

She would have got him, too; Mollie had no doubt
about that. Senga had never failed yet, and beneath
the defence he had built up Angus was lonely. Senga
would have got him and she would have broken his
heart. And that might have spelled disaster for him
and Jennet, as well as Mollie. She would rather spend
the rest of her life without him than see that happen.

She was quite proud of herself for having tricked
her streetwise sister into making a play for Joe instead.
Once she left Bute he had come back to Mollie like
a naughty dog begging for a second chance, but she
wasn't at all minded to agree to that. Why should she
take back her sister's leavings, she thought resentfully.
But at the same time there was a certain amount of
pleasure in letting Joe court her.

Angus even returned to ploughing, hoisting himself
up onto the tractor seat with increasing dexterity.

'D'ye think it's safe?' Mollie asked anxiously as
she and Jennet watched him drive off down the lane.

'What's got into you? You're the one that nagged him until he got back on his feet, and now you've started fussing over him driving the tractor.'

'I'm not fussing, it's just that these machines can be dangerous. I've heard all about Drew Blaikie's accident.'

'Drew was unfortunate. Angus's been driving a tractor since before he was ten, and if it's something he wants to do I'll not argue with him the way Gran did. She took the heart out of him and I'm going to put it back, even if it kills him.'

For all her brave words Jennet secretly worried herself sick that first time, and when she heard the tractor roaring and rattling back to the yard a few hours later it was all she could do to stroll – and not run – into the yard to see him arrive. Angus, exhausted but triumphant, slithered down to the ground and reached up for his crutch, which had been wedged in behind him.

'I've not lost the knack,' he told his sister, grinning.

'I never thought you had,' she retorted sharply. 'It's like being on a bicycle – you never forget.'

'That's elephants,' he said, and tugged on her long curly hair as he limped past her into the house.

Celia, who never missed a Sunday service unless it was unavoidable, always insisted on a proper family attendance at Harvest Thanksgiving. This year Mollie went with them, as did Jamie, wearing a little sailor suit that Jennet had bought for the occasion. With his face scrubbed until it shone like an apple, his shoes shined and his hair dampened with tap-water before being brushed into place, he perched on the hard wooden pew between his mother and Mollie, staring wide-eyed at the stained-glass windows. He tilted his head so far back to look up at the vaulted roof that it bumped against the high back of the pew, and then he asked in awe, 'Who lives here?'

'God,' Jennet whispered back.

'Is he playing the music?' Jamie tempered his own clear voice to a loud whisper.

'No, that's Mr McLennan that used tae teach our Sam at the school,' Mollie murmured.

Jamie craned his neck to see the pulpit, surrounded by piles of apples, turnips and cabbages, leeks and flowers and potatoes, all carefully arranged and backed by sheaves of golden oats and barley.

'Getting our dinner?'

'We'll be going to Aunt Ann's for our dinner afterwards. Just sit quiet and be a good boy,' Jennet urged.

She had arranged to sit by the aisle, ready to whisk him outside if he became restless or tried to talk too much, but Jamie sat quietly for most of the time, mesmerised by the splendour of the place and the sight of all the worshippers in their Sunday best. When the hymns were sung he accepted a book, opened it at random and stood on the pew, quietly singing his favourite songs and making things difficult for Mollie, who had to give up singing in order to stifle her giggles.

When the congregation filed outside afterwards several women eyed him with interest.

'They usually favour the man,' Jennet heard one sharp-faced woman murmur to her companion. 'I feel myself that that's the Lord's way of making sure that the men don't get off with it entirely.'

Her friend shushed her and then came to gush over Jamie, as if to make up for the unkind words. 'He's just a wee picture,' she enthused. 'And a credit to you. So well behaved, weren't you, little man?'

'We didn't get dinner,' Jamie informed her, 'Getting it at Aunt Ann's.' Then, spotting a friend, he suddenly let go of Jennet's hand and dashed over to the Blaikies. 'Struan!'

'Hello, wee man!' Struan picked him up, beaming, and Jennet had no option but to join them.

Lizbeth Blaikie's handsome face was rigid with disapproval as she watched her son toss Jamie up in the air. 'Jennet . . . Angus . . . er . . .' She nodded vaguely to Mollie. 'It's rare to see you at the church.'

'We always come to Harvest Thanksgiving,' Angus reminded her. 'The rest of the time we're usually too busy taking care of God's earth for him.'

Struan gave a muffled sound, which he turned into a cough. His mother glared at him.

'Allan's not with you today?'

'Not today, Angus, he had business in Glasgow.'

Angus nudged his sister and then, as she said nothing, he soldiered on. 'You'll be pleased to see him back on the island.'

'It's always good to see your own kin again. Speaking of kin,' Lizbeth said heavily, 'I'd a letter from your grandmother the other day.'

'So did we. She seems to be enjoying herself in Largs.'

'She deserves her rest. That woman,' Lizbeth said pointedly, 'has had a hard life, and I should know, being her friend for more years than either of us can remember. She's a saint. There's not many like her.'

'You're right there,' Angus said, and Struan had another coughing attack.

'She's worked her fingers to the bone for her family . . .' Lizbeth Blaikie was continuing when Jennet, making some excuse about keeping her aunt and uncle waiting, took Jamie from Struan and fled, with Angus at her heels.

'Why didn't you help me?' he hissed as they went. 'Standing there with your mouth shut and leaving me to do all the talking!'

'I can't bear to speak to that woman! She ignores my Jamie and she always does her best to make me feel like a criminal. But she's right, Gran did work her fingers to the bone for us.'

'And her poor leg, too,' Angus said, and the two of them, walking among the folk all dressed in their Sunday best, with their Sunday manners, began to giggle.

20

'If you ask me,' Mollie said, 'it looks evil.'

'I'd hate to be in it with all that water above my head,' Jennet said, and Mollie squealed, clapped her hands to her ears, and spun away from the edge of the pier, where the two girls were contemplating the British submarine on show as part of Bute Thanksgiving Week.

'Don't . . . it gives me the shivers just to think about it!'

The boat, long and narrow and dark, gave Jennet the same feeling, but young men had had to entomb themselves in it, deep below the sea's surface, in order to fight in the war. She marvelled at their courage and endurance.

'Joe wanted me tae go on board with him and see round it,' Mollie said from where she now stood a few feet away from the edge.

'Are you going?'

'I told him that if he wanted someone to hold his hand on board that thing he'd have to invite Senga.'

'You're being rotten to that lad!'

'That's what he says, but tae my mind he deserves it. I might allow him tae take me out again eventually, till someone better comes along. But even if I do, it'll be a while before I let him forget the way he mooned after that sister of mine. Come on, we'll go and have a look at the flower show. That's better than a submarine any day.'

'You're right.' Jennet reached down to take Jamie's hand and discovered that the little boy, who had been by her side a moment ago, was no longer there. 'Jamie?' She looked wildly round the crowds on the pier. 'D'you see him, Mollie?'

'He was here a minute ago. He can't have gone far.' Like the town's streets, the pier was crowded with folk, most of them local, but sprinkled with a few late holidaymakers and people who had taken the ferry over from the mainland for the day. A small boy, not much higher than the average adult knee, would easily be lost in that throng.

Jennet's blood ran cold. 'You don't think . . . he couldn't have fallen in the water, could he?' She edged forward to peer down at the narrow strip of black water between the pilings and the submarine.

'No, of course not, someone would have seen him, or heard him. He was here not a minute ago,' Mollie said urgently. 'He can't have gone far.'

'He's so little, and yet he can move so fast . . . You stay on the pier and I'll run up towards the street, just in . . .'

'Is this what you're looking for?' Allan Blaikie said just then, moving into Jennet's line of vision. Jamie, beaming, was perched on the man's shoulders with his chubby legs dangling and his hands gripped firmly in Allan's.

'Look at me, Mummy,' he crowed, 'I'm up high!'

'The king of the castle,' Allan agreed.

'You naughty boy, you know you're supposed to stay beside me or Mollie!'

Recognising her anger, Jamie's excited smile died and tears of surprise and shock began to fill his eyes. 'Don't be too hard on him,' Allan said swiftly, 'I'm sure he didn't mean to wander away. It's difficult for a wee bairn, in among all those legs . . .'

'Are you trying to say that I wasn't looking after him properly?'

'I just meant that he wasn't doing anything wrong.'

'Of course he was. He knows that he must never run away from me or speak to strangers.'

Allan's eyes narrowed. 'I'd hardly class myself as a stranger.'

'You are as far as Jamie's concerned.'

'There's no harm done, Jennet,' Mollie interceded. 'The laddie's safe and that's all that matters.'

'Give him to me!' Jennet reached for her son, but when Allan freed his hands, Jamie clutched at the man's hair.

'I want to stay up high!' His lower lip began to jut in a way that would have made Celia smack his legs.

'You'll do as you're told!' Jennet reached up and

began to untangle the small fingers, heedless of the pain she might be causing Allan.

'Another day, eh?' He lifted the little boy over his ducked head, then put him into Jennet's arms. 'Time to go back to your mummy, son.'

Once Jamie was in her grip, Jennet pushed her way past Allan and then along the pier, shoving through the crowds and not halting until Mollie caught at her arm.

'Slow down, Jennet, before you get yourself killed, and Jamie with you!'

Jennet stared at her uncomprehendingly and then looked around. She had reached the road, and if Mollie had not stopped her she might have plunged across it in front of a horse-driven cart.

'Where is he?'

'Allan Blaikie? Back on the pier, probably. You didn't need to be so harsh with him,' Mollie said, puzzled. 'He was trying to help us. If he hadn't found Jamie and brought him back, we'd have been in a right pickle. You nearly scalped the poor man, pulling Jamie away from him like that, and you've frightened the wee soul, too.'

It was only then that Jennet realised that her son was shaking, his face wet with tears.

'It's all right, pet, Mummy just got a fright when you went away.' She took the handkerchief Mollie offered and mopped his face and then her own.

'I'll take him for a wee while. We'll go and get a nice drink of juice, eh, Jamie?' Mollie suggested as she gathered him into her arms. 'And then we'll have a look at all the pretty flowers. And when we get back home mebbe you'll draw some flowers for me, eh?'

Jennet followed them along to the ice-cream parlour, her heart still thumping. At the sight of Allan and Jamie – laughing together, enjoying each other's company – all the pleasure had suddenly gone out of her day.

Although the days were getting shorter there was still plenty to do before winter arrived. The largest field had to be ploughed to allow the winter frosts to kill off any weeds before the spring planting, while other fields had to be manured to encourage the clover and grass that would eventually become hay. The dry-stane dykes had to be repaired and the dairy herd checked over. The older animals, their milk yield now low, had to be replaced by heifers, which then had to be put to the bull, for they would not give milk until they had calved.

Now that Helen McCabe was there to look after the house and Jamie, Mollie was free to help Jennet with some of the outdoor work. Together they cleaned out the cowshed, heaving bales of straw across the yard to be broken up and spread about the floor just before the animals came in.

'And they'll no sooner be in there, nice and dry and clean, than we'll have to clean it all out and pile it here,' Mollie mourned as she and Jennet turned to the next task, using big wooden forks to heft manure

into the cart. 'All these years in Glasgow I never knew
what went into growin' stuff tae eat. I think I liked it
better that way . . . not knowin'.'

'Nothing's wasted on a farm,' Angus said from the
bed of the cart, where he was levelling the manure.

'Ye're right there. I'm just glad you've got a proper
lavatory instead of makin' us all use the dung-heap!'

'In the old days that's just what you would have
had to do,' Jennet said. 'As Angus says, nothing gets
wasted on a farm.'

'Only the folk.' Mollie paused to catch her breath
and ease her shoulder muscles, looking down in
dismay at her clothes, spattered with mud and dung.
'I'd do anythin' for a nice hot bath and half a bottle
of Evening in Paris!'

Jennet knew just what she meant. It was at times
like this that she wondered why she had been so determined to stay on the farm. But then again, she thought
as she forked another load of manure and heaved it
up onto the cart, then bent to lift another forkload,
farm life had its compensations: bringing in the cows
on misty early mornings when the sky admired its
pearl-grey reflection in the placid surface of the Sound
of Bute; the dew on the spiders' webs that made the
hedges glitter gold and silver; and the birds stirring in
their nests and just beginning to break into sleepy song.
The memories kept the routine – stoop, dig in, stand,
lift, empty the fork, stoop, on and on and on – bear-
able. And finally the cart was full.

'Last load for the day.' Angus picked up the reins.

'Thank God for that. Tell you what, Jennet, I'll race you when we get back to the field. The one that shovels the most sh . . . manure can get off doing the dishes after supper.'

'She always manages to stay cheerful,' Jennet marvelled to Angus that evening when Mollie had gone upstairs to luxuriate in the bath she had been craving all day.

'Too much, if you ask me.'

'She works hard, too.' For once she was taking time to leaf through the newspaper and now she tapped at the page as an item caught her eye. 'The Farmers' Dinner's being held on the nineteenth in St Blane's Hotel at Kilchattan Bay.'

'What about it?'

'You'll have to go.'

'Don't be daft.'

'Angus, you're the farmer here now. You should go to it.'

'You're the farmer, too.'

'I'd go in a minute, but it's always just the menfolk, so it has to be you.'

At first he was adamant in his refusal, but after a few days of arguing, as well as a visit from Andra Blaikie to suggest that Angus should go to the event with him and Struan in his car, he finally agreed. Jennet was pleased, for Martinmas rent day was approaching, and to her mind, Angus needed to do all he could to establish himself with the other farmers as the new tenant at Westervoe.

She and Mollie aired and brushed his one and only good suit and Jennet went into Rothesay and bought him a new shirt for the occasion.

'You look very smart. I'm proud of you,' she said when he came into the kitchen that evening.

'I feel daft.'

'You don't look it. I wish Mollie could see you.' Mollie was staying overnight with her mother and brother.

'I'm glad she can't. She'd probably say something sarcastic.'

'She wouldn't!' Then, as she caught the sound of a car in the lane, Jennet called out, 'Here they are!'

When Angus had gone off with the Blaikies, both scrubbed and dressed in their best, she settled down to relish an entire evening on her own. She found some pleasant music on the radio and was halfway through the first chapter of a book borrowed from the library in Rothesay when Gumrie began to bark out in the yard.

He wouldn't bark for Bert McCabe, who would be in his cottage with Helen at that time of night. Jennet put the book aside and opened the door to find Allan Blaikie outside.

'Angus's out,' she said at once, and began to close the door. He stopped her with a hand on the panels.

'At the Farmers' Dinner. That's why I knew it was safe to come over. Can I come in?'

She hesitated and then said reluctantly, 'For a minute, just.'

'Thanks. Your hospitality overwhelms me.'

'You're lucky I didn't slam the door in your face.' She stalked back into the room and he followed, closing the door.

'Will you scream for help if I take my coat off?'

'Go on,' she said grudgingly, and then when he had taken it off and hung it neatly over a chair, 'I suppose you'd better sit down.'

He glanced at her book, lying on the floor beside Celia's big chair, then sat down opposite. The last time they met, at Rothesay pier, he had been in flannels and a shirt under a sleeveless Fair Isle pullover, but tonight he was in the suit he had worn when he visited Westervoe shortly after his return to the island.

'I wanted to say I'm sorry if I upset you when we met in Rothesay, though I have to admit that I don't know what I did to deserve the way you treated me.'

She drew a deep breath and sat down, her hands folded primly in her lap. 'I don't want you to be around Jamie. I don't want you calling him "son".'

'But he is my son.'

'No, he's mine. You had your chance a long time ago, before he was born, but you didn't want him then.'

He stared down at his hands, then said, 'Jennet, what I did then was . . . it was a terrible thing. But I didn't realise it.'

'What you did when?' she asked coldly. 'When he was conceived here on the island, or when I told you in Glasgow that I was carrying him?'

'Both times. The first time, down by the water, I was so scared that I was near out of my mind. I'd just seen the state Angus was in, and between that and not seein' myself coming out of the war alive . . . And you,' memory suddenly softened his voice, 'so understandin' and carin'. You were the only person I knew who'd understand. And I . . . I lost my head.'

'And afterwards? If you had done the right thing by me when I told you about Ja . . . about the baby,' she said, her anger beginning to rise. 'If you'd married me, or even put a ring on my finger and told your parents and my grandmother and Angus that the bairn was yours . . . if you'd just done that, my life would have been a hell of a lot easier than it's been since then.'

'I know.' His voice was little more than a whisper. 'I let you down and I'll never forgive myself for it.'

They had met in a teashop in Sauchiehall Street on his next leave. On his way back to his regiment Allan had called in at the nurses' hostel, where at that very moment Jennet had been trying to write a letter telling him that she was pregnant. It had been such a relief to be able to tell him in person. Together, she had thought in her naïvety, they could work something out.

But instead his face had turned chalk-white and he had said, 'God, that's all I need!'

'All you need? What about me?'

'I'm due to report back tomorrow morning, Jennet. I could be thrown into prison if I don't turn up; shot mebbe. If it's marriage you're after, there's not enough time!'

The words 'you're after' had struck a chill deep within her, but she had struggled on, desperate to find an answer to the situation in which she now found herself.

'We could get engaged. Then at least I could tell Gran and your parents that we'll be married as soon as you get your next leave . . .'

His pallor had turned to a sickly grey. 'Tell my mother? I can't, Jennet, not right now, not so soon after . . .'

'After what?'

It was only then that she had found out that Drew had been crushed to death beneath his father's tractor while ploughing Gleniffer's top field.

'But . . . my grandmother never told me,' she whispered in disbelief.

'She didn't want to say it in a letter. She asked me to break it to you. That's why . . .' he stopped suddenly.

'That's why you came here.' Only for that reason; not to see her. For a moment Jennet had thought she was going to be sick.

'She thought it best,' she had heard Allan say as the wave of nausea ebbed away, 'since you and Drew had been walking out together . . .'

'But it's not Drew's child I'm carrying,' she had flared across the table at him. 'It's yours!'

'And that's why I cannae tell my mother the truth right now, what with her being broken-hearted over

losing Drew. They all think of you as his sweetheart,'
Allan had said wretchedly. 'They'd think we betrayed
him.'

'Mebbe you'd prefer it if I just let them all think
that it's Drew's child. That way your mother would
have her grandchild and you'd be spared the bother
of marrying me.'

The words had been heavy with sarcasm, but for a
split second as he looked up at her she had seen hope
flaring in his eyes at the suggestion. Then it died and
he said, 'Don't be daft, I'd not . . .'

Jennet had pushed her untouched tea away, so angry
that for two pins she would have thrown it over him,
uniform and all. 'Go back to your regiment, Allan
Blaikie,' she had told him as she got to her feet, 'and
don't worry about me. I'll manage, somehow.'

And she had walked out of the teashop, ignoring
his attempt to call her back, oblivious to the curious
eyes of the other customers, and had taken to her
heels, running and running until she was too worn out
to run any more.

His letter had arrived a week later. She let it lie
for a whole day, trying to summon up enough
determination to destroy it unread. Finally she opened
it. He had apologised, then suggested that an abortion
might be the best solution for them both.

'I know that it is possible at a price,' he had written,
'because being with lads all the time, I hear about
such things. They say that it is safe, if you go to the
right place. I am enclosing all the money I can put

together – I hope it will be enough. Let me know if
it costs more.'

He had ended with a promise that he would not
return to Bute or try to contact her, if that was what
she wanted.

'I was going to have an abortion,' she said now, in
the cosy warmth of the Westervoe kitchen. 'But then
I couldn't go through with it.'

'Thank God for that.' When she looked up,
surprised, there was horror in his eyes. 'Imagine wee
Jamie not bein' alive. I never thought of it that way
when I wrote the letter.'

'I spent the money.'

'What?'

'The money you sent. I could have returned it, but
instead I took all the other nurses out to a nice hotel
for their dinner the night before I came back here.'

The shadow of a smile brushed his mouth. 'I hope
they enjoyed it.'

'They loved it. We never got enough to eat at the
hostel or the hospital.'

'Jennet, let me make up for what I did.'

'It's too late for that. D'you know what folk call a
woman who has a child with no man willing to give
it his name?' The anger began to come back. 'D'you
want to hear what my grandmother said about me
when I came back here?'

He winced. 'I can imagine.'

'She thought – they all thought, your mother as
well – that the father was some serviceman I'd met

on a dark street one night. Mebbe not even British, my grandmother said. Mebbe I wouldn't tell her his name because I never knew it myself.'

'You can now. Marry me, Jennet.' He reached over and put his hand on hers. 'Let me give you and Jamie my name and look after you both.'

Although the kitchen was warm enough, his hand was cold. She withdrew her fingers from beneath it and then brushed it from her lap as though it was an unwanted piece of fluff.

'I needed to hear you say that three years ago. I don't need it now.'

'I wish to God I had said it three years ago! When you were tellin' me then . . . it was just words then, it wasnae real.'

'It was real enough to me, but then it's easier for men,' Jennet said bitterly. 'They can just walk away and get on with their lives. Women can't. But I survived, and Jamie was born. And now, just when we're managing fine, you turn up. Why couldn't you have let the two of us be?'

'I meant to, even when my uncle decided to send me back here. I thought we could live our separate lives and not get in each other's way, but then . . .' his voice faltered slightly, 'then I saw Jamie and he wasn't a word any more, Jennet, he was flesh and blood.'

'He's been flesh and blood since he was conceived.'

'Marry me, Jennet . . . please.'

At one time – on several occasions, if she was honest – Jennet's heart would have sung to hear those words from Allan Blaikie; now they just angered her further.

'Why should I do that?'

'To give Jamie a father, for one thing.'

'That's exactly what your brother said.'

'Struan?' Allan asked, astonished. 'Our Struan asked you to marry him?'

'Not long after he was demobbed. I told him the same as I'm telling you . . . I've no wish to marry anyone.'

'But I'm not Struan! Jamie's my own son and I . . .'

She was on her feet and raining open-handed blows down on his head and shoulders before she knew what was happening. 'Don't you ever call him that, d'you hear me?' she panted as she flailed at him. 'He's mine, and that's the way it's going to stay!'

He got up, but stood still, taking the blows. Then, as they showed no sign of abating, he tried to catch her wrists.

'Jennet . . .' he began, then yelped as one flailing hand caught the side of his face and the nail dragged a long scratch from his ear to the corner of his mouth. Jennet stopped, horrified by her own violence, and stepped away from him.

'You deserved that,' she said breathlessly.

He had taken a handkerchief from his pocket and now he dabbed at his cheek. When he took the handkerchief away she could see blood on it. 'That, and more,' he said.

'Go away, Allan.'

'You said, that night . . . you said you loved me.'

'That's more than you said to me,' she reminded him cruelly, and he winced.

'Do you still love me, Jennet?'

'You ask me that after all that's happened?'

'I want to know if it's still true.'

'No, it's not.'

'Are you certain of that?' he asked, and then when she said nothing, 'I've grown up a lot in the years since we last met. I want us to . . .'

Jennet walked to the door and opened it. 'We've nothing more to say to each other, Allan,' she said. And after a moment's hesitation he nodded and went past her and out into the night.

November arrived, bringing with it the farmers' rent day, and to Jennet's relief Angus went to the factor's office and officially put his name in as the new tenant of Westervoe.

'Yours, too,' he said when he got back to the farm. 'It was your idea and you should have a share of the place . . . warts and all.'

She had been fretting as the day approached, worrying in case he changed his mind at the last moment. Now that he had made the decision to move forward independently of their grandmother, that was all that mattered to her. It was not until the following morning, as the two of them, still half asleep, trudged down the lane to bring in the cows in a cold, wet dawn, that the reality of it struck her.

To one side a ploughed and manured field glistened beneath the rainwater; to the other the cows' hooves churned up mud around the gate as they gathered for milking. Raindrops dripped from the hedges, now stripped of their leaves, and the Sound of Bute was lost beneath a dreary grey mist that reached up from the water's surface to bond itself with the clouds above. Gumrie slunk alongside, wet and too miserable to run ahead as usual, and at each step that she and Angus took their feet sank into watery runnels in the lane's ruts and had to be hauled out in order to make the next step. It was as though the entire world was made of cold drops of water, falling from the sky and dripping from their noses and oozing slowly down their necks.

'It's ours,' she said, and Angus, reaching out to open the gate, gave her a sideways glance, blinking rain out of his eyes.

'What is?'

'All this.' She gestured to the cows and the mud and the river beyond the dim outline of the dry-stane dyke. 'Westervoe. It's our responsibility, our home. Ours.'

'Aye,' Angus said gloomily. 'Aye, we've gone and done it now.'

21

All other farm work, apart from milking and seeing
to the livestock, came to a standstill when the
threshing mill that travelled round the farms without
a machine of their own reached Westervoe in mid-
November. Threshing was a job that involved
everyone on the farm, and in her younger days it had
seemed to Jennet that the machine, with its belts and
cogs and wheels, took over the farm like a dirty, noisy
god feverishly worshipped and tended by the farmers
and farmhands feeding bales of oats into its hungry
mouth and gathering up the grain, chaff and stalks
that it spat out at them.

In the week or so since the night of the Farmers'
Dinner Allan Blaikie had not made any effort to
contact Jennet. On the day he was due to collect the
pigs she arranged to take Jamie to visit the Logans,
being careful to stay away until the evening. She
was just beginning to think that she was free of him
when, to her consternation, he and Struan arrived

from Gleniffer to help with the Scotts' threshing.

'I thought your father was coming,' she said to Struan when Allan was out of earshot.

'Ach, he'd other things to do, and Allan was keen. He misses the farming a bit.'

'Then he should have stayed in farming,' Jennet said sharply, and told Helen McCabe to keep the little boy by her side all day.

'I'll certainly do that,' the girl said earnestly. 'Threshing mills are no place for wee bairns.'

There was nothing more that Jennet could do, other than stay well away from Allan as they gathered round the mill to hear Angus's instructions. Mollie was set to clearing the chaff and cavings – short bits of straw – from under the machine as it worked.

'We could do that between us,' Jennet suggested.

'I need you on the rick, with Bert. Struan can cut the bales loose and Allan can feed the corn into the thresher. Norrie and me'll pass the bales up.'

'But clearing chaff and cavings at the same time is hard work for one person.'

'If it's too much for Mollie, she can help Helen with the wee fellow instead and Norrie can take over her job.'

'I'll manage fine,' Mollie said at once.

'Mind and wrap up well, for the chaff gets everywhere,' Jennet advised her before clambering up the ladder to where Norrie stood on the rick.

'Manage?' he asked cheerfully, reaching down to give her a hand.

'I know what I'm about.' She took hold of a bale, making sure that she was not standing on any part of it. Snapping at folk seemed to be the order of the day, she thought as she braced herself to lift the bale free. When she let go it landed in front of Angus, who had come up with the idea of propping his shorter right leg on a wooden box so that he could stand upright without having to use his crutch. He dug the prongs of his pitchfork into the bale and tossed it up to the thresher, where Jem deftly caught it and then swung it on up to Struan. He slashed the bonds and Allan then fed the loose corn into the drum where it was stripped of its grain.

Threshing was largely a matter of teamwork, made easier if they all cooperated with each other and with the chugging rhythm of the mill. They soon fell into the right pattern, and from then on the work was continuous, without time to talk or even rest for a moment. Once, when Jennet snatched a second to swipe an arm across her perspiring face, she caught Allan's eye. He looked away at once, but the momentary diversion must have thrown him off his rhythm for the machine's steady thrumming suddenly changed to a deeper, harsher note, indicating that too much corn had been fed into it.

'Mind what you're about, man!' Angus roared up at him as the mill tried to cope with the added load.

'Sorry,' Allan shouted back. It was clear who was in charge at Westervoe, Jennet thought with a rush of pleasure. She craned her neck precariously to see how

Mollie was getting on, but the other girl was hidden from sight by the machine's bulk.

Threshing was the nearest Mollie McCabe had ever been to hell. Chaff and bits of broken straw spewed out beneath the machine at a frightening rate and she had to work hard to pull them free before they gathered and clogged up the machinery. Above her head grain was pouring into a stretched tarpaulin, while the stripped straw was thrown out from another part of the mill to be used as animal bedding. But all Mollie could see was the area where she worked, raking and shovelling, throwing filled bags over her shoulder and hurrying them into one of the sheds before rushing back to start all over again. The chaff found its way everywhere – down her neck and inside her blouse, up her nose and down her throat and into her eyes. Fortunately she had had the sense to tie a headscarf turbanwise round her head and push all her hair beneath it, but even so she felt her scalp itching; whether because of chaff, or just in sympathy with the rest of her, she had no way of knowing. Her back, arm and leg muscles ached and, despite the cold wind, sweat poured from her.

On the way to the shed with yet another full bag of chaff she stumbled slightly and Angus, the muscles on his forearms standing out as he forked bales of corn up to the rick, shouted, 'Are you all right?'

'Yes.'

'D'you want Norrie to take a turn there? You've

done well,' he added as she stared at him from below
lashes encrusted with chaff.

'I'll go on as I am,' she yelled back and stamped
on into the shed, where she threw the bag down. He
had deliberately given her the worst job of all in the
hope of humiliating her in front of everyone and she
was determined to stay at it for as long as she must.
Her eyes watered with tears of tiredness and frustration, and then watered even more when, rubbing the
tears away, she only succeeded in getting a piece of
chaff in one of them.

'Damn it!' She blundered back into the yard,
blinking, and got on with the job, leaving the fresh
tears to pour down her hot face in the hope that they
would also clear and soothe her eye.

It was still stinging when they stopped for the
midday meal, trooping into the kitchen where Helen
waited for them, each one trailing chaff and straw
over the flagged floor.

'Here . . .' Allan stopped her, taking her face in his
two hands. 'That eye's sore-looking; did you get chaff
in it?'

'Aye, and in every other part of me that it could
find! Bits I didnae even know I had myself,' she said,
and he grinned.

'As to the rest of you, you'll have to see to that
yourself, unless you're determined to make me do it,'
he said, 'but I can help with the eye. Give me a bit
of clean cloth, lassie,' he ordered Helen. Then to
Mollie, 'Come back outside for a minute.'

In the yard he held her head steady with one hand and made her roll her eye up as far as she could. 'Now hold still,' he commanded, and she felt his breath light and warm on her cheek as he put his face close to hers, concentrating on probing her eyeball with the corner of the clean cloth.

'I can see it . . . No wonder your eye was sore, it must feel like a boulder.'

'Like Ben Nevis,' Mollie agreed.

'And rubbing it in didnae help, you should never do that. Be still for a minute . . . There!' he said triumphantly and stepped back. 'How does that feel?'

'Better. Much better,' she said gratefully, while fresh tears poured into her eye. He caught her wrist as she raised her hand to wipe them away.

'Don't start it up all over again! Let the tears clean it, then get the lassie to tip some castor oil into it from a spoon,' he ordered. 'That'll help it to heal. And now that's done, I'm ready for my dinner!'

'I thought,' Jennet said when the two of them re-entered the kitchen, 'that you'd given up farming for the butcher business, Allan Blaikie.'

'I have, but it's good to keep my hand in now and again.' He pulled up a chair by Angus's side and started on his dinner as though he had not eaten all week. 'By God, there's nothing like working out of doors to give you an appetite!'

'He's nice, that Allan Blaikie,' Mollie said that night. The long day's threshing was over, Jamie and Angus

were in bed, and she and Jennet, having indulged
themselves with deep, hot baths ('What your grandmother and the authorities don't know is perfectly
legal,' Mollie had said firmly) and having washed the
chaff and cavings from their hair, were lounging
before the kitchen range in their pyjamas with mugs
of cocoa.

'He's a charmer, like his father.'

'I've never thought of Mr Blaikie as charming,'
Mollie said, surprised. 'Let's have some more cocoa.
My mouth feels as if a wee furry animal's moved into
it.'

'I'm fine as I am. It's the chaff; you'll be sneezing
it and spitting it for the next two days.'

'I suppose Mr Blaikie's quite good-looking in an
old man sort of way. But not charming.'

'I don't mean like Charles Boyer, I mean like . . .'
Jennet searched for the right words. 'Just full of life,
making folk think that they have some happiness
secret that nobody else has. Grandmother always had
a soft spot for Andra Blaikie.'

'Your gran never had a soft spot for anybody,'
Mollie scoffed, returning to her chair with her refilled
mug. 'So . . . did you have one for Allan Blaikie?'

'No.'

'A good-looking man like that living not half a mile
away, and you were never sweethearts?'

'Allan preferred the more mature girls. Why are
you so interested? D'you fancy him yourself?'

'He's not my type.' They had put the lamp out and

the room was lit by the glow from the range. Molly was lounging on the big wingback chair that had been Celia Scott's, one arm above her head, her legs stretched out before her and her bare feet on the cloth rug. 'This is the life,' she said contentedly. 'Where could I find a rich man, d'ye think? I fancy bein' able tae do this whenever I feel like it.'

'If I find a rich man I'll keep him to myself.'

'Some friend you are,' Mollie said, and they grinned at each other.

'I'm for my bed,' Jennet decided five minutes later, draining her mug and getting up to rinse it under the tap.

'I'll be up in a minute.' Mollie cradled her mug in both hands, reluctant to move. 'And don't you dare waken me in the morning, I'm going to sleep for weeks. I bet poor old Rip Van Winkle had been threshing before he dozed off for all those years.'

After Jennet had gone upstairs Mollie nodded by the fire, rousing herself when a coal rattled in the grate and telling herself that she must get to bed at once; then drowsing again to waken with a start, splashing cold cocoa over her wrist, when Angus said from the inner doorway, 'Jennet? Are you still up?'

'It's me.' She drew the lapels of her very respectable pyjamas together and pulled herself upright in the chair, muffling a yawn. 'Jennet's gone to bed.'

'What are you doing up at this time of night?'

'I was too tired to be bothered going to my bed,

so I was looking at the pictures in the flames. D'you want something?'

'A drink of water, just. That chaff's all down my throat.'

'Mine, too. Would you like some cocoa?' She began to get up, but he waved her back into the chair.

'Water's fine. I'll get it. D'you want anything else yourself?'

'No.' She gulped at the cold cocoa, making a face when the skin that had formed on the top clung to her upper lip. She wiped it away with the back of her hand. 'I should be getting to my bed.'

'You did well today,' Angus said from the sink. 'It's a miserable job, clearing the chaff from beneath the mill.'

'So I discovered.'

He brought his cup of water over and sat down opposite her. He too was in his pyjamas and bare-footed. 'I should have set someone else to help you.'

'Why didn't you?' she challenged, and then when he said nothing, 'Did ye want tae show me up as a city girl in front of all those farming folk?'

He started to deny it, then said, 'To tell the truth, I don't know. If I did, I was proved wrong.' Then, unexpectedly, 'What sort of pictures? In the fire, I mean,' he added as she hesitated, unsure of his meaning.

'Oh, them. Castles and dragons and fairies . . . the usual things.'

'Usual?'

'Did you never see pictures in the fire when you were wee?'

He gave her a grim smile. 'In this house, anyone caught staring into the fire was malingering and given something more useful to do.'

'Try it now,' she suggested. 'That's a castle over there, a tall thin one on a bit of a mountain. And that wee tongue of blue flame's a dragon in front of its cave. See? If we look hard enough we might see a maiden in distress and a handsome knight riding to rescue her.'

Angus leaned forward, then admitted after a minute or so, 'I can't see a thing.'

'Look harder, and closer.'

He leaned further down, so that their heads were almost touching as they both gazed into the red coals behind the range's black iron bars.

'Don't *try* tae see anythin', just keep your eyes on the fire and let the pictures come tae you.'

They sat silently, Angus staring into the fire while Mollie, her face turned towards the range, moved slightly in her chair so that she could flick occasional glances at him. She rarely got the chance to look at him properly. His face had rounded out slightly in the past few months, and the extra fullness suited him. The summer sun and long hours spent out in the fields had given him a tan, and the small flames danced in his grey eyes while the fire's ruddy glow outlined his features like an artist's pencil, highlighting and shading to show the strong slope of his nose, the permanent pain-lines etched on his forehead, the sweep of his cheekbones and his flat, strong cheeks. His hair, tousled from contact with his pillow, drew soft shadows about the harder lines of his face, and Mollie's fingers itched to smooth it back.

Instead she asked, 'What do you see?'

'Guns firing and buildings on fire.' His voice was sombre. He straightened, leaning back in the chair, his eyes closed.

'No dragons or knights? You're going tae have tae learn tae read the flames properly, Angus Scott!'

'Mebbe I'm too old for it.'

'You're not old at all. You've got all your life in front of you.'

'You think so?'

'I know so,' she said almost fiercely. Then, when he opened his eyes and looked at her, she added, flustered, 'Besides, it's never too late tae learn. I'll teach you.'

'I can just see Jennet doing all the farm work outside while you and me sit in here staring into the fire,' he mocked and raised the cup of water to his lips. His good foot, long and narrow, the toes straight and well tapered, stretched out on the rug, coming very close to her own. Mollie hastily withdrew both her feet, tucking one beneath her in the big chair and moving the other back so that it rested on the balls of her toes beneath the chair.

'The winter's comin' . . . long dark nights and plenty of fire. We can practise then. And once you learn, you can help wee Jamie to learn to see the pictures.'

He gave her a lazy smile. 'You make it sound sensible!'

'We all need some magic in our lives, no matter what age we are.'

His damaged leg was shorter than his good leg, but not much shorter, she noticed now. The lower part, protruding from his pyjama leg, was thin and the foot, twisted slightly, drooped like a flower in need of sustenance. She wondered if exercises might help to strengthen the wasted muscles.

'You'd not say that if you'd been raised by my grandmother.'

'Mebbe that's what's wrong with her,' Mollie said. 'Mebbe she needed some magic.'

'She needed something, that's for certain.' He lifted the cup again, draining it and then lowering it to say, 'On the other hand, mebbe she was right to be so practical.'

'There's nothing wrong with being practical,' Mollie said lightly, settling back in the chair. 'I keep meanin' tae try it myself some day. But it surely needs tae be tempered with a bit of fun.'

'Or a bit of magic?' The gleam in his eyes did not owe everything to the firelight. For once he was completely relaxed as he leaned back, his hands spread over the arms of his chair.

'Either . . . both.' Tired though she was, Mollie felt that she would be happy to stay there for ever, alone with Angus in the firelit room. 'But at least one of them.'

'I don't know, Mollie.' He was staring into the fire again, but she knew, by the set of his jawline and the deepening of the lines across his forehead, that his gaze had turned inward, to his mind. 'To tell the truth, I'm wondering already if I did the right thing, taking over this place.'

'Of course you did the right thing!'

'A farm takes an awful lot of work.'

'Are you doubting your own ability?'

'I'm doubting my own strength.' His wounded leg twitched slightly. 'I can't put too much on Jennet's shoulders.'

'They're strong, and so are yours. And you've got our Bert working for you now. You're talkin' as if your grandmother's the only person who can run this place.'

'She's more able than me.' He slapped at his damaged knee, a gesture that she had often seen before.

'For pity's sake,' Mollie said passionately, 'if she could do it at her age, surely you can do it at yours. Anyway, the rent's paid and the matter's decided. And Jennet's pleased, so you might as well just leave it at that.'

'And stop whining at you? I didn't mean to do that.'

'You're not whining, it's just . . . you've been raised to believe that you can't do anything without your gran's support, but you're a man now, Angus

Scott,' Mollie said. 'Is it not time you proved her wrong?'

As soon as the words were out of her mouth she wished them back. The last thing she wanted on this magic night was to anger him. But to her surprise his tension suddenly ebbed away and he grinned.

'You're right. I'll go ahead . . . but you'll have to answer to me if things go wrong.'

'They won't, I promise you.' Mollie yawned, as much from relief as from exhaustion, and reached for his cup. 'Give me that and I'll wash it along with my own.'

'No, I'll wash them while you get to your bed.' He hoisted himself to his feet. 'You deserve your rest.'

Thinking that the kitchen was empty, he had left his crutch in his room and now, carrying the two cups with a finger through their handles, he used his free hand for support as he moved around the table towards the sink. He moved fairly easily, but without the crutch the inch or two of difference in the length of his legs gave him a lurching gait.

'You know,' Mollie said thoughtfully, recalling the way he had worked that day with his bad foot propped on a wooden block, 'you might be able to have a special boot made, with a built-up sole and heel to it.'

She knew immediately, by the sudden chill in the air, that she had said too much. Angus paused before taking the final step towards the sink, where he dumped the two cups noisily on the draining board before turning, supporting himself against the edge of the sink with both hands.

'When are you going to learn to mind your own business?' He was too far away from the fire for her to see his face, but she could tell from the cold, hard voice and the rigid set of his shoulders against the dark grey of the window that it would be twisted with fury.

'I . . .' She moistened her lips. 'I just thought, after seeing how well you did at the threshing . . . I thought it might help.'

'Is it not enough that you pestered me like a wasp round a rotten apple until I got onto the one crutch? D'you know what an effort that was? And here you go again! Are you going to be buzzing round my ears for the rest of my life, wanting me to do this and do that?'

'Angus . . .'

'Why don't you look to your own life, Mollie McCabe, instead of trying to change mine? You're a grown woman, you shouldn't be hanging around this place as though you've as much right to be here as me and my sister.'

'D'ye want me to go?'

'There's little sense in you staying, is there? The fact is,' Angus said cruelly, 'it suited me very well when you took yourself off to Rothesay. It was Jennet who was so determined to get you back when our grandmother got hurt, not me.'

Mollie got to her feet. 'I'll go tomorrow,' she said through stiff lips, and walked out of the kitchen, her sudden fragile happiness just as suddenly smashed to pieces.

22

Jennet was dismayed by her friend's decision to return to Rothesay. 'But why now, when the holiday season's over and you're not needed at Aunt Ann's?'

Mollie flinched inwardly at 'not needed'. She was beginning to think that she wasn't needed anywhere.' Aloud she said, 'The same could be said for this place. The work's slowing down now that winter's coming; the deep-litter house is doin' fine and the cowshed's ready for the beasts comin' in. And Helen's a trained farm servant, Jennet, she's of more use tae you than I am and she's desperate tae work in return for livin' in the cottage.'

'What are you going to do?'

'Your auntie and uncle are lettin' us stay on in their house, and Sam'll be working with Mr Logan, repairin' the boats, paintin' them and learnin' about how to build them, too. He's fair looking forward tae that. And Mam and your auntie need me tae help them tae get the house all done up for next summer. And

STAYING ON   337

I want tae get a job too . . . in a shop, mebbe.' She
babbled on. 'I'm missin' the dancing, too; I'm not
from a farming family like you, remember.'

'Mebbe not, but you're as much family as anyone
can be. Tell her, Angus,' Jennet appealed to her
brother, who sat at the breakfast table, almost hidden
by his newspaper. 'Tell her we want her to stay!'

'If the lassie feels the need to go,' he said from
behind the paper, 'then you should leave it at that and
not go on at her.'

'That's right.' Mollie busied herself with clearing
the table, avoiding Angus's side of it. 'I'll only be in
Rothesay, so you can come in on the bus and see me,
and I can come . . .' She broke off, then said, 'Look
at the time already. I'll see tae the hen mash today,
and you do the dishes, Jennet. Come on, Jamie Scott,
you can help me.'

'She never said a word about this last night when
we stayed up together,' Jennet said when her friend
had gone into the yard. 'D'you think something's
upset her?'

'I think,' Angus said, folding his paper with swift,
sharp movements, 'that she's a grown woman and
well able to decide for herself where she wants to be
and what she wants to do with her life. And I think
you're making too much of a song and dance about
it.'

He slapped his hands flat on the table, levered
himself from his chair and snatched up his crutch.
Outside, he could hear Jamie chattering in the little

shed where the hen food was stored. Angus went on through the yard and out to the tractor shed. He would finish the ploughing while the weather was right for it; it was a job that would keep him busy all day, and the mood he was in, that suited him fine.

The morning was cold and it took a while to get the tractor engine going. Once it was chugging away Angus climbed into his seat, using the series of blocks that Jem had set up, under his direction, to assist him. The sight of them reminded Angus of Mollie's suggestion the previous night, and a sharp stab of anger went through him at the memory. He would be glad to see the back of her. It was high time she went back to her own family.

But she was in his mind all day, and even though she was gone by the time he returned to the house that night, he kept thinking that each time he glanced up he would see her sitting across the table, or helping wee Jamie with something, or turning from the sink or the range. And each time she wasn't there he felt empty inside.

When Jennet had gone to her bed that night he sat on in the kitchen opposite the big wing chair in which Mollie had been sitting less than twenty-four hours earlier. Narrowing his eyes, he could still see her there, leaning back, her legs stretched out and her bare feet on the cloth rug, her hair shimmering like polished bronze in the firelight. He could even smell her freshly washed hair, the way he had last night when, heads together, they had stared into the flames.

His eyelids began to ache, and when he relaxed them and opened his eyes fully she was gone. He wrenched his gaze from the chair and stared into the fire, but he could see no castles or dragons or knights in shining armour riding to rescue maidens.

There was no magic there at all – only the dying embers.

The floor of the big cowshed was liberally covered with clean straw and the feeding troughs filled before the cows left their field for the last time that year and came to winter indoors. The remaining arks were moved to a slight rise in their field, to lessen the danger of flooding in bad weather, and the farm's busy daily routine slowed as the days shortened.

With animals to tend every day there was still work to do, but less than in the other seasons, and now that Bert McCabe was working for Westervoe, Jennet had more time to devote to Jamie. From the first she had given him as much of her attention as possible, tying a shawl about her body to act as a sling in which she could carry him while she attended to her farm duties, then buying a second-hand pushchair as he got too heavy to carry.

Her grandmother had told her that she was spoiling the child, and it was character-strengthening to leave him to his own devices, but Jennet had insisted on doing things her own way, talking non-stop to her baby as she worked, even when he was asleep with his face almost hidden in the folds of the shawl; and taking time each evening, no matter how tired she was, to read stories to him. As a result, Jamie was chattering like a lintie by the time he reached his second birthday, and he had developed an interest in everything and everybody.

All too soon, she thought, watching him as he stood on a chair, helping her to bake scones, he would be going to school, and when that happened she would lose him to his teachers and his new friends. That was the way it should be, but until then he was hers, and she meant to make the most of every minute.

She had another reason for keeping him close; although he had not made another attempt to be alone with her, Allan Blaikie came about the farm occasionally and Jamie had taken a liking to him. Whenever they met, the little boy clamoured to hear the mouth organ, and for his part, Allan was clearly besotted with the child. It was impossible to keep them apart without telling Angus her secret, so Jennet had to settle for the occasional visit, making sure that she was always there at the time. To his credit, Allan had never attempted to see Jamie behind her back. On the few occasions when he had called at the farm and found Helen and Jamie alone at the house, Helen reported, he had gone away again.

'Ye'd make a good father,' Angus joked one day when Allan and Jamie were kneeling on the kitchen floor, making a toy farm out of cardboard boxes. 'I never thought I'd live to see Allan Blaikie playing with a wean.'

'Nor did I, but I suppose it comes to us all. See, Jamie, this one would do fine for your cows, would it not?' Allan picked up one of the boxes and handed it to the little boy, who considered it carefully, then said, 'No, for my friends that went away.'

'Your friends?' Allan looked at him blankly, then at Jennet, who mouthed, 'The pigs.'

'They runned away,' Jamie said. 'All lost.'

'Mebbe they're having a wee holiday,' Allan improvised.

'No, got lost,' Jamie said sadly; then, picking up one of his toy pigs, 'This one won't, 'cos I'll smack it if it does.'

'I was wonderin'. . .' Allan said casually to Angus over the child's bent head, 'have you never thought of raising beef here at Westervoe?'

'Why would we want to do that?'

'There's money in it, for one thing. Now that the war's by, the Government'll be easin' up on the need for crops, and this farm could do well with beef cattle.'

'The local butcher would do quite nicely out of the idea, too,' Jennet put in from the table, where she was kneading bread. His blue eyes met her grey stare unblinkingly.

'It's your interests I'm considering more than my own, though I'd not deny that it would be of benefit to me, as well as to Angus . . . and you.'

'We've always had the dairy herd, and we've always grown the crops to feed and bed them. That's the way Westervoe works.'

'I don't know, Jennet,' Angus put in thoughtfully. 'Allan might have a point.'

'The point is that we've just taken over this place. We have to run it as it is for a year at least before we start trying to change things.'

'What about the deep-litter house?' her brother asked mildly, but with an amused glint in his eye.

'That's different.'

'That's what women aye say,' Angus challenged, and she slammed the soft bread dough down on the table.

'It *is* different! Those old arks wouldn't have seen us through another winter and we didn't have the money to buy new ones. The stable wasn't being used and it made sense to get some of the hens into it.' She almost threw the dough into the loaf tin, saying over her shoulder as she put the tin into the oven, 'We stay as we are, for at least a year; that was our arrangement, Angus. I stay for a year till we get settled, and after that I go back to my training and you can do what you want with the place.'

Allan, who had been sprawled on the floor helping Jamie to move the herd of small wooden cows that had once belonged to Angus and Martin, sat upright on the floor. 'You're planning on going back to Glasgow?' he asked Jennet.

'Mebbe. If I want to.' She turned on the tap and began to wash her hands.

'It's the only way I'd agree to take this place on,' Angus explained. 'Jennet's got her own life to lead and I don't want to see her stuck on the farm the way our grandmother was.'

'And I've told you that perhaps that's what I want for myself and for Jamie. He likes farming.' Jennet nodded at her son, totally absorbed in laying out his little cardboard-box farm.

'You could come back here after you've finished your training, if you're so set on it. At least you'd have a trade to go to, if things didn't work out here.'

'They will.'

'You're as stubborn as the old woman,' Angus grumbled.

'Are you trying to get rid of me? Is that it?'

'I'm trying to look out for you. Tell her to finish her nursing, Allan, mebbe she'll listen to you.'

'I doubt if she'll mind a word I say,' Allan said. Then, getting up, 'I'd best be getting back to Gleniffer. My mother doesnae like it if any of us are late at the table.'

Jennet took advantage of the quieter working days to take Jamie to Rothesay as often as possible. She felt that it was good for the little boy to be with other folk, and it meant that she could spend time with Mollie, who seemed reluctant to visit Westervoe.

'I'd just be in the way there,' she said when Jennet wanted to know why.

'How could you ever be in the way? You're one of the family now, surely you know that?'

'I'm not certain that Angus would agree with you.'

'You know he has his moods. They don't mean anything.' Jennet had found Mollie painting one of the guest bedrooms, while her mother whirred away at the sewing machine in the kitchen, repairing some bedding, and Ann turned out another guest room. They could hear her now, shifting furniture about. Alice had taken Jamie off to the workshop where her father and Sam were getting the boats ready for the next holiday season. Joe, a summer employee, had found other work in town for the winter.

'Angus works hard and he deserves peace and quiet when he's in the house.'

'He can get it in his own room if he wants it. I think he's missing you,' Jennet said, and Mollie, applying cream paint to the frame of the door, paused and glanced over her shoulder.

'Has he said anything?'

'No, but I know Angus. He's awful quiet.'

'He always is.' Mollie returned to her work.

'Quieter than usual, I mean. Is there another brush?' Jennet wanted to know. 'I'm not used to doing nothing.'

'You can sandpaper that skirting if you like.' After a long pause in which she concentrated on smoothing the paint evenly while Jennet, on her knees, worked away at the skirting board, Mollie went on, 'I'm walking out with Joe again.'

'That's nice, I like Joe. You took your time forgiving the poor lad.'

'I'm not sure I have forgiven him. I don't really care one way or the other.'

'Why are you going out with him, then?'

'He kept asking, and he's a good dancer. And I don't like going to the pictures on my own,' said Mollie, who had found work in one of the Rothesay shops.

Jennet gave a startled exclamation as the little bit of sandpaper she was holding hit against a knot in the wood, catching her fingernail. She stuck it in her mouth and then said round it, 'That doesn't sound very romantic.'

'I've given up on romance,' Mollie said. 'And I suppose Joe's better than nothing.'

'Does he know that?'

'Of course not, you know how easily hurt men are.'

'You and Jamie go, and stay on if you like,' Angus said when Jennet announced after one of her trips to Rothesay that Ann Logan wanted to celebrate the first peacetime Christmas with a family party on Christmas Eve. 'I'll stay here and see to the place.'

'You're not going to miss Christmas, surely?'

'I'm not bothered; you know we never do much at Christmas anyway.'

'You mean Grandmother never did much.' Jennet rubbed tears from her eyes with the back of a gloved hand. She was helping him to repair one of the gates, which meant that they were right out in the open and in the path of a biting wind. 'We're on our own now and we have to make our own rules. And Jamie needs a proper family Christmas,' she argued.

Her brothers had never been as close to their aunt and uncle as she was, although they had helped out with the boats occasionally and they had been friendly with Geordie Logan and had enlisted alongside him when war broke out. As Jennet had said to Mollie, Angus seemed to be lonely these days, and she dearly wanted to draw him into the warmth of the Logan family circle.

'It'll be grand,' she pushed on. 'Bert and Helen will be there, and Alice and her young man, and Sam's girlfriend and . . .'

'And Aunt Ann and Uncle George and Mollie, and mebbe that fellow Joe that Mollie's sweet on.'

'I don't think she's sweet on him; she just goes out with him for company. If you ask me,' Jennet said thoughtfully, 'there's someone else on her mind.'

Angus's head, bent over his work, came up suddenly. 'Why? What did she say to you?'

'Nothing at all – that's what makes it so strange. Mebbe he's married already. I hope not,' Jennet fretted. 'It would be terrible for her.'

Angus went back to his work, driving a nail into the gate with hefty blows of his hammer. 'It sounds to me as if you're letting your imagination loose.'

'I wish she'd stayed on here, with us.'

'We'd no need of her here.'

'I had need of her.'

Angus gave the gate an experimental push. It swung

slowly into place and he latched it. 'That's that done. Come on, let's get out of this wind.'

'You'll come to Rothesay with me and Jamie on Christmas Eve?' Jennet nagged as they hurried back to the farmhouse.

'Mebbe. I'll see.'

'And we'll have a proper time of it here, too, for Bert and Helen as well, if they want to spend the day with us. I'm going to bring out the decorations we used to put up, and make a pudding and get some mincemeat for pies. Struan's offered to bring a wee tree over for Jamie.' Jennet put a gloved hand on her brother's arm. 'Imagine, Angus, this'll be his very first proper Christmas!'

If it hadn't been for his accident, Angus Scott might well have married the Saltcoats lassie he had been courting before the war. She had certainly been willing enough, and on his way to see her, immediately after enlisting in the Army, Angus had intended to ask her to be his wife. He liked the thought of knowing, while he was away fighting for King and country, that she was waiting for him at home, his ring on her finger.

But the train had never reached the station and on the girl's first, and last, visit to the hospital Angus had looked into her eyes and read his own future in them . . . a useless cripple, no good to any woman. Watching her walk swiftly from the ward and knowing, although she had not been able to bring

herself to tell him to his face, that she would not be
back, he had given up for ever on his dreams of one
day having a wife and family of his own. Then Mollie
McCabe had marched into the farmyard, clutching an
untidy brown-paper parcel in her arms, limp red hair
flopping about her pale face as she ordered his grandmother to call Gumrie off.

At first she and her family had simply been an
unwelcome invasion, one of the necessary evils of
war as far as Angus was concerned; then, as Mollie
began to nag him into becoming mobile again, she
had become a nuisance, a stone in his shoe or, he
thought as he lay in bed that night, trying to read, the
grain of sand that irritates the oyster.

Clearly imposed on the printed page before him he
could still see her dazzling smile on the day he walked
round the kitchen table using only one crutch. Then
the picture changed, and kept on changing. Mollie
lugging heavy pails of pig food out to the sty was
swiftly followed by Mollie tossing Jamie up in the
air, Mollie frowning with concentration, the tip of her
tongue sticking out from the corner of her mouth, as
she carefully fluted the edge of the pie she had just
made.

He blinked hard and began to read his book,
concentrating on the first line, the second and half of
the third before she swam back onto the page, this
time leaping from the kitchen chair in a swirl of long
tea-tanned legs, cream petticoat and floral skirt on the
day he had walked in to find Jennet drawing a mock

seam up the back of her legs. Then came Mollie struggling out from beneath the threshing mill, exhausted and covered with chaff, but refusing to give in and give up. And Mollie later that night, her glowing freshly washed hair swinging round her face as she looked for pictures in the fire.

Angus laid down the book and rubbed at his face with both hands. The fanciful comparison between her and the oyster's grain of sand had been nearer the point than he first thought, for Mollie had, in time, become a pearl.

'Jennet's not the only reason I love this place,' she had said to him in Nero's stable as Jennet went to tell their grandmother that she wanted Angus to be allowed to run the farm. Startled, unable to believe that Mollie could possibly be trying to say that she cared for him in the way he cared for her, he had turned his back. And later, like a fool, he had sent her away from Westervoe.

He groaned aloud and threw his book across the room so vigorously that the back of his hand connected with the solid cupboard by his bed, sending a bolt of pain up his arm from the bruised knuckles.

He had shied away from the Logans' Christmas Eve invitation because he could not bear the thought of having to watch Mollie with her sweetheart; despite what Jennet had said earlier about her friend looking on Joe merely as good company, Angus was convinced that the young man was just the sort to suit someone as lively as Mollie McCabe. But now, rubbing his aching fist with the fingers of the other hand, he knew that he had to go, for not seeing her at all would be worse than seeing her with Joe.

His mind made up, Angus turned out the lamp and then wished he had kept it on, because all at once the darkness was filled with images of Mollie.

23

Sam McCabe opened the door to Jennet and Jamie on Christmas Eve, and immediately pulled them through the hall and into the Logans' front parlour.

'Look at this!' He scooped Jamie up into his arms. 'Look at the pretty things, Jamie!' he said, and the little boy's eyes rounded as he looked up at the ceiling, where homemade paper chains hung from corner to corner and looped across the top of each wall.

'They're in the kitchen too, and out in the hall. I helped tae make them,' Sam told Jennet proudly. 'Me and Alice, mostly. And look at this . . .' He led her to the bay window to show her the small tree, hung with silver balls. 'We've all been collectin' silver paper for ages. Isn't it bonny?'

'It is.' Jennet's eyes were on the tiny wooden Nativity scene . . . Mary and Joseph, the child in the manger, the shepherds and wise men and the animals. Her cousin Geordie had carved all the little figures several years ago, and they were brought out every year.

'Did you bring presents?' Sam asked anxiously, beaming when she assured him that she had. He helped her to take them out of her bag and lay them with the others beneath the tree, while Jamie looked on, stunned by the colour and the excitement; silent for once and sucking at one of his woollen mittens.

Mollie hurried into the room, then stopped short at the sight of them. 'Jennet! I didnae know you'd arrived.' She clapped a hand to her head, which was covered in rag curlers, her eyes searching the room, then said, 'Is Angus not with you?'

'He'll be along later with Bert and Helen, once the milking's done. What's this?' Jennet nodded at the curlers and her friend flushed crimson.

'I just fancied a change, that's all.'

'She's getting all prettied up for Joe,' Sam smirked, and Mollie glared at him.

'I'm nothing of the kind. And why didn't you tell us that Jennet and Jamie were here?'

'We were just comin' along tae the kitchen. I wanted tae show them the decorations and the tree first.' Sam took Jamie's hand. 'Come on up to my room with me, wee man, you can help me to make some more chains.'

'Don't get him all covered with glue,' his sister called after him, and then, to Jennet, 'He's not all that grown up, even if he does have a girlfriend. He's been as excited as a bairn all week. Right enough, we've never had a Christmas like this. It's goin' to be great!'

Nesta, Ann and Alice were in the kitchen, stirring

and mixing and rolling for all they were worth. The gas oven and all the gas rings were in use, and chilly though the day was, the door leading out to the long back garden with George Logan's workshop at the end of it lay open to let some air into the hot, stuffy room.

Jennet assured them that Helen was bringing the leg of pork and the baking that the two of them had prepared at Westervoe, then she took her coat off and set to work along with the others. By midday the preparations were almost complete, and after a quick snack to keep them going Mollie insisted on taking Jennet upstairs to help her with her hair.

'I should really take Jamie off Sam's hands,' Jennet said, 'for the poor lad's been looking after him for the past two hours.' Sam and Jamie had arrived downstairs in search of food, then gone into the parlour.

'Ach, he'll be enjoying himself now he's got someone of his own age to play with at last,' Sam's sister said callously; then, opening the parlour door, 'I hope you two aren't making a mess in here.'

'I'm teaching him tae play Snap,' Jennet heard Sam declare proudly. She looked over Mollie's shoulder to see both boys sitting cross-legged on the carpet, surrounded by playing cards.

'Aye, well, just remember that he's wee, so there's no gamblin' allowed,' his sister told him while Jamie yelled 'Snap!'

'That's no' fair, I wasnae lookin'!' Jennet heard Sam protest as Mollie closed the door.

Going upstairs she indicated the banisters, fes-
tooned with paper chains. 'Would you look at that?
He's covered the whole place! Bless him, it's the first
decent Christmas he's ever had and it'll take him
months to get over it.'

Five minutes later, looking at her reflection in the
small mirror, she wailed, 'Straight as a stair rod! I've
been in agony all night with these curlers and I've
not got a single curl tae show for it!'

'But your hair's lovely,' Jennet said truthfully.
'Look at the way it falls.'

'Aye, straight down from top tae bottom. I wish I'd
been born with curly hair like yours. Even our Senga
has a bit of a curl in her hair, but not me!'

Jennet tugged at a handful of her own hair, held
back today by a blue ribbon that matched her skirt
and the embroidery on her white blouse. 'I wish you'd
this hair too,' she said ruefully. 'Yours is more . . .
stylish.'

'Humph. It's not worth putting on my new dress
now.'

'Of course it is. Let me see it,' Jennet commanded,
then gasped when Mollie brought it out from behind
the curtain that filled in as a wardrobe. 'Oh, Mollie,
it's lovely!'

'D'ye like it?' Mollie held the dress out at arm's
length. 'The material used up all my clothing coupons,
and Mam helped me to make it. I just wanted tae have
somethin' special for once.'

'Put it on,' Jennet ordered. Then as Mollie pulled

her jersey and skirt off and reached for the petticoat spread over the bed, 'You've lost weight.'

'Only a wee bit.' Mollie's rounded arms were definitely thinner, as was her waist; her face, Jennet suddenly realised, was thinner too, the cheekbones more prominent.

'Is there something wrong? Are you not eating properly?' Mollie had always had a good appetite.

'Like a horse, same as usual. And I'm fine.' Mollie slipped the petticoat on, then the dress. 'How do I look?'

'Wonderful,' Jennet said, and meant it. The dress, in a soft, woollen material that shaped itself to Mollie's body, was a pale oatmeal colour – a surprise in itself, since Mollie tended to like patterns. Trimmed with dark green velveteen at the hem, it had a V-shaped collar, cuffs on the short sleeves and wrapped around to button down one side to the hem, with large buttons a shade lighter than the trimming. A tie belt of green velveteen accentuated Mollie's trim waist and the straight skirt made her look tall and elegant.

Mollie twisted and turned, trying to see herself from all angles in the small mirror. 'D'you not think it would look better with curls?'

'Don't be daft, your hair looks just right with it.'

'If you're sure . . .' Mollie studied her reflection, chewed nervously at her lower lip and then, as though coming to a decision, began, 'Jennet . . .'

'What?'

'Is that the door knocker?' Mollie jumped to her feet. 'Mebbe it's Angus. Come on, let's go down.'

Joe, dressed in his best and with his hair oiled and smoothed back, caught up with Angus, Bert and Helen as they walked along to the Scotts' door. He and Bert greeted each other like old friends, and Angus's hope that the young man was bound for another house faded as Joe turned in at the gate with them.

Alice opened the door and as they all surged into the narrow hall, Joe, one step ahead of Angus, looked up and gave a long, admiring whistle. Following his glance, Angus stopped in the doorway at the sight of Mollie standing halfway up the stairs, the creamy shade of her dress complementing her red hair, which lay about her face like a cap of autumn leaves.

For a moment Angus's world stood still and then Joe, moving forward to lean on the banister, said, 'You look good enough tae eat!'

'I always thought that was a daft thing to say,' Mollie said tartly, continuing on her way down to the hall. 'Angus, are you goin' tae come in and close the door, before Sam's paper chains get blown down from the ceiling? The men are all out in the workshop at the back if ye want tae go through. We'll call you when the dinner's ready.'

Before the war, whenever they could slip away from the farm and from their grandmother's control, Angus and Martin had enjoyed helping their uncle and their cousin George with the boats; but so much had

happened to change Angus's life since then that his
teenage years had become more of a dream memory
than reality. He had not visited his uncle's workshop
for years, and he had forgotten how soothing the
mingled smells of paint and varnish, sawdust and glue
could be.

The boat George Logan was building with Sam's
help took up most of the space in the centre of the
shop. The men gathered around it while Jamie, who
had found a pile of sawdust, pawed through it gleefully. After a few minutes Angus retreated to the bench
alongside one wall, where he sat listening to his
normally shy uncle talking animatedly about his boats.

Joe detached himself from the group and came to
sit on the bench, offering his packet of Woodbine.
Angus, who had not smoked for years because his
grandmother disapproved of the waste of money, hesitated and then took one. The workshop was already
filled with fragrant blue smoke from Bert's cigarette
and George Logan's beloved pipe.

Joe struck a match and lit Angus's cigarette, then
his own. 'Too strong for you?' he asked as Angus
began to cough.

'It's fine, but I've not smoked for a while. There's
never time for a cigarette on a farm.' Angus took a
second drag, and this time the smoke went sweetly
down into his lungs.

'Ye'll be glad Mollie's moved back here,' Joe said.
Then, as Angus stared at him, puzzled, 'It means that
now you don't have me callin' in and botherin' you.'

'Oh, it wasn't a bother,' Angus lied.

'She said it was. She was always gettin' on at me about it; she said you didnae like folk hangin' around the place. But I couldnae stay away. I missed her,' Joe confessed. He glanced at the others and then turned back to Angus, edging along the bench and lowering his voice. 'I made a bit of a fool of myself when her sister was over for Bert's wedding. Mollie was ragin' about it; she'd not talk tae me for weeks after. She mebbe told you about it?'

'We didn't talk all that much,' Angus said uncomfortably. 'She's my sister's friend.'

'I know.' Joe had been looking wretched during his confession, but now he summoned up a faint smile. 'She told me about the two of them bein' skin sisters. You'll know all about that,' he swept on while Angus struggled to make sense of the phrase, 'the two of them tryin' tae mix their blood when they were younger, and the knife bein' blunt and them not havin' the courage tae go through with it, so they just say they're skin sisters instead of blood sisters. Mollie thinks a lot of your Jennet, and she thinks a lot of you, too.'

'Does she?'

'Oh aye.' Joe moistened his lips with the tip of his tongue and glanced round again to make sure that he was not overheard. 'That's why I wondered if you knew what she thought about me, because I want tae ask her tae marry me and I'd not like tae set her off again by askin' at the wrong time. You've known her a lot longer than I have, so I wondered, what d'you think?' He finally ended the rush of words and peered hopefully into Angus's face.

'When . . .' Angus started, then coughed as the words caught in his throat, and tried again. 'When were you going to ask her?'

'My ma always says that the New Year's a good time for new beginnings, but I'm not certain.' Joe pulled a shred of tobacco from his lip. 'I was thinkin' of waitin' for a month or two more, for the thing is, Mollie can be right sharp when she's put out and I'd not want tae do the wrong thing. Has she ever said anythin' tae you about her feelin's for me?'

'Mebbe you should ask my sister about that,' Angus said, and Joe's eyes widened.

'I couldnae ask her, she'd only tell Mollie and then the two of them would get a right laugh. I know about lassies, I've got two sisters of my own and they're never off the gossip. I feel right sorry for the lads they go out with. I think I'll go ahead and ask her,' Joe said. 'I'm ready for settlin' down and I've been offered work at a garage in Rothesay, with enough pay tae cover the rent on a wee house. I'd work hard for Mollie, and I'd respect her and take care of her, ye neednae worry about that.'

'I'm sure you would,' Angus said. Five minutes earlier, at the sight of Mollie on the stairs, his world had stopped; now, in the smoky atmosphere of his uncle's workshop, he felt as though it was ending altogether. Best, perhaps, to get the misery over with.

Perhaps the knowledge that Mollie was lost to him for ever would help him to start looking forward instead of back.

'Mebbe the New Year would be the best time,' he said to the man who was dashing his hopes so cruelly. 'As your mother says, it's a time of new beginnings.'

'Ye think so?' Joe reached out and shook him warmly by the hand. 'Thanks, Mr Scott, for your advice. I appreciate it. It's grand tae be able tae talk tae an older man at a time like this,' he said.

Helen, considerably bulkier now than she had been at her marriage only weeks earlier, had insisted on helping in the kitchen despite Ann's attempts to get her to rest before the party began.

'This kitchen's awful hot for a lassie in your condition and there's a nice sofa in the parlour,' she coaxed, but Helen shook her head.

'I'm best to be workin', and anyway, Satan finds mischief for idle hands.'

'If that's an orphanage upbringing for you, I'm glad I didnae have one,' Mollie murmured to Jennet and Alice.

Ann, who had sharp ears, glared at her and then asked, 'Have you heard from your gran, Jennet?'

'A letter and a wee card, and some money to buy presents. We sent her a cardigan and a nice card.'

'She'd no thought of coming over for Christmas or the New Year, or mebbe having you over to Largs?'

'We couldn't leave the farm, and from what she says she's got no notion to come back to Bute,' Jennet said thankfully. That was one worry over . . . like Martin, her grandmother had clearly given up all claims to the farm and now all that she and Angus had to worry about was keeping the place viable.

When they finally got back to Westervoe Jennet carried Jamie upstairs and put him to bed, while Angus went out to make sure that the animals were comfortable. She went downstairs just as he returned to the kitchen.

'It was a grand party.'

'It was all right.'

'Did you not enjoy yourself?'

'I'm not one for parties, you know that.'

'Mebbe if you made more of an effort,' Jennet said, irritated by his scowl, 'you'd have enjoyed yourself better. If we'd all spent the evening sitting in corners the way you did, nobody would have had a good time.'

'You wanted me to go, and I went,' he snapped back at her. 'Just be grateful for that!'

'I am, but I wish that . . . D'you not want a cup of tea and a bit of cake?' Jennet asked as he made for the inner door.

'I'd prefer my bed and my own company.' The door slammed shut behind him on the last word, leaving her to wonder what could have happened to put him in such a bad temper.

Fortunately he was in a better mood in the morning,

though he looked as though he had not slept well and
he stayed behind while Bert took the others to church,
crowded together in the cart with Nero between the
shafts.

After the service Struan and Allan both slipped
parcels to Jennet when their mother's attention was
elsewhere. Allan's, she discovered when she got
home, held a small mouth organ for Jamie, and
Struan's gift to the little boy was a wooden tractor.
His parcel also contained a smart pair of ladies'
gloves. She pushed them hurriedly into her apron
pocket, then hid them later in a drawer in her bedroom
and fretted about them for several days. Clearly,
Struan had not given up his hopes of marrying her.

'Be kind tae him, you said. He's a decent lad, you
said. And what thanks do I get for bein' kind?' Mollie
wanted to know, then answered her own question. 'He
turns round and asks me to marry him!'

'But surely it's nice to get a proposal of marriage?'
Jennet had taken Jamie along to Rothesay to wish
everyone a happy New Year and had scarcely had time
to drink her aunt's homemade ginger cordial and
savour a slice of Nesta's rich fruit cake before Mollie
whisked her out for a walk, pleading a headache and
the need for fresh air. Now the two of them marched
briskly along the Esplanade in the teeth of a howling
and icy gale.

'You didnae think it was nice when Struan Blaikie
asked you to marry him, did you? Anyway, I'm still

angry with Joe over the way he went running after Senga.'

'He should mebbe have waited for a few months longer.'

'Or until hell froze over,' Mollie snapped, walking even faster.

'I hope you didn't say that to him?'

'No, but I did say that I'd not fancy standing there in my wedding dress and veil watchin' my bridegroom makin' eyes at Senga.'

'Oh, Mollie! Hold on, I've got a stitch.' Jennet clutched the railing with one gloved hand and pressed the other deep into her side. 'Does your mother know?' she wheezed when she had caught her breath.

'No, of course not.'

'I won't tell.'

'Is that stitch not gone yet?'

Jennet took her fist from her side and walked a few steps. 'It's easier, but I'm turning back to the house now, for I'm frozen!'

'You mean she turned him down?' Angus asked, astonished, when she told him.

'She says he's not the right one for her. I think there's someone else she cares about, but I can't think . . .' Jennet began, then stopped as she saw that Angus had lost interest and had disappeared behind his newspaper again.

24

Struan Blaikie made his move towards the end of January, arriving at Westervoe on a miserably wet day. The hens, unable to get out to scratch about, sulked in their arks and in the deep-litter house, while Gumrie stuck like glue to the kitchen range, whining pitifully when Angus tried to make him go outside.

'Call yourself a working dog?' he had finally roared at the animal. 'It's time we got ourselves a proper dog for this place!'

'He's good at his work.' Jennet had tried to defend Gumrie, who crouched by the range with his ears back and his tail flopping gently in apology for his own weaknesses, 'And if you'd to fetch the cows in, he'd be there with you no matter the weather. You know that.'

'I know that we've put up with his nonsense for long enough. Another dog . . . then you'll not be needed any more!' her brother hissed at Gumrie before limping out into the downpour.

Jamie, anxious to play with the small second-hand tricycle they had bought him for Christmas, grizzled all afternoon and Jennet was almost at her wits' end with him when Struan arrived, shaking rainwater from his jacket and taking care to wipe the worst of the mud from his boots before stepping into the kitchen.

'Angus's gone off to see about buying in seed potatoes,' Jennet informed him.

'If this weather settles in it'll be a while before we can plant them.' Early potatoes were planted in the first two months of the year and lifted in June.

'There's time yet. We're nearly finished getting the field ready. Jamie, stop that,' she added to the little boy, who was following her around and tugging at her britches.

'Want to go out!'

Jennet glanced through the window and saw that the rain had eased to a light drizzle. 'All right, if you must, you must. Go and fetch your jacket and your boots.'

'Are you sure?' Struan asked doubtfully as the little boy, beaming, hurried to the short passage between the farm kitchen and the rest of the house. 'It's still raining out there – he could catch his death.'

'He'll not melt, and he'll be back in as soon as he starts to feel miserable. In the meantime, at least I'll have had a bit of peace.' Jennet knelt down to help her son as he came staggering back to the kitchen, the wrong arm through one sleeve of his jacket and his boots tucked precariously beneath the other arm.

'Stand still now, for the sooner you're ready, the sooner you'll get out.'

'The bike's in the wee outhouse, d'you think you could get it for him?' she asked Struan, and by the time she had dressed Jamie and clapped a cap on his head, ignoring his protests, Struan was wheeling the tricycle into the yard.

'He seems quite happy out there in the wet,' he said when he returned.

'He's of farming stock, he might as well get used to the weather.' She went on with her baking. 'Do you want to see Angus about something? He'll not be back for a while.'

'Nothing important.' He went to the window to peer out. 'Jamie's splashing through all the puddles,' he reported.

'I've no doubt of that.' Jennet put the scones into the oven and dusted some flour from her hands.

'He's fairly growing, Jennet.'

'Aye, and more of a handful with every day.' Jamie had become livelier since Celia Scott's departure. Now that there was no need for him to be seen but not heard, Jennet found herself having to put him in his place regularly.

Struan moved away from the sink to let her wash her hands and then asked, his voice carefully casual, 'Did the gloves fit all right?'

'The . . . ? Oh, yes, they're lovely.' She had almost forgotten about his gift. 'I'm sorry, I never got the chance to thank you for them.'

'That's all right, I just wondered because I'm not used to buying things for women,' he said. Then he rushed on, 'I got a letter from Martin the other day. He said he'd written to you as well.'

'That's right. He seems well settled.' Martin had written just before Christmas to tell them that he and the girl he fancied now had 'an understanding'.

'He says he's not coming back.'

'We knew that already.'

'That's a pity. Angus could mebbe do with his help.'

'Angus – and me – are managing fine without him.'

'But it puts a lot on your shoulders, Jennet.'

'Away you go; plenty of women on Bute have run their own farms.'

'But is that what you want?'

'For the moment, yes, it is.' Jennet took one of Angus's shirts from the clotheshorse, where it had been airing, and began to fold it. 'We've agreed that if I want to go back to nursing after that, Angus can manage on his own with Norrie and Bert and a bit of help from Jem, if needed.'

'You're thinkin' of leavin' the island again?'

'I don't know for sure.' She picked up a pair of Jamie's trousers, noted that they needed patching and put them aside instead of folding them. 'I'm giving this place a year before I make up my mind as to what to do next.'

'Have you thought any more about my offer?' Struan asked, and her heart sank.

'I've thought about it a lot and the answer's still

the same. I've no notion to marry anyone just now. Mebbe not ever.'

'I'm not just asking for myself,' he said. 'My mother wasnae too good at Ne'erday, she couldnae stop thinking about our Drew. I know it's been a few years now, but my father says it's preyed on her mind every Ne'erday since, and with me and Allan both back home, and Drew not with us, it was worse for her this year.'

'I'm sorry to hear that, but I doubt if you marrying me would make her feel any better.'

'Are you certain sure, Jennet,' he said, 'that that wee lad out there isnae our Drew's bairn?'

Jennet, about to put the clotheshorse away, banged it down again. 'I've told you he's not and if I have to, I'll swear to it on the Bible! And even if he was . . . which he's not,' she added swiftly, 'I don't think much of you wanting to marry me just so that you can give Jamie to your mother as a ready-made grandson!'

'It's not the only reason . . .'

'It seems to me to be a strong one, though. It makes you a good son, Struan, but a poor husband, so why can't . . .'

'I love you,' he said loudly. Then as she stopped, letting a silence wash over them both, he cleared his throat before saying it again, quietly this time. 'I . . . I love ye, Jennet. It's not an easy thing to say, but there it is.'

The shock of the declaration left her speechless.

'I should mebbe have said that when I asked ye before, but words like that don't come easy tae a man like me,' he blundered on while she was still trying to collect her thoughts.

'I know that, Struan, and I'm touched by what you say. But it doesn't make any difference to the way I feel.'

'So ye'll not have me.'

'I'm not the right one for you . . . I'm not,' she insisted as he opened his mouth to protest. 'If I was, I'd surely feel the same way about you. But I don't. I like you as the friend you always were, but that's all.'

'So. Well.' He shuffled his feet uncomfortably, then said, 'I suppose I'd best just get back to Gleniffer then.'

'Yes.' She followed him to the door, wishing she could find something else to say, but knowing that any attempt to comfort him would probably lead him to think that he might still have a chance of breaking down her resolve.

Instead of lessening, the drizzle had become a downpour again; rain teemed down from a low, grey sky, to bounce on the cobbles and splash into the puddles. The hens and cats that were usually scattered about the yard had found shelter and the only living creatures left in the place were Struan's dog, huddled against the house wall, and Jamie, careering round and round on his tricycle and screaming with pleasure every time the wheels ran through a puddle,

throwing up a bow-wave of water. He showed no signs
of becoming miserable. His cap, discarded, lay near
the farm door and his light brown hair, normally as
curly as his mother's, was darkened by water and plas-
tered to his neat little skull, making him look entirely
different.

'Look at me,' he shrieked when he spotted his audience, circling the bike round and away, laughing back
over his shoulder at them, one eyebrow lifted and his
grinning mouth, from that angle, seeming to tilt more
at one corner than at the other.

Struan, pulling on his own cap, suddenly tensed.
From where she stood close behind him and slightly
to one side, Jennet could feel the muscles and bones
of his back stiffen. He stood motionless, his hands
by his head, until Jamie had rounded the top of his
circle and was coming back towards them, grinning.
Then Struan lowered his arms and turned to Jennet,
his eyes boring down into hers.

'I'm such a fool,' he said. 'God, you must have
been laughing at me all this time!'

'Why should I laugh at you?'

'Not Drew,' he said. 'You told me the truth when
you said it wasnae our Drew. But I knew as soon as
I looked at him that he was a Blaikie. He's Allan's
bairn, isn't he?' Then, as she stared back at him, mute,
'Ye cannae deny me this time, can ye? I've been such
a damned fool!'

'Struan, wait!' As he called his dog and strode away
from her, splashing across the yard, Jennet ran after

him into the rain, then had to give up as he passed
Jamie without a glance and stormed into the lane.

'Look, Mummy,' Jamie clamoured, the bike wheels
throwing water over Jennet. She didn't notice, but
stood in the rain, staring after Struan.

Struan was halfway along the road that led to
Rothesay when he remembered that it was early
closing day, and his brother would probably be back
at the farm. He swung round so abruptly that he
almost fell over the dog trotting close to his heels.

'Out of my way,' he roared at it, and began the
walk back to Gleniffer. By the time he reached the
farm the persistent rain had soaked its way through
his clothing and chilled his skin, but he ignored the
discomfort as he threw the door back on its hinges
and marched into the big kitchen where his mother,
as usual, was working at the range. Allan sat at the
table, paperwork from the shop spread out before
him.

'Struan, would you look at the mess you've brought
in with you,' Lizbeth Blaikie yelped, staring at the
spreading pool of water about his feet. 'Get back
outside to the wee porch and take your boots and your
coat off this minute!' Then, taking in the water
cascading unchecked from his hair to run over his
face and down his neck, 'You're soaked through, man,
where have you been?'

'Visitin',' he informed her, his eyes on his brother.
After glancing up Allan had returned to his paper, but

when Struan went on, 'Visitin' . . . with his bastard', Allan's head jerked up again.

'Don't you dare to use such language in this house!' Lizbeth said sharply. 'I'll have no blaspheming here.'

Struan turned his head to look at her, spraying her jersey with droplets. 'It's only blasphemy when it's a lie, Mother,' he informed her. Then, looking back to Allan, 'And this isnae a lie. I've been over at Westervoe . . .' a forefinger came up to stab towards Allan, 'visitin' his bastard and his whore!'

'Catherine,' Lizbeth rounded on the new maid, who stood at the inner door, her eyes wide in a shocked face, 'go upstairs at once and make the beds!'

'I made them hours ago, missus.'

'Then make them again. Go on when I tell you,' Lizbeth shrieked as the girl hesitated. Then when she had fled, 'What's going on here? Where's your father? He's never here when he's needed.'

'He's not needed now,' Struan tossed the words at her. 'I can handle this. Well, Allan, are ye going tae deny what I'm sayin'? Goin' tae call me a liar, are ye?'

Allan, on his feet now, glanced at his mother. 'Come outside, Struan. This is something best discussed between the two of us.'

'I think my mother should hear what you have to say.'

'So do I.' Lizbeth's normally ruddy face had turned as white as milk. 'What's he haverin' about, Allan?'

He ignored her, concentrating on his brother. 'What did Jennet tell you?'

'Don't fret, she didnae spill yer secret. She's been loyal tae ye, though God knows why. It was the bairn himself . . . I could see it in his face from the time I came back home, but I thought he was Drew's bairn. That's why I wanted tae marry her, tae give him his rightful name . . .'

'*You* want to marry Jennet?' Allan asked.

'What's wrong with that?'

'What's wrong with it?' his mother chimed in. 'You were going to bring that lassie and her . . . her . . .'

'The word's bastard, Mother,' Struan said clearly.

'. . . into my house? How could you?'

'Oh, don't fret; she turned me down, the first time I asked and again the second time. Mind you,' Struan said, his mouth smiling thinly at Allan though his eyes were murderous, 'who can blame her? It's one thing, our Drew not bein' able tae acknowledge his own bairn because he's dead, but it's another for you tae leave him without a name.'

'Hold your tongue!'

'That's just what I'll not do, now that I know. I looked at him today, Allan, and I saw your face lookin' back at me as clear as if you'd been standin' there. And Jennet couldnae deny it when I challenged her. So I'm not goin' tae hold my tongue at all. I'm goin' tae see that this whole island knows what ye've done, and how ye deserted her and the bairn.'

'It's not just me you'll shame, it's her and the wee one as well.'

'Jennet's been shamed since the day you fathered

the bairn on her. And he was shamed the day he was conceived,' Struan said. 'But you've got away with it until now. Not any more, Allan. I'm goin' to see that you're shamed the length and breadth of Bute. I'll see you hounded off this island and out of my . . .'

The words became a gurgle as Allan caught him by the throat, shaking him so hard that raindrops from his hair and clothing sprayed the kitchen.

'Stop it,' Lizbeth shrieked as Struan fisted his hands, then chopped them upwards from his side to break his brother's grip. He sucked in air and would have lunged at Allan there and then if his mother had not pushed her way between them.

'I won't have this in my house, between my two sons! For pity's sake, is it not enough that I've lost Drew without you two trying to kill each other?'

'Outside.' Allan, ignoring her, pushed his brother in the chest and as Struan staggered back he followed, pushing and nudging until Struan was through the open door and into the porch. Before Lizbeth could get through the door the two of them were in the yard and Struan was struggling with his jacket, hauling the sodden weight of it free, then throwing it down onto the ground. Allan stood back until the jacket was clear before launching himself at his brother, who met him halfway.

'Andra!' Lizbeth screamed at the top of her voice. 'Andra, for the love of God . . . !' Then, as her husband emerged from the stable, she flew over to him, dodging her sons as she went, and clutched his arm.

'What's goin' on here?'

'Struan came home with some nonsense about Jennet Scott and the wee . . . He called him a . . .' Lizbeth gabbled. 'And Allan tried tae choke him and now they're . . . Stop them, Andra, stop them before they kill each other!'

'You're gettin' soaked, woman, you'll catch the pneumonia. Come in here.' Andra pulled her into the shelter of the stable, a hard task since she resisted every step of the way.

'Never mind about me, put a stop to them . . . now, Andra!'

As Struan's bunched fist missed his brother's jaw and hit his shoulder, Allan twisted away, caught his heel on a raised flagstone and staggered back, arms windmilling, towards the stable. His father reached out and grabbed at the bottom half of the stable door, swinging it shut.

'Lizbeth,' he said, shooting the bolt home just as his son crashed against the door and then fell to the cobbles, 'I'm gettin' tae be an old man now and it's more than my life's worth tae try tae separate these two, now their blood's up. They're all muscle, the pair of them.'

'But they'll kill each other!' his wife wailed as Allan rolled away from Struan's determined rush and gained his feet, before launching himself back across the stones to grapple with his brother.

'Mebbe not, and even if they do, ye'd not want tae see me dead an' all, would ye?' Andra put an arm about her sturdy shoulders. 'Not after all these years we've spent together. Whatever's botherin' them, it's best tae let them work it out atween their two selves. Then, when the fires have damped down, you and me can chastise the both of them. That's what parents are for, is it no'?' he added soothingly.

As his sons rolled over and over on the wet ground, Allan trying to gouge Struan's eyes out while Struan attempted to bring his knee up into his brother's groin, and his wife had hysterics at his back, Andra Blaikie leaned his folded arms on the top half of the door and prepared to watch one of the bonniest fights he had seen in many a long year.

'Allan Blaikie?' Angus was saying incredulously in the Westervoe kitchen at that same moment. 'Allan Blaikie?'

'Aye, Allan Blaikie. You know who I mean, surely.' After keeping her secret so well for so long, Jennet had found it hard finally to admit the name. But she had no option . . . There was little hope of Struan keeping his mouth shut, and Angus had to hear it from her rather than from one of the Blaikies.

'I thought I knew him, but now I'm wonderin' if I really do.' Angus sank into a chair at the table, staring at her. 'And the same goes for you. I didnae even know that the two of you were . . .'

'We weren't. It was just the once, a daft mistake when he was upset about being a soldier and I was upset about . . . worried about Martin being away from home.' She couldn't admit to Angus that her worries at that time had been for him.

'Why didn't he marry you? Did you not tell him when you found out that . . . you know.'

'I told him, but the way things were we decided against marriage.'

'Both of you? I doubt that,' he said, an edge to his voice. 'You might as well tell me the truth, for if you don't I'll have to go over to Gleniffer and get it out of him.'

She bit her lip and then admitted, 'Allan was just about to be sent overseas when we . . . when I found out that Jamie was on the way. He thought he was going to be killed and he was scared of what his mother would think . . .'

'What his mother would think?' her brother asked in disbelief. 'You were carryin' his child, and you werenae married, and he was more worried about what his mother would think than about you and Jamie? What the hell sort of a man is he?'

'It wasn't as clear as that, not at the time.' She would never have believed, that terrible day in the Glasgow teashop, that she would end up defending Allan and seeing his point of view. 'Drew had recently been killed and you know that the Blaikie boys were nearly as scared of their mother as we were of Gran. He panicked.'

'So you came home on your lone. And you let Grandmother say all those terrible things about you and about the man that fathered Jamie, and you didnae say a word in your own defence?' Anger began to take over from shock. 'Why, in God's name? You should have told us, and the Blaikies. You should have told me, if nobody else, and let me deal with it. It was the least he deserved!'

'You weren't well and, anyway, I didn't want to talk about it! Can you not see that? I was ashamed, and there was no sense in causing more trouble than I already had. I might have set Gran and the Blaikies against each other and I didn't feel strong enough to cope with that sort of thing.'

'So you'd all the worry and Allan got off scot-free.'

'If he survived the war he was going back to work for his uncle in Glasgow. He'd not have been back here, and I thought it was better for me to have Jamie all to myself. D'you think I wanted Mrs Blaikie interfering all the time, criticising the way I was bringing her grandchild up? If Allan's uncle hadn't decided to buy a shop here on the island, and send him over to run it, nobody would ever have been any the wiser.' Her head was throbbing; she put her hands up to support it and felt her way into a chair.

'How did Struan find out?'

'He saw a family likeness in Jamie when he came back from the fighting.'

'I've never seen it myself.'

'When you look at him you just see Jamie, same as me. When he was just born,' Jennet admitted, 'I thought I saw Allan in him, but only in those first hours, and nobody else noticed it, not even Gran. But

Struan did, and it made him think that Drew had fathered Jamie. That's why he asked me to marry him.'

'Struan asked you to marry him?' Angus, gripping the edge of the sink, had been staring out at the darkening afternoon beyond the kitchen window; now he spun round to face her. 'You never told me that, either!'

'Why should I? I turned him down.'

'When was this?'

'Not long after he came home. He knew that Gran wanted to let the farm go and he thought that if I married him the two of you could run Westervoe together. And he wanted to give Jamie the Blaikie name, for Drew's sake.'

'It's Allan who should be offering you marriage, not Struan.'

'He did, when he came back to the island and saw Jamie.'

'He . . . ! Jennet,' Angus said, sitting opposite her, 'is there anything else you've been keeping from me? Because if there is I want to know it now.'

'There's nothing.'

'When Allan offered marriage . . . ?'

'I turned him down because I'm happy the way we are, Angus, with the two of us working the farm together. And Jamie's happy too – he's got you and me, and he's loved.'

'First thing tomorrow I'm going over to Gleniffer to tell Allan what I think of the way he's treated you.' His hands clenched on the table. 'I just wish I was able tae give him the thrashing he deserves.'

'Don't you dare! I just want things to go back to the way they were before.'

'I doubt if you'll get that wish,' Angus said as Jamie, who had been sent off to the parlour with some sheets of paper and some crayons, marched in, his towelled hair still damp, to show them his artwork.

25

———————

Angus vanished the next morning, returning in time for the midday meal. It was late evening before Jennet was able to find out that he had indeed gone to Gleniffer to confront Allan.

'I asked you not to!'

'Nobody's going to treat my sister the way Allan Blaikie treated you, and get away with it. I had to catch him before he went to the shop. Not that he'll be going there today,' Angus added with a touch of satisfaction creeping into his voice, 'for he's a right mess and so is Struan.'

'They had a fight?'

'One of the best, according to Andra. Allan's covered with cuts and bruises and I gave him a right tongue-lashin' into the bargain. I can tell you, Jennet, that he's sorry he ever clapped eyes on you.'

'How is Mrs Blaikie?'

'She's never been as nice to me in her life. She's black affronted by the way Allan's treated you. She sent some of her home preserves over – pickles and jellies. I put them in the kitchen press.'

'So can we just let the whole thing blow over now?' Jennet asked hopefully.

'We can, but I expect the rest of the island's goin' tae have a grand time of it figuring out what happened to set the Blaikie lads against each other.'

The following morning Norrie hurried into the yard to report that on his way to work he had seen Struan, '. . . in a right old mess! His face was like one of those maps we used to have to study at the school, all red and black and blue,' Jennet heard him report gleefully as she came out of the kitchen with a steaming bucket of mash for the hens.

'I wonder what sort of trouble's come up between them two?' Jem said, puzzled.

'A woman, sure as day,' Norrie told him with all the authority of his sixteen years.

'Or money,' Bert hazarded as Angus led Nero from his stable.

'More likely a woman. Struan had a right swollen lip . . .' Norrie was elaborating when Angus intervened.

'And you'll have empty pay packets if you don't get on with your work. The potato field won't get itself ready, and there's silage to fetch and oats to bruise for the animal feed.'

'Wait a minute, Angus, they might as well know the truth of it.'

'Jen . . . !'

'The news will get round sooner or later and I'd as soon our own men heard the right story.' Jennet started to put the bucket down. Then, catching sight of two of the farm cats lurking nearby in hope, she hung it on a hook by the stable door before going to stand by Nero, stroking his strong warm neck for comfort. The horse's breath plumed from his nostrils into the cold morning air.

'Folk don't want the truth, Jen, they prefer to make up their own way of things.'

'I'm tired of keeping secrets. Struan and Allan were fighting because of me,' she told the three men confronting her, 'because Struan found out that Allan fathered wee Jamie.'

There was an uncomfortable silence during which all three farmhands stared at the flagstones as though they had discovered something interesting in the cracks. Then Bert cleared his throat before saying awkwardly, 'It's none of our business, is it?'

'No, it's not, but I thought you should know.'

'And now that you do,' Angus said, 'you can get on with your work.' As the men scattered, grateful for an excuse to be on their way, he asked his sister, 'Did you have to do that?'

'I'm fed up of secrets. The sooner this business is out in the open and gossiped over and then forgotten, the better.' Jennet collected the pail. 'Did you see their faces? They were so embarrassed they didn't know where to look. That means that if someone else

mentions it to them, they'll feel embarrassed all over
again, so they'll not want to talk about it.'

'I doubt if the Blaikies'll thank you for parading
their business all over the place.'

'If I can face folk, then surely they can as well.'

'Somehow,' Angus said, 'I don't think Mrs
Blaikie'll have your courage.'

'That's her worry. Now that I've told Bert,' Jennet
suddenly realised, 'I'd better go and confess to Aunt
Ann and Aunt Nesta and Mollie.'

'What about Grandmother? If you don't tell her,
Mrs Blaikie will.'

Jennet sighed. 'I'll write a letter as soon as the hens
are fed, and post it in Rothesay. Helen'll have to look
after Jamie and see to the meals today, since I'll have
my hands full.'

'Ye've had a bad time of it, pet,' Nesta McCabe said
when Jennet had told the whole story to her and Ann
Logan.

'And you've handled it well,' Ann agreed.

'I don't know about that.'

'You'll stay for your dinner? You might as well,'
Ann said as her niece glanced at the clock. 'By the
time you get back home it'll be the afternoon.'

'Yes, I'll stay. I'll walk down and meet Mollie on
her way back from work.'

'I wish you'd told me before, Jennet,' Mollie said.
'You know I'd not have breathed a word to anyone.'

She gave her friend's shoulders a comforting squeeze, then asked, 'Is it terrible, knowing that everyone knows?'

'To tell you the truth, it feels grand. They'll talk about it for a week and then they'll get tired of it and I'll be free as a bird. No more secrets, no more worrying about someone guessing. Struan's done me a good turn,' Jennet said, and meant it.

'Jennet!' Angus called from the foot of the stairs that evening.

'In a minute.' She had just settled Jamie for the night, and she was helping him to say his prayers.

'Now would be better, Jennet! There's . . . there's somethin' needs seein' to in the yard!'

'What?' Jamie said at once, unfolding his hands as his mother reached the window in time to see Lizbeth and Andra Blaikie, both dressed in their Sunday clothes, crossing the yard.

'It's just a cat that's come to the wrong farm,' she improvised, trying to keep her voice steady. 'I'll go and shoo it away before our cats fight with it.'

'Me, too.' He began to struggle out from beneath the blankets and she hurried to tuck him back in.

'No, I can manage. Come on now . . .' She caught his hands and held them together within hers, 'Nearly finished. God bless Great-Grandmother and Great-Great-Aunt Rachel, Amen.'

He scrunched his eyes up and repeated the words in a meaningless gabble. 'Don't hurt the cat,' his voice followed her to the door.

'I won't. I think it's gone now anyway.' If only it was as easy as shooing a cat, Jennet thought as she paused before the parlour door, her heart hammering against her ribs.

Lizbeth Blaikie was perched on the edge of an armchair while her husband spilled his bulk over the shiny leather sofa. Angus hovered by the fireplace, his hands in his pockets.

'Jennet,' he said with relief, 'here's Andra and . . . and Mrs Blaikie come to see you.'

She smoothed her apron, wishing that she had thought to take it off, then sat down on a chair. 'You've come about me and Allan. I suppose he's told you all about it.'

'Not so much Allan as Struan,' Andra put in. 'The lad came tearin' in yesterday and tried tae kill Allan. He might have managed it, too, if they'd not been so well matched. In the end they just wore themselves out and once they were lying out on the flags in the rain, Lizbeth here went for Allan with the yard brush.'

'He was lucky I didnae get my hands on the pitchfork first,' his wife said bitterly.

'I'd tae haul her off.' Andra looked at her proudly. 'But she got in a good few wha . . .'

'That's enough, Andra. Our Allan deserved everything he got, Jennet, for he's done you a terrible wrong.'

'I think that's between me and Allan.'

'We got the whole story out of him eventually. He's that ashamed of himself for not marrying you right away and giving the bairn his proper name.'

'Jamie does have a proper name,' Angus put in, moving to stand behind Jennet. 'He's a Scott.'

'I never thought a lad of mine would have failed in his duty tae the lassie that carried his bairn. Look at me and Lizbeth here,' Andra went on earnestly. 'As soon as we knew she was . . .'

'It's not too late for him to put things right,' Lizbeth cut in sharply.

'Allan asked me to marry him not long after he came back to Bute, but I told him that I'm happy as I am, and so is my son.'

'Aye, he told us, but you can't let the wee one grow up as a . . . a . . .'

'I've never thought of him in that way, Mrs Blaikie. I left that to other folk,' Jennet said clearly, and the woman coloured.

'He's loved and cared for,' Angus put in, 'and he always will be.'

Lizbeth hesitated and then said, 'Could we . . . d'you think I could see him, Jennet?'

'He's asleep and I'd not want him disturbed.'

'It seems to me, Mrs Blaikie, that you've got a right nerve, asking a favour like that,' Angus said coldly. His hand landed on Jennet's shoulder, the fingers tightening. 'You've never looked in Jamie's direction because you thought his father was some unknown stranger. He doesn't look any different just because he's Allan's son. As we said, we'll manage. Nothing's changed at all.'

'So . . . we'd best leave it at that and not cause any more trouble,' Andra told his wife, rising to his feet.

'But . . .'

'Be told, Lizbeth. Ye've had yer say and Jennet's had hers, and that's an end of it.' He pulled his cap on over his grey hair. 'We'd best be gettin' home now.'

On the way out through the kitchen Lizbeth hesitated, staring at the tin bath, still waiting to be emptied, and at the toys scattered over the floor. Then she said to Angus, 'Thank you for hearin' us out at least.'

'We don't believe in bein' uncivil to neighbours,' Angus told her.

'I can't just let her go like that,' Jennet said suddenly as the two of them stood in the doorway and watched the older couple walk away. 'Look at her, Angus.' Mrs Blaikie's shoulders, normally as erect as a sergeant major's, were slumped and, as they watched, her husband put a supportive hand beneath her elbow. 'There were tears in her eyes when she saw the mess Jamie had left in the kitchen. When all's said and done, he's her grandchild!'

'And I'm your brother and if you call her back now I'll do a better job on you than Struan did on Allan.' Angus caught her arm and pulled her into the kitchen, shutting the door and leaning back against it. 'Are you mad, woman? She was one of the old witches who talked against you the most when you came home, even though Gran's her friend. And it's made my blood boil, the way she's looked at you every time you met since, and the way she ignored the wee one.'

'I think she's learned her mistakes the hard way.'

'Give the likes of her half a chance and she'd take all three of us over, and the farm intae the bargain.'

'No, she'd not. She couldn't, for we'd be the ones with the power. We have Jamie and we could always threaten to stop letting her see him if she started taking advantage.' Jennet began to gather up the toys.

'I don't know . . . Best to leave things as they are, if you ask me. At least sleep on it,' Angus suggested. 'You might feel different in the morning.'

Later, when she was ready for bed, Jennet drew the low nursing chair up to the cot and sat watching Jamie, fast asleep and blissfully unaware of the upheaval that his existence had caused. Lizbeth was right when she said that he had Blaikie blood in him. Perhaps it would be unfair to deny the people who, after all, were his grandparents the pleasure of seeing him now and again.

On the other hand, Angus was right when he said that Allan's mother had treated both Jennet and Jamie cruelly. Even so, Jennet recalled the sudden tears that had come to Lizbeth Blaikie's eyes as she looked at the tin bath with its cooling water, and the few wooden and rag toys on the carpet.

The really bad thing about having a child of your
own, she decided as she got up and made her way to
the big bed, was the way it made you realise that
mothers – even mothers like Mrs Blaikie – could hurt
badly where their own were concerned.

The following afternoon Lizbeth Blaikie opened her
kitchen door to find Jennet and Jamie standing on the
step.

'We were out for a wee walk and we thought we'd
just come and say hello,' Jennet said brightly. She had
almost turned back half a dozen times, and she had
had to force herself to walk down the Gleniffer lane
and then enter and cross the large, neat farmyard. But
she had managed it, and now there was no turning
back.

Lizbeth's eyes widened and even more colour than
usual rushed into her cheeks. She gulped audibly
before saying, 'Oh . . . that's nice. Come in.'

The kitchen was almost exactly as Jennet remembered it from her visits as a child; walls and shelves
massed with bowls, pans, crockery for everyday use,
jelly pans and jelly bags and moulds, and the pretty
painted plates that she had yearned after. She had
always promised herself plates like that when she
grew up, but they had not yet materialised and she
was beginning to doubt that they ever would.

The Women's Rural Institute that Lizbeth and Celia
Scott had clung to all their lives was represented by
the rag rugs on the floor and hand-knitted cushion

covers on the fireside chairs and the small sofa below
the window. But for all the items in the big square
room, it was neat and spotlessly clean, as always, even
down to the snowy runners on the backs of the chairs
and across the chenille-covered table. A far cry from
Westervoe's kitchen, Jennet thought ruefully as she
followed Mrs Blaikie in, with Jamie clinging tightly
to her hand.

'You'll have some tea?'

'I'd love a cup. Not that we're staying long,' Jennet
warned.

'Even so, it's good to see you . . . both of you.'
The woman beamed as she ushered Jennet to a chair.
'The kettle's just on the boil. D'you like buttermilk,
wee man?' she added to Jamie.

'Aye,' he said in his gruffest voice.

'Yes, please,' Jennet reminded him.

'Yes, please,' he said, adding, 'Helen gives me
buttermilk – it's good for me.'

'She's quite right. I'll get you some, and a wee bit
of shortbread . . . if that's all right with your mother.
How is Helen?' Lizbeth asked Jennet.

'She's fine.'

'She's a good lassie. I was vexed with her when I
heard . . . but I'm glad you've taken her and Bert in.
It was kind of you. Now then, my wee man, what
about that buttermilk? And after you've finished it,'
Lizbeth said tremulously, 'we'll go and see the new
puppies, if your mother says it's all right.'

* * *

There was no sense in trying to keep the visit to
Gleniffer a secret from Angus. Jamie was full of it,
and he could not wait to pour out the story about the
nice lady with the big farm and the puppies that the
little boy had been allowed to play with.

Angus listened and smiled, commenting in the right
places, but as soon as his nephew trotted into the yard
to play with Gumrie he said to Jennet, 'I just hope
you've not made a mistake, Jennet.'

'I did what I had to do.'

'You didnae have tae do it at all! Not after the way
she behaved. And now that you've made friends with
his mother, Allan'll probably think that the coast's
clear for him.'

'He won't. I went to see her when I was sure that
Allan and Struan wouldn't be around, and I made it
clear to Mrs Blaikie that it would only be the occasional visit and that I'd not changed my mind where
Allan was concerned. She's really mortified by what
he did, Angus. I felt quite sorry for her,' Jennet
admitted, and he groaned.

'That's just the beginning, you mark my words.
She'll be getting the wee one to call her Granny next.'

'That's not going to happen, either . . . Not until
he's old enough to understand and make up his own
mind about it.'

'You think so? Once that woman and Grandmother
get together they'll have nothing else in their minds
but making a decent woman of you.'

'She's not even written to Grandmother yet.' Mrs

Blaikie had tentatively asked if Jennet had notified her grandmother, and when she replied that she had, the older woman had nodded.

'It's the right thing to do, lassie,' she had said. 'I write every week, but I was holding my own letter back to give you a chance to tell her your news. I'll write tonight and tell her about your visit, if I may.'

Celia Scott's letter arrived two days later. Angus had gone to Rothesay, so Jennet put it, unopened, behind the clock, where it managed to catch her eye every time she stepped into the kitchen. The day seemed to drag by, and it was a relief when she was finally alone with him, and able to hand it over.

'You read it first.' He slid it across the table to her when she put it down by his hand that night. 'It'll concern you more than me.'

'D'you want me to read it aloud?'

'No, just read it then pass it back.'

Surprisingly, the first half of the letter was just the same as usual; a dry report on the weather, Celia's health and her sister Rachel's health, and a mention of their daily outings to the shops. Then came the final paragraph: 'I was surprised to read of your sister's news; it is a great pity that she did not see fit to tell us sooner than this. It must have come as a great shock to you, Angus, and I am disappointed in Allan Blaikie. I had expected more of him, but at least you now have the satisfaction of knowing whose blood runs in the child's veins.'

Jennet read the entire letter, then handed it to her brother and began to gather up the used supper dishes. As she reached the sink a strangled grunt told her that he had scanned the page.

'At least she's been told,' she said, laying the dishes down by the side of the sink, 'and I can get on with my life in peace.'

'The old bitch!'

'Angus!' She whirled, a hand flying to her mouth. 'That's no way to speak of your grandmother!'

His face was crimson with anger. 'I could think of a lot worse words, but I'll not dirty my mouth with them.' He held the letter out, slapping the back of his free hand against it. 'Is that all she has to say about you and the wee fellow? She spent more words on the weather than she did on you! And she has the cheek to say that I've got the satisfaction of knowing Jamie's got Blaikie blood in him . . . as if I was bothered about his father. As far as I'm concerned, he's your bairn and my nephew. And that's all that matters!'

'You know what Grandmother's like . . .'

'I always thought I did, but I never realised she was such a wicked old . . . witch!' He got up and limped to the range, where he stuffed the letter between the bars of the fire. 'There,' he said with satisfaction as the sheet of paper flared up and then turned to ash, 'that's where it belongs!'

'Angus, I'll have to answer that letter and now you've burned it!'

'You don't have to answer it at all, and if you take my advice you won't. But if you must, just tell her about the weather. That's all she deserves,' Angus said. Catching the back of a chair for support, he bent and picked the poker up from the hearth, using it to push the remains of the letter deep into the glowing embers.

26

Because Helen McCabe's baby was due in a week or two Jennet thought it safer to arrange for her aunt to take Jamie when the time came for planting the early potatoes. Helen was not at all pleased, nor did she take it kindly when Bert and Jennet united to ban her from helping out in the field.

'All that bending and straightening for hours at a time . . . you'd never manage it,' Jennet said, while Bert chimed in with, 'Not in your condition, pet, you might harm the wee one.'

'What am I to do, then, with Jamie away?'

'There's the food to get ready for everyone – that's a full job in itself,' Jennet pointed out, and Helen finally had to give in, although she insisted on toiling out to the field regularly with a basket of food and bottles of cold tea.

Inching her way along a row, dibber in hand and with her booted feet sinking into the clinging, freshly ploughed earth, Jennet wished with all her heart that she, too, had the excuse of being heavily pregnant. The sackful of potatoes tied about her waist certainly helped her to feel as though she was.

It began to rain almost as soon as they started work, and each time she straightened to fetch more potatoes from the sack the cold sleety drops stung her in the face before running down her neck. Despite the sacking she had wrapped about her head and neck for protection, the rain found its way in to trickle down her back as she bent to make evenly spaced holes with the dibber, dropped the potatoes in and then straightened. Two sideways steps later she had to bend her aching back and start it all over again. There was some pleasure in reaching the end of a long row, but that was swiftly offset by the knowledge that she had to move forward and tackle the next.

When she finally rubbed the rain from her eyes and turned stiffly to monitor her progress it seemed as though she had scarcely gained more than a yard or so, though she felt as if she had been working for hours. Through the grey wet mist she could see other figures dotted about the field; some casual farm labourers had come along for the sake of a day's work, and Andra Blaikie had sent Struan and another of his farmhands to help.

When Struan first arrived, clearly unsure of his welcome, Angus had stuck his hand out and said bluntly, 'If I've got a quarrel it's with your brother. No reason why you and me should let what's happened get in our way.' Struan, his face flushing

with relief, had almost wrung the proffered hand from
Angus's wrist.

'I made a right fool of myself,' he said gruffly to
Jennet as they sat in the cart on their way to the field.
'I've no regrets about tryin' tae batter the life out of
our Allan, for he deserved it. I'm talkin' about askin'
ye . . .' He stopped, too embarrassed to say the words.

'Struan, it was a kind offer and I'm just sorry I'd
to turn you down. But you deserve better than me.'

'I don't know about that. It still sticks in my craw
that ye prefer Allan tae me.'

Dear God, Jennet thought, is this nonsense to go
on for ever?

Allan had called in at the farm a week earlier and
when she saw the butcher's van bumping along the
lane, her first inclination had been to snatch Jamie up
and run with him into the farmhouse and bolt the
door. Instead she stood her ground, calling the little
boy to her side.

'I'm not here to cause trouble, Jennet,' he said as
soon as he was within earshot. 'And I'll be gone in
a minute. I just wanted tae thank you for lettin' my
mother see the wee one now and again. It means a
lot to her.'

'It didn't seem right to deny her, considering
she's . . .'

'It's a kindness anyway, and one that's appreciated.'
His face was still patched with the yellow remains of
bruises, and there was a fresh scar over one eyebrow.
'And I wanted you tae know . . .'

'Allan,' Jamie clamoured, ducking away from the hand Jennet had laid on his shoulder in order to tug at the man's trouser leg. 'I can play my . . .' He struggled for the right word, and Jennet said, 'Mouth organ.'

'Aye!'

Allan squatted down, his face close to the child's. 'Can ye? That's clever.'

'I'll show you.' Jamie turned and scuttled into the kitchen. Allan watched him – it was more like holding him with his eyes than just watching, Jennet thought later – until he had disappeared through the door.

'He likes it, then.'

'He does, but me and Angus are beginning to wish you'd thought of something else,' Jennet said wryly. 'He thinks it's music, but it's just a noise.'

When he laughed, he was the Allan she had known before the war. She even felt the sudden lift of the heart, the sudden catch in her throat that she had known in those carefree days when she had had a teenage crush on him. Then he said, 'I'd best go.'

'What was it you wanted me to know?' she asked as he turned away.

'Eh?' He swung back, frowning, then remembered. 'That I'll not bother you again,' he said. 'I've done you more than enough harm.' Then, his voice low and urgent, 'Jennet, I'd give anythin' to be able to turn the clock back. If I'd only kept my wits about me that time I saw you in Glasgow . . .'

'We'd all like to turn the clock back, but it can't be done,' Jennet said.

'Where's Allan?' Jamie asked a few minutes later when he found his mother alone in the yard.

'He had to go away,' she said, and Jamie's face fell.

'Wanted him to hear me. When's he coming back?'

'I don't know, son,' Jennet said.

It was only later that she recalled Allan's words: 'If I'd only kept my wits about me that time I saw you in Glasgow.'

At least he had not wished Jamie's life away.

'I'd keep an eye on that wee heifer if I was you,' Jem said before he left that night. 'She's shiftin' about an awful lot. I'm thinkin' that she's about ready tae drop her calf.'

'I'll move her into the wee shed and keep an eye on her during the night,' Angus said, and the old man nodded.

'Call Bert if ye need help. He's got good strong arms.'

Jennet offered to take her turn at looking in on the heifer during the night, but Angus would have none of it. 'No point in both of us having broken sleep and you'd the worst of the potato planting. I was on the cart, just. I'll call you if I need you.'

After her day in the potato field Jennet's back was aching and her blistered hands stung. She was glad to crawl, rather than tumble, into her bed, and as soon as her head touched the pillow she was asleep. It seemed only minutes before the harsh jangle of the alarm clock jerked her awake.

When she looked into Angus's room on her way to the kitchen she saw that it was empty, the bedclothes thrown back. In the kitchen the quilt from his bed had been tossed onto the big wingback chair, indicating that he had dozed there between visits to the cowshed. The fire had been kept going, and the kettle was steaming on the range.

Jennet, stiff from the previous day's work, started the porridge going, then took two mugs of hot strong tea to the shed, determined to take over and send her brother back to the warm kitchen for something to eat before the milking.

As she stepped into the shed she met Angus on his way out, his face strained and shadowed by lack of sleep. 'Jennet, go and fetch Bert.'

'Is the calf coming?'

'No . . . that's the trouble.' Behind him, she could hear the heifer's harsh, uneven breathing. She put the tea down on the window ledge.

'Can I not help?'

'Mebbe, but I need Bert too, so just go and get him!'

She was halfway to the cottage when the young farmhand burst out through the door, his shirt half buttoned and twisted about the shoulders as though it had been thrown on in a hurry.

'Jennet, thank God you're here. It's Helen, I think she's started . . .'

'So's one of the heifers. Angus needs you in the shed.'

'But Helen . . .' he began.

'You see to the heifer and I'll see to your wife. Go on now!' She grabbed him by the arm and almost threw him towards the shed before running to the cottage where Helen was stooped over the small sink, one hand clenched on the single cold-water tap and the other fisted and rammed into the small of her back. The tap had been turned on full force, soaking Helen and the surrounding area.

'I'll . . . be all. . . right . . .' she gasped when Jennet put an arm about her. 'Just leave . . . me be for a while and . . .'

'And you'll drown or die of pneumonia. Let go now.' After a struggle Jennet managed to prise the girl's fierce grip from the tap and turn it off. 'The front of your gown's sodden. You'll need a fresh dry one.'

'Upstairs.' The pain was beginning to ease and Helen transferred her grip to the edge of the sink. 'In the top drawer in the bedroom. I'll just sit here for a minute.'

'You'll not; you'll come upstairs with me if you don't want your bairn birthed on the floor or the table. Come on now . . .'

Step by step Jennet coaxed Bert's wife up the narrow staircase. A fresh bout of pain struck Helen when they were half a dozen steps from the top, and Jennet had a difficult time unclasping Helen's grip from her arm and guiding the girl's hands to the wooden rail screwed to the wall. Once that was done she herself was able to move down a step or two in the hope that, if Helen lost her balance and fell, she would be able to prevent her from tumbling all the way back to the kitchen.

Eventually she got the young woman to the bedroom and latched her clawed fingers to the iron bedstead while she scrabbled in the drawer, disturbing the neatly folded clothing, and found another night-dress. Then she eased the soaked gown away from the girl's body, which was so thin that it was child-like apart from the huge swollen belly, slipping it over her head and replacing it with the dry one.

'There, that's much better. Now, onto the bed with you.'

Helen resisted. 'The quilt . . . take the quilt off.'

'It's nice and soft, you can lie on top of it,' Jennet coaxed, but the girl shook her head.

'It was a wedding gift from the mistress.'

'Mrs Blaikie?'

'Aye. I'll not have it soiled.' She was so insistent that Jennet was forced to remove the quilt and place it, folded, in the small wardrobe. Only then would Helen consent to lie on the bed.

'Catch hold of the bedstead if you need to, I'll be back in a minute.' Jennet skimmed downstairs, her aching back and blistered hands forgotten, and out into the yard in time to see Norrie disappearing into the shed. She rushed in after him.

'I need Norrie.'

'Norrie?' Bert asked, shocked. 'Is Helen . . .'

'She's having the baby and I need Norrie to go for the nurse. You can use my bicycle,' she added to the lad. 'How's the heifer?'

'Not so good,' Angus threw the words over his shoulder. 'On your way to the nurse's house, Norrie, stop off and ask Jem to come in and lend us a hand.'

'Tell Jem on your way back,' Jennet put in. 'Attend to the nurse first. Then when you get back here you can start getting the cows ready for milking. I'll come and help you as soon as I can.'

Back at the cottage she filled the kettle and a pot and put them onto the small range, then stoked up the fire before splashing some water into a large baking bowl and snatching a clean dish towel from the clotheshorse. In the bedroom Helen lay writhing and moaning on the bed.

Thank goodness Jamie was in Rothesay, Jennet thought as she dampened the towel and wiped the girl's face and hands. Nesta was due to bring him back that morning; perhaps she could be persuaded to stay on for a day or two, since Helen would not be fit for work. She dried Helen's face, brushed out her long dark hair, tied it back loosely, and tried to make her comfortable on the two pillows. Then she found some clean towels and laid them beneath the girl's hips.

'There now, is that better?'

'Yes, thank you.' Helen's voice was weak and flat; now she lay on the bed like a rag doll and, when another wave of pain caught her, she jerked and

twitched so severely that Jennet was hard put to keep
her on the bed. Once it was over Helen went limp
again and Jennet stood looking down at her,
concerned. She had only a hazy recollection of
Jamie's birth now . . . Nesta, who had helped to deliver
him, had told her that it was Nature's way to wipe
such memories from women's minds, because if they
remembered every detail of childbirth they would
probably refuse to go through it again. Even so Jennet
was sure that she had had to struggle to push him into
the world. Helen showed no sign of doing that.

She wished with all her heart that Nesta would
come soon, or that the nurse would arrive, for she
was beginning to feel that she badly needed help and
advice. When brisk footsteps clattered up the wooden
stairs she hurried to the door, almost in tears of relief.
But it wasn't the nurse or even Nesta. It was Lizbeth
Blaikie.

'The lad met Andra on the road, and Andra fetched
me. We both came over. He's with Angus in the
cowshed,' she said shortly. 'I thought you'd need help.'

'I do, Mrs Blaikie!' Jennet could have kissed the
woman.

'Well now, Helen, yer time's come, has it?' Lizbeth
moved past her to stand by the bed. 'How are ye?'

'I made her put the quilt aside, Mrs Blaikie,' Helen
said feebly, and Lizbeth turned to raise an eyebrow
at Jennet, who shrugged and shook her head helplessly.

'I think a wee cup of tea would be a good idea for

all three of us,' Lizbeth said. 'First bairns usually take their time. Would you mind making it, Jennet?'

While Jennet was dealing with the tea, Norrie arrived at the door, breathless, to announce that the nurse was off delivering someone else's baby, but word had been sent and she would be there as soon as she could.

'What about the heifer?'

'I think the master's right worried, and Mr Blaikie too,' the lad said, and Jennet's heart sank. She and Angus could ill afford to lose an animal from their herd, or the money that the calf would bring when it went to the auction rooms. She sent Norrie back to the shed with tea for the men and instructed him to tell Bert that his wife was doing fine.

By the time the tea was half drunk Helen's contractions had become stronger and more frequent. They had tied a sheet to the bedstead, and she was pulling at it so hard that the entire bed frame creaked.

'She should be further on than she is,' Lizbeth said to Jennet in a low voice when one of the bouts of pain had eased. 'She's not workin' hard enough. I'll be glad when . . .'

'Bert . . .' Helen moaned

Jennet bent over her. 'He's helping Angus. D'you want me to fetch him?'

'No!' Helen said fiercely. 'Don't let him come in. Don't let him see me like this, it'll frighten him.'

'It didnae frighten him tae get ye intae this pickle, did it?' Mrs Blaikie said grimly. 'I sometimes think men should see the results of their labours . . . Not that I'd ever want one of them at a birth, gettin' in the way.'

'Tell him I'm sorry to have been . . . a nuisance,' Helen said.

'Ye can tell him yourself, lassie, when your bairn's here,' her former mistress advised her.

'Will it be all right . . . the bairn?'

'Of course it will.'

'Then I'll not be here.' The other two women looked at each other, puzzled.

'Of course you will, Helen,' Jennet said gently, taking one of the girl's hands in hers.

'No, it doesnae work like that! My mother died givin' life tae me,' Helen whispered, 'and I always knew that I'd die givin' life tae my own bairn.'

'That's nonsense, lassie,' Lizbeth told her firmly.

'Beggin' your pardon, Mistress Blaikie, it's not. A life for a life. One comes and one goes.'

'If that was true, we'd all only have one bairn and they'd be motherless.'

'It's true for me. My mother . . .' Helen said, and closed her eyes.

Two contractions later she was exhausted, and the birth was no further on. Her helpers retired to the window to watch in vain for the nurse and to confer in low voices.

'It's as if she's made up her mind,' Lizbeth said. She had tried coaxing and hectoring, but neither had helped.

'Mebbe I should fetch Bert.'

'Only if we have tae. He'll just get intae a state and make things worse for us all. Anyway, he'll be covered with muck from the cowshed. Even if she changed her mind, he'd be carryin' enough dirt tae kill her and the bairn both. If she'd just work along with the pain,' Lizbeth said, 'instead of lyin' there like a useless lump, the bairn'd be here by . . .' She stopped and hurried back to the bed as Helen's sudden sharp cry signalled the onset of another contraction.

Ten minutes later, with the child no nearer being born and still no sign of the midwife, Jennet decided that it was time for a different approach.

'Helen,' she said clearly from the foot of the bed, 'you're having a baby and you're perfectly healthy. It's time you got on with it, because you're not going to die.'

'I am.' Helen's voice was just a whisper. 'I know it.'

'How d'you know it?'

Helen's fingers plucked at the sheet, now more like a rope than a stretch of linen. 'I told ye,' she said irritably. 'I'm just like my mother, and she died.'

'Who told you that?'

'My auntie that put me intae the orphanage.'

'Did she have any bairns?'

'No, she wouldn't take a man because she didnae want tae die in childbirth like my mother.'

Jennet and Lizbeth looked at each other, appalled at the stupidity of the woman who had terrorised the young Helen with her nonsense. Then Jennet said, 'Never mind your auntie, just listen to what I'm telling you. You're not going to die . . .'

'I . . .'

'No, you're not, because if you do die I'll put Bert out of this cottage. I will,' Jennet said steadily as the girl's eyes flew open. 'I'll put him and the bairn out the minute your funeral's over.'

Helen found the strength to raise herself on her elbows, her eyes frantic. 'Ye cannae . . .'

'I can, for it's my cottage. Bert's no use to us without a wife, and I'm far too busy to look after a newborn as well as my Jamie. They'll have to go, Helen, both of them. They can live in Skeoch Woods, for all I care. And it'll be your fault, not mine.'

'No!' Helen wailed, then as a fresh pain gripped her she fell back, the wail rising to a scream. Lizbeth moved forward.

'Come on now, lass, let's get this bairn out into the fresh air. A big push . . . now!' And as Helen bunched her fists and pushed until colour flooded her pinched white face, the older woman winked at Jennet. 'Well done,' she said to both of them. 'Now then . . .'

Five minutes later she spun round and handed a limp, blood-streaked little bundle to Jennet. 'Clear its mouth and get it breathin',' she said tersely before turning back to the bed. Panic-stricken lest she drop the little thing, Jennet scurried with it to the chest of drawers where she had laid out a folded sheet and a towel in readiness. Laying the baby down, she managed to get a finger into the tiny mouth and clear it of mucus, then she lifted its feet in one hand and smacked its buttocks once, twice, three times without success.

'Mrs Blaikie,' she whispered in a panic, 'it's not . . .' She smacked again, then a fifth time.

'Take it downstairs quickly. A basin of cold water and a basin of hot. Dip it . . . aahh!' Lizbeth said as a thin wail filled the room. 'D'ye hear that, Helen?' she asked her patient. 'That's yer wee . . . er . . .'

'Boy. It's a boy!' Jennet carolled joyfully.

'Yer wee laddie. Wrap him up warm and put him in the cradle, Jennet, then come and help me. There's an awful lot of blood,' the woman whispered when Jennet moved to the bed after settling the baby in the cradle she had loaned to Helen and Bert. 'I'm thinkin' that she left it too late tae start gettin' the wee one out.'

'No!' Jennet looked at Helen's face, waxy against the pillow beneath her head, her sunken eyes closed and her mouth a thin grey line. She looked more like a corpse than a living being. A chill ran down Jennet's spine. Mebbe the girl had been right after all. If she died, the last words she heard would have been Jennet's, threatening to throw Bert and their new motherless baby out of the home that Helen had so carefully prepared for them. And she would have to carry that memory with her for the rest of her life.

Tears were flooding her eyes as the door knocker rattled downstairs and a voice called, 'Yoo-hoo!' The nurse had finally arrived.

* * *

'In the nick of time,' Jennet said an hour later. 'I'll never be able to thank you!'

'Och, I don't know about that, lassie. You and Mrs Blaikie were managin' and I doubt if you'd have killed her, though she's had a bad time. It'll take a good week before she's on her feet again,' the nurse said. 'There's not much of her, and it's a fine big baby.'

'She can have as long as she likes.' Bert was upstairs with his family, having taken a minute to tell Jennet that the heifer had produced a bullock and they had both survived. Lizbeth had bustled along to the farm kitchen to feed the men.

By the time Helen was settled and the nurse was on her way, leaving Jennet free to return to her own kitchen, her knees felt so weak that she had to walk close to the wall for support. Everyone had eaten and left, and Angus was there on his own, washing the dishes.

'We kept some dinner for you,' he said over his shoulder.

'There's Bert and Helen, too.'

'I know, there's enough for them as well. The Blaikies had to get back to Gleniffer. It was a bit of a worry, but it all worked out. A nice wee bullock, Jennet.'

'A nice wee McCabe, too.' She lowered herself carefully onto a chair.

'It's a good thing we got the potatoes in yesterday. If we'd decided on today for it we'd have been in a right pickle.'

'Mum! Angus!' Jamie carolled from halfway across the yard.

'Is that the time already?' Jennet looked at the clock just as her son burst in through the door, hurling himself at her and immediately starting a long story about all the things he had seen and done in Rothesay. Over his head, Jennet saw Mollie standing in the doorway.

'I thought Aunt Nesta was bringing him back.'

'She wasnae feeling too well, so I said I'd do it.' Mollie hovered, as though unsure of her welcome. Her gaze moved from Jennet to Angus. 'I'll get the next bus back,' she said while Jamie left Jennet and ran to throw his arms about Angus's knees.

'No, wait. Can you stay for a day or two, mebbe a week? Helen's just had her bairn and she's not well, and it's so good to see you here, Mollie!' Jennet got up and put her arms about her best friend, her skin sister.

'Of course I'll stay,' Mollie said. Then, looking at Angus over Jennet's shoulder, 'If it's all right.'

He put a hand on Jamie's curly head, his eyes drinking in the sight of Mollie, her hair blown about and her cheeks and nose wind-reddened.

'Stay,' he said.

27

Although her baby thrived, Helen McCabe had lost a lot of blood, and it was indeed a week before she was strong enough to leave her bed. Mollie was indispensable and appeared to possess the ability to tend to Helen and her baby, Thomas, see to the cooking and cleaning, keep Jamie happy and care for the hens at one and the same time.

She was surprised to find that Lizbeth Blaikie had begun to come to the farm more regularly and was even prepared, when she visited, to roll up her sleeves and get on with some work.

'Who waved a magic wand over her?' Mollie wanted to know.

'Helen would have died if she hadn't been there when the baby came. And I've been taking Jamie over to Gleniffer now and again because, when all's said and done, the Blaikies are his grandparents. Not that he knows that, of course.'

'What about Allan and Struan?'

'We don't see much of them, thank goodness. And I don't let Mrs Blaikie take any liberties where Jamie's concerned,' Jennet added. 'He's my bairn and she has to be kept in mind of that.'

'Don't worry,' Mollie assured her. 'I'll keep her in mind all right.'

She had given up her job in order to help out at the farm, assuring Jennet and Angus that she would be able to find work again when she needed it. 'Specially once the holiday season comes in again.'

Angus's suggestion that she should be paid for her time at Westervoe was immediately turned down. 'I'd not think of taking a penny, so don't offend me by offering again. I'll be happy with my food and some-where tae sleep. And mebbe a kind word now and again,' she added, giving Angus a sideways look.

He said nothing, much to Jennet's relief. She was anxious to keep Mollie at Westervoe for as long as she could, and she had been afraid that Angus would make it difficult; but he seemed content to get on with his own work and leave Mollie alone.

As the better weather came in there was plenty of outside work for Jennet to attend to. The second preg-nant heifer dropped her calf early one morning, calmly and easily, needing no help, which meant that there were two new calves to care for. Arks had to be cleaned out and shifted to another field so that the hens had fresh grass to scratch on, and the pigsty prepared for its new occupants.

'Another Jack and Jill,' Jennet said as she, Mollie

and Angus finished work on the sty.

'Not again,' her brother protested. 'What about Hansel and Gretel for a change, or Buster and Keaton?'

'Or Rumpelstiltskin and Ermintrude,' Mollie said. 'It's only Jack and Jill because Jamie can say those names. It'll be nice to see the baby pigs settled in here.'

'In their own way they're every bit as lovely as wee Thomas McCabe, or the calves,' Jennet agreed. 'It's a shame to think that . . .'

'Don't,' Mollie turned from the sty, eyes closed and hands clapped to her ears. 'I can't bear to think about it.'

'It's what farming's all about,' Angus pointed out. 'We raise them, feed them, keep them happy, then they repay us. They might have short lives, but they're contented lives.'

'I suppose so. And it's a long time till Nov . . . Who's this?' Mollie said as they walked back towards the yard. A man was coming down the lane to the farm.

'A tink?' Jennet guessed. His clothes were odd; a long loose coat, trousers that flapped about his legs, a floppy hat clapped on top of his head. A sack, or possibly a bag, was slung over one shoulder. 'We've got soup to spare, haven't we?'

'And new-made bread and cheese and pickles,' Mollie agreed. No traveller was ever turned away without a parcel of food.

They met the man at the entrance to the yard. 'Afternoon.' He took his hat off and wiped an arm across his forehead. His grey hair was long enough to be unfashionable, and when he bent to put down his bag Jennet saw that there was a perfect ring of shiny hairless skin right in the centre of his skull, like a monk's tonsure. 'Mild, I thought when I was on the ferry, but when you've been walking for a while it's downright warm.'

'There's tea,' Mollie offered. 'Or lemonade if you'd prefer.'

Instead of answering, the man took a long moment to study her with interest. His skin was weather-beaten and his grey eyes were surrounded by a mass of fine wrinkles, as though he had spent a lot of his time screwing them up against a bright light.

'No,' he said at last, pointing a sturdy index finger at her, 'I can't place you. You're not . . .' Then, as his gaze moved to Jennet he gave a smile of pure pleasure. 'It's you, isn't it? You're Jennet.'

'Yes,' she said cautiously.

'I knew by the hair,' he said, then turned to Angus, his eyes widening as they took in the crutch and then moved up to Angus's face.

'You're . . .' He paused, one eye almost closing as he concentrated.

'I'm Angus,' Jennet heard her brother say, his voice suddenly cool. 'And you're my father. You're James Scott.'

*   *   *

It was an awkward reunion. Tactfully Mollie took herself off to the cottage where Helen was looking after Jamie, and Angus left almost immediately after that, pleading urgent farm work.

James pushed his plate away and got up from his seat at the table to watch Angus cross the yard. 'He's not pleased to see me back.'

'He'll be fine. He doesn't find it easy to talk to strangers.'

'Did he get hurt in the war?' James asked. Then, when Jennet gave a brief explanation, 'Worse for him than being wounded in the fighting, eh? And what of Martin?'

'He did go to war, and he survived; but afterwards he decided to go to England. He's working on a farm there, we hear from him now and again.'

'I must write to him, or mebbe visit before I go home. Mebbe,' James said, 'he'll understand why I left, since he's done the same thing himself and no doubt for the same reason.'

'You'll have to visit Grandmother, too,' she reminded him. On coming into the farmyard he had hesitated, surveying the house doubtfully, and had asked, 'My . . . your grandmother . . . ?' On being told that Celia had moved to Largs, the tension had suddenly left his thin shoulders. Now a shadow passed over his face.

'Has she changed?'

'You're still afraid of her, aren't you?'

'D'you blame me?' he asked and then when she

shook her head, 'What has she said about me?'

'She feels that you deserted her. So did your father, and Martin.'

'My father had the best excuse of the three of us, for he died young, poor soul. You, Angus and Martin must have grown up hating me for walking away from you the way I did.'

'Mebbe, at times; but we got over it. We've managed to build our own lives. Where's home?' she asked casually, pouring out more tea.

'France, in the Loire valley.'

'You've been there all this time?'

'Just for the past few years. I was everywhere before then, but I think I'm finally settled now.'

'In France, you mean?'

He smiled at her. 'Aye, in France. I've no intention of moving back here . . . For one thing, you and your brothers have made your own lives, and for another, I'd not have the right, after what I've done to you.'

So he wasn't back for good. Jennet felt relieved to hear it; having fought hard to give Angus his proper place, she would not have welcomed the idea of their father being the new tenant.

He had taken his tea back to the window. 'It's not changed at all, it's just as I mind it.'

'Shabbier, mebbe. We've not had the time or the manpower to look after it properly.'

'Who's that?'

Jennet joined him, and saw Jamie circling the yard on his tricycle. 'That's my son. You might as well be told now as find out later from one of the gossips,' Jennet went on steadily, 'that Allan Blaikie's his father, but I'm not married to him.'

'Allan Blaikie of Gleniffer? Andra's lad?'

'That's right.'

His eyes narrowed. "It's not like one of the Blaikies to let a lassie down like that. Is he married to someone else? Is that the way of it?'

'No, he's not. It's just the way things are, and there's no bad feeling between us.'

'So I don't have to go and knock young Allan's head off because he's betrayed my only daughter?'

'No, you don't.' Jennet crossed to the open door. 'Jamie, come here a minute.'

'Jamie . . . ?' her father said wonderingly. She turned to see that his grey eyes had suddenly taken on the pearly glow that the waters of the Sound reflected on a soft sunless day. It was as though they had been lit up from within. 'You named him for me? I don't deserve that,' he said when she nodded, 'but I thank you for it, lassie. And I'm doubly glad now that I came back to seek you out.'

Then Jamie was in the room, making straight for the protection of her legs when he realised there was a stranger there.

'Jamie, this is your grandfather, come to visit us. Say how d'you do.'

She nudged him forward and as he held out his hand obediently James took it in his brown clasp, very gently, as though afraid that his blunt fingers might

crush the small hand. 'I'm very pleased to meet you
at last, Jamie,' he said huskily.

'I suppose I'd best see the Blaikies,' he mused when
Jamie had gone back to his tricycle. 'And are the
Logans still in Rothesay?'

'They're still there and still hiring out boats. They
lost Geordie, though. His ship was torpedoed.'

'I must visit George and Ann. They were good folk.'

'They still are.'

'Gold never tarnishes,' James said. Then, collecting
his mug and the plate he had eaten from, he took them
to the sink. 'I'm not here to make more work for you,
and I'm sure you've got more important things to do.
Don't let me hold you back from them.'

'Would you mind keeping an eye on Jamie for me?
I'll not be far away if you need me.'

'Mebbe they'll want to put him into the cottage,' Helen
said anxiously when Mollie told her about the
newcomer.

'I doubt that. You and your Bert are worth more to
them than a father they've not seen for years and
years. Is it just Scotsmen that aren't always very good
at being fathers?' Mollie wondered thoughtfully,
hanging the last of Bert's shirts on the clotheshorse
to air and putting the iron onto its rest to cool, 'or
does it happen in other countries, too? There's your
father that you never knew, and mine that me and
Mam and the rest of us would have been better not
knowin', and Jennet and Angus's father goin' away

when they were little, and even wee Jamie's father denyin' him just when Jennet needed him most.'

'My Bert's not like that.' Helen looked down at the sleepy, milk-sated baby in her arms and stroked his cheek with the tip of a forefinger. 'Thomas has the best father in the world, haven't you, my wee bird?' she cooed to the baby.

'Which proves that some Scotsmen can be good fathers. The thing is,' Mollie said thoughtfully, 'you have to make sure you pick the right man. Give me a shot.' She took the warm little bundle from Helen and cradled him in one arm, gazing down at his tiny face. 'Isn't he perfect? Every wee fingernail and toenail and his wee nose and everythin'. It's a right miracle, isn't it?'

'Aye,' Helen agreed, smiling at her sister-in-law over the baby's head. 'It's the best thing that ever happened tae me, apart from meetin' Bert. It'll be your turn one day.'

'I doubt that,' Mollie said.

'It will. Why wouldn't it?'

'I'll put him in his crib, will I? Then I'll get out of the road so's you can have a wee lie down before he wakens up and starts yelling for more food.'

'I'm feeling much stronger.' Helen folded the blanket that had turned the table into an ironing board. 'I'll soon be able to start looking after the farmhouse and Jamie again.'

'Are you sure? You don't want tae tire yourself out too soon and make yourself ill again.'

'I'm fine. I took longer than most to get over his birth, but the nurse is pleased with both of us and I'm all right now.'

'Helen pet, listen . . . I'd count it as a favour,' Mollie said carefully, 'if you'd just take your time over gettin' back to work. There's no hurry at all and ye might as well enjoy bein' on your own with the wee one while ye can. I'm not in any hurry.'

She spaced the last four words out carefully, and Helen, who had been staring blankly, suddenly smiled. 'You mean you want to stay here longer,' she said, and just as Mollie started to nod, she added, 'near Angus Scott.'

'Angus? Why would I . . . how do you know?'

Helen gave her a long, slow, almost sensual smile. 'When ye love someone as much as I love your Bert,' she said without a trace of self-consciousness, 'ye see more than ye ever did before.'

'So he's not going to stay for ever, only for a month or two at the most,' Jennet reported to Angus that afternoon. 'He lives in France now and that's where he wants to be.'

'That's something, I suppose.'

'At least we'll get to know him properly while he's with us.'

'It's too late for that, Jen. We're adults now, not bairns; we don't need him any more.'

'I do. Now I'll be able to say that I know what my father looks like and where he is. And there's

Jamie . . . Now he has his own grandfather.'

'And what good will that do him? Fetch Mollie, will you?' Angus put an end to the conversation. 'It's time to put the cows back to pasture and we might as well do it now as tomorrow. We could do with her help.'

James Scott was sitting on the bench outside the kitchen door, sketching on a large pad balanced on his knees. The tricycle had been deserted and Jamie was leaning heavily against his new grandfather's shoulder, his curly brown head close to the man's tumbled grey hair and his tongue sticking out from between his teeth as he concentrated on following the swift crayon strokes.

'Go and fetch Mollie, Jamie. Tell her we're taking the cows out.'

'I'll help.' James put the sketchpad aside and got to his feet.

'You don't have to.'

'Lassie,' he said with a grin, 'this is a farm. Everyone helps.'

Acclimatised to being indoors, the herd emerged timidly from the cowshed at first, but as they smelled the fresh spring air the animals became excited, jostling each other in their hurry to get along the lane to their allotted field. Once the gate was opened they rushed through, galloping about the grass like teenagers instead of respectable matrons.

'It's all right for them,' Mollie said as Angus closed and latched the gate. 'They don't have to clean out the shed after a winter's occupation. Sometimes animals can be more trouble than the holiday folk at Mrs Logan's house.'

In the lane, James was drinking in the view over the river. 'The Sound of Bute,' he said softly. 'I've kept that picture in my mind for all these years and it's still true. The Clyde never changes. It's still one of the most perfect places on earth.'

'Yet you were happy enough to leave it,' Angus reminded him coldly.

'I'd not say that I was happy to go. I felt I had to leave because I lost your mother and everywhere I turned I was reminded of my loss. This is a beautiful island, but the thing about it is, it's small. Throw a stone on Bute and you're bound to hit someone,' James said, then turned to lean his folded arms on the gate and watch the excited animals.

'Freedom. There's nothing like it.'

'Some of us,' Angus continued relentlessly, 'never find out about that.'

'But you already have, lad. Mebbe you don't know it yet, but this is your freedom, here at Westervoe. You and your sister have done a grand job with the place so far, and you've all the time in the world. You'll do even better.'

Angus turned with a muffled snort of disbelief and started to limp back along the lane.

'Anger,' James said as he and Jennet followed along behind, 'is like pus in a wound. When it's finally drained out of him he'll be able to see the truth of

what I'm saying. Then he'll know that everything he
wants and needs is here, right under his nose.'

In the kitchen that night Jennet stared at the skilfully
executed crayon sketch of Jamie, head down and face
half hidden, cycling in the yard. Although the drawing
was rough there was no mistaking the identity of the
child, or the background details. The sweeping lines
even managed to convey the movement of little boy's
legs and the tricycle wheels.

'That's just like him!'

'I'd a good subject,' her father said, smiling.

Mollie reached for the pad, studying it in the lamplight. 'You could make a living doing that.'

'I do . . . well, not much of a living,' James
admitted. 'We manage though, between selling the
occasional picture and growing vegetables, and
keeping chickens and ducks and a pig and a goat.
What we can't use ourselves is bartered for the other
things we need.'

Angus had not taken any part in the conversation,
but now he raised his head from his newspaper to ask,
'We?'

'I haven't told you yet about Anna, my wife.'

'You're married?' Surprise put a squeak into
Jennet's voice.

'A year or two now. She's Yugoslavian. We met
when I was there during the war.'

'Yugoslavia was occupied during the war,' Angus
said, and his father nodded.

'And a lot of the people took to the countryside, living in the hills and in caves. Wonderful people!' he said warmly, taking the sketchpad back from Mollie and turning the pages until he found the one he was looking for. 'This is Anna.'

Mollie went to stand behind Jennet so that they could study the portrait together. Anna, sitting by an open door with a basin of potatoes in her ample lap and a knife in one hand, had dark hair tucked beneath a triangular kerchief. Her round face was calm but her eyes, looking directly out of the picture, danced with amusement and the corners of her full mouth seemed to tremble, as though she was just waiting for the crayon to be laid down before breaking into a full-bellied laugh. This time, the strong sweeping curves indicated warmth and serenity.

'She didn't come to Scotland with you?' Jennet carried the sketch over to Angus.

'Anna's had her full share of wandering. It was her decision that I should come back here to see what was happening to you all.'

'Her decision?' Angus pushed the pad back at his sister after giving it a swift glance. 'You're still taking orders from women, then?'

'Anna and I usually decide things between us, the way it should be between a man and a woman,' James said calmly. 'But yes, she was the one who persuaded me to come here. My own feeling was that it was too late.'

'That's my feeling, too,' Angus told him, and

Mollie, after a swift glance at his closed face, got up and moved towards the inner door.

'I'm off to my bed. You need tae be free tae speak about family business.'

'No, please stay,' James said. 'I'm sure that there's nothing any of us would want to keep from you. After all, you belong here.'

'I don't, I'm just here tae help Jennet . . .'

'Mebbe so, but it's clear to me at any rate that this is where you belong,' the older man said gently, and after a moment's hesitation Mollie sat down at the table.

'So you came to find out what had happened to us,' Angus said from the fireside chair. 'Well now, Father . . .' he said the word harshly, as if it were an insult, 'the story's easy told. Jennet had a fatherless bairn and you werenae here to make things right for her and see to it that the man responsible married her. I couldnae do it at the time for I was still a pitiful invalid after the train crash that chewed up my leg. You werenae here for that either, were you? Just as you werenae here to persuade our Martin to come home after the war . . .'

'Angus!'

'I don't see why we should make a big fuss of the man, Jennet. We might have killed the fatted calf if he'd come back sooner, when he was needed, but not now. As he said himself, it's too late!' Angus snatched up his crutch and made his way to the door.

'He's right,' James said when his son had stormed

out. 'And mebbe that's part of my reason for coming back. He needs to get rid of that anger and, since I caused most of it, it's best that he vents it on me and not on either of you.' He smiled at both girls. 'I think Anna was right after all. It was time for me to come back. But for now it's probably time you two were in your beds.'

'I'm afraid that you'll have to have Grandmother's old room,' Jennet said; then, seeing the sudden apprehension in his eyes, 'All her possessions have gone to Largs, and Mollie put the place to rights and made the bed up with fresh linen this afternoon.'

'At least there's no danger of her haunting the place since she's still alive,' James said, getting to his feet. 'I'll manage fine in that room.'

'It'll be better than a cave in Yugoslavia,' Mollie said, and he looked at her in surprise and then grinned.

'You're right there, lassie,' he replied.

28

'She . . . Anna isn't in the least like our mother,' Jennet said to James the next morning. He had slept late and Mollie had taken on her outside duties so that Jennet was free to talk to him when he finally came downstairs. She had asked him if she could look through the pad and he had brought it down to the kitchen, then got on with the food she put before him while she turned the pages one by one.

'No. There was only one Rose,' he said now, his face soft with sudden memories. 'D'you mind her at all? You were only wee when she . . . when we lost her.'

'Aunt Ann has a picture of the two of them in her front parlour. I look at it every time I visit. And I have a drawing of her,' Jennet said, 'a sketch, like these. You must have done it.'

'You've got one of my pictures?'

'There's a pad with several in it, in my bedroom. I'll fetch it.'

When she brought it downstairs he pushed the crockery to one side and laid it on the table, going over each page intently.

'Here's Rose.' With the tip of a finger he traced the young face, the mass of curly hair, so like Jennet's, the smiling mouth and slim neck. Jennet couldn't see his downbent face, but the love and longing in his touch were clear to see.

'I wanted to take this with me when I went away,' he said at last. He glanced up at her and she saw that his eyes were damp. 'But I couldn't find it. I thought my mother had burned it, the way she burned all the other drawings I made when I was growing up. She thought it was a terrible waste of time, farming folk drawing pictures.' He leafed through the pad with its sketches of the farm, and of children . . . Martin and Angus playing in the yard, a baby that Jennet took to be herself sitting at the table, held firmly in her chair by a long scarf looped crosswise about her chest and tied to the chair back. Then he turned back to the portrait of his dead wife and asked, 'Where did you find it?'

'In Gran's room when I was packing her things.'

Astonishment jerked his head up. 'She kept it?'

'I should have put it in with the other things being sent to Largs,' Jennet confessed. 'But I wanted to keep it here, where it belonged. I kept waiting for her to ask for it, but she didn't.'

'She couldn't, because she'd not want to admit she'd kept it,' her father agreed. 'I can't believe she did. Mebbe there's hope for her yet.'

'Take the pad with you when you go.'

'No, it's yours . . . but I'll do a copy, though,' he said. Just then Jem burst in, beaming for once, to shake James by the hand, and the two of them went off together.

The first people to descend on Westervoe when word got out about James Scott's return were Lizbeth and Andra Blaikie. Lizbeth swept into the kitchen in her usual way and was completely confused when James gave her a hug and a smacking kiss on each cheek.

'What d'ye think you're at?' she squeaked, freeing herself and trying in a flustered way to smooth her hair.

'It's the way we do things in France.'

'Aye, well, it's not the way we do things on Bute, is it, Andra?'

'It might be a good idea, at times,' her husband said, grinning. 'How have you been, man?'

'Not too bad. And yourself, Andra?'

'Much the same.' To Jennet, it was as though they had been meeting every day for the past twenty years.

'I hear, Lizbeth, that you and me are grandparents to the wee lad playing out there. Who'd have thought it, eh?'

Lizbeth's flush deepened. 'James, it was as much a surprise to us as it was to you. I cannae tell you how ashamed we are of our Allan – is that not right, Andra? He got a tongue-lashing, I can tell you, and

if he'd been ten years younger I'd have taken the belt
to him for what he did!'

'If he'd been ten years younger he'd not have done
it, Lizbeth,' her husband pointed out, while James
chimed in with, 'I didn't mean that. I meant, who'd
have thought that we'd share a grandchild. I was sorry
to hear about your Drew, it's a terrible thing to lose
a bairn, even when they're grown.'

'Struan's a great comfort,' Lizbeth said.

'I'm sure he is. I'll need to come over to see him
. . . and Allan, too. I suppose I'd best have a word
with him.'

'I told you, it's all been sorted . . .'

'Whist now, Jennet,' James said amiably, 'I'm still
your father for all that I've been away for a while.
It's my duty to speak to the young man.'

'It is that, and I hope you give him a right flea in
the ear,' Allan's mother said warmly. 'Speaking of
family duty, when are you going to Largs to see your
mother?'

James tugged at his ear and shuffled his feet. 'I've
written to her and said I'd go over next week.'

'Not till next week?'

'To give her time to get used to the idea of seeing
me,' James explained feebly.

But Celia Scott was not minded to wait for a full week
before confronting her wayward son. Washing the
dishes after the midday meal the following day, Jennet
glanced out of the window to see her grandmother

and her great-aunt advancing across the yard. She gave a horrified yelp and James, who had been working on one of his sketches, this time one of her and Mollie and Jamie, jumped to his feet and hurried over to join her.

'Is it the wee chap? He's not hu . . . Oh God, it's her! I'd best get myself tidied up,' he panicked, but he had only got as far as the inner doorway before his mother, showing no signs of her earlier injury, marched into the kitchen.

'So it's true, then. There you are, James,' she snapped. Then, acknowledging her granddaughter with a brief nod, 'Tea, Jennet, we're both parched after that long journey.'

'Would you not like some dinner, Gran? We've all eaten, but there's . . .'

'Just tea, and mebbe a scone or some shortbread. And we'll be off when I've had a word with your father.' Celia sat down at the table, drawing her gloves off. 'Andra kindly brought us from the boat, and he's comin' to take us back to the pier later.' She looked at the pad, then pushed it aside. 'I see you're still scribbling!'

'Aye, I am. Did you not get my letter?' James asked as Jennet hurried to make tea and butter some scones. 'I was going to visit next week . . . Good afternoon, Aunt Rachel.'

'You surely didn't think I was going to wait until next week? I've been waiting for more years than I can remember for an explanation of your conduct,

James Scott, and I was certainly not of a mind to wait another week. How's the farm coming on, Jennet?'

'We're managing fine.'

'I see you got that big hen house you were always on about.'

Jennet put a plate of shortbread down on the table. 'It's worked out well.'

'Are the new potatoes in?'

'Yes.'

'They've done a grand job,' James put in. 'I'm proud of them both.'

His mother fixed him with an eye as sharp and almost as painful as a well-honed dagger. 'That's very nice for you, James,' she said. 'I just wish I could say the same about you.'

'That's not . . .' Jennet began hotly, but James put a restraining hand on her arm.

'It's all right, pet, I can speak up for myself. And I can see to the tea as well, so you go and look to those hens of yours.'

'And tell Angus I'll want to see him before I go,' Celia called after her as Jennet made her escape.

'I don't want to see her,' Angus grumbled when Jennet delivered the summons. 'Nor her sister.'

'You can't let her come all the way here, then go all the way back without seeing you!'

He had been grooming Nero, one of his favourite tasks. Now he put the currycomb down. 'Look, Jen, I'm tired of being told what I should do on my own farm.'

'Our own farm!'

'All right, ours. Only it seems to me that it's not ours any longer, the way folk treat it. Thanks to you we've got Mrs Blaikie in and out of the place these days, and then there's this father of ours, and now Gran's back with Great-Aunt Rachel in tow.'

'Only for a few hours, to see Father.'

'You see? Not to visit us and ask how we're doing, but to see him. The sooner the pack of them get out and leave us in peace, the better,' Angus said savagely, snatching the currycomb up again.

'I'll come and get you when they've had their talk,' Jennet snapped back at him. 'You can surely be pleasant to them for five minutes!'

When she had gone he closed his eyes and leaned his head against Nero's solid, warm flank and then jumped when Mollie said from the doorway, 'I should be gone by the end of the week.'

'What?'

'I was tending to the calves . . .' Because the light was behind her he couldn't make out her face, but as she jerked her head to indicate the calf shed through the wall he could see flashes of dark red as fronds of her hair lifted and then settled. 'I could hear every word you said and you're quite right. How can you see to the farm properly with all of us about? Helen's much stronger now; she'll be able to get back to her own duties in a day or two.'

'I didn't mean . . .'

'It's all right, Angus, I know it's been difficult for you. I'll explain to Jennet that I've had the offer of a job in Rothesay.'

'Wait.' He ran a trembling hand along Nero's side for comfort and support. His last chance had come, and he knew it. 'That day you brought Jamie home, when I said to you to stay, I didnae just mean for Jennet's sake,' he said in a rush of words. 'I said it for me, too, and now I'm sayin' it again.'

'I could be all coy and confused,' Mollie said with a catch in her voice, 'but if I did that, you'd probably take fright and say you meant somethin' different. Then we'd be back where we were before and I couldnae bear that. So I might as well come out and say it. Are you askin' me to marry you?'

'I suppose I . . .' he began and then as Nero turned and looked at him, 'Yes. Yes, I am.'

'Then say it.' Mollie ventured a few steps into the stable. 'It's only going to happen once in my life, so I want to be able to tell my grandchildren and it needs to sound right.'

'It's not the first time, surely? Joe Wilson told me at Christmas that he was going to propose to you.'

She stiffened. 'He did, did he? And why should he say that to the likes of you?'

'He wanted my advice . . . as an older man.'

'He's got a right cheek on him, that Joe Wilson. What did you tell him?'

'To go ahead and ask you.'

'That was a daft thing tae do, considerin' you wanted me for yourself.'

'I thought he'd be the better man for you.'

'I know best about who's best for me. And you know fine and well that I'd already made my choice, though you've been too stubborn to admit it.'

'Until now,' Angus said. 'Now I'm admitting it and it's taking all the courage I have. So hurry up and tell me once and for all: will you marry me, Mollie McCabe?'

She moved closer and put one hand on Nero's burnished coat, close to his, then considered him with her head to one side.

'For God's sake say something!'

'I should ask for time to think, or something like that. It would be . . . proper. But if I did, you might take fright again,' she said. 'Of course I'll marry you, ye daft fool of a man!'

'Poor Joe,' Angus said when he finally got the chance to speak again.

'Ach, he'll find someone else easy.' Mollie's voice was muffled against his chest. 'I'd never have married him anyway, even though I'd almost given up on you when he proposed. I'd as soon have been an old maid as married to him, or anyone else.'

'You don't need to be one now.'

'I know,' she said happily. 'I'm so pleased, because I don't think I'd have been very good at it.'

'Mollie . . .'

'Mmm?'

'I've arranged to go to hospital next week to see if they can make a special shoe. If it works, I'll be a lot more mobile.'

She drew his face down to hers and kissed him long and hard. 'Who cares whether it works or not, Angus Scott?' she said when the kiss ended. 'You're perfect just as you are!'

'That caused quite a stramash,' James said thoughtfully as they all watched Celia and her sister drive away in Andra Blaikie's car two hours later. 'I just wish you two had made your announcement earlier, then I'd not have had to face my mother's interrogation at all.'

'We'd have announced it earlier if I'd had my way,' Mollie told him. 'A good six months earlier.' She giggled. 'Your gran's face was a picture, Jennet. And so was yours, come to think of it.'

'You might have told me! I thought we always told each other things like that.'

'This was different, Angus being your own brother. Come on, Jamie . . .' she pounced on the little boy, sweeping him up into the air, 'let's go and help Uncle Angus finish making Nero look all nice and smart.'

'How did you get on with Grandmother?' Jennet asked her father as they walked back to the farmhouse.

'Difficult at the start, but I held on to the thought of Anna and that kept my courage going. D'you know, Jennet, it's easier talking to her as an adult than as her son. We came to a better understanding than we'd ever had before,' James said. Then with a swift change of subject, 'That lassie's going to be the best thing that ever happened to Angus.'

'When the two of them walked in together, Grandmother looked as if she was sucking on something nasty.'

'She'll come round to the idea. In any case, it's none of her business.'

'You didn't seem to be surprised when Angus told us they were to be married.'

'I could tell it from my first day here, by the way they looked at each other. Even the careful way they didn't look at each other,' James said thoughtfully. 'Love was almost hanging over Westervoe like a mist.'

'You should be a poet.'

'No,' James said, 'I have trouble enough just being an artist.'

He spent a week in Rothesay with the Logans and then came back to Westervoe for one night before going to England to see Martin.

'I'll mebbe look in on my mother before I set off. That way she'll not be able to say I ignored her. And that reminds me, Angus, I hope I can tell her you'll be inviting her to the wedding.'

'It's just going to be a quiet wee occasion,' Angus protested. 'All we want to do's get wed and get on with our lives.'

'Even so, your grandmother enjoys a good wedding party. It gives her a chance to dress up a bit.'

'Gran . . . dressing up?'

'Oh, I mind the way she used to dress for special occasions. You never know . . .'

'Make sure Angus asks your grandmother to his wedding,' James reminded Jennet as she and Jamie walked with him to the bus stop at the end of the lane. He had refused to let her go as far as the ferry because, he said, he hated goodbyes.

'I think Mollie'll see to that. You'll be back some time?'

'I don't think so. I've done what I came to do, and Angus's still finding it hard to forgive me, which is his right. His anger's easier carried on my shoulders than on his. At least you've forgiven me . . . and no doubt you've forgiven young Blaikie for any harm he did you as well.' He touched her cheek swiftly and gently. 'You're your mother's daughter, Jennet; when life was cruel to her she could always put the hurt behind her and look to the future. I wish I could have done that when she died.'

Her heart sank as she heard a familiar sound from further along the road. 'Here's the bus coming.'

James bent and scooped his grandson up, hugging him and giving him a kiss on the cheek, despite Jamie's protests. 'Be a good laddie now, and take care of your mother for me,' he said.

There was still so much to say, so many questions to ask, but the bus had come into sight and the final minutes were swiftly melting away to seconds.

'A word of warning, Jennet,' James said as he put the little boy down and picked up his old canvas bag. 'Don't bury yourself here just because you think Angus needs you. He can manage fine on his own now, with Mollie to keep his spirits up.'

'But I love Westervoe!'

He squinted at her through half-closed eyes in the way that he had. 'Even so, you still have to make sure that living here is what you want forthe rest of your life. Not what's best for Angus or even for Jamie, but what you want for yourself.' He held up a hand to stop the bus. 'We've only got one life and it's wrong to give it over to someone else entirely.'

'D'you not think,' Jennet asked evenly, 'that you've left it a bit late to give me fatherly advice?'

The bus ground to a halt. The people on board stared through the windows as James Scott took his daughter into his arms and kissed her on one cheek, then on the other.

'I have indeed,' he said into her ear, 'and you're quite right to slap my knuckles. But think on.'

Then he climbed onto the bus, and went out of her life for the second time.

29

Angus and Mollie managed to fit in their wedding after haymaking and before it was time to bring in the harvest. Jennet was Mollie's Maid of Honour, and to Angus's surprise, his grandmother and Great-Aunt Rachel accepted their invitation and arrived 'dressed to the nines', as Lizbeth Blaikie put it.

'Celia always did know how to put on style when the occasion demanded it,' she told Jennet approvingly.

'I never knew that.' Jennet found it hard to believe that the elegant old woman in a dark blue costume with the small-brimmed, feathered hat over hair set in soft grey waves was the same Gran who had stamped about the farm in wellington boots, a long raincoat and a man's hat.

'You never gave her the chance, did you? If you'd had a wedding of your own . . .' Lizbeth began and then, realising her mistake, she flushed and changed the subject, nodding at Mollie and Angus. 'They seem to be right pleased with each other.'

'And so they should be, for they're perfect together.'

In the two months between his engagement and his wedding Angus had been back and forth to the mainland, and soon he was going to receive a specially made boot, which would help him to move about more easily. As it was, he and Mollie and his single crutch had done a good job of taking a turn or two round the church-hall floor when the dancing started.

He was going to be all right now, Jennet thought thankfully as she watched the two of them together. Everything had come right for him and she herself was free to consider her own needs . . . hers and Jamie's.

Her father's parting words – 'We've only got one life and it's wrong to give it over to someone else entirely' – had echoed in her ear every single day since they were spoken. 'Not what's best for Angus or even for Jamie,' he had said, 'but what you want for yourself.'

He had made his peace with Martin and had returned to his wife and his vegetables, his animals and his art. He wrote regularly, illustrating his letters with tiny sketches in the margins to amuse Jamie and to bring his everyday world to life for his son and daughter.

'So, Jennet,' Lizbeth broke into her thoughts just then with uncanny timing, 'what does the future hold for you now that Angus's settled?'

And without stopping to think Jennet replied, 'I'm going to complete my nursing training.'

* * *

It was so much easier now that Mollie was at Westervoe for good, and more than willing to look after Jamie while Jennet was in Glasgow. Once the decision had been made, everything seemed to fall into place, and at the end of August Jennet left Bute for Glasgow.

Angus was too busy to leave the farm and Ann Logan and Nesta McCabe were rushed off their feet since it was holiday time again, but Mollie and Jamie went with her to the ferry.

'The good old *Duchess of Fife,* bless her,' Mollie said as they watched the steamer coming in. 'That's the boat we came over in all those years ago. Who'd have thought that a German bomb could be the best thing that ever happened to me? Now, mind and write every week, and I'll write to you every week . . .'

'You'll be too busy being a farmer's wife.'

'I'll stay up all night if I have to,' Mollie said self-righteously. 'I have to let you know how Jamie's coming along. And you'll be sure to come home every chance you get?'

'Of course I will.'

'Good. Then I'll be able to make you help with cleaning out the deep-litter house and the byre, the way you always made me do them.'

'And I'll whine and complain all the time, the way you always did.'

'That,' said Mollie, 'was before I was a married woman. It's different now.' She moved her hand slightly, as she often did these days, to let the light catch the plain gold band that Angus had put on her finger.

Jennet knelt to hug Jamie. 'Be a good boy and I'll be back soon,' she said huskily, but he only had eyes for the great bulk of the steamer as she was skilfully brought alongside the pier.

'He'll be fine,' Mollie assured her. 'Angus and me'll see to that. And you'll be home before . . .'

Her voice trailed away and she stared at a point above and behind Jennet, who released Jamie and turned to see Allan Blaikie, dressed in his best suit, among the folk waiting on the pier to greet new arrivals or take the ferry back to the mainland.

'Allan!' Jamie rushed to greet him, then towed him back to Jennet and Mollie.

'I'm off to see a customer in Largs,' Allan said when he reached them. 'Are you taking this ferry too, Jennet? I didn't realise that it was today you were leaving. Well . . .' he held his hand out. 'Good luck with your training course.'

'Thank you,' she said feebly.

'They're starting to board, Jennet, you'd best go,' Mollie advised.

'Yes.' Now that the time had come, Jennet was not sure that she was doing the right thing. 'Mollie . . .'

'It'll be fine,' her sister-in-law hugged her hard. 'And if it's not, there's always Westervoe to come home to.'

'Let me take this on board for you.' Allan picked

up Jennet's case as she knelt to kiss Jamie for the last time.

'Be a good boy and do what Mollie tells you. I'll be back soon,' she said, then turned swiftly and headed towards the ferry.

'Noooo!' she heard Jamie wail as she walked away, and her heart sank. This was what she had feared ever since deciding to return to Glasgow. Although he had had his third birthday, Jamie was still little more than a baby, and they had never been apart in his short life, other than for his two brief sojourns with the Logans.

'Jamie . . .' she turned back, knowing that she could not bear his misery and prepared to stay if necessary; but as he struggled in Mollie's arms it was not his mother Jamie was pointing at, but the paddle steamer behind her.

'Boat,' he was yelling. 'Want to go on the boat!'

'Not today,' Jennet heard Mollie try to soothe him. 'We'll all go on the boat another day. Go on,' she mouthed at Jennet, who hesitated while people hurried past her to board the steamer.

'Why don't you let him go over to Wemyss Bay with you?' Allan suggested. 'We'll see you onto the Glasgow train, then catch the ferry back and I'll deliver him to Westervoe safe and sound. I promise I won't kidnap him,' he added as she hesitated.

'I don't . . .'

'It's a good idea, and very kind of you,' Mollie thrust the little boy into Jennet's arms. 'It'll give you a wee while longer with him, Jennet, and it'll be a treat for him. What do you say, Jamie? Would you like to go on the boat with Mummy and wave to her when she goes on the train?'

'Want to go on the boat!' Jamie locked his arms about his mother's neck.

'Mollie . . .'

Her friend, sister-in-law and skin sister gave her a smug little smile and went on to Jamie, 'You can go on the boat twice if you come back home with Allan, like a good boy.'

Jamie nodded his head, and the battle was lost as far as Jennet was concerned.

'What are you doing?' she hissed at Mollie as they followed Allan to the gangway.

'Keeping Jamie happy. And I like Allan Blaikie; even though he treated you badly, I think he deserves a chance to make it up to you.'

'I don't want him to make it up to me!'

'He wants to, badly. And you're just like Angus. He never knew what he wanted either, till it was almost too late. So think on . . . and enjoy Glasgow,' Mollie added, giving Jennet a push towards the gangway.

As they watched Bute slide away Jamie waved frantically at Mollie. Then, as Jennet put him down, he turned in a slow circle, looking at the deck, the seats, the railings, the people and the ever-present seagulls keeping pace with the steamer as she ploughed her way through the water. He heaved a great sigh of pure pleasure.

'Isn't he grand?' Allan said in awe. 'Can I take him down to see the engines? That was always my special treat.' Then, as an afterthought, 'Come too, if you want.'

Jennet shook her head and they went off hand in hand, leaving her free to lean on the railing and watch Bute become smaller before it finally slid aft of the steamer.

Wemyss Bay Pier, with its handsome Victorian glass-roofed railway station, was appearing on the horizon by the time the two of them returned, Jamie almost incoherent with excitement.

'We'll go and see the engines again on the way home, after we've settled your mother on the train,' Allan promised. Then, to Jennet, 'That should help him to see you off without wanting to go with you.'

'I suppose that's part of having a son,' she said ruefully. 'Only three years old and already he's more interested in engines than he is in me.'

'That's the way it is.'

'What about your customer?' she asked as they went to sit on one of the benches, with Jamie standing up between them so that he could see everything. 'Will Jamie not get in the way?'

'What customer?' Allan asked, and then, remembering, 'Oh, the one I have to see in Wemyss Bay?'

'You said you'd to see someone in Largs.'

'No, I said Wemyss Bay, and it'll not take me a minute. Jamie won't get in the way.'

'There isn't a customer at all, is there?'

'I'm sure I could find one . . . if I have to.'

'Allan, what are you doing on this boat?'

He looked at Jamie, then out across the water and then, finally, at her. 'Spending a wee bit of time with you before you go away. It was the only way I could think of,' he said. Then, as she opened her mouth to speak, 'I like your father.'

'You met him?'

'Oh, yes. Did he not tell you that he gave me a very hard time over the way I'd treated you?'

'He'd no right to do that! I told him that everything had been . . .'

'He'd every right, Jennet. I deserved it, and more. Since he didn't tell you about it, I don't suppose you know that when he'd finished with me I asked him for your hand in marriage.'

'You did what?' Astonishment made her voice overloud, and some people standing by the railing turned and looked at them.

'I thought it was the right thing to do, and I wanted him to know that my intentions are honourable. Late, but honourable.'

'Very late.'

'He said that, and he also said that I'd not find a better wife if I travelled to Timbuktu and back,' Allan continued as bells rang and the paddles began to slow. 'He's right, of course. I'm staying put on Bute, and if you decide to come back to live there then at least I've got your father's permission to court you properly.'

'Allan . . .'

'I just wanted to tell you. I behaved badly all those
years ago, Jennet,' he said, his face suddenly serious.
'I was a daft laddie then, but I've grown up now, and
I've changed. When you feel like it, give me the
chance to prove that to you. Have faith in me. I'll not
let you down again.'

He got to his feet and lifted her suitcase. 'Come
on, Jamie, let's you and me go and see them putting
the gangway in place.'

She watched them go, hand in hand. 'Have faith,'
he had said, while her father had advised, 'Decide
what you want for yourself . . .' What Jennet wanted
right now was to provide a good future for herself
and for Jamie. But after that part of her life was
settled . . .

Mollie had kept faith with Angus, even when it
seemed that he would never reciprocate. Helen had kept
faith with Bert, loving him and having his child, even
though through all the long months of carrying wee
Thomas she had had to live with her secret belief that
the child's birth would mean her own death.

'Come on, Mummy!' Jamie yelled from the
gangway, where he waited, one hand in Allan's, the
other beckoning to her.

She looked at the two of them – one so tall and the
other so small – and was struck by their resemblance
to each other. Jamie's eyes were grey, but when he
was happy, as he was now, there was a blue sparkle
to them. His hair was lighter than Allan's, but darker

than hers. And his mouth tended to lift more at one side than the other, just like Allan's. They looked right together . . . father and son.

Perhaps, when she had completed her training and returned to Bute, as she knew she would, it would then be time to put her faith in Allan. He had let her down once, but she knew that he would not let her down again.

Bibliography

———————

All Muck, No Medals: Landgirls by Landgirls by Joan Mant. Published by The Book Guild, Lewes, 1994.

The Buteman and West Coast Chronicle. Printed by The Buteman Ltd, Castle Street, Rothesay, Bute, 1945. File now in Rothesay Library, Bute.

The Farmers of Bute: For Sixty Years and Beyond by William B. Martin. Printed by The Buteman Ltd, Castle Street, Rothesay, Bute, 1951.

Graips & Gumboots (Memories of the Women's Land Army) by 'Alex', WLA No. 906, and 'Bea', WLA No. 1223. Printed by Admin Systems, 1993; published by SMI and RSH, Dumbartonshire, 1993.

History of Bute by Dorothy N. Marshall, MBE, FSA, FSA Scot. Revised edition 1992 by Dorothy N. Marshall and Anne Speirs, BA, FSA Scot. With an account of Rothesay Harbour by Ian Maclagen, LLB,

FSA Scot. Published by Bute Print, 15 Watergate, Rothesay, Bute, 1992.

The Isle of Bute by Norman S. Newton, photographs by Derek Croucher. Published by The Pevensey Press, Newton Abbot, Devon, an imprint of David & Charles, 1999.

They Fought in the Fields – The Women's Land Army: The Story of a Forgotten Victory by Nicola Tyrer. Published by Sinclair-Stevenson, London, an imprint of Reed International Books Ltd, 1996.

sphere

To buy any of our books and to find out
more about Sphere and Little, Brown Book Group,
our authors and titles, as well as events and
book clubs, visit our website

www.littlebrown.co.uk

and follow us on Twitter

@BtweentheSheets
@TheCrimeVault
@LittleBrownUK

To order any Sphere titles p & p free in the UK,
please contact our mail order supplier on:

+ 44 (0)1832 737525

Customers not based in the UK should contact
the same number for appropriate postage
and packing costs.